MERCY OF THE DRAGON

MATT MEMEMARO

BRIMINITE PUBLISHING HOUSE

To Nakita,

Your MOTD is much better than mine and you know I am envious because of it. Thank you for pushing me to do better.

Also by Matt Mememaro

The Toldar Series

Voyages of the Kaliban's Cradle Series

The Four Worlds Series

The Kai Flint Series

Pursuit of Glory

St. Nick

Shadows of the Dragon

Revenge of the Dragon

Desolation of the Dragon

The Diego Gaudin Anthology

Ironrock
The Haven
Windrise
Talon's Peak
Bloodstone
Travion's Roost
Desacourt
Nestlewood
Ashenfort
Sinibad's Lair
Thornton Grove
The Tomb of Chilijo
The Obelisk
The Dragon's Gore
Kressin
Gatestone
Montemayor
The Commonwealth

ONE

Elanor Sunfire stood transfixed as she watched the dragons ascend into the sky one at a time. A hollow feeling washed over her, starting at the base of her stomach, which then wound up into her throat. Loss filled the air around her, and she could taste defeat unlike any other that she had experienced on her tongue. The world would never be the same as the enormous golden dragon shrunk on the horizon, leaving a path of destruction behind it. The worst feeling was that there was nothing she could do about it. Her eyes were locked onto the retreating form of the much smaller white dragon, Azura.

Pain shot through her body as she watched Azura's retreating form. Ayr had been backed into a corner, and he had no other choice. Right? Azura was in no state to question Ayr or change his mind. It was evident to Elanor that since they had become a bonded pair of dragon and rider that there was a less than mutual power struggle that existed between them. If Ayr wanted something, then he would get it regardless of what Azura thought or wanted in return. Having been close with Azura for years before she had picked him as her rider, Elanor was now concerned for her second favourite dragon.

With nothing she could do to call them back, Elanor at last pulled her eyes away from Azura. All around her dragons roared in pain and suffering, their cries echoing what they had just lost. They were not alone. As the ashes and rubble continued to settle around them, Elanor's focus shifted closer to her. There was a ringing in her ears and a numbness over her entire body. The loss of Ayr and Azura weighed heavy on her but now there was one other that was all encompassing.

Evor still lay on his side, his laboured breathing filling the mountain side with an energy that it did not have before. He was weak, the effects of the wound from Sinibad taking a heavy toll on his body. Even though she was so close to him, there was nothing that she could do to ease his pain. Evor's laboured breaths were at least consistent, and Elanor could still feel his energy pulsing through his body, full of ancient magic. Evor would not die for the moment.

Evor.

He will not kill me.

Can you stand? We need to go.

Go where, Elanor? Sinibad has destroyed our home. We have nowhere to go.

Evor was right. Elanor could feel the pain coming through in his thoughts. The dust of the Obelisk crashing into the ground was still swirling around her. There was too much going on around her for her to fully process just what had happened. Evor filled her mind, his pain becoming hers. Elanor could feel the deep wounds that Sinibad had inflicted upon her across her body as if it was her own.

If it was not something that she was used to, Elanor would have collapsed when Sinibad inflicted the wounds upon Evor, but she knew that Evor was a master of masking his pain and only shared it when it was too great for him to handle. As the minutes passed, Evor continued to groan, and Elanor fed him encouragement, in an attempt to help him back to his feet. It was evident that Sinibad had inflicted serious damage, and Elanor started to climb up the mountain towards where Evor rested.

The steepness of the slope was the only thing that kept her from Evor, and Elanor stretched out, using whatever branches and the trunks of trees that she could get her hands on. Using them to propel her forward, Elanor felt like she was making progress towards Evor as he continued to writhe in pain. She reached him moments later, despite it only being one of his massive feet. It would be enough.

Evor sighed as Elanor's hand touched his foot and, in an instant, everything that he felt shot through her body. Elanor almost recoiled as the shock flooded her body, but she remained strong, flexing her calves as the red-hot electricity surged through her. In this moment, she was stronger than Evor, despite her body wanting to give out on her. She screamed in protest as she took on his pain, but as she settled and the initial pain wore off, Elanor started to transfer her power to Evor.

Elanor...

Her focus was solely on Evor and his wounds. If she could do something that would reduce his symptoms so that he could fly again, she would have done her job. She did not have the amount of magic within her system that would be able to heal him within a day, this would need to take place over the course of the coming weeks, just as Dalton and Sinibad had intended. Elanor grit her teeth in frustration. This would be the last time that Evor fell to Dalton and his will.

Come on, come back to me, Evor. How I wish I had dragon's tears.

You are my rider, Elanor. You support me in every way that you can.

Just hearing his voice in her thoughts was enough to keep her focused on siphoning his pain away. Elanor continued to work with her magic, not wanting to let him down. If only she had more available to her, but she knew that she could not push herself past her limits unless she wanted to be in the same situation as he was. The magic was a slow release, no more than a trickle, but it was having a small impact on him. Elanor remained calm as she continued to channel her power into Evor until he interrupted her thoughts.

Elanor. Look to the skies. We have company.

Frustrated, Elanor hissed and turned back towards the open expanse of where the Obelisk had once been. Two somewhat familiar dragons were making their way towards them, both much smaller than Evor, but they would still pose a threat if their intentions were aligned with Dalton's.

Can you fight?

I will do what I can, should they prove hostile. Keep transferring your power to me. I need every drop of energy if I am to recover.

They still had moments before the new arrivals joined them, and Elanor closed her eyes. She was trying to push herself to the brink of exhaustion. If Evor could not fight against these two dragons, then they stood no hope of surviving. They would tear both him and her apart without a second thought. With her eyes closed, Elanor could only hear the wingbeats of the new dragons as they approached, and Evor let out a low, mournful roar, one that did nothing to prove that he was capable of combat. If this was a fight waiting to happen, Elanor would need to face down both dragons and their riders.

Elanor...

I know, Evor. I will face them.

With a heavy sigh, Elanor turned her back on Evor and she could feel him trying to grant her strength. Elanor refused the gesture, fully knowing that Evor needed every bit of power available to him. Her only hope was to pray to Chilijo that these dragons were not in the servitude of Dalton and were in fact coming from the Obelisk. Wishing she had more magic at her disposal, Elanor steeled herself, drawing up to her full height as the dragons came into land. Both were as graceful as the other, touching down without causing Elanor to lose her balance. If they were hostile, they would have engulfed her in flames without a second's thought.

"Lady Sunfire! Are you injured!"

Elanor recognised the voice. As the dragon tilted its head down towards the ground, Elanor saw the familiar figure of Marcello peering over it. He had removed his helmet, and his face was full of concern.

Without feeling the need to respond verbally, Elanor shook her head, but this answer did not calm Marcello, his tone still panicked. The other rider on the back of the other dragon could only be his brother, Malachi. How ironic that the Marshadow brothers had come to her aid considering their family's affinity with the Ashbourne line.

"No, I am not. But Evor is."

"Where is Lord Ashbourne?"

The empty pit in her stomach opened up even more than it already had. There was nothing she could do to stop him from leaving even if Evor had been fully fit. Shy of pinning Azura to the ground, but against the dual threat of both Onoss and his brother's new dragon, Evor would have struggled even though both vicious dragons were still so young. Dalton had come prepared. How had he destroyed the Obelisk so easily? Even a dragon the size of Sinibad would not have been able to collapse it with such ease.

"Gone."

It was all she could manage to croak out. It was as if she could not fully believe it, but the retreating figures high above her that were only slipping over the horizon with each passing wingbeat brought her closer to reality. Marcello turned his head skyward and sighed.

"I wish we were not delayed. The arrival of Sinibad was frightening. We barely escaped the Obelisk as it came crashing down."

"I know, I was on the Obelisk when he landed."

"That dragon poses a threat that we can't contain. If Drementhol didn't stand against it, I'm not quite sure what we can do."

"We still have assets available to us."

Marcello clicked his tongue and drew in with a deep breath. "I'm not so sure about that, Lady Sunfire."

"Stop speaking in riddles, Marcello. What do you mean?"

"The Obelisk was destroyed, Elanor. I don't care what you say. The riders are now on the backfoot thanks to one action by Dalton Ashbourne. How can you say that we still have assets available to us?"

"Neither of us are dead, are we?"

"No, but Evor may be close."

Elanor wanted to extend her hand and swat him out of the saddle. Marcello's face carried concern, but his worry was not what she needed right now. "Evor will not die. If Dalton wanted him dead, he would have commanded Sinibad to end his life. He wants something more from us."

Malachi leaned forward in his saddle and spoke for the first time since landing. "I would have thought he'd have wanted all the Sunfire's dead. Why did he leave you alive?"

"He wants me to become a Dragon Lord."

The Marshadow brothers both turned to look at each other before they turned back to Elanor. "You, a Dragon Lord? He'd have you elevated above your father's position?"

Elanor nodded, the only motion that she was able to muster. Her voice was giving out on her the more she spoke. She could still see the crumbled remains of Grace's body further down the hill. Elanor closed her eyes, trying to forget the sight of Dalton's knife at her neck. There had been nothing that she could do. At least it had not been Evor.

"Then we need to ensure Evor does not die, Marcello."

Marcello nodded, his eyes filled with more panic as he agreed with his brother. "Sinpac and Esher will help Evor regain his footing. Are you happy to ride with one of us, Elanor?"

"No, Evor needs me. I will not leave him."

"He can't stand."

"He will."

Elanor turned her back on the wyrmguard and their dragons. She reached out and touched the base of Evor's foot. He shuddered with her touch, and she left a surge of power radiating through his body. Evor groaned but there was movement under her hand. He raised his head and glared at the two Marshadow dragons.

"Help me up."

Elanor vaulted up Evor's leg and ran along it towards his head. With each step she took, she could feel more life returning to Evor's body. It still was not enough, and he was still not sure if he could stand. He groaned in pain once more as Elanor reached his head, the saddle calling her name. Sinpac and Esher made their way over towards Evor, their bodies cramming the space over Evor's head, blocking out the sun.

As one, the two standing dragons bent and shifted their weight underneath Evor. With a groan, Evor moved with them, putting weight on his legs as they tilted him upright. Elanor gave Evor all of the encouragement that she could, channelling magic through her hand which flowed into Evor's body. It was a struggle, the two smaller dragons doing what they could to help him, but within moments, Evor rose, now standing on all four feet. The progress was slow, but now that he had his feet under him, Elanor felt more confident that he was ready to take on whatever challenges either Dalton or members of the Commonwealth would throw at them.

I need more magic, Elanor.

It will come. Can you fly?

Evor groaned again as he stretched out his wings, almost hitting Sinpac and Esher in the process. They scampered back away from him, and for the first time since Sinibad's attack, Evor was now standing of his own accord. Whilst he did not show any outward sign of pain, it was all throughout his mind. Elanor tried to calm him, to take the pain away from him, but the largest wound was underneath his right wing.

Yes, Elanor.

Don't lie to me, Evor. I can feel it. You can barely walk.

We're not safe here. We need to return to the Obelisk and the other riders.

There's nothing there, Evor. Our home has been destroyed.

Then I look forward to bringing destruction onto the ones that brought it down.

TWO

With his focus now solely on the loss of the Obelisk, Evor was moving freer than before. His pain was fading, despite the wounds still being so fresh, but Elanor continued to pump her magic into his system. She knew that it would not be enough, but it would do for now. Sliding into the saddle, Elanor reaffixed her mask to her face, able to smell the sulphur and blood stains in the air. She looked to the spot where Ayr's brother had instructed his dragon to murder Draxion, swallowing her whole. That would be an image that would haunt her, but at least it had not been Azura.

When would they see her again? Evor had been far too focused on his wounds and on the loss of the Obelisk, but Elanor thinking about her for the briefest moment, caused Evor to turn his attention to her.

When will they be coming back, Elanor?

I have no answer for you Evor. When Dalton Ashbourne says so.

I will kill that man.

Evor's sorrow turned to anger in a flash, and even though she could not see his eyes, Elanor could feel his face tighten into a scowl. Evor turned his head towards where the retreating dragons had vanished to over the horizon, his eyesight far better than hers. As she looked through his eyes, she could see that they were almost past the point of no return for him as well, Sinibad no larger than an ant flying towards the horizon.

You're not in a state to fight, Evor. You need to rest.

Yes, you are quite right, Elanor. I am thankful for this armour plating. I believe it saved my life.

Good. Let us pray to Chilijo that it will not be needed again.

Evor reverted his attention to Sinpac and Esher, the two wyrmguard dragons watching him with apprehension. He hissed at them and then took a thunderous step forward. As he placed his foot on the ground, Evor was shaky, and Elanor sent another surge of magic into his body. He shuddered underneath her touch but steadied as she wanted him to. As he looked to the sky, Elanor could make out dozens of dragons flying around the shattered remnants of the Obelisk, that had still not come down to land as the dust was settling. Several were headed their way, but was it for them or a means to escape the destruction of the Obelisk?

Elanor wanted Evor to fly, but she could sense from his muted movements that he did not want to put his wings out or could not. He was too proud to tell her that he could not fly, so instead, he grumbled as he waited for the dragons approaching them to arrive. Elanor leaned forward in the saddle, rubbing her hand against his scales.

You can just tell me if you can't fly.

I will not let you down, Elanor.

You never have.

I know who those dragons are. They would call themselves our new Dragon Lords.

Great.

Hearing confirmation from Evor only made Elanor groan in response. Out of all the riders that survived the fall of the Obelisk, she did not want to speak to these the most. Why were they coming here, rather than helping survivors from the Obelisk. Elanor steeled herself and settled into the saddle. Evor groaned again and stumbled, his legs shaking underneath him. With the groan he started to lower himself towards the ground and both Sinpac and Esher made their way to help him.

"Let me rest!"

The smaller dragons backed away, and Elanor cast a glance at the Marshadow brothers who were both seated high in their saddles. Their faces were unreadable underneath their helmets, but Elanor did not need to see them to understand what their intentions were. They kept their eyes locked on her and Evor and remained unmoving. If she did not know where their true intentions lay, she may otherwise have directed Evor to attack them and chosen to explain her actions later.

Whilst she was familiar with their new arrivals, she was not familiar with their dragons at first sight. Baldur Cole was the first to touchdown on the ground atop his enormous yellow golden dragon that was only a few shades darker than Sinibad. On either side of Baldur, the two other dragons touched down. A sleek crimson red that belonged to Leyla Argoss and a thick deep aqua dragon that was ridden by Romulus Khan respectively.

Baldur's yellow dragon took a step towards them, and despite being on Evor's back, Elanor felt small in comparison. Their presence was not what she wanted or needed right now. As a result, she was furious. Elanor felt Evor shift underneath her, as he joined with her emotions, giving her more fuel to her fire. She rose out of the saddle, feeling what fury he could muster behind her.

"What the fuck are you three doing here? Why are you not helping those in the Obelisk?"

Baldur leaned forward in his own saddle, as his dragon stepped closer. He flicked his mask from his face and shook out his greying hair in the process. "We thought it would be in our best interests to see what had caused the elder dragon to depart from the Obelisk. We should have known it was you. Let me guess, Dalton Ashbourne was here?"

"And what if he was? Evor is hurt. The elder dragon almost destroyed him whilst Dalton murdered my mother in cold blood."

Baldur bowed his head as his jaw tightened. "That is a great loss that will be felt throughout the Commonwealth. We will bring him to the ground."

"Will you listen to yourself and look around, Baldur?"

"Our backs are against the wall. Kaladin spent his time as Overlord strengthening our defences, but it is clear to me that his efforts were in vain. We have not seen him since the Obelisk fell."

A lump formed in Elanor's throat as she recalled the events within her father's old office moments before Sinibad had come crashing through the ceiling of the Obelisk. "Kaladin's dead. Gundrag is gone."

"Kaladin's dead? How? Have you seen the body with your own eyes?"

Elanor's throat was drying out faster than a desert now that the last memories of him being inside her were now rushing back to her. Evor sensed her anguish and tried to flood her emotions with his own thoughts and feelings, but he had not been there for her. Guilt filled Evor and his memories flooded into Elanor, but all she could now feel were Gundrag's teeth against her own neck. She was still pinned and as helpless as before.

"Yes. I saw the body. He was among the first to fall in the attack. Sinibad destroyed the Lord Chairman's chambers when he arrived."

"Did he now? It wouldn't have had anything to do with you, would it Elanor?"

Elanor sucked in a deep breath of air and stood up straighter as she stared Baldur in the eye. "No. You know Kaladin loved me; he threw himself at me which protected me from the rubble falling."

Baldur did not seem convinced. He shifted in his saddle and cast a glance at Layla and Romulus. "A likely story. Kaladin would not have succumbed to something so trivial. Regardless, we have business to attend to."

"Yes, why are you here? Should you not be helping those out of the Obelisk that can't help themselves?"

"We came to investigate what Dalton Ashbourne was doing here. There is nothing more important to this piece of the puzzle than him. If we could have caught him, this would all be over."

Elanor was defeated and raised her hand gesturing towards where Dalton and the rest of the dragons had at last slipped past the horizon. "Then chase him down for all I care."

Romulus raised his head and sneered in Evor's direction. "He has too much of a lead. Your dragon can't fly. That is of as much concern if we need to consolidate our assets."

"Then he can walk. Go and help the others. Do something!"

Leyla's head snapped towards the wyrmguard that still stood behind Elanor. Her eyes narrowed and she gestured for them to step forward. "Wyrmguard, the Lady Sunfire has indicated she does not need help. Come with us."

"My lords?"

Marcello seemed hesitant from his voice, but he patted Sinpac on the side and the dragon rose to its full height, ready to rise into the sky. Elanor wanted to turn around and berate the wyrmguard. She knew where his loyalties lay, but disobeying a direct order from the soon to be Dragon Lords would only put his head on a pike above the Haven. With a snort coming from his dragon, Baldur replaced his mask, pulling it over his head with a short, swift motion. He slid back into the saddle properly and the dragon started to turn away.

"Do as you're told, wyrmguard. If there is anyone left inside the Obelisk, we need to dig them out."

Marcello now understood and had no further questions. "Sir!"

One by one, Baldur and the others all rose into the air, their dragons spreading their wings and taking flight. Elanor and Evor could only watch them go. She heard Evor grumble underneath her, his frustration shining through as he tried to flex his wings again. Instead, as he grumbled, he was forced to watch on as Baldur and the others all made their way back to the Obelisk.

Considering that Evor could not fly, the journey back to where the downed Obelisk now lay was a long one. What they could have covered in minutes in the air, was now reduced to a slow and cumbersome affair. With most steps that he took, Evor tried to take off into the air, but considering that Elanor could feel him shaking underneath her, she cautioned him against it.

You need to stop, Evor.

Elanor, I must return to the sky.

No, you need to rest. The fact that you survived an encounter with Sinibad is impressive enough. Asking more out of you is unbecoming of me as a rider.

I cannot afford to be weak, Elanor.

You are not weak, Evor. Stop trying to fly, there is nothing we can do.

Elanor turned her attention from Evor, for the first time since their argument had begun to what had once been the largest structure in the entirety of the Commonwealth. It was remnant of Evor, broken and dejected, now no longer standing proud and tall like it once had. As they approached the Obelisk, Elanor could make out streaks that shot through the sky, dragons all flying in every direction and as they got closer to the Obelisk, she was beginning to hear their roars.

None of them were anywhere near the audacity of Sinibad's, but their mournful nature shook her to her core. Evor was still in denial of what he had seen with his own eyes, but the wounds that scarred his side and back were a stark reminder of what had occurred here. Elanor could hear dragons roaring, calling out for help, their roars an echo as they rumbled up from inside the shattered Obelisk. Half of the city was obscured from her view as Evor walked towards it, with a thick layer of dirt and debris covering many of the buildings that she could see.

Dragons roosted atop everywhere that they had a vantage point, most of the smaller dragons diving in and amongst the rubble, doing what they could to search for survivors. With the lack of dragons that were returning with other dragons, or even riders, Elanor was beginning to lose hope. It was still early and the Obelisk was a structure that few could traverse within moments and considering the destruction that had been brought upon it, Elanor could only assume that most of the regular corridors and passageways through it had been cut off.

As they drew nearer, Elanor continued to watch the dragons dive amongst the ruins. Grief was flowing through both her and Evor, unable to believe what they had witnessed. Those in the town below the Obelisk had not fared any better either. For every dragon and rider that had been affected, there were dozens of regular citizens of the Commonwealth that would have either been crushed or trapped by the Obelisk's fall if they had even managed to survive for that long.

The dust was still settling all around them, a thick layer of silt building on the ground. The sky was still burned orange from Sinibad's flames and there was a sense of dread as they approached the massive figure of the Obelisk. Elanor saw Baldur land on Rotang at the highest point of the Obelisk. Whilst the structure had fallen and was shattered into pieces, it was still just as imposing as it had been.

Romulus and Leyla landed beside Baldur, each of them staring down at the ongoings with disdain. Elanor hoped that it was for the actions that Dalton had taken against them. Whilst she could only see their dragons from this distance, were the riders speaking and scheming working out what their next step was? Nothing this diabolical had ever been achieved in the lifespan of the Commonwealth, not even in the first war with Chilijo.

They were nearing the city, and the destruction was becoming more evident. The Obelisk had created a crater around it, and from her position on Evor's back, she could see where it had ended. Half the city was destroyed and she paused, examining the damage. She could see no bodies even though it was clear that everything was broken. Elanor continued to step closer to the Obelisk and then she did see something that tore her heart apart.

Elanor closed her eyes, not wanting to see it. From underneath the Obelisk she saw a massive granite-like protrusion jutting out from the ancient stone. The shape remained motionless against the shifting dust, and as Evor took another tentative step closer, her breath caught in her throat. What she had mistaken for mere stone revealed itself to be a colossal dragon's head, almost as large as Evor. The head was unmoving, the dragon deceased, crushed as it had tried to flee the failing Obelisk.

Magjer!

Terror and horror filled Evor, as he recognised who was half buried underneath the rubble of the Obelisk. He picked up his pace, running towards the unmoving figure of the dragon that lay before them. Evor bit into the stone, trying to uncover more of Magjer. As he started to dig, scraping away pieces of the Obelisk, Elanor could already tell that Magjer would not rise again.

Just like the other dragons that Sinibad had taken out of the sky, Magjer had decades, if not centuries of experience. But all that mattered for nothing, his life snuffed out in an instant. Evor was beginning to come to the realisation that Magjer was not going to recover from this traumatic event. Mourning filled Elanor's mind as Evor slowed in his digging, his claws no longer chipping away at the very most outer layer of the Obelisk.

We were too late, Elanor.

There was nothing that we could do to save him, Evor. Sinibad saw to that. I just dread to think how many more dragons lay underneath the ruin.

I will kill Sinibad for what he has done here today.

You need to rest, Evor. You can't hunt Sinibad now with the state that you're in. Are you forgetting what he just did to you?

I did not have Azura with me. Together with her newfound power, we would crush him.

I admire the confidence, but Sinibad just destroyed the Obelisk and left you crippled, Evor.

You would be surprised what two promised dragons can do together.

I will take your word for it.

Evor's talons had become bloodied in the desperate assault on the Obelisk. With his chest heaving, he dragged himself backward, away from the pulverized stone and Magjer's mangled corpse. A guttural, primal sound tore from Evor's throat, a roar that dissolved into something worse. The keening wail that pierced Elanor to her marrow, vibrating through her body like the death knell of all hope.

As Evor's anguished howl shattered the air, the Obelisk trembled, sending cascades of dust and stone fragments raining down around them. Dozens of dragons launched from their perches, wings unfurling with thunderous cracks as dragon after dragon joined his mourning cry. Their combined voices created a deafening tempest that made the very foundations of the ancient city quake beneath their fury.

Even though you are now a part of his plan, Elanor, we will have our revenge.

Yes, Evor. Dalton Ashbourne will pay for what he has done to us.

THREE

The corpses of dead dragons and their riders lingered all around them. These had been the unfortunate ones who had not been aware of what was about to befall their great structure, either too busy in their work, too deep in the Obelisk to find their way out before it collapsed, or those that had simply been asleep. Either way, time had not been on their side, and it had run out.

Elanor wondered just how many had perished in the collapse of the Obelisk and knew that the number would likely never be confirmed. It mattered little, the loss of life here had been more than what was acceptable for both dragons and their riders alike. It also would not have been just dragons and riders either. With half of the city underneath the Obelisk shattered like a steel sword across a blacksmith's anvil, Elanor could only imagine how many people that supported the riders had been lost.

These were the people with no access to a dragon and no way to escape the fall of the broken, towering structure that now laid across the expanse of the Seminary of Fire. Even the great wars and Chilijo himself had not seen the Obelisk fall, but now through the actions of one man, the riders were homeless.

The day dragged on and Elanor was exhausted. There was no clear organisational structure and the three riders that were going to be calling themselves Dragon Lords were concerned with their own dragons, rather than the safety and wellbeing of those around them.

Elanor snarled up at them, frustrated with their lack of action, but realistically, what could they do in this situation?

Each of their dragons were far too large to fit into the collapsed hallways of the Obelisk yet still could have been useful trying to dig through the ancient structure. She had instructed Evor to rest, the digging to try and save Magjer alongside the wounds from Sinibad were still taking their toll on him. At least now with the lack of activity his breathing had returned to normal, and he was seemingly better than he was only a short while ago. However, it was clear as much as he might have tried that flight was an impossibility for him considering his injuries.

As the day dragged on, more dragons pulled themselves from the rubble of the Obelisk, many with the assistance of others. Elanor remained in Evor's presence, watching as the survivors gathered their bearings and then assessed any injuries that they had sustained in the collapse. There were less survivors than Elanor had hoped for, but she only had a small window to look into what was coming from the Obelisk.

There were less larger dragons compared to smaller ones, many of the smaller dragons only the assistants that floated around and conducted business within the libraries. Elanor's heart sank, full well knowing that these dragons would never bond with a rider and therefore never reach their full potential. They would be of minimum use in the war to come with Dalton, especially considering that they could not even contend with one of the many wyvern that Dalton had at his disposal.

As the sun started to set across the Obelisk, Elanor spotted Marcello's dragon, Sinpac dragging another corpse from the wreckage. It had been a common sight all across the day as the dust had continued to settle around them. Evor grumbled beside her, raising his head to investigate who Sinpac had just brought outside. It was a blue dragon, much like the colour of Azura's eyes. A twang of guilt shot through Elanor, fuelled by Evor's emotions as he remembered her face, bringing it to the forefront of her vision.

That's Dallanor. What a shame, I would have thought he'd have made it out.

I haven't seen his rider either.

Considering how deep in the Obelisk their quarters were, I'm not surprised that they did not make it out, Elanor.

There's so many. What a waste of life. I thought Dalton didn't want to kill off all of the dragons and their riders.

I cannot discern what his motives are. He seems to say one thing and then does the other.

He kept you alive though. Why?

You are still valuable to him, Elanor. That is why I live.

As Sinpac took a proper hold of Dallanor, clenching his jaws around his neck, Esher landed beside them and assisted his brother in lifting Dallanor off the Obelisk. Elanor and Evor could only watch as the two dragons moved their counterpart towards the pile of bodies that had become larger as the day dragged on. It was a mixture of dragons as well as their riders that had not made it out of the collapse, and already the pile was beginning to smell of death.

From what Elanor could see, it was not the only pile either. There were at least another four positions that dead dragons and their riders were getting placed on, that were all just outside of the city. Mournful dragon roars filled the air, echoing out from the gaps in the Obelisk and they did not get any easier to hear as the day went on. As Dallanor's body was placed on the ground near them, Elanor had seen enough.

We need to go, Evor.

Go? Go where?

We can't stay here anymore. I need to get started with the task that Dalton set me.

Becoming a Dragon Lord?

As much as I don't want to, yes. But with Kaladin out of the way, it should be easier.

Do not underestimate Baldur and the others. He is just as dangerous, if not more so than Kaladin.

And look at what happened to him, Evor.

Don't let an achievement that was not yours go to your head, Elanor. Ayr is not here to protect you this time.

A hot flush of rage swept over Elanor, and she cast a side eye at Evor. He just rolled his in response, knowing full well the range of emotions she had gone through when Kaladin had forced himself onto her. Whilst he had been busy dealing with Gundrag, the pain had still passed through from her to him. He should have known better than speaking about something that should have remained unspoken between the two of them.

You're very funny, Evor.

Apologies, Elanor. I should know better.

Yes, you should, Evor. You know that Kaladin was always a sore point. Even more now.

I am glad that Kaladin is dead. He was not the man to lead the Commonwealth.

No, he was not. We could do a better job.

We? What are you saying, Elanor.

We could remake the Commonwealth in our own vision. You and me, together at its head.

You would have to outmanoeuvre those new Dragon Lords. You have the pedigree due to your family lineage, but would they be convinced you are the best choice as Overlord?

Elanor glowered at him, and Evor conceded, noting the fire in her eyes. She felt him rise up to match hers and for the first time since Kaladin's assault, her power was returning to her.

Yes, Evor. The world will be what we make it.

Then what is your plan?

We'll approach Baldur and the others if you can manage it.

Yes, Elanor. I can manage. Climb aboard and I will see you to them.

Evor groaned as he stretched out his wings, the pain still radiating through his body. Elanor's eyes caught the wound that pained him and she shook her head, wishing that she could do something for him. She did not have enough magic left in her system to even heal so much as a molecule of one of his scales, which would regrow them in the blink of an eye. The wound was also far too big for her to do anything. If only Ayr was here. She sighed as she clambered up Evor's side, making her way back towards her saddle.

Evor did not move until Elanor was in place. As he stood up, Elanor could feel that his legs were shaky underneath him, but Evor groaned, pushing himself to stand. Elanor gave him a push of magical energy that surged through his body yet went immediately to his injuries. Still, Evor steadied himself and rose to his feet. Elanor had seen Rotang vanish behind the other side of the Obelisk only moments ago and knew that that is where he would be. Evor headed off in the direction, back towards the south of the Obelisk.

As they rounded the city, they saw, for the first time, the true destruction that Sinibad had brought upon the Obelisk. The summit that her father, Crassus had once called home was no more. She remembered where Sinibad had brought his foot down onto it, the enormous dragon seeming like he was only inches away from her head. The moments since then had been a blur and she was exhausted, but there was still much more to do.

Evor's progress was slow, but as he took each new step, he was steadier and surer of his body and the control he had over it. Elanor did what she could to soothe him, and for now it was enough to keep him on track. They circumnavigated the city, until both Evor and Elanor saw Rotang standing over Baldur. He was an enormous red dragon that rivalled Evor for size. The two other prospective Dragon Lords stood speaking to Baldur on the ground. Their dragons also stood overhead, two that Elanor did not recognise on sight. The first on the left was a bronze dragon with eyes that were as dark as storm clouds, while the other was a vibrant green, brighter than Baindussa.

That's Tempura and Gravu. They are bonded to Romulus and Leyla. I do not trust them, Elanor.

Hmm, I see. We have no choice if we are to ally with them in this fight.

Not only did they commit many crimes in the rebellion, but they were also thought to have torn their fellow hatchlings apart once they broke free from their eggs.

You can take them, can't you?

Not without the little one by my side. We'd best be careful.

Yes, Evor.

Rotang was the first to notice them, turning his head to greet Evor. "Ah, Evor, I see that you have returned to us. Can you fly?"

"Not yet, but I will return to the skies. My rider wishes to speak with Baldur and the others."

Rotang's eyes narrowed at her, and she felt the full force of his fury for the first time since having only met Baldur once. She felt uneasy, much like she had done many times in the presence of Gundrag. She had not seen him since Evor had chased him away, and she had kept her eyes to the sky hoping that he would not come back. So far had not seen the purple dragon reappear. It was only a few that rose out of the Obelisk that were his colour.

Rotang snorted and then leaned back. "The Lady Sunfire wishes to speak to Baldur? Fine, but make it quick."

A rumble rolled from Evor's tongue. "Thank you."

He lowered himself to the ground and allowed Elanor to climb down his neck. She hit the ground and found all three prospective Dragon Lords staring at her. She straightened her tattered and bloodied uniform before pulling herself up to her full height and closed the distance between them. It was odd being outside the city and the Obelisk on the ground, but this was no normal situation.

"Lady Sunfire!" Baldur's voice carried across the open space between them. "Fancy seeing you here."

"Baldur, I don't have the time for your games. Why are you three plotting and not helping the survivors?"

Leyla cut across Elanor. "We've done what we can, Lady Sunfire. I don't see you or your dragon helping out either."

Elanor just glared at her and Evor snarled from behind. Leyla was not put off by Evor, but instead just smiled up at him.

"And just what do you think you are going to do, Evor? Gravu will rip you limb from limb if you can't fly."

"We don't have time to trade pointless jabs, Leyla. Baldur, I came here to put my name forward as the fourth Dragon Lord. I think my credentials speak for themselves."

She was greeted by laughter from both the dragons and their riders alike. The dragons all homed in on her as the riders continued to laugh. She stood in between the three of them, her fists clenching into fists as she waited for one of them to speak. Romulus was the first to come to his senses.

"You, a Dragon Lord? Elanor, please forgive me, but your dragon is barely airborne. I don't think that gives you the right to demand a seat on this council."

"Evor will return to his full strength soon. You know as well as I do that I was groomed for this position. I can help."

Layla scowled. "None of us were appointed by either the Overlord or the Dragon Lords due to their untimely deaths and whilst I do not agree with the Lady Sunfire on many things, she is qualified. Should her dragon heal, she is as powerful as any of us."

Baldur leaned back, his eyes cold and calculating, running her up and down. For as powerful and as ancient as he was, he was still a man that could be manipulated despite his demeanour. If she had moved Kaladin to love her, perhaps there would be a slither of that with Baldur to help her get what she wanted. There would be nothing between them other than a purely political motivation on Elanor's behalf. Ayr was not here anymore.

"At this stage, I do not think that we are in a scenario where we can refuse a more than skilled hand. Her lineage is proof of that. For all the Sunfire's flaws, her father was still an excellent and powerful rider, and he no doubt groomed her to succeed him."

"Then let her be Lord Chairwoman, not a Dragon Lord."

Baldur was firm in his decision. "No. There should always be four Dragon Lords. This way we can also keep a closer eye on her. We know that her promised is Ashbourne's dragon. Who knows what she will do should he come calling."

"A wise decision, Baldur. Perhaps you should put your name forward to become Overlord."

Baldur shook his greying head and cast a gaze towards his dragon that let a puff of smoke rise from his nostrils. "Rotang will not allow it. I cannot be afforded to hide behind a mound of paperwork and ceremonies when there is action to be taken. Nor do I want the role, unlike some."

"Then who can lead as our figurehead? Who has the pedigree?"

Baldur turned back towards Leyla and a thin smile spread across his lips. There was no warmth to it. "When we were summoned to the Obelisk, I could sense a change in the wind. I requested that the Hormook join us. With the new way that Dalton has waged his war against the Commonwealth, it was clear to me we need outside help."

Romulus shifted in his chair, looking like he had just sat on a thumbtack while Leyla's face twisted into a grimace. "The Hormook? Are you sure, Baldur? What in Chilijo's name could come from inviting them back to the Commonwealth."

Leyla cut across him. "Nothing good by my reckoning, Romulus."

"When Kaladin told me of his plan to wake the Keeper, it was the only decision that I could make. Out of all the riders in the world, they are the most apt at being able to contain that threat."

"If there are even any left alive!"

"Unless something has happened in the past few weeks since I last saw them, then there are two Hormook still left alive. They are Terenas and Athel. Those are the last two that remain."

"Baldur!" Romulus raised his voice. "You can't bring them here! They will destroy us."

"Not when their magic is directed at an appropriate target. Both the Keeper and Dalton Ashbourne fit that criteria."

"There's a reason why they weren't called to assist us during the Ashbourne rebellion."

Baldur's eyes flashed a shade of red as he rounded on Romulus. "This is not the Ashbourne rebellion, nor will I allow it to become another. Dalton has his allies, and I have mine. The Hormook will make their presence known here in the Commonwealth. I will cut the head off the snake before it can strike at us again."

"This is a terrible idea, Baldur."

"Are you sure about that, Lady Sunfire? I was not aware that your position at your father's beck and call made you privy to the situation in the north."

Elanor snarled and snapped back like a ripcord. "Just because I was heavily involved with the Obelisk and the ongoings in the Seminary of Fire does not mean that it was my only focus. I have had a lot of time to study our manuscripts and texts."

Baldur leaned forward, a smirk widening across his face. "Then by all means, tell me. What do you know of the Hormook? They are only mentioned in a handful of texts. Have you ever seen them in person before?"

"I know enough. I know they are uncontactable. But they are a myth, more than anything. How were you able to reach them?"

Baldur's smirk remained etched across his face. "A myth? Hardly. Before I was recalled by Kaladin, I took liberty to reach out. I have reason to believe that they will be with us presently."

"You know they pose a threat to the Commonwealth."

"They may, but when it comes to Dalton Ashbourne and this elder dragon, I am not willing to take that risk."

"You've just made things worse, Baldur."

"A necessity if we are to win this war."

"And what then if Dalton should defeat them?"

"Dalton Ashbourne will fall, Lady Sunfire. I did not put my hat into the selection to become a Dragon Lord only to fail. Dalton is a threat to our democracy and our way of life and must be stopped at all costs."

"Any threat to the Commonwealth must be stopped. But forgive me, Baldur, if we are to defeat Dalton, should we not go about this the proper way."

"Drastic times call for drastic measures, Lady Sunfire. Your father and Anton understood that. They did what was necessary when the time called for it."

"I am not my father."

"Nor would we expect you to be. Crassus was a one-of-a-kind sorcerer, the likes of which we will not see again."

"I know one that can be."

Baldur shook his head, staring down his nose at Elanor as a blood vessel looked ready to pop in his forehead. "I will not hear of the

Ashbourne boy's skills. He has chosen to side with his father. The fact that you think he is still on our side is absurd, Elanor."

"He was forced to go with Dalton; he didn't want this."

Romulus groaned from beside Baldur. "We need to keep her close to keep an eye on her. If she goes running off to him, then we can put her head on a spike. Her last name will only add legitimacy to our claim, Baldur. We can claim that Crassus wanted us as Dragon Lords before he died."

Baldur frowned and shot a glance at Leyla. Elanor could see him calculating the risks, weighing up the pros and cons of the situation. Baldur's throat tightened and his eyes darkened. There was something about him. Perhaps it was the decades of experience, and his sternness, but with the events that both Baldur and Rotang had been a part of, there had to be a trauma underneath that hard exterior somewhere. He would be a harder wall to break than Kaladin had been, even if she was to use her charms on him. Perhaps Romulus would be an easier target, but considering his physical appearance, even though he was younger than Baldur was less attractive. There was something about Baldur's grizzled and ragged appearance that she liked despite his demeanour. She cut across before he could speak again."

"I will be able to take on the mantle of Dragon Lord."

"And what of your dragon? He can't fly."

"Do we have access to the dragon's maw?"

Baldur's frown remained etched on his face. He glanced around at Romulus and Leyla with a tired expression. "There is one in the city, yes. We will be able to use it to transport Evor to the Haven, should no other dragons need it first. Meet us there when you are able, Elanor as we usher in this new age of the Commonwealth."

"Should I take this as a notion that you'll accept my ascension to the position of Dragon Lord beside you?"

A loud sigh came from Romulus, and it was his turn to stare at the other two, dejected. "What choice do we have? If Evor is fit, he is among the most powerful dragons in the Commonwealth. We need action now! You may prove to be a valuable asset as well."

Baldur rounded on him. "You do not decide for us, Romulus!"

"The Lady Sunfire is correct. We need to act now. If she fails in the role, we can remove her. The new Overlord that we install will be able to remove her, Baldur."

Baldur shook his head, but Elanor could see his expression was softening. "Fine. Usually, I would not be for such a brash course of action, but our backs are against the wall. The riders have never been weaker."

Leyla nodded her agreement. "Ready your dragon, Lady Sunfire. We will prepare the dragon's maw and have the surviving wyrmguard bring you to the Haven for our ascension."

FOUR

Ayr Ashbourne had never seen eye to eye with Dalton Ashbourne. Ayr knew better than to question his father, but everything about what he was doing seemed against what Ayr wanted to do. Yet here he was, following him once again. There was not a choice. If he chose to disobey, then Evor would have been killed right in front of them, or worse, Elanor. Dalton already had blood on his hands and Ayr wanted to avoid more of it being spilled. Even though she had not verbalized it yet, Azura thanked him for his compliance, knowing what his refusal would have brought down upon Evor.

There were no words that needed to pass between them for the majority of the journey. Ayr's decision weighed heavily on his mind. This had always been part of the plan though. Elanor and Evor had been the distractions, and the one thing that Dalton had not accounted for. Ayr kept his thoughts to himself, blocking Azura from his mind as she flew. Even she knew at the moment now was not the time to pry.

There were mixed emotions coming from Azura and even though Ayr had barred her entryway to his mind, he could still feel her every thought. There was everything from anger and resentment towards him, back to the realization that Evor would have been killed without him choosing to follow Dalton. If only any other dragon had picked him and not her. Why had the one dragon in the offering that had been promised to Evor chosen him?

Ayr closed his eyes and sighed, leaning back in the saddle, allowing the wind to rush around him. He cast his mind back to Elanor and how she had stood there, watching him leave. The hurt and betrayal she felt came through Azura, a direct message from Evor. If he stood up to and fought back against Bryne and Dalton as well as their dragons, all four of them would have been killed. Even though leaving Elanor had been the only correct option to get them out alive, it had not been easy.

He had half a mind to direct Azura back towards the west and back towards the fallen Obelisk to where Elanor and Evor would have been waiting. Yet the Obelisk was now in pieces, broken by the enormous golden dragon that flew ahead of them, just within the horizon. If Sinibad was not the unstoppable behemoth that Ayr knew he was, he might have respected the giant more. Instead, he cowered in fear, unable to work out how anything could stop him, considering the next largest dragon, Evor, had fallen before Sinibad like a child's toy.

As Ayr lulled in his musings, Sinibad changed course ahead of them. The golden dragon turned, almost in a one-hundred-and-eighty-degree circle, before turning and heading to the northwest. Ayr was confused, as was Azura and she reached out to him, probing against the barrier he had put in place.

Where is the monster going now?

We can't be heading back towards the Obelisk. There's nothing left there for him to destroy.

I don't think we are Azura.

The more that they turned to follow Sinibad, it was evident that the golden dragon was not headed back towards the Obelisk. In fact, they almost passed within sight of it, the Seminary of Fire passing underneath them. The volcano that the Catalyst had been completed on was directly underneath their path. His mind fell back to when Azura was much smaller, when he was much weaker and the conflict that had taken place on the mountain top. He pictured himself throwing Gable off it, the first time he thought he had killed him. Azura entered his mind with a sigh.

That memory should not haunt you, Ayr. You just killed that rider. Yet his dragon still remains.

Onoss will be of no threat to us. You have killed the dragons of the Dragon Lords, Ayr. That spawn of Sinibad is nothing by comparison.

Thank you for the reassurance, Azura.

It seems that you need a lot of it at the moment. Sit back and enjoy the ride. We are together. That should be enough for you, Ayr.

She pushed her way into his mind, and Ayr was too exhausted, not willing to fight. He slumped back in the saddle as Azura's presence overwhelmed him. Whilst he had shut her out previously, there was now no point. His only options were to sit here and accept his fate or leap from the saddle; the latter would only lead to either Dalton or the fall catching him and neither sounded savory to him.

His mind was elsewhere. Azura still filled it, but it was now with her calm, soothing tone, a single melody that let Ayr focus his thoughts. All he could see were the fall of the Obelisk, Sinibad striking Evor from the sky, and the death of Draxion and Grace as Elanor begged for Dalton to release them. He had no mercy, but this was all part of the plan. Dalton had told him as much before he had sent him to the Seminary of Fire. But Bryne, Bryne was new. Ayr had considered him not yet ready and that was why Dalton had sent him headfirst into the Seminary. Ayr had not wanted his brother to receive a dragon, but it was clear that others in the Ashbourne line demanded a bond.

The time slipped by and Ayr had lost track of it. Night was falling when Sinibad started a descent towards the ground. Bryne and Dalton followed him on Zaurien and Onoss respectively, dipping into a deeper dive. Ayr finally saw what they were seeing and Azura followed as they made their way towards a massive lake that was of a similar size to Sinibad. Zaurien and Onoss landed, and before Azura had, both riders had already dismounted. When Azura touched down, Dalton was already waiting for them with his hands on his hips.

I will follow your lead, Ayr. You've got to be the one that can stand up to your father.

Can't you just eat him, and we can be done with this?

You know as well as I do, he's too magically gifted to not see me coming. I would if I had the chance to.

Perhaps one day.

One day, Ayr. You should speak to him.

I don't think I'll have a choice.

Azura shook her head as Ayr began the climb down from her back. Each step he took down Azura's side was getting heavier as the realization of what he had done. There was no barrier between them now and there was no protection offered by anyone other than Azura. He knew that Dalton would not have brought him all this way just to harm him. Dalton remained standing as Bryne moved into position behind him. There was a clear direction from Zaurien to stand behind him. With Onoss standing behind them, they cut an imposing figure against the golden lit surroundings of the lake they had landed beside.

"So, you haven't turned and run away from me yet."

Ayr stooped into a low bow, paying respect to Dalton. "Why would I do that, father? Was this not part of your plan? To have us reunite and to have Bryne with a dragon of his own?"

Dalton's mouth twisted into a thin line. It was clear that he was not pleased with Ayr's response. "You know full well that it was not the plan. I should strike you down where you stand!"

"And why would you do that, father? The Commonwealth has still not been destroyed like you wanted."

"No, but this was just the first step of many. You were not supposed to fall in love with the Sunfire woman!"

"She is my dragon's promised rider. What was I supposed to do? I can't help that Azura was bonded with Evor!"

Dalton raised his finger and his tone in response. "You are a fucking Ashbourne, boy! The rules do not apply to us! You should have resisted her!"

Ayr...

I know. I want to, Azura.

You will only grow stronger as he will grow weaker over time. Now is not the time to strike. We will be able to soon.

Knowing that they were outnumbered, Ayr listened to the calming voice for Azura in his head. Every fibre in his body wanted to reach out with his magic and strangle both Dalton and Bryne. The latter sat back on Zaurien and allowed the events to play out in front of him. He removed his mask which was decorated in the pattern of a deer, which Ayr thought was an odd choice for him.

Bryne shook out his hair and was evidently happy as he stared down at Ayr. Ayr wanted to launch an attack at him, just to at least knock him off his dragon, but if he did, Dalton would smite him. The fact that Bryne now had a dragon after mocking him for the weeks leading up to Ayr's insertion into the Seminary of Fire and how he would not be chosen as a dragon's rider. Now that Ayr had the better dragon, he knew that the rivalry between the two of them would only be renewed with more vigour and fire. He glared back at Bryne, trying to let his displeasure be known through his eyes as Dalton continued to berate him.

"You'll fall into line. Just because you have physically left her side does not mean you are free from her attachment. I will break this bond that you have brought upon yourself so you can live free like Chilijo intended it to be."

The name of the Commonwealth's deity perked Ayr's curiosity, and he took a small step forward.

"Why father?"

Dalton's eyes narrowed. "Why what?"

"You bring Chilijo's name into the conversation. I have heard many conflicting things about the great dragon that once won them the war. Why do you think that he intended for the dragons to live free?"

Dalton exhaled and pressed his hand to the side of his head. "I don't have much time left, Ayr. I can feel my magic beginning to leave my body."

Ayr rolled his eyes. "Spare me the pity. I know your reasoning for wanting to take the Commonwealth by force and it has nothing to do with you running out of time. You want vengeance, and nothing else."

"If that was my only concern then I would have succeeded in my task by now, Ayr. Stop being so narrow minded. I should have pulled you out of the Seminary the moment I suspected you falling for Elanor."

"You needed me there. Without me, you would not have gotten your claws as far into the Obelisk and their command structure as you did."

Dalton snorted heavily and started to laugh. Above him on Zaurien, Bryne mimicked his sounds. "I needed you? Boy, I walked into Crassus' chambers unopposed. I walked into the Haven untouched. If you think I needed you, you are mistaken. You are just another tool."

"Then why did you go through all that effort to get me there?"

"It is clear to me that you still don't understand what is necessary for me to achieve my goal of a reform across the Commonwealth. You have much to learn. Your magic may have shown it's potential when you killed the Dragon Lords, but potential is nothing. Get back on your dragon."

"I'm not finished speaking to you."

"I am. We have somewhere to be, Ayr. Don't force my hand."

Ayr grit his teeth and he could feel the power surging behind Dalton's eyes. He knew that he was too valuable for Dalton to kill, but that did not mean that Dalton could not make his or Azura's life miserable until they reached their destination. As he took a step back, Ayr felt the atmosphere around him begin to return to normal. The hairs on the back of his neck were still erect as Azura entered his mind again.

Stop! Don't let him get under your skin. Just tell him what he wants to hear.

Ayr bowed his head in submission. Dalton pulled away and turned back towards Onoss who had his head also bowed. He placed his neck onto the ground and allowed Dalton to grab onto one of the jagged spines that were dispersed along his neck. One of them just in front of where Dalton had placed his hand was snapped off, jutting out like a plateau. It was odd seeing a rider board a dragon without the need for a mask, but having seen it before from Dalton, Ayr was not surprised.

It was uncanny, still seeing both Dalton and Bryne on the back of dragons that looked so out of place. Yet even as they watched him retreat to Azura, Ayr could feel the burning eyes of Bryne on his back. There would be no escaping his gaze until it was clear to him that he had fallen in line. Before coming to the Seminary and to the Obelisk, it would have been easier, but now that he had Azura, he was going to have to put on quite an act.

Ayr traced his footsteps back to where Azura was waiting for him. Despite all that had happened, she still looked magnificent, her white scales still flawless against the green and brown background she stood against. The armour that she wore was still embedded in her body and there was nothing more that he could say to her.

Patience, Ayr. We will have our moment.

FIVE

Ayr and Azura continued to follow Dalton and Bryne as they flew north. Dalton was as forceful and as pushing as Kaladin had been when Ayr had been flying towards the Keeper's lair. This time it was different. There was no looming threat of Kaladin wanting to kill him or Azura hanging over him anymore, but he suspected that Bryne would be more than willing if Dalton gave the word. They were spread across the sky in an equal formation. If they had been approaching the Haven with Sinibad at the helm, terror would have overtaken the city without a sizable dragon to tackle Sinibad now that Drementhol was gone.

It had been a week since the fall of the Obelisk and Ayr had a suspicion that the Haven was where they were going. Yet as the familiar opening landscapes around the Haven came into view, Sinibad, who was still leading them, turned and headed more west. They were nearing the outskirts of the Commonwealth, heading towards the border of it when Sinibad made another turn to the north.

Where in Chilijo's name is he going?

I have no idea, Azura. Nobody ever comes this far northwest.

Your father does.

They continued the ride in silence, the wind lapping around Azura's wings and breaking over the saddle. There was nothing he could do as this journey continued. It was clear to him that Dalton had a plan, something that required them being near the Haven, but not too close.

Was his goal to destabilise the riders first and then launch an attack on the Haven whilst they were at their weakest? Their fortresses to the east held more strength, holding back the hordes that threatened the Commonwealth, but their true strength lay in the dragons that roamed the skies.

As the day grew longer, Sinibad was finally starting to descend from cruising altitude. He cast a glance back over his shoulder for the first time, ensuring that he was still being followed. Ayr felt uneasy as he watched Sinibad comb through the mountains like he owned them and he wondered if this is where the elder dragon had been hiding for all the years. He seemed to know his way around every nook and cranny and the canyon that they were in began to narrow as it rose up around them.

Ayr narrowed his eyes, spotting something in the distance. He felt like he was approaching the Keeper's lair once again, but as they neared the figure on the horizon, it was not only covered in snow, but there was more to it than one spire. Nestled in the middle of the canyon, protected from the elements stood a city that seemed to almost rival that of the Obelisk.

However, the towering spires that were in the centre of the city greatly resembled those that had been in place at Ashenfort. As they neared the new city that was rising out of the ground in front of them, Ayr frowned and Azura, curious, probed his mind.

What is wrong, Ayr?

This looks exactly like Ashenfort but it's not. Has Dalton conjured a replica out of thin air?

I would not put it past him. Do you know how many allies he is likely to have with him? If he has not been alone this whole time, then it is possible he could have conjured the city through the labour of men.

I was never privy to his plans. He could have thousands at his disposal. I imagine after twenty years of scheming, he would have allies.

The Marshadow brothers proved that Dalton still has allies everywhere within the Commonwealth. I would imagine that once more people hear that he has returned to the world they will flock to his cause.

Do you think we will be the only riders?

You may have only been a child when the war broke out, but I can still remember it. If those that returned to the Commonwealth after his defeat have seen what he's done, I doubt it. We will have to see.

I worry what the future will look like, Azura.

We are only playing his game now, Ayr. We will learn more of his plan in the coming days and weeks.

Stay close to Sinibad whilst he is not hostile to us. I don't know what awaits us here.

We will be fine. You are your father's son after all.

Some days I don't know about that.

Sinibad dove low towards the city. Considering there was no alarm from it, Ayr assumed that the city knew that they were coming. Sinibad's roar announced their arrival if it had not already. Yet unlike what he had experienced at the Haven, no weapons of any kind turned towards them to shoot them out of the sky. They were present in the city however. Dalton had invested in a similar ballista to the Commonwealth, each of them with their deadly points aimed at the sky, but remained locked in their position.

The walls rose up around them and Sinibad flew off into the distance, towards the largest mountain peak that was behind the city. Sinibad settled upon the peak, his talons gripping at the ancient stone as his muscular tail wrapped thrice around the mountain's circumference. From this angle, the mountain appeared as if carved by Chilijo himself specifically to cradle the golden dragon, whose scales now caught the light and cast a beacon visible in every direction. With Sinibad settled into his roost, Azura followed Onoss and Zaurien into the city.

There was a clear-cut strip of grass beside one of the larger buildings that appeared to be a dragon stable. Onoss and Zaurien were headed towards it and were not slowing down. From underneath the stable, Ayr saw a large blue head moving, one that would have almost matched Evor for size. It strolled out into the sunlight, its eyes narrowed as it glanced up at them. Ayr saw that its left eye was bruised and swollen, a cut on the scales just above it.

Do you know who that is, Azura?

Hmm. She does look familiar, but I have not seen her at the Obelisk in years. That's Manir, no wonder why I have not seen her. Her rider is Kita Stromguarde. They went missing on a regular mission investigating one of the border cities. Nobody has seen them since.

Went missing? How is that possible? Would the watchers not see it go wrong?

The watchers are not always right, Ayr. I guess she came here.

Ayr frowned, running the name through his head. It did not seem familiar to him, but Dalton had told him about many allies that he had in the first rebellion. Yet her name was not one that came to mind.

That would explain why nobody foresaw the fall of the Obelisk then.

Is Dalton strong enough to block their magic?

Maybe he killed them first. Surely, they still would have told their riders.

You and I both know that communication is not one of the Commonwealth's finest assets, Ayr.

Ayr snorted as the tallest buildings now towered over them. He laughed at Azura's joke, her humour still incredibly dry despite all the time she had spent around both dragons and riders at the Obelisk. She was using it as a coping mechanism, but he did not blame her. All he could do was support her and try to take some of her grief from her. Whilst he had not spent long at the Obelisk, he still felt the loss through her.

Onoss touched down on the grass strip first, followed by Zaurien and then lastly Azura. Now that they were on the ground in this strange new city, Ayr felt no more at ease than he had when they were flying. With Sinibad looming over them like a giant guardian, he still felt uncomfortable. He could picture the monster standing over the wounded form of Evor, and he knew what the golden dragon was capable of if Azura ever got in his path. The tall blue dragon that had seen them enter the city approached them, and the smaller dragons were all dwarfed by her.

Her voice was as smooth as Azura's, but deeper most likely due to her size. "Dalton. It is good that you return to us. Was your trip eventful?"

"You can see we have returned with the white dragon, Manir. Of course it was eventful."

Manir turned her attention towards Zaurien and her voice softened. "That is good then. And who is this?"

Zaurien puffed out his chest as he stood up taller. He still barely came up to her chest, but it was clear to Ayr that he was trying to impress her. Azura sniggered at the gesture.

"I am Zaurien, my lady. Dragon to Bryne Ashbourne."

A sparkle came into Manir's eyes as she glanced down at him. Their eyes met and something unspoken passed between them. "Another Ashbourne dragon? That is very interesting indeed. Kita will be very eager to meet you."

Dalton cut across the conversation with a commanding boom in his voice. "Manir, where is Kita?"

"She awaits your arrival in the war room."

A look of annoyance came over Dalton's face as he sighed. "Of course she does. I didn't expect anything less. Come with me, my sons. Let us see in this new age in the Commonwealth's timeline."

Questions were burning on the edge of Ayr's tongue. His jaw clenched tight, muscles twitching beneath his skin as he fought the urge to demand answers. What exactly was Dalton's plan now? He had achieved his vengeance on Grace and the others that had wronged him. What role would Ayr play in this dangerous game? The Commonwealth was still not defeated by any stretch of the imagination. The weight of uncertainty pressed down on his shoulders like the massive wings of Sinibad. Ayr drew in a deep breath, steadying himself. The time for hesitation had passed and the act that might save them all or condemn them, had to begin now.

"What is this place, father?"

A smirk spread across Dalton's face as he slid down from Onoss' neck. He glanced around at Manir and the rest of the city.

"This is what I built. This is what Ashenfort should have been all those years ago before it was destroyed. It's called Ironrock."

"Why here?"

"We loom in the shadows of the Haven, Ayr. How else do you think I could strike at it so quickly, and then fade back into the abyss? When I have completed my goal, this will be the new seat of power."

Manir spoke over the top of them. "And it will be glorious. This is what Chilijo envisioned for us when he first began the Commonwealth all of those years ago. I am glad that we now have all the remaining Ashbourne family under one roof."

Dalton's smirk remained etched upon his face. "I couldn't agree more, Manir. Now we need to organise our next strike against the Commonwealth."

"What are you planning, father?"

"Never mind that, Ayr. You've done enough already. Now come."

Dalton landed on the ground with both of his boots squelching, the thick grass underfoot. He stormed away from them, leading them towards the hall that Manir had emerged from. Bryne slid down the neck of Zaurien and landed with a heavy thud. Not wanting to be left behind and chastised for it, Ayr dismounted from Azura and followed Dalton.

The dragons lingered, Azura feeling unsure as of what to do until Manir turned her head and spoke again. "Follow me, little ones."

Onoss bowed his head in response. "Yes, matriarch."

The ground was shaking as the dragons started to walk behind the riders and Ayr was taking in more of the city. He had brief memories of what Ashenfort had looked like when he was a child, the perfect white stone of the mountain carved into the architecture that surrounded it. The streets were wide enough to accommodate even the largest of dragons, all except Sinibad, but he did not need the roads when the sky was his. The surrounding city was sparsely populated for its size, and Ayr wondered just how many people were in it and if any of them were phantoms summoned by Dalton.

They were all clad in thick black robes, much looser fitting than the riders uniform that he still wore, and he did not get close enough to any of them to investigate them properly. There was the proper and fluid movement of a person, but Dalton's ability with magic did not give Ayr the answers he was seeking. For a man that made shadows like a second skin over his body, he did not put it past him.

The room was pitch black; the darkness so complete it seemed to swallow the sounds of their boots reverberating off the floor. When Dalton clapped his hands together, an amber light bloomed from nowhere, spreading like liquid fire across the ceiling. The glow pulsed with the rhythm of a sleeping dragon's breath, casting dancing shadows that revealed ancient stone walls etched with draconic runes. Heat radiated downward, warming Ayr's face and he felt more at home.

Dalton continued moving forward unhindered, and unspeaking. He burst through the threshold of the hall, and for the first time since he had dismounted from Onoss, did Dalton look small. The hall was as expansive as the one that the late Dragon Lords had resided in and it was almost as if Dalton had it copied, except as they neared the rear room, there was only one chair present.

The throne, which was a massive obsidian structure with dragon scales etched into its surface, dominated the room, wide enough to seat three armoured men shoulder-to-shoulder or accommodate a juvenile dragon curled in repose. A tall blonde woman who Ayr could only assume was Kita, reclined across it like a predator at rest, one leg dangling over the armrest, the other stretched along the seat's polished surface. Between her slender fingers twirled a dagger that caught Dalton's light with every rotation, while her other hand absently rolled a jade-green apple across her palm.

Her features mirrored Elanor's with the same high cheekbones; the same full lips curved into a knowing smile. But where Elanor's hair fell in dark waves, Kita's cascaded like spun gold to her waist. A black leather eyepatch covered her right eye, the strap cutting across her otherwise flawless face. Her remaining eye was a pale blue like winter ice over deep water, several shades darker than Azura's and watched Ayr with predatory intensity. Dalton spread his arms out wide as he drew within earshot of the throne.

"Dearest Kita, what have I said about taking liberties whilst I am not here? Just because Manir is the power of this place while Sinibad takes his leave, does not make you ruler of my Commonwealth."

Kita's voice was soft, low and husky, like a whisper carried through mountain fog. Each word rolled off her tongue with unfamiliar inflections. Her vowels stretched where they should not have been, consonants clipped short or lingering too long. The cadence reminded Ayr of ancient songs sung by travellers who claimed to have journeyed beyond the Commonwealth's southern borders, where the traders spoke of lands untouched by dragon fire.

There was a glint in her eye, like the fire from Manir's belly radiated within her. "Dearest Dalton, what have I told you about the fact that I don't care? You were gone for two weeks. I was so bored here without you."

"You should have been watching the skies, Kita."

"Manir does that for me. Besides, I could be doing worse than sitting here minding your seat for you."

"You know you're not supposed to touch it."

"Just like I wasn't supposed to touch you?"

"You have never been one to follow directions, Kita."

A high-pitched, raspy cackle that Ayr recognised, echoed from the rafters. He glanced up to see a sleek obsidian shape detach from the shadows, with its wings unfurling with a leathery snap as it spiralled down through the air. The miniature dragon was no larger than a house cat but with scales that gleamed like polished onyx. He landed with practiced precision on Dalton's left shoulder. It was Chorru, his serpentine tail coiling possessively around Dalton's neck. A wisp of smoke curled from his nostrils as Dalton snorted appreciatively at his companion and reached up to scratch the sensitive spot beneath Chorru's scaled chin, eliciting a rumbling purr that vibrated against his master's ear.

"It's good to see you, old friend."

"I've tried to keep her in line, Dalton, but she just won't listen."

"Remove yourself from my throne, Kita. You're not my wife."

Kita pouted as she sat up properly, biting into the apple and then stabbing it with her dagger. "I should be."

Dalton's demeanour shifted, and his eyes darkened. "Do not disrespect me, Kita. Just because you came to me seeking power, does not mean that I am willing to give it to you. You will do as you are told or Manir will be broken."

Kita moved herself off the throne fully now, the pout more prevalent as she drew closer to Ayr. Dalton approached the throne and passed Kita. He had not taken his eyes off her and did not until she had passed him. Kita removed herself from his gaze the moment she neared him and instead fixated on both Ayr and Bryne. The little fire in her blue eye told Ayr that there was no doubt there was a silent conversation happening between herself and Manir and she was plotting something less than pleasant.

"You need us, Dalton. We will bring more riders into the fold."

"You forget your place, Kita. May I remind you of what awaits outside."

Kita threw her hair back and Ayr caught a glimpse of a split dye underneath the blonde. She glared at Dalton. "I have not forgotten, I am merely choosing to ignore it."

"And that will be your downfall. Leave us. I would like to speak to my sons in private."

SIX

ita slinked away, her boots quiet against the tiled floor. Manir turned and followed her without a word, and then the only sound that filled the hall was Manir's footsteps. Dalton moved back towards his throne with Chorru still resting on his shoulder. When Dalton reached the throne, he paused to inspect it and Chorru clambered down from his arm onto it. With Chorru coiling around the throne, Dalton turned his back and sat down on the throne, spreading himself out, but not as wide as Kita had been.

With the room emptied of Kita and Manir, it became silent as a grave. Dalton stared at both Ayr and Bryne. Ayr felt uncomfortable as Dalton's eyes drifted over him, assessing him properly for the first time since Dalton had made his presence known at the Obelisk. His eyes were ice cold, void of any warmth and he felt like he was a child, once again back under Dalton's gaze, unable to do anything to defend him.

Now is not the time, Ayr.

I know. We know nothing about what his intentions are yet.

Ayr cut the communication off, waiting for someone else to speak. The silence was uncomfortable, until Dalton broke it.

"Well done, Bryne."

Out of the corner of his eye, Ayr saw Bryne smirk. He was Dalton's mirror image. It was everything from the sharp cut of his jawline to the slight asymmetry of his eyes, but where time had etched deep lines into

Dalton's weathered face, Bryne's skin remained taut and unmarked. It was the difference between aged leather and fresh parchment.

"Thank you, father. What have I done now?"

"You now both have dragons. It is clear to me that you have much yet to learn."

Ayr stood up straight, feeling Azura's presence at his back. "I was still learning plenty, father. You had no reason to destroy the Obelisk. If you had given me more time, I could have access to all of their records."

Dalton shook his head and snorted. "If you think they would have given you access, then you have another thing coming. You are delusional, Ayr."

"I had the ear of Elanor. She was going to become a Dragon Lord like you wanted her to. Then you had to go and harm her dragon!"

"She needs to be kept in line. And like I said to you, you were not supposed to fall in love with her."

"I didn't. I was using her."

Ayr!

Dalton raised his left arm, the sleeve of his dark robe falling back to reveal a forearm etched with swirling runes that pulsed with violet light. It was unlike his dragon tattoo that Ayr knew was emblazoned across his chest and was not something Ayr had seen from him before. Ayr's windpipe constricted as if gripped by invisible talons, the magical force crushing against his throat until black spots danced at the edges of his vision. His boots scraped against the polished stone floor as he was wrenched upward, suspended in the air like a puppet.

With a flick of Dalton's wrist, Ayr shot forward, the room blurring around him until he jolted to a stop mere inches from the ornate throne. Dalton rose with predatory grace, his shadow stretching across the floor between them. Chorru arched his scaled neck and hissed, revealing needle-sharp fangs before his forked tongue darted out, the wet tip grazing Ayr's cheek with a touch cold as winter.

Don't panic, Azura. He won't harm me.

I can't free you from his magic!

Don't do anything!

"Don't lie to me Ayr! You fell for her and have been smitten ever since. I know what effects a promised dragon has on another's rider."

"That wasn't my intention."

"Yet it was what you achieved none the less, boy. Your failure almost cost me."

"You've had us at your beck and call ever since you made your presence known with Sinibad in the cave. I have only ever done as you have asked."

"Yet you failed to kill Crassus. That was your one task. Without me, you would have failed."

"You know what I did, don't you?"

Dalton shook his head and snorted. "Poisoning the book? It could have been years before he touched that."

"You didn't specify how the job had to be done!"

Ayr left a snap in the back of his mind, and Azura was gone from it as if she had been snuffed out of existence. He felt no connection to her, even though she was standing just behind him. It was as if Dalton's magic had severed the bond between them. Ayr tried to reach her, but there was nothing but a block in place between them. He could not even turn his head to see where she was. There was nothing between them. Dalton took a step closer and did not raise his voice.

"How dare you go against my orders. Your brother would not have hesitated. All you had to do was drive a blade between his shoulder blades and vanish. That was your task!"

"They would have hunted me."

"You've been hunted your entire life, Ayr. I think you've lost your edge. The woman made you soft."

"I killed the new Overlord without hesitation."

Dalton stepped around Ayr, his eyes not moving from his face. "Major Kaladin Dawnscar? The man that flattened Ashenfort with his dragon? I wonder what motivation you had for that, Ayr. I am well aware of the fact that he was involved with Lady Sunfire before you went to the Seminary of Fire."

"He and I had issues."

Ayr felt Dalton's rage coil around him like a vice, his throat growing ever tighter. Ayr was finding it difficult to breathe as he felt Dalton's breath on the back of his throat. The pressure against his throat felt like iron bands tightening with each passing second, his pulse hammering against the magical restraint. Dalton's hot breath, reeking of contained fury, ghosted across the nape of Ayr's neck, raising goosebumps along his skin despite the suffocating heat of the moment.

"Issues? He fucked your woman, and you wanted him gone. I could not trust you to bring the Obelisk down on your own. Thankfully Bryne was better trained."

"Then who's failure is that, father?"

A hot needle-like sensation erupted down Ayr's back as he felt Dalton lash out again. Ayr crumbled underneath the blow, despite resisting, trying to do everything he could to stand against it. He heard Bryne's snide laughter behind him as Dalton appeared in front of his face once again.

"You were the eldest! You were supposed to be the one that would claim my legacy first. Instead, your brother had to come in to accelerate the plan."

"Accelerate the plan? Father, you always intended on inserting Bryne into the Seminary of Fire. That was what we agreed upon."

"I did, but when it was clear you did not wish to do what was necessary, it was time to play my backup plan. I am disappointed in you, Ayr."

Dalton's voice shook him to his core. Without his connection to Azura prevalent, all he had to rely on was himself. With Dalton and Bryne present, however, Ayr was not confident he could beat both of them. In response, Ayr hung his head in shame. He needed to know what Dalton's next move was before he made it.

"Apologies, father. What can I do? I don't want to fail you again."

"And you won't. You will remain here with me until I deem you ready to venture out into the world again."

"I am already more powerful than any other rider in the Commonwealth, father. I can handle myself should they attack me."

Dalton snorted again. "If only your power was what I was concerned about. You proved yourself powerful enough when you helped me murder the last Dragon Lords, however I don't think that was because you wanted to."

"Elanor was in danger I had to respond."

"I thought so."

The constraints around Ayr's neck loosened and as they fell away, he could feel himself starting to breathe once again. His feet touched the ground as if he had stepped onto a cloud, but his knees buckled underneath his weight, forcing him into a kneeling position. Ayr tried to push himself up, but could not, instead he was forced to stare up into Dalton's eyes as he kept an arm raised over Ayr. There was nothing he could do to fight his way out of this predicament.

"You used your power, not because you wanted to, but because you wanted to save your dearly beloved."

Ayr grimaced and spat through his teeth. "My promised."

"It matters not, Ayr. I intend for there to be one final strike against the Commonwealth. Neither you or Bryne are completely ready to take over my legacy. You need more training, especially now that both of you have dragons of your own."

"What would you know, father? You have never had a dragon of your own bonded to you."

"Ayr!"

A boot flattened Ayr before he had the chance to defend himself. He was on his back, staring up at the ceiling as Dalton moved over him. Even though no new magic had been used on him, Ayr felt stunned, and unable to move. Dalton sneered down at him.

"I spent decades studying dragons and their magic. I was taught by someone of the highest order to understand it and use it to bend the world to my will. Speak to me like that again and I'll remove your dragon's head."

The pain made Ayr's chest feel like it had collapsed as his ribs pulsed from the impact. Dalton took a step back away and Ayr tried to stand but found himself unable to. There was something holding him to the ground. Instead, his voice was the only tool he had available to him. Without Azura, Ayr felt like his magic was completely cut off.

"Don't, I would turn on you without her."

"Then perhaps you should consider your next words carefully. You know I already intend to sever your bond with Azura. Perhaps you need to prove yourself to me that you are worthy of keeping her."

With Azura not in his head, she spoke out for the first time. "I will incinerate you, Dalton!"

Despite the threat from Azura, Dalton was still calm like there was ice in his veins. "You'll do nothing. You've seen what I can do!"

Ayr went to turn, to make sure that Azura was alright, but as he did he felt her coming back to him. It was like a rush of adrenaline that took over his entire body, like a wave surging to flood his entire body. Dalton had released the block and Azura shot into his mind.

"What did you do?"

"You two control nothing here. Everything is as I will it to be. Now, I want to see something from you, Ayr. Bryne, step forward."

Ayr looked up and saw Dalton throwing a knife that he had summoned at him. It was not blade first, but rather it had been thrown in a way that he could catch it by the hilt. Ayr extended his arm and heard Bryne moving on the tiles behind him. Ayr spun as the knife touched his flesh, but it was almost too late. Bryne was coming down over him, with a silent roar as he stabbed down with his own blade. Ayr was already on the backfoot, and Bryne's dagger missed his face by inches, but Ayr was not so lucky with the rest of his body.

They came together with a grunt and Ayr was thrown back to what seemed like a lifetime ago, when he had accosted Bryne in the halls of the Obelisk, screaming that his name was something else. However, now their roles were reversed, and Ayr was the one in the disadvantaged situation. Something told him that Dalton was not going to jump in and save him. Azura roared overhead, as did Zaurien. She leapt forward, but Zaurien did as well, cutting her off.

Ayr!

Dalton's voice ripped across the room, louder than either of the dragon's roars. "Use your power, Ayr! Show me something!"

There was no anger and no flow of magic that came from Dalton, but Ayr needed to do something. Bryne's face hovered inches above his, sweat beading on his forehead and dripping onto Ayr's cheek. Bryne's lips curled into a wordless snarl, revealing his teeth that were stained yellow, as he leaned his full weight onto the hilt. The polished steel of his blade pressed against Ayr's collarbone, threatening to slice through his flesh and bone with each laboured breath.

Azura and Zaurien snarled overhead, the former trying to get past the latter, with Zaurien doing whatever he could to block her movements. He nipped at her, but Azura did not want to press past him. Ayr could see her vision in his own mind, and he urged her forward, but even though he was younger, Zaurien was already larger than she was. The fact he was not attacking told Ayr that he still had a chance here. He grunted, and shifted his weight, moving to the side.

Bryne slipped off him and Ayr felt the dagger push by his side, running down his arm. Ayr got his legs out from underneath Bryne and kicked away from him. Incensed, Bryne brought the dagger down again and this time it stabbed the ground between Ayr's parted legs. Ayr kicked back at Bryne and shot to his feet as Bryne tried to avoid the blow. With his feet underneath him, Ayr stood up and beckoned for Bryne to come at him.

Bryne obliged him and climbed to his feet. He ran forward, swiping and snarling as he came, Ayr being able to parry and step back with each swipe. Bryne kept coming, and Ayr thought back to the dozens of times that they had sparred. Bryne was as skilled as Ayr having spent almost as long being pushed by Dalton in their training. Whilst Bryne was not Dalton, he was still a threat and Ayr's magic still felt constricted, even though Azura was back in his mind. It was not how Dalton wanted this fight to go.

Their stalemate erupted into a dance, steel flashing under the dim light as Ayr parried Bryne's vicious overhead swing. Sweat beaded on Ayr's forehead, trickling down his temple as he countered with a desperate thrust that Bryne dodged. Neither man wasted breath on taunts or threats. There was only the harsh rasp of laboured breathing and the metallic ring of blades humming through the air. Deep within, Ayr felt Azura's magic coursing through his veins like liquid fire, sharpening his reflexes. It kept him alert, keeping him up to the pace when Bryne feinted left then slashed right. Ayr arched his spine backward, the blade whistling mere inches from his throat, before his fingers clamped around Bryne's wrist with crushing force, yanking his opponent off-balance and into striking range. His dagger was inches away from Bryne's heart.

"Stop!"

Dalton's voice cracked beside them like a bullwhip striking stone, each syllable that he spoke reverberating through the chamber. Ayr's muscles seized together, his body becoming as rigid as if encased in ice. When he managed to exhale, the warm breath caught in his constricted throat, he saw Bryne's arm extended toward him, the blade reflecting the dull glow of Dalton's conjured light. The razor-sharp edge hovered an inch from the base of Ayr's neck, where his pulse hammered beneath his sweat-slicked skin.

"Look at the pair of you. Barely more than forty summers between the both of you, and you are always at each other's throats. However, I can see that one of you has the edge and the other does not. Competition has always brought out the best in our family."

Ayr glanced down at Bryne's blade that had not moved from his throat. "I'm not going to kill my brother to prove myself to you in a training exercise."

"You don't have to. I can tell from your body language that your intent is not there. I'm disappointed in you, Ayr."

Ayr tossed his blade to the side, and saw it evaporate the moment that it left his hand. Dalton had no further use for it. "So, you'd rather I injure or potentially kill one of your most valuable assets? I thought Bryne was your favoured son."

Dalton stepped closer to him. "Yet I trained you first. You have your part to play in this as much as he does. You're not good enough for what comes next. You'll remain here, in the city under my supervision until you prove yourself capable. Am I understood?"

It was pointless to argue with him. Agree Ayr, we can bide our time. His fall will come when he least expects it.

Ayr could not find a fault in her argument and took her advice. Dalton's latest spell uncoiled like a serpent releasing its prey, the invisible tendrils of magic receding from Ayr's limbs one by one until the tingling sensation of returning control flooded through him. His fingers twitched, testing their newfound freedom. The urge to lash out at Dalton burned hot in his chest, but Ayr swallowed his pride, forcing his shoulders to slump in submission.

He pivoted, the stone floor cold and unyielding against his knee as he sank down in feigned reverence. Dalton's thin lips curved into the barest hint of a satisfied smile as Ayr lowered his gaze, hiding the defiance that still smouldered in his eyes.

"I will do whatever you ask of me, father."

"You still have much to learn, my son."

SEVEN

We are almost there, Elanor. Wake up.

Elanor was rocked by Evor's voice as she slept in the saddle. It had been one of the longest flights of her life, outside the recent trips she had taken with Ayr and Azura as well. However, this time, Evor had not been flying. The dragon's maw that had first brought her and Evor to the Haven was in use once again, and they were suspended between a handful of the wyrmguard dragons. Due to the use of the dragon's maw, the flight had been slower, and Elanor wished that Evor was able to fly again.

His healing would take time, but a week had not been enough. There were no resources that they could utilize at the Obelisk, many of them destroyed in the collapse or otherwise needed on dragons that were more wounded than Evor. Those that could fly had done so in the days before the future Dragon Lords and the wyrmguard had left, but even their numbers were diminished.

There was a school in place that was constantly training those to replace the wyrmguard that were already in service, their skills of a higher level than what the Obelisk could provide. And there would be many suitable riders to be used as replacements once word reached the Haven. Above them, Elanor knew were the Marshadow brothers, along with the Lord Chairman Barrett. There was no point in him maintaining the role at the Obelisk given that it was no longer left standing. Nobody had any idea as to how best to restore the Obelisk to its former glory, but without the structure in place, the surrounding city was left in ruin.

The decision had been made to leave it behind, uprooting everyone's lives that still lived there. With half of the city destroyed, it was no longer suitable for habitation. Dust from the Obelisk had settled throughout every inch and facet of the city and it coated every surface with a thick blanket. The protection that it offered was now diminished if Dalton Ashbourne chose to attack again. The city's defences were also crippled, and those dragons that had fought against Sinibad were either dead or dying. Over the coming days as everyone had tried to figure out the next step, some had succumbed to their wounds.

Dozens of dragons were in the air all around them, carrying multiple passengers along with whatever supplies they could carry. The journey was slow, due to the dragon's maw not only being in use for Evor's sake. There were three more present, some of them carrying several dragons in each. It was a poor excuse for a convoy, but it was all that they could muster. Elanor did not feel like they would be able to stand up to Sinibad and Dalton's horde of wyvern if they chose to come back. Evor did what he could to calm her mind.

You are being irrational, Elanor. Why would Dalton attack us again? Trying to find us flying through the skies, even at this slow pace would be extremely hard to do.

You know how well he can control magic, Evor. What's to say he doesn't have a spell that can locate us?

Elanor, we're almost at the Haven. He is not going to be waiting behind a mountain just to strike at us.

Elanor rose up out of her slouched position and sat in the saddle properly. Evor was laying flat against the floor of the dragon's maw, and was somewhat comfortable, unlike he had been during their last trip in the massive logistical device. Due to his injuries and his size, Evor was alone, with the other maw's packed to the brim with smaller, yet less injured dragons. Some could fly, but most of them could not, especially given the severity of their injuries and the duration of the flight.

She wished that he was free to roam the skies, and that they were moving to the Haven under his own steam. But instead, she was just grateful that Evor was alive. Sinibad could have ended him in a heartbeat and for whatever reason, Dalton had spared him. Yet she could not be grateful to the man that had taken everything else away from her. Evor was now the only family that she had left, and she needed to avenge the ones that had passed on.

With nothing left to her name, Elanor was a shell. With nothing left to do except wait for their journey to be over, Elanor relaxed in the saddle, attempting to push magic into Evor's veins to help him heal. It had been her daily ritual, draining herself whilst they had been inside the dragon's maw, taking the time to replenish her energy throughout the rest of the day. Despite her efforts, Evor was only a fraction better than what he had been a week ago. Each night when they landed, Elanor spent an hour holding herself against Evor, draining herself to the point of exhaustion. She was not the only rider that had repeated the process with their dragon. Those riders that were in a similar situation to her were also helped by those around them. The more capable riders brought the riders meals, while their dragons brought deer from the surrounding areas for others nourishment.

The progress had been slow, but now the end of their journey was in sight. The walls of the Haven were just within sight of the horizon. It was not home, the place that Elanor wanted to be now nothing more than distant memories that lingered in the past. The dragon's maw was set down a short while later and the city rose up before them. Elanor could only watch as the wyrmguard dragons let the thick netting down around them, falling away from them like a cage.

It is time we returned to the skies, Elanor.

Evor yawned as he stood up from his prone position in the net, and almost immediately tried to unfurl his wings and take flight. He managed one step, and then another, regaining his footing. Evor was hesitant but he wanted to be in the sky. Elanor gave him the push he needed and Evor took another step forward, flapping his wings as he stood on the ground. The pain radiated through him and shot into Elanor as a result. Evor grunted and tried again, only for the same result to occur.

You still need to rest, Evor!

I will rest when I am dead, Elanor.

You're lucky you're not already. Can you walk?

My strength is not that far removed from me. Of course, Elanor. Where are we going?

Elanor glanced up at the sky just in time to see Rotang and the other dragons of the Dragon Lords flying overhead. Elanor sighed, exhaling through her nose as she shook her head. They had been forgotten about once again. Evor entered her mind, seeing what she had seen.

Do you want me to follow them, Elanor?

Of course, Evor. They won't forget about us.

Evor grunted as he took another massive step, this time he was out of the dragon's maw. He grew in confidence, each time another foot touched the ground was another success in his mind. Elanor reassured him and guided him forwards, still pumping what remained of her magic into his body as best she could. The road that they had landed beside was wide enough to support him, as were the gates that barred entry to the Haven.

Dragons lined the walls as they always did, and the gatekeepers were tracking them from the moment they had landed. The gates to the Haven were not usually opened on the account of dragons being able to fly over them, however in this instance it was needed. The main

gate of the Haven had three different levels to it to better help control
the flow of traffic that was coming through it. The first was a small
door that only had room for Evor's head.

The second was another layer that had enough room for a dragon
the size of Azura to pass through unencumbered and then the third
was what needed to be opened now. As Evor approached the gate, the
dragons that guarded it wrenched back on the controls, allowing it to
open. The controls were too big for any human to operate, and they
required the assistance of dragons to open. The only way that a human
could open the gates were if they were magically gifted akin to the
power of Dalton and Ayr.

As they passed underneath the open gate, Elanor locked eyes with
the dragons that sat atop it. They stared back down at her, but she
could feel them only looking at Evor. The dragons made her feel
smaller than what she was, her reflection and Evor's evident in their
eyes. Evor turned his head towards them, eyeballing them until he had
passed them. They stood by, their silent judgement evident and Elanor
saw them recoil as they noticed the wounds on his back.

"He survived the elder dragon?"

Both Elanor and Evor heard their whispers, but Elanor kept
Evor focused on moving towards their destination. She kept his head
straight, even though she could feel the doubts creeping into his mind.

You are stronger than most, Evor.

She continued to track the new Dragon Lords towards their destination, which appeared to be nowhere else except for the hall which
was where they would base their operations from. Elanor urged Evor
on underneath her, desperate to catch the Dragon Lords before they
left her behind once again. Evor quickened his pace, cutting through
the Haven like an overgrown snake, careful where he placed his tail.
They passed numerous dragons, all of whom stared at Evor's wounds.

That was the least of their concerns, however. Elanor could see Rotang and the others landing in front of the hall. Evor increased his pace into his run and let loose with a roar that broke across the sky. All three of the Dragon Lords turned to face them, their dragons snorting a puff of smoke from their nostrils. Despite being the smallest of the three, the largest smoke plume came from Gravu. She continued to snort as Evor ran towards them, desperate to catch up as their riders dismounted.

"Late as always, Evor."

Evor was out of breath from the running, the wounds on his back still causing pain to radiate through his body. Elanor reached down from the saddle and patted Evor, pushing her last remnants of magic into his body. He groaned as he received the magic, his focus solely on Gravu as she taunted him.

"It was unlike you to help me, Gravu. I saw how you treated the others at the Obelisk that fared less fortunate than yourself."

Gravu's usual shade of green was a touch darker for a moment as her scales flushed with anger. She leaned forward as Leyla slid from her neck, helping her rider closer to the ground. Leyla touched on the ground in front of the hall with grace, flicking her hair out behind her as she shrugged her mask from her face. The other two Dragon Lords were mirroring her actions as Gravu spoke.

"At least we can fly, Evor."

"Now is not the time to be comparing ourselves to each other, Gravu. Dalton Ashbourne has struck at our core, or did you forget that? My home, as well as yours, has been destroyed. I did not realise that lordship put you above the rest of us. I am here to help you."

Tempura stepped forward to greet Evor, Romulus on the ground beside him. "We are grateful for the assistance, Evor. And we're sure that Elanor will in turn become a great Dragon Lord."

"We will do whatever we can to assist the Commonwealth in achieving their goals."

Rotang frowned down at Evor, his eyes narrowed to a point. Elanor felt small before him as Evor lowered his head towards the ground. She began the descent down his side, as the other Dragon Lords awaited her arrival.

I wish Ayr and Azura were here.

So do I, Elanor.

Can you sense her?

No Elanor, since she left the Obelisk, I have not been able to sense her. Either she is too far away from us, or Dalton is shielding her presence.

What are the chances that they are close by and that it is the latter.

I cannot see into the mind of the madman, Elanor. Only yours and Azura's.

Stay alert for me, Evor. If you sense her, we may be in danger.

Of course, Elanor.

Elanor's boots struck the packed earth with a dull thud, her knees bending to absorb the impact as she dismounted. The leather of her riding gear creaked as she straightened, her muscles aching from hours in the saddle. Across from her, Baldur's weathered face remained impassive, his steel-grey eyes fixed on her without blinking, his scarred hands hanging motionless at his sides like those of a statue.

"You would be late to your own ascension as Dragon Lord, Elanor?"

"What, we're doing it now? Shouldn't we wait for everyone to be assembled?"

Baldur glared down his nose at her, his lips thinning as he thought over his next words. "We have wasted more than enough time on the journey back here. Now that we are in the correct place, there is no time. Once we are appointed, we can go about our business."

"You need the Overlord to appoint us."

Romulus shook his head in disagreement. "Not in times like these. There are others who can fill that role."

Elanor frowned. "Who? Nobody sits above the Overlord."

Romulus raised his hand towards the sky, his finger pointing to the horizon. "There are two that do. The Hormook come for us now. They will appoint us as Dragon Lords."

EIGHT

E lanor followed Romulus' outstretched finger as her breath caught in her throat. Two monstrous dragons approached, their wingspans casting moving shadows that swallowed entire city blocks. The Haven was large, especially given the size of some of the dragons that it housed, but buildings that had seemed grand moments before now looked like children's toys beneath the colossal beasts. Their scales were polished obsidian, darker than midnight and reflecting sunlight in prismatic bursts along their underbellies. As they crested the Haven's walls, their jaws gaped wide, revealing rows of teeth like ivory claymores. Their synchronized roar vibrated through Elanor's chest, rattling windows across the city and sending birds scattering from every rooftop in panicked clouds. Each of the dragons rivalled the size of Drementhol and due to their size, would have been centuries old.

Is that the Hormook?

Evor grunted at her, his voice filling her head. I never thought that I would see the day that they would return to the Commonwealth.

It looks like that day is today, Evor.

We are in grave danger. Baldur will answer for this decision.

Let me become a Dragon Lord first.

We should move out of the way. These dragons do not care about other's lives if they get in their way.

Are they that full of self-importance nothing else matters?

Indeed, Elanor. There is a reason why they are so long lived.

It appeared that Elanor was not the only rider that was having the conversation with her dragon. The riders moved towards the entrance to the hall, and their dragons made their way towards the roof of the hall. Whilst Evor groaned as he unfurled his wings, but there was no need for him to fly as he climbed up the side of the building. Elanor watched him work his way up behind Gravu, before settling in beside her. They watched as Hormook approached, their beating wings almost in synchronisation. The dragons slowed down, approaching the hall of the Dragon Lords.

Side by side, the obsidian behemoths landed with such force that cobblestones cracked beneath their massive talons. The impact sent tremors through the Haven's foundations, rattling windows and dislodging roof tiles that clattered to the ground like broken pottery. Elanor's knees buckled, her hand shooting out to try and grip onto something to steady herself.

The first dragon swung its wedge-shaped head toward the riders, it's nostrils flaring with plumes of sulphurous steam, and its pupils constricting to thin slits in eyes that gleamed like polished amber. The second beast's sinuous neck arched upward, jaws parted to reveal its teeth that were as long as swords, its gaze fixed on the dragons perched along the rooftop. Above her, Elanor felt Evor's muscles coil as tight as bowstrings.

I have a bad feeling about this, Elanor.

The dragons themselves were ghastly apparitions of decay. Their massive frames were twice the size of Evor and were covered in obsidian scales that hung from their emaciated bodies like armour several sizes too large. Each scale overlapped the next in jagged, uneven patterns, creating a patchwork of dark plates that rattled when they moved. Deep crevices between the scales revealed glimpses of sickly grey flesh beneath, as if the creatures were slowly decomposing despite being very much alive. When they exhaled, a sulphurous miasma escaped from between their yellowed fangs, each tooth longer than Elanor's arm.

Elanor could not see the Hormook riders from her position on the ground, but she could see through Evor's eyes that they did not sit in a saddle. Rather than that, both Hormook riders stood, clinging onto one of their dragon's scales as if they were directing the dragons by their hands. Elanor had never seen such an intimate connection between a rider and their dragon. The dragons responded to the rider's touch and then moved towards the ground, much like most other dragons did when their riders wanted to dismount. The Hormook riders slid down their dragons and came to land upon the ground a moment later.

Elanor's breath caught in her throat as the Hormook riders dismounted. They towered at least seven feet tall, their limbs unnaturally elongated and thin beneath their armour. When they removed their masks, Elanor's hand moved to her belt, even though she had no weapon. Their skin hung in loose folds from sharp cheekbones, the colour of old parchment left too long in the sun and was not quite white, not quite grey. Their eyes were set deep in hollow sockets, glittering like wet stones in shadow. No lips framed their mouths, just taut skin stretched over yellowed teeth that seemed too numerous and pointed. The air around them carried a faint scent of something acrid and ancient, like disturbed tomb dust.

Baldur was the first to move as the Hormook dragons breathed down smoke around them. He raised his arms and stepped forward with a beaming smile that was very unlike him.

"Terenas! Athel! Welcome to the Haven!"

The taller Hormook's eyes were amber with vertical slits like that were much like a reptile. He followed Baldur's every movement with predatory intensity. This one was evidently male, with silver hair cropped so close to his ashen skull that individual bristles caught the light like tiny blades. Three parallel scars lined his forehead, diagonal cuts that had healed into ridges of discoloured tissue, deep enough to suggest they had once exposed bone beneath. They looked ancient, as though they had been carved there centuries ago by some massive talon.

"Baldur, you're fortunate that we came."

"And I am forever grateful that you answered the call, Terenas. How was your flight?"

Terenas appeared to have no patience for Baldur or his formalities, instead opting to be short and blunt. "Fine. Now can we get on with business? I was under the impression that you would be eager to get this over with quickly so we can get on with hunting Dalton Ashbourne sooner rather than later."

Baldur bowed his head in what Elanor thought was a first. This man never bowed to anyone, not even the Overlord or the Dragon Lords that had come before him. Yet here he was, standing before the Hormook, ready to bend the knee for them.

"And how did you fair, Athel?"

The female Hormook carried herself with the same imperious demeanour as Terenas. Her spine was rigid, and she carried her chin tilted upward with ancient pride. Her silver hair caught the light like polished metal, flowing past her shoulders in rippling waves that framed her gaunt face. Unlike Terenas' cropped style, hers cascaded down her neck in elaborate braids interwoven with what appeared to be small obsidian beads, matching the colour of her mount's scales. When she moved her head, the ornaments clicked together, creating a sound like distant rainfall on a stone. Even her tone was reminiscent of Terenas.

"Fine. As Terenas said, we have business to conduct. Will you take us to the dais?"

Baldur bowed his head even more and gestured behind him towards the hall. "Come with me then, please. We will get underway when you are ready."

"We are ready now, Baldur."

Before Baldur had turned and directed them into the hall, Elanor was already making her way inside. Evor had his head down on his legs as he rested, sucking in every ounce of oxygen that he could. The next part of this journey would be only one that Elanor could undertake. The Hormook moved behind them, their footsteps, if they had any were silent. Elanor could not see their boots underneath the dark robes that they wore on their bottom halves, and little was known about them.

Baldur strode ahead of the group, his shoulders tense as he guided the prospective Dragon Lords and the towering Hormook through the grand hall. Marble columns stretched toward the vaulted ceiling where ancient murals depicted dragons in flight. Instead of turning toward the ornate double doors of the council chambers where the Dragon Lords traditionally convened, he veered sharply left, leading them down a dimly lit secondary corridor. Torches flickered in iron sconces along the rough-hewn stone walls, casting long shadows that danced across the worn flagstones beneath their feet. The ceiling here was low, and it was commented upon by Athel.

"It is a good thing that we don't need our dragons here to complete your coronation."

Baldur turned his neck to glance back to check over his shoulder on their guests. "Apologies that our facilities don't match your expectations, Athel. You have not graced us with your presence in centuries."

"Nor have we had reason to, Baldur. The concerns of the Commonwealth are not ours. You should know that better than anyone."

"Yet you came when I summoned you."

"We could feel the world's upheaval when you called upon us. If it was not for that turmoil, we would not have come. You should not expect anything else from us."

Baldur bowed his head again as he returned to face forwards, pushing on the door in front of him. "Noted. I'll be sure to bring it up with the new Overlord when we appoint them."

"Is that sarcasm, Baldur?"

The corners of his mouth did not move. "I'm not sure what you mean, Athel. This way."

The door opened at Baldur's touch and the group filtered inside, with the Hormook bringing up the rear. Elanor had not yet stepped into this secondary room and found it to be a smaller version of where the Dragon Lords held council. Instead of there being the chairs lined up on the podium in the centre of the room, there was a dais that housed a small altar, no wider than Elanor's shoulders. On it was a single chalice, similar to what she had drunk out of all those years ago at the Obelisk right before she and Evor had been bonded together.

The two Hormook moved towards the dais, their silver hair gleaming under the torchlight as they stepped up onto the ancient stone platform. Athel's weathered hand rose in a commanding gesture, directing the prospective Dragon Lords to stand in formation before the dais. Meanwhile, Terenas with his face half-hidden in shadow, moved with deliberate slowness around behind the platform, his long fingers trailing across the carved runes etched into its edge.

Terenas' skeletal fingers were as pale as moonlight against the midnight fabric, and they disappeared into the folds of his robes. The whisper of silk against skin broke the silence as he withdrew a crystalline vial that caught what little light existed in the chamber. The container was as long and slender as a rapier's hilt, contained a swirling liquid that seemed to pulse with its own inner luminescence. It was neither fully liquid nor gas, but something caught between states of matter.

He reached out towards the chalice, his long fingers curling around its ornate stem. Terenas unstopped the vial as his silver eyes flicked upward, meeting the stern gazes of the Dragon Lords who watched from their lowered positions, before he tipped the vial. The contents slithered out, thick and dark as midnight blood before coiling into the chalice with a soft hiss that seemed to echo in the chamber's tense silence.

"The blood of Chilijo."

Elanor's back straightened like a bowstring being drawn taut, her spine rigid with tension as Terenas lifted his ancient, hooded gaze from the ornate chalice. His pale eyes were as cold as winter frost, and they locked with hers across the chamber. It was a silent challenge that made her throat go dry. The moment stretched between them until Athel raised her slender hand, adorned with silver rings that caught the torchlight, and pointed one long finger deliberately toward Baldur, who stood motionless as stone at the edge of the dais.

"This process should be swift. Would the first nominated step forward. Baldur Cole."

Baldur grunted with a sound like gravel shifting beneath a boot, and stepped out of line. His weathered face betrayed nothing as he moved toward the dais, his footfalls echoing against the stone floor. The torchlight caught the silver threads in his dark hair as he approached Terenas, whose pale fingers extended the ornate chalice. The vessel gleamed with and seemed to writhe in the flickering light, the liquid within dark and still as midnight. Baldur kept his eyes locked onto Terenas as he stretched out for the chalice.

"By taking this oath, you will become a Dragon Lord of the Commonwealth. You will do your best to defend her borders and see her interests protected. Do you swear to uphold this oath?"

Baldur nodded with conviction. "I do."

"Then drink and see it done."

Baldur took the chalice from Terenas, without breaking eye contact. With one firm arm, Baldur raised the chalice to his mouth and drunk from it. A drop of Chilijo's blood spilled onto his face as Terenas tried to take the chalice away, but it was clear from his facial expression that Baldur wanted to keep drinking. When he removed the chalice, Terenas raised a clawed hand, pushing Baldur back.

"May the next nominated step forward."

It was clear to Elanor that even though Baldur was acting normal, Chilijo's blood had changed something about him. He walked slower, and seemed unfocused, but there was no time to ponder what had happened to him as Leyla and then Romulus. Each of them, repeated the process and oath that Baldur had undergone before walking back off the dais to stand back in line.

"Will the next nominated step forward. Elanor Sunfire."

Relax, Elanor.

Elanor inhaled through her nose and walked forwards up onto the dais. Terenas held the chalice out for her and as she approached, she could see over the lip of it. The blood of Chilijo stained the edges, but she could see that there was much less than what had originally been in there. Terenas stared at her as she approached before Elanor's hands rested on the chalice as she waited for him to say the words.

"By taking this oath, you will become a Dragon Lord of the Commonwealth. You will do your best to defend her borders and see her interests protected. Do you swear to uphold this oath?"

Elanor nodded with conviction, mirroring the other Dragon Lords that had made their ascension. "I do."

Terenas' eyes filled her with a sense of dread as he pushed the chalice towards her. Yet she was in this position now and there was nothing she could do to get out of it. She was so close to achieving one goal that Dalton had set her. This was for her safety, and Evor's.

"Then drink and see it done."

The memories of her bonding ceremony with Evor came surging back to her. Elanor raised the chalice to her lips and let the thick, dark blood slide between her lips. It ran down her throat and was smooth. She could feel the ancient magic in the blood as Evor entered her mind once again. He encouraged her to drink with his gentle probing, and Elanor continued to chug the liquid until Terenas placed his hand on the chalice, lowering it from her lips.

She could feel the blood working down her throat, and there was a chill that ran down her spine that coincided with the blood's movement. Terenas raised his hand and pushed her away. Knowing that it was now her time to retreat, Elanor stepped off the dais and returned to stand beside the other newly appointed Dragon Lords. Terenas placed the chalice back where he had found it, before he looked out towards them.

"Congratulations, Dragon Lords. You now have bound yourself to the ancient magic that Chilijo spread across the world. You by his divine right, now have the authority to guide the Commonwealth however you see fit. Our job here is done."

Baldur spoke up, clearing his throat. "Forgive me, Terenas. Would you not stay here whilst we make preparations to take the fight to Dalton Ashbourne?"

Athel's gaze sharpened as she glared down her nose at Baldur. "We granted you one favour, do not push your luck, Dragon Lord."

"I merely thought that you would want to see order returned to the world before you departed once again."

"We will see order restored, but we will do it at our own pace. Do not push us."

Baldur bowed his head. "Of course, forgive me."

Terenas stepped down away from the dais. "We're done here. Enjoy the rest of your day, Dragon Lords."

Both Terenas and Athel made their way out of the room, bowing their heads to leave. Elanor watched both of their forms become nothing more than shadows. The Dragon Lords stood in silence, until the ghastly figures of the Hormook had left their hall before Evor crept into Elanor's mind once again.

Congratulations, Elanor. This is something nobody in your family has ever achieved.

I don't feel any different. I thought like when we bonded that I would feel new power or something that would just mark my ascension.

You just took an ancient oath, one that very few riders take. You've just tied yourself to the other Dragon Lords and the Commonwealth. Will you do what is necessary to ensure its survival?

I will do what must be done, Evor. I have to ensure your survival and mine. We have to live for Ayr and Azura, otherwise Dalton will rule over us all.

We need to play the game well, so they trust us.

I will work on the dragons; you work on the riders. Together, Elanor, we are unstoppable.

NINE

Romulus was the first of the Dragon Lords to speak as his gravelly voice shattered the oppressive silence like a hammer through glass. The physical world around Elanor seemed to snap back into focus as Evor's rumbling thoughts continued to echo through the corridors of her mind. She pushed against his presence, feeling the familiar resistance like trying to close a door against a strong wind, before turning her full attention to the half-circle of Dragon Lords with their weather-beaten faces and calculating eyes

"Well, that was interesting. I never thought that I'd see the day that the Hormook made their presence felt here."

Baldur's eyes narrowed as he followed the path of the Hormook out of the room. "If they leave the city, we will be worse off because of it. Our power is scattered thanks to the efforts of Dalton Ashbourne and his elder dragon."

"We're not going to be able to stop them from leaving the city if they want to leave us. The Hormook have their own agenda."

Leyla scoffed from beside Elanor. "And yet we beg them to come and help us. What's to say they won't side with Dalton in the war?"

"We don't know, Leyla. But we need to decide upon our next steps."

It was now Baldur's turn to scoff at Romulus. Even though they had all ascended together, Elanor felt like each of the new Dragon

Lords was trying to position themselves above the others. This would not be sustainable as they needed to support each other.

"Romulus, we have nothing. The Haven is not what it used to be, despite the additions that Kaladin made to the city, we can't defend against a force like that. We don't have the riders we once had either."

Elanor had heard enough and stepped forward. "Where is your leadership, Baldur? You had no qualms when you were flying out destroying villages that had pledged their alliance to Dalton. What's stopping you from that now? Is it because you don't know where the next attack will come from?"

Baldur rounded on her, a glare flashing in his eyes. "Just because you are a Dragon Lord does not mean you can overstep, Elanor!"

"I'm a Dragon Lord, the same as you. I took the oath. The Commonwealth is mine to rule over as much as it is yours now, and I will serve it well. Before I die, I want this place to be better than how I found it!"

Baldur stared at her for a moment, considering her words before he chewed on his bottom lip. "Then we need to get on the same page if we are going to defeat Dalton Ashbourne."

Elanor breathed a sigh of fresh air. This was all she had wanted from them and if Baldur was realising the error of his ways, the other two would come around as well. "Where do we begin, Baldur? I'll follow your lead if you have a plan."

"We need to send out scouts that can give us reliable information. The sooner we know where Dalton's base of operations is, the better. Due to the limited number of wyrmguard we have readily available, we will need to delve into the academy to elevate more. I would send the Marshadow boys, but I want them to stay close to me, I do not trust them."

Romulus raised an eyebrow as he questioned Baldur. "Do you want me to go to the academy then? These are unprecedented times. I can find the recruits we want to give this mission to. A task force of six riders should suffice should it not?"

Baldur nodded and turned his back on the rest of the Dragon Lords. "Yes, now that we no longer have access to many watchers, we need to direct what we do going forward. I will entrust you with this. Elevate them all, Romulus. Even those that aren't ready yet."

"I'll take my leave then."

Elanor watched as Romulus pushed past Baldur and followed the same path out of the room as the Hormook had. Silence fell over the room again as those remaining looked at each other. Leyla scuffed her boot on the ground before walking out behind Romulus without another word. It left only Baldur and Elanor in the room together. He stared at her again.

"I'm sure you've got your own agenda for wanting to become a Dragon Lord, but I will not have you sowing division amongst us. Do whatever you need to do to ensure that you are prepared to hunt Dalton."

"You do the same then. We should not sit around like our predecessors."

The lines around Baldur's mouth narrowed. "I will, Lady Sunfire. Best of luck to you. I pray to Chilijo that we can get through this alive."

As Baldur finished speaking, he bowed and stepped away, exiting the room like the others had done so before him. Now Elanor was opening her mind once again to Evor and he entered it without permission, but she needed his comfort.

We have a job to do, Elanor.

I'm not doing anything until you can fly again, Evor. You are my number one priority.

Evor's quiet chuckle filled her mind. *You are far too kind, Elanor. I will need the time to heal on my own, but I will gladly accept any assistance you can offer me.*

I want you back in the sky sooner rather than later.

I will fly again soon, Elanor. I can feel it.

Then prove it. I will come to you.

I will come to you Elanor, then we can leave the city for a moment.

Hold on.

Something flickered in front of Elanor's vision in the darkness. She readied what little magic she had remaining in her body, and summoned what little flame she could, holding it in front of her face. As she moved it overhead, a dark shadow dropped down from the ceiling. Elanor leapt back out of the way as the shadow made it's presence known. Elanor rolled her eyes, realising what was in front of her.

"How fares dearest Evor, Elanor?"

"You can ask him yourself if you weren't that much of a coward and ventured to the roof. What are you doing here, Chorru?"

Chorru laughed, smoke "And face the other dragons that reside there with him? I don't think I will."

Elanor grit her teeth together out of frustration. Of all the creatures that she had expected to see today, Dalton's annoying and constant companion was not among them. She took a deep breath as Chorru flicked his tongue in and out of his head. She wanted to grab it and drag the smaller dragon to her, throttling him before he had a chance to defend himself. But if he was here, Dalton wanted something.

"What do you want, Chorru?"

"Dalton sent me to check on your progress. I must say, the ascension to lordship was one that was very lacklustre. I was expecting more. The Hormook however, that is something worth noting."

"That wasn't my call to make."

Chorru smiled at her, his tongue increasing its frequency in movement. "No, but it happened all the same. You should be grateful. Not everybody gets to see those monsters in their lifetime."

"They were here for a purpose. I've completed one task Dalton has sent me. Now do you have something valuable for me, or did you just come to annoy me?"

"Dalton wishes to apologise for the harm he caused your dragon, but he knows he needed to send a message to you to get his point across."

Elanor was growing impatient with Chorru as the smaller dragon continued to chatter. She wanted Evor to crash through the roof and grab him, but in doing so would expose what her true intentions were here to the other Dragon Lords.

"I don't have all day, Chorru. Tell me what you want me to do."

"Dalton wishes that you reveal his location to your friends soon. He wants the full strength of the Commonwealth brought down upon him so he can bring an end to this war."

"Where is he?"

Chorru curled in the air around her and Elanor felt his presence on her shoulders. She wanted to shrug him off, but any movement might cause the small dragon to attack her. With Evor not able to reach her, that was something she could not afford right now. Instead, the hairs on the back of her neck stood up as Chorru breathed on her.

"Dalton waits in the city he has created from his own vision. Ashenfort was lost to him, so he created a new one. Ironrock lies to the west, hidden amongst the mountains, where the golden dragon watches over it."

"And what will I say when they ask how I know where he is? That's not something that I can just pull out of nowhere, especially considering that Evor is not able to fly."

"You will know when to divulge that information. Evor will be able to take his time in recovering, but if you say you have had a premonition from your mother before she died, I would think that would suffice as an answer, would it not?"

"Some premonitions from watchers can take months or years to resolve. Why am I taking advice from you?"

"Out of everyone here, who wants you to succeed, Elanor?"

He has a point, Elanor.

I know, but we can't trust him.

Ayr and Azura are not here. We need to make this decision ourselves. Do we not want to ensure our survival. It sounds like he wants to lead what remains of the riders into a trap.

We can't leave the Commonwealth. Not without Ayr and Azura. You're also not ready yet.

Get rid of the whelp and then I will show you how ready I am, Elanor.

Elanor steeled her gaze at Chorru as the world came back into full focus. He was back in front of her, hovering inches away from her face as he beat his wings in a steady rhythm.

"You do, Chorru."

Chorru peeled his lips back to reveal his rows of jagged teeth that were like daggers. The smile unlike Evor's was not pleasant, and she wished to slap it off his face. Even though he was an annoyance, he was still correct in what he was saying and he knew it.

"I'm glad you accept your fate. This is part of your task that Dalton has set you."

"How many does he intend to kill?"

Chorru's eyes flashed bright in the darkness. "All of them."

"Is there anything else or will you continue to shadow me until the job is done, Chorru?"

"No, not for now. I will send a message back to Dalton. You should expect to see me throughout the city. You know I enjoy tracking your progress."

"You better pray that I don't end up with my magic returning to me."

Chorru openly mocked her. "Or what? You'll smite me with the might of Chilijo? You'll do nothing, Elanor."

"Get the fuck out."

"As you wish, Lady Sunfire."

With one final long beat of his wings, Chorru was gone, soaring up into the ceiling. Elanor lost sight of him almost instantly as his scales blended in with the darkness. Evor entered her mind, grumbling his dissatisfaction with Dalton's messenger.

That whelp needs to be scorched.

You're telling me. Are you ready for me now?

I have been waiting for you since you were anointed Elanor. Come, let us move onto happier thoughts.

You couldn't fly an hour ago, what makes you think you will now?

I am invigorated by your ascension to lordship, Elanor.

This is a bad idea.

Come.

She was compelled to return to Evor and could sense his presence above her. He was moving from the roof, as were the rest of the Dragon Lords. Rotang and Tempura had already departed, with Leyla now mounting Gravu. The Hormook dragons had already left the Haven, and in Evor's vision they were nothing more than dark specks on the horizon as they flew over the city. When Elanor stepped out into the daylight, she saw Evor above her, perched on the roof like an oversized bird. There was something different about him, his movements more fluid than they had been in the last week since his injuries.

Elanor's tone was light and warm towards him. "Get down here, you old man."

"Old man? Elanor, I am not part of the species that has an expiry date no longer than a breath of wind. Dragons can live for thousands of years."

Evor crawled down the side of the wall and splayed his claws out on the ground in front of her. Whilst she watched him move, she realised he was in fact moving freer than what he had been seemingly only moments ago. Evor's wing still looked to be in an uncomfortable predicament as he moved, but it was at least moving more in tune with the rest of his body. The motion gave Elanor some hope that he would be able to fly. Evor extended his neck towards the ground, and Elanor reached up latching her hand around one of his spines underneath his neck.

Evor lifted her into the air, and Elanor shook her way up towards the top of his neck and towards her saddle. When Elanor was seated, Evor shook his head out and his wings started to unfold on either side of her. Knowing what was coming next, Elanor reached into her jacket pocket and retrieved her mask from it, pulling it over her face. The world changed once again, her vision now switching between her own and Evor's.

Evor took a step forward and there were no words spoken between them. He was full of confidence and ready to fly. How had her ascension had this much of a change on him? Evor faced the cliff face and picked up his speed. Usually, he was faster shooting up into the air, but Elanor understood he wanted more speed before flying. Evor shot forward and in the next breath, Elanor felt the all too familiar sensation of flight overwhelm her.

It felt right, and Evor felt powerful underneath her as she readjusted herself in the saddle. There was no need for her to lock into place as Evor was not hitting peak velocity. This was a test, one that she was certain that he would be able to pass. The earlier shakiness had left his body, at least for the first few wingbeats, but his injuries were not yet healed. Evor soared over the first row of buildings underneath them, but Elanor felt his breath catch in his throat a moment later.

I am feeling stronger, Elanor.

Can you keep flying?

I am not sure, Elanor. The injury seems to have healed.

If you're not sure you need to land.

No, Elanor, let me fly.

Evor's confidence would be his undoing. No sooner than he had spoken, Elanor felt him shudder again, except this time it was not from his breath. Evor titled to the right, towards his injured side, and Elanor jolted in the saddle, placing her hand at her side, to try and push whatever energy she could towards him.

Then land before you undo all of the healing that you have done.

Evor grumbled underneath her, knowing that she was right. He searched for a landing space amongst the structures of the Haven and soon spotted an open space that was surrounded by half a dozen other dragons. They each looked up at them, and from their elevated positions, they were all growing in size as Evor shot towards them. Both he and Elanor braced, the landing uneven and not pretty, much like Evor was like a hatchling once more. He groaned as he hit the ground, his limbs buckling underneath him. There was a steady realisation washing over him now that he had safely landed and had his feet underneath him once again.

Perhaps I do need more of your power before we can fly properly once more, Elanor. That was not wise of me to exert myself beyond my capacity.

You just want what's best for us, Evor. We can try and fly again in a few days when your strength returns to you.

TEN

Ayr remained standing before Dalton, expecting something else to come from his father's mouth. Instead, Dalton dismissed him, with a swift wave of his hand. There was no direction from him, and Ayr was left standing in an abyss. He could feel Bryne moving behind him and he heard Zaurien snarl as the other dragon moved away from them with his rider in step.

We should go before he changes his mind, Ayr.

Go where? Dalton's given us no direction.

We will find our way in this new place. We just need to leave. Climb aboard.

Ayr nodded as Azura straightened her neck, bringing it down to ground level for him. Ayr cast one final side glance towards Dalton who was tracking back towards the throne. Dalton sat down as Ayr climbed up Azura's neck and she turned away, not allowing him to look at the source of all his problems any longer. Azura was swift, exiting the way that they had come into the room, not turning her head back to check on Dalton.

As the light started to spill into the corridor, Ayr could once again see the outside world and the city that awaited them. He grew excited about the prospect of being free in this new city but did not know what dangers Dalton would throw at them from here. If he had instigated a fight between the two brothers, did it mean that Bryne would try and kill him at any opportunity he got? The white pillars of the buildings were coming into view and as Azura stepped out into the bright sunlight, a new shadow that was far too large to be Zaurien stepped towards them from the side.

A sapphire-scaled behemoth cut through the air toward them. It was none other than Manir, her massive wings creating wind currents that buffeted Ayr's face even from this distance. Atop the dragon's muscular neck sat Kita, her blonde hair whipping behind her like a battle flag, her single pale blue eye fixed upon them. Manir encroached on Azura's space, which forced Azura to try and sidestep her, but Manir surged forward with the speed of a striking viper, cutting off her path. Azura let loose with a roar that sounded more like a bark as she was surprised that Manir was standing over her.

Kita's voice projected down from the saddle with the same gravitas and authority that Dalton had. "Just where do you think you're going, little Ashbourne?"

Ayr glared up at her. "Away from Dalton."

"Is that what you want to do? Has he given you orders yet?"

"Why do you care?"

Kita leaned back in her saddle, the leather creaking beneath her weight as she revealed a wicked smirk that split her face from ear to ear, the expression a mirror image of Elanor's but with a cruel edge that made Ayr's stomach turn. Manir's massive blue form cast a shadow over Azura, her scales gleaming like polished sapphires in the harsh sunlight. The dragon's presence pressed down on them like a physical weight, just as overpowering as Evor's aura but lacking any trace of the gentleness or warmth that Evor showed toward Azura. Instead, Manir's golden eyes tracked Azura's every movement with the calculating patience of a predator.

"I would have thought that Dalton would be taking care of you, rather than letting you fend for yourself."

"You don't know him that well, do you? What's your purpose here, Kita?"

"We came here seeking a better life. One that only Dalton could provide."

"And you worked your way into his bed?"

"That as well as many other things. I hold his ear close to my mouth."

I do not trust her at all, Ayr.

Neither do I, Azura. I feel like she would eat us in a heartbeat if she was given half a chance.

Keep your magic prepared then. For both of our sakes.

"So, what do you want with me then?"

Kita's smirk relaxed into a more warm and friendly smile rather than a sinister smirk. "I want to help you Ayr. You have not navigated Dalton's world whilst you have had a dragon by your side."

"What difference does it make? I've navigated the Commonwealth's world without one."

Manir snorted down at them, smoke from her nostrils dissipating just above Ayr's head. "All the difference, Ashbourne. Come with us."

Considering the only other option that they had was to go back inside towards Dalton, Azura reached into Ayr's mind and pushed him towards the only decision that was viable to them. If Kita and Manir were going to show them this new city that they were unfamiliar with, it would not be a bad thing. Perhaps she could divulge some information regarding what Dalton's next steps would be. Knowing that Azura was bending to their command, Manir's expression softened and she turned away from them.

Azura followed Manir, and for a brief moment, Ayr thought that he was following Evor. Azura took several steps for every one of Manir's as the two dragons walked side by side. There was no conversation between them, but instead, Kita set about giving Ayr an in-depth history lesson of the new city that Dalton had conjured from nothing but the whims of his own mind.

"After the war concluded, Dalton was exiled, having simply lost far too many casualties to be able to continue."

Ayr rolled his eyes, he had heard this all before. "I know this, Kita. How did the city come to be? How did you get here?"

"I was always on the side of agreeing with Dalton, but due to my position within the Commonwealth, could never truly join him. I was always watched by others around me and I didn't want to be thrown into the Tower of Echoes for no reason. It was only when I heard whispers that Dalton Ashbourne had returned to the world, did I take my chance and seek him out."

"You came here? Dalton was always moving around."

"I came across him when you and your family were hiding out in Nestlewood."

Ayr raised an eyebrow. "Nestlewood? That was where we went after Ashenfort fell. That was well over a decade ago. What took you so long to get here?"

"I was told to wait. You know as well as I do that your father is patient."

"What has Dalton done here?"

"You should know him, Ayr. Dalton had a vision. A life that he wanted to lead before the Commonwealth took it from him. He's rebuilt Ashenfort in his image. What it would have been if he won the war."

Ayr snorted. "If he won the war? He was never going to."

"Do you know? Were you there? If only he had not alienated Crassus early on."

"He's remedied that situation now."

Kita cast a side eye at Ayr with a snort of her own. "I'm well aware of that fact. Who do you think told him he needed to kill Crassus first?"

"So, what, are you his advisor now?"

"Among other things."

They passed under a tall archway, one that bridged the gap between two towers in the centre of the city. Ayr flinched as he heard a high-pitched squeal from above him. Ayr raised his head towards the sound and hanging from the bridge was a jet-black wyvern that was snarling at them. He raised his hand towards it, but a flicker of magic from above him cut him off before he had finished forming his spell.

"Don't!"

"What?"

Kita frowned at him from above on Manir's head. "We don't do that here. The wyvern that you will see within these city walls are all under the command of Dalton."

"They're dangerous!"

"This is what I mean. You are not familiar with Dalton's world now. Before you went to the Seminary, Dalton was still very much in hiding, now his power has reached a level where he does not have to. With the threat of Crassus and Anton gone, he has come out of the shadows."

"That was always part of the plan."

Kita flicked her split dye hair over her shoulder with a laugh. "If you say so, little Ashbourne."

"Where are you taking me?"

"There is much to discover here."

They fell into silence again, the only sounds reaching Ayr's ears being that of the dragon's feet as they crashed into the path below. Considering that Dalton had likely raised this city from the ground up, the attention to detail was impressive. It in every way resembled what Ayr had remembered of Ashenfort when it had been in all its glory, and he wondered if Dalton had been the one to construct that city as well.

Magic was in the space all around him and it was thick unlike anywhere else he had been. This place was an anomaly.

Kita and Manir turned through the streets, snaking through them, their movements showing that they both knew exactly where they were going. For the first time since being here, Ayr saw others that were neither Kita or wyvern. There were people without dragons going about their day-to-day business. They scurried with purpose, moving through the rows in the buildings, some speaking to each other, whilst others carried or moved carts.

There were people of all ages, ranging from greying men and women all the way down to toddlers that would not have remembered the day before. Ironrock was a functioning city with its own economy and had attracted those that believed in Dalton's cause. This was a city within the Commonwealth, but governed outside of it. Kita led Ayr and Azura down a wide path that could fit at least six large dragons across it. Ahead of them, Ayr heard another dragon roar and then in the next moment, saw one rising above the towers that loomed in the distance. It was a green dragon that reminded Ayr of Baindussa.

"Where's that dragon going?"

"I'm not sure. Dalton has his own watchers here that were battling with the ones inside the Obelisk. We still function very much like the riders of the Commonwealth."

"Were battling?"

"Do you really think that after the collapse of the Obelisk that Dalton would let the watchers live when they are among the Commonwealth's greatest assets? They are the one thing that would be able to stop him."

"The watchers weren't that powerful. They could only see snippets of the future."

Kita smirked at him. "Keep telling yourself that little Ashbourne. The future holds the balance of power. Just because you can't see the future doesn't mean you should dismiss it."

"It didn't help me when Elanor and I ventured into the cave of Sinibad."

"Stop being naïve, Ashbourne. The Commonwealth has taught you that they have their own set way of doing things, but under Dalton, we have our own. Sometimes the world needs to change for the better and the wrong side wins in the first place."

Another dragon came into sight, standing tall over the marketplace. It towered above the stalls and had its eyes locked on Azura as they approached. It was a strange shade of purple, mirroring Gundrag, but Ayr could tell based purely of its body language that this dragon was not Kaladin's mount. Manir stepped in front of Azura, diverting the dragon's attention away. It flicked its orange eyes towards her and snorted.

"What are you doing bringing her here, Manir? She does not belong here."

"Never you mind, Nagahal. The little Ashbourne is my concern. Not yours."

"Dalton will want to have words with them."

"Who do you think brought them here? He's already had words. Move aside, or I will move you myself."

There was no rider present on Nagahal's back, but he moved with purpose between the arcs of the buildings, taking care not to step on anyone below. He climbed up on the tower beside him and slinked around it so that he was taller than Manir.

"As you command, my lady. Enjoy whatever you are doing today. The white dragon looks like her and her rider would make for a nice snack."

Manir snorted at him and beckoned for Azura to follow her. As Ayr passed underneath the shadow of Nagahal he once again felt small but knowing that Manir would not take any flak from Nagahal, he felt secure. It was no different than what they had experienced at the Obelisk, with the hostility of other dragons and their riders. Yet, considering his relation to Dalton, Ayr thought they would have been welcome. When he had grown up throughout the Commonwealth he had needed to lie, but with Azura by his side, he was now a known commodity. Evidently, words about him had spread far and wide, touching places he had still not been yet.

"Keep your thoughts to yourself, Nagahal. She and her rider are under my protection whilst they are here. You will answer to Dalton if anything happens to them."

Nagahal leaned back with a smirk playing on his lips. "If he ever found out. I answer to no human."

Manir snorted and turned her head to glance up at Sinibad who was still resting at the peak of the mountain. For the first time since Ayr had encountered him, Sinibad appeared tranquil; his enormous, scaled chest rose and fell in slow, rhythmic movements, each breath causing small avalanches of loose stone to cascade down the mountainside. His leathery eyelids remained closed over eyes that had previously tracked their every movement through the winding streets of the city below.

Manir and Kita continued to lead them through the market stalls that reminded Ayr of his time in Nestlewood and every other major city he had lived in the Commonwealth. From what he could see from his perch on Azura, the people were very much real and interacting with each other. He was surprised by that, knowing that Dalton was the master of illusions. This must have been one too large for him to pull off with any success.

As they neared the end of the marketplace, a new structure loomed in the distance that they headed towards. It was of a similar make to the Obelisk, however much smaller and with less dragons crawling all over it. There were only three present, each of them sunning themselves, and they paid no attention to the new arrivals. When they made their way underneath the shadow of the Obelisk-like structure, Manir turned back to them, and Kita was smiling down at them.

"Welcome to what is going to be your new home whilst you're here."

Ayr was unimpressed. "This is just the Obelisk. Dalton has created nothing new here. I thought he wanted to overthrow the Commonwealth, not just make a new one in his image."

"Outside of your training did you ever speak to your father, Ayr?

"Not particularly. He was always busy with one thing or another. He never had much time for Bryne or I."

A sad smile came to the corner of Kita's mouth. Her face darkened and she nodded in understanding. "That makes sense. He always kept you at arm's length, didn't he? Come with me, little Ashbourne. I'll make you feel at home."

Manir turned back towards the Obelisk and then continued to walk towards it in silence. With the sun now blocked from her scales, Manir turned into a dull shade of blue. With the blue dragon moving into the Obelisk on the ground in front of them, Ayr sought comfort in Azura. Azura was inside her own head, still not wanting to believe the events that had befallen her home not that long ago.

I wish Evor and Elanor were here, Ayr.

So do I, Azura. I miss them too.

ELEVEN

I don't like this, Ayr.

Neither do I, Azura. This seems like it is a trap.

If it looks like a trap and feels like a trap, then it probably is a trap. Humans are a dubious race at the best of times, Ayr. When the stakes are this high, I do not think that we should be trusting of anyone here. Whilst this city is your father's what's to say that anyone here holds that same loyalty to you?

Dalton has our best interests at heart. He would be foolish to put us into a situation that ends up in us dead.

Does he, Ayr? Because everything I have seen thus far has seemed to be the opposite. I only know your father through your memories, but from what I have seen, he will never let you have peace or seek out anything that you truly want to do in your heart of hearts.

I have been bred for this. This is my life's purpose.

Have you ever wanted more?

Yes, Azura. I always thought that there was more outside the Commonwealth. Dalton always made mention of it.

Then perhaps once this is all over with, we should go there.

That sounds nice.

"Hey, Ashbourne. Eyes up!"

Ayr came out of the conversation with Azura as she continued to plod forward, but as he did, he saw a beam just above his head. Azura had veered off course and was about to run them into a wall. Ayr laughed as Azura corrected herself and brought them back on course. Manir snorted and shook her head in amusement.

"Come on, little one, focus."

Ayr felt Azura freeze underneath him. *That's what Evor calls you.*

I know, Ayr. I do not trust Manir as far as I can throw her.

I somehow don't think that would be very far. Have you seen the size difference between the two of you?

With your magic at my disposal, Ayr. I somehow do not think that would be a problem. Do you?

The little bit of humour broke up the seriousness of their situation. How did Manir know about Azura's nickname? Ayr quite liked the image of Azura tossing Manir around with magical blasts, but they were for now, both on the same side. Manir led them down the corridor, and took a sharp turn left at the end of it. She walked up the ramp that was identical to what was in the lower bowels of the Obelisk, and the further they ventured, the more that Azura felt uncomfortable.

Ayr did what he could to soothe her, but Azura felt out of place regardless. She pined for Evor, but there was nothing that they could do now. Their fate was sealed, and they were now trapped in this new Obelisk, following Manir with obedience. When they crested the ramp, Manir turned to the left and Ayr saw Kita again who was smiling at him.

"Welcome to your new home, little Ashbourne."

Once again, she led them into a room that was identical to what their lodgings had been in the Obelisk, down to the straw bed and

"Did Dalton create this with magic?"

"Does it matter? You're here now. This will be where you train."

"And who's going to train us? Dalton?"

"Me, for now. Dalton will see you when he believes that you're ready."

"He'll see me when he believes that I'm ready? So he'll have me locked up here until then? This is no better than how the Commonwealth treated us."

"There is a reason why Dalton does what he does."

Ayr snorted. "And that's why he wanted you off the throne when he returned? What are you to him? Just an escort?"

Kita's eye washed over him, and he could feel her entering his soul. Her eye held anger, but the rest of her expression was more forgiving. Her smile came easy and as mischievous as ever, her lips pulling back to reveal her pointer teeth as she ran her tongue over them. Ayr shuddered at the sight. Her confidence radiated through her entire core.

"Dalton wishes I was just a simple escort. It would be much easier to get rid of me if that was the case."

"You're not going to replace my mother."

"I'm not planning to. I will be everything that she was not to him."

Ayr scowled at her. "I think you underestimate just how valuable she was to him."

Kita snorted. "Considering he just carried out vengeance against Grace Sunfire, a woman he had not courted in decades, just how important do you think your mother was? It's a good thing she's gone from this world."

Rage overcame Ayr, but Azura was decisive in trying to override his emotions. She brought him down off the cliff face that he was on, even as he raised his hand. Kita's smirk remained etched all over her features and was even echoed by Manir.

"A good thing? She was twice the woman that you are."

"I'm sure I'll change your mind, little Ashbourne. It is because of me that Dalton knew exactly where to strike into the heart of the Haven."

"So you specialise in underhanded tactics. I'm not sure what else I expected of someone like you, Kita. You're a traitor. I'm not sure what else I can learn from you in that regard."

Kita laughed as she began to remove herself from her saddle. Her body was fluid and graceful, moving in a similar fashion to Elanor. Whilst their attire and hair differed, Ayr could almost picture Elanor in her place. She moved towards the ground and beckoned for Ayr to do the same. Ayr was apprehensive, but his environment told him that it should have been comfortable. The uncertainty was still flowing from Azura. He did what he could to push it from both his mind and hers. When Ayr touched his boots down onto the ground, Kita was already walking towards him.

"I'm going to test you in every aspect of your life, little Ashbourne. There's a reason why Dalton has kept me close to his side."

Ayr was curious, unable to read her facial expression. She drew close, almost within arm's reach and Ayr saw something flicker under her hand out of the bottom of his eye. He stepped backwards as she lunged forwards and saw the strange light of a magically conjured dagger being thrust towards him. Kita's lips curled into a snarl as she jabbed forward again. Azura screamed out in his mind, her concern that this new Obelisk was a trap all but confirmed.

Ayr had no time to defend Azura, as by the time Kita was stabbing forward again, he had already summoned his own knife. It was the length of his forearm and only as wide as his small finger, but it was enough to defend himself. Kita came at him again, in an unrelenting assault that forced Ayr to give ground. As a smile came over Kita's face, Ayr realised that she had been testing him. It was just like sparring Elanor. She was just as fast and just as powerful, and Ayr had his work cut out for him.

Manir was not exuding any threat towards them and Azura stood, watching the action with intent. She entered into Ayr's mind and tried to probe him, but he was too focused on the fight. He welcomed her in, her awareness only an increase to his reflexes that would help him in the fight. Kita was fast, but he felt confident matching her. There was no doubt in Ayr's mind that she was using Manir to her advantage as well.

Their blades came together again, and Kita pulled Ayr past her. He tried to swipe at her, but instead received a slash across his shoulder blades. Ayr grunted as he pulled away from Kita, finally putting space between the two of them. His hand flung to his back and Ayr knew that the cut was not deep. He spun back, but Kita was already striking at him again. She grabbed his wrist, controlling his blade and pulled him close. Her hand moved below his belt and Ayr cried out in alarm.

"What are you doing?"

"The rule is, if I beat you, I get to fuck you."

"It's a good thing that you haven't beaten me yet."

Ayr stepped forward, shoving her backwards. Kita was grounded and only took a step back as Ayr's dagger came flying at her. He tried to skewer her in the stomach, but such a simple strike was one that was anticipated by her. Kita pushed it away and struck back, as she spun. Ayr let her go past his body and grabbed at her free wrist. Her momentum pulled her to him and Ayr's blade found it's way to her throat.

"You were saying?"

I love seeing a little bit of Ashbourne magic.

Don't tell her that. She'll kill me in my sleep.

I feel like we've gone back in time, Ayr. It's not killing that she wants to do.

Would that even work considering what I have with Elanor?

I'm no expert in the subject.

Kita lowered her eye to the blade and snorted. There was nothing that she could do to stop Ayr from striking if he was inclined to do so.

He had half a mind to thrust it forward, but striking at any of Dalton's assets before the time was right could have catastrophic results. And if he was the only one that could be labelled as the murderer, Dalton would come down harder on him than anyone in the Commonwealth had done so thus far. Kita's smirk was still etched all over her face as she assessed him.

"You think you're good, little Ashbourne."

"Who do you think trained me?"

"I'm well aware of the training that you had as a child. From all accounts you failed at a lot of it. I'm surprised to see that you've improved since then. The Seminary and the Obelisk are not the best teachers."

"Dalton wouldn't have sent me to the Seminary unless he thought I was ready."

"You were ready and it's a shame that you had to become involved with Elanor Sunfire. What were you thinking?"

Ayr rolled his eyes as Azura snorted overhead. "What are you? My father in disguise? I've been here not even a day and I've had enough of you people trying to drive a wedge between my promised and I."

"Is that you or your dragon talking, little Ashbourne?"

Azura spoke for him this time. "There is no difference. We are the same."

"Hmm. I look forward to seeing your growth over the coming weeks and months."

"Months? Is that how long we're going to be here for? Are you going to spend all that time training us?"

"That's going to be up to you. Dalton will ultimately decide your fate."

"Why do I get the funny feeling you'll be heavily involved in that decision making process?"

Kita backed away from him, her knife dissolving in her hand at her command. Her smirk faded as she moved away. "Because I report directly to your father."

"That's not the only thing that you do from my understanding."

"That tongue of yours will get you into trouble if you keep letting it waggle without restraint."

"Is there anything else, Kita? Or can you leave my dragon and I alone in peace?"

"I'll let Dalton know that you're settling well into your new place."

It was now Ayr's time to turn his back on Kita, and Azura shoved past Manir, cementing her place in their room. Manir looked taken aback but then stepped aside and allowed Azura to pass her. There was a glance of understanding as they passed, and Ayr was just glad that he was finally seeing the back of what was either going to be a new nemesis or ally. Azura echoed his thoughts.

You and I need to be very careful, Ayr.

You and I? As long as I can control Kita, we have nothing to worry about.

Manir is powerful and I do not think that we should be overlooking her. Kita has not revealed the full extent of her power yet. Do you think your father would keep her around if she was not useful to him?

Hmm. You raise a good point, Azura. Perhaps we should ponder this over a meal.

We should, and I need to tend to your wound.

It's not deep, Azura. I can tend to it myself with magic.

Yet I should tend to it all the same. How do we know for sure if her weapon was not contaminated? I know you're talented, but this will make sure of it.

You're right again.

I always am, rider.

Ayr sighed a breath of relief as he heard the door shut somewhere behind him. He and Azura were alone at last. He heard Azura moving behind him and the shadow of her head dimmed the light that came in through the raised windows at the far end of the room. Unlike their lodgings at the Obelisk, this place seemed to have no entry available to them from the outside. Was this an oversight on Dalton's behalf or was it something that he had intentionally designed?

Take off your jacket. Ayr did as he was told, feeling Azura move into position behind him. Then he felt her against his skin, one of her scales the size of his torso. Hold still.

We've done this before.

Not when I was this big.

The last time Azura had tended to one of his wounds properly, she had been much smaller and easier to move into position. Now he could feel only a portion of her face against him. He remained still, allowing her to move to the point where her eye was just above his wound. Ayr felt the single tear drop from it and into his open wound. The tear once it mixed with his wound turned cold, and Ayr felt like ice was shooting through his veins. Azura moved away from him, and he could hear the satisfaction in her thoughts.

There, now there's no risk of infection.

Thank you, Azura. Where would I be without you?

Probably dead.

TWELVE

The room that Elanor and Evor shared together seemed less full of life now that it was shared by only half of the occupants. The bed that Elanor had shared with Ayr seemed unusually large, and she had grown used to his presence. As she rolled over, she caught the first rays of the morning sunshine coming in through the window. Seeing Evor curled up without the additional mass of Azura by his side was also unusual. What warmth the extra two bodies provided was gone and their absence was making Elanor's heart grow fonder. She stretched out, trying to enjoy the time they had alone, but Evor rolled his head over and grumbled at her.

You need to relax, Elanor. I can feel your anxiety beginning to get to me. There is nothing that we can do until the Ashbourne's choose to reveal themselves once again.

We know where they are, Evor, Chorru told us as much.

That does not mean that it is the correct course of action, Elanor.

I would rather stay here and make sure that you're healed. Why would I fly out and fight Dalton and Sinibad when you are not at your full power?

It does seem to be a foolish decision if we were to do that.

Then what ails you, Evor?

Whilst you are all I need Elanor, I miss the presence of the little one as the days go by.

Can you feel her?

I reach out into the void at least three times a day. Azura's magic is strong, but no, I cannot sense her yet. If she is to return somewhere near us, I will be able to sense her.

I pray to Chilijo that it happens sooner rather than later.

Elanor noticed that Evor's mood was improving as he thought of Azura. She could see Azura shifting into his memory as he brought thoughts of her to the forefront of his mind. Whilst Evor was focused on her, Elanor noticed something else. In any vision of Azura, whenever Ayr appeared, she was drawn to it and Evor noticed.

You miss him.

He is the rider of your promised. If I wasn't missing him, I would be concerned. Our emotions mirror each other.

Forgive me, Elanor. I will stop thinking about her.

No, don't. She is your promised. Keep calling to her and bring her back to you.

Of course, Elanor. She is all that matters.

Elanor's frustrated groan echoed off the stone walls as an unfamiliar voice invaded her consciousness, cutting through the familiar rumble of Evor's thoughts. She rolled over on the stiff mattress, her muscles aching from the previous day's exertions, and lifted her gaze to the vaulted ceiling. There, perched on one of the ancient wooden rafters, with his obsidian scales gleaming like polished stone in the dim torchlight, was none other than Chorru. His amber eyes, narrowed to slits, seemed to pierce through the shadows as he observed her with predatory stillness.

"Good morning, Elanor. How are you faring on this fine day?"

"What do you want, Chorru? Fuck off!"

"I am here to make sure you're doing your job as instructed. I haven't seen much change in the Haven these past few weeks. I would have thought you'd be using your high station to improve the situation here. Yet all I have seen is more uncertainty and hesitation from you."

"You can tell Dalton that he should not have injured Evor then. That has set us back weeks! If he can't fly, then I won't travel."

"Dalton does not make mistakes, Elanor. You know that."

"He will when I rip him limb from limb."

"You need to make good on your task, Elanor. I want you to report on Ironrock today. Take Evor for a flight beyond the city. Tell them what I have told you and then plan accordingly."

Elanor stuck her chin out, defiant. "And if I don't?"

"I don't need to threaten you with anything. You know what happens should you not deliver on what you have promised."

"Evor is already injured."

"Yet I saw you trying to fly yesterday. Is he that injured?"

Evor's rumbling voice cut across the room. "It is none of your concern what I can and cannot do, whelp."

Chorru hissed, baring his needle-sharp fangs as he swivelled his serpentine head towards Evor. His scales rippled with an iridescent sheen in the dim light, his eyes narrowing to venomous slits. Elanor could feel Evor's muscles tensing along with a rumble building in his massive chest. If he was not disciplined there would have been nothing that she could have done to contain the primal urge to lunge forward, jaws agape, and swallow Chorru whole. Yet they both knew that removing Dalton's slithering agent here would only serve to bring his volcanic rage down upon them with the force of an avalanche, crushing what fragile position they still maintained.

Now is not the time, Evor!

I know.

"Well then Evor, I expect to see you back in the sky sooner rather than later. Dalton is most eager for the war to begin, sooner rather than later."

Evor snorted at the smaller dragon. "If Dalton wants this war, he can start it at any time. If he needs us to start it for him, is he really as powerful as he thinks he is?"

"You've seen enough of his power to know that I speak the truth."

Elanor could feel Evor's rage building out of control. If she did not do something about it now, it would spill over and Chorru would be on the chopping block. And right now, considering her position with Dalton, she could not afford to risk this asset, as much as she wanted Evor to devour him.

Evor...

He angers me.

Now is not the time. Stop!

Evor froze for a moment as his chest heaved. His anger was filling Elanor's entire mind, and she tried to push him down from his heightened position like she would push down an angry dog. Evor was not often one to anger easily, but now as Elanor tried to bring him down, he did so, his anger turning into a simmer.

As you wish, Elanor. You are correct, this is not the time, but he will burn.

We have bigger targets to worry about.

We do.

Chorru flipped back up into the air above Elanor's head with a maniacal laugh. "You two need to get your shit together. If Dalton had no patience for you, he would have ended it all by now."

"Nothing stopped him when he came to destroy the Obelisk. What is stopping him now?"

"His son."

Elanor felt a pang of guilt in her chest. "What's happened to Ayr?"

Chorru laughed again as he spun in the air once more. "Nothing has happened to him. He is not ready yet. Dalton intends to release him from his bond."

"With Azura?"

"Dalton will break the chains that bind dragons to riders. They will only serve the rider should they choose to."

"Evor serves me because he chooses to."

Chorru's laughter continued to ring around the room. "Does he serve willingly, or because the ancient magic of Chilijo chooses it for him? Change is coming, Elanor. Now are you going to inform the Dragon Lords of what you know? Or do I need to report to Dalton that you are failing with your task."

Elanor grit her teeth and snarled at the smaller dragon. "Fuck off, Chorru!"

"You're most welcome, Lady Sunfire!"

"We need to go, Evor!"

Elanor turned away from Chorru, headed towards the wardrobe where she knew that a new freshly pressed uniform was waiting for her. As she changed Evor pushed himself off the floor with a groan, snapping at Chorru as he flew around in the rafters, laughing. Elanor tried to ignore him as she changed but found it almost impossible to. She was already out of her bed garments and into her uniform within moments and was pulling her boots onto her feet as Chorru let loose with one final laugh.

"Good luck, Elanor. I will give Dalton your regards."

Elanor sneered at Chorru as he slipped out of the small gap in the windows. There would be no calling him back now. Elanor sighed as she saw his tail vanish, and she knew what had to be done. She grabbed her mask from beside the bed, and with nothing further to do here, crossed to where Evor stood waiting for her. He lowered his neck and Elanor climbed aboard, using the armour plating that still remained along his body as leverage and for an easier path to climb up him.

With a gentle nudge of his head, Evor wedged the window open and prepared to leap from it. Elanor felt his wings open behind her, however due to the confines of the room, he could not open them until he teetered on the threshold. The sun crept into the room, and for the first time in several weeks, Elanor felt optimistic about what awaited them outside. Whilst the threat from Chorru loomed over them, Evor felt powerful. He stepped forward and stretched out his wings, allowing them to catch his falling body weight.

Evor let out a triumphant roar that shook the very stones beneath them, his massive, scaled chest expanding with the force of it. As Elanor pulled her mask on, the cool fabric slid against her flushed skin, and the familiar weight settled over her features, she could not help but indulge in the sensation with Evor, feeling his savage joy course through their bond like liquid fire in her veins.

How do you feel, Evor?

It is still not yet fully healed, but I can at least fly again.

This is a good start. How far can you go?

Each day I go a little further, Elanor. Soon I will be able to fly longer distances again.

Can you manage a day?

Not yet, but soon.

Excellent.

Elanor leaned back in the saddle and smiled as Evor directed where they were going. Even though he still felt like he was not yet at full capacity, his movements were fluid and smooth. He was so close to returning to his full power. It was now time to act. Evor soared over the Haven, and the dragons that rested on the rooftops beneath glanced up at them. Realising it was a dragon that had come from within the city, they paid them no mind, dropping their heads as soon as they had raised them.

Today, the Dragon Lords were venturing out into the city as a means to see what was still required to arm it significantly against a Dalton Ashbourne attack. The looming forms of Rotang and Gravu were spotted from a distance and Evor turned towards them. Rotang was the first to notice Evor and bellowed out in greeting. Evor responded in kind and within moments was making his descent towards them. As Evor crashed down to the ground, Rotang and Gravu made their way towards them, the former with smoke steaming from his nostrils.

"Evor, it is good to see you flying once more."

Evor was hesitant to answer at first, wondering why Rotang was being so polite towards him. "Thank you, Rotang, I was not sure I would be able to."

"It was a grievous wound that Sinibad inflicted upon you."

"Without my rider it would have been impossible to heal from. She has given me the extra strength required."

Rotang bowed his head. "I assume your rider is here to see Baldur and the other Dragon Lords?"

"She is. Where are they?"

Rotang raised a taloned foot and pointed it towards the nearest building without further explanation. Whilst it was no hall of the Dragon Lords, it was still sizeable and from what Elanor understood, a recent addition to the Haven. Kaladin had ordered it constructed in what was another effort to keep Dalton from attacking the city. It made sense to Elanor why Baldur and the other Dragon Lords had taken to this keep being used as their war room as they prepared. The hall was sacred and should not have been used for such matters. Elanor stepped inside to find a round room in the entrance that was sparsely occupied, only by Baldur and Leyla.

Baldur glanced up from the table that they were working on and almost rolled his eyes. He'd have known that she was coming, Rotang having given him the information before she'd even walked in the room. Strangely, Romulus was absent, however if he was busy ensuring that the wyrmguard recruits were ready, then he would be at the academy, toiling away preparing them.

"What do you want, Lady Sunfire? I thought you would be tending to the mighty Evor this early in the morning."

"I've got something important to tell you."

Leyla raised a curious eyebrow as she stepped around into view next to Baldur's shoulder. "By all means then, tell us. Anything you know could be useful in the war. But I'm not quite sure what you could have learnt from being stuck in your room for the past few weeks as Evor heals."

Elanor drew in a breath and then continued. There was no point in holding back now. "Dalton Ashbourne is in a city called Ironrock just to the west of us here. He has the elder dragon and thousands of wyvern at his disposal. That's how he managed to kill the Dragon Lords. He has an easy position where he can strike at us from."

Baldur turned his head to glance at Leyla who mirrored his emotions. "If Ironrock is where his stronghold lies, then we will break it. He brought the fight to us; we can do the same thing to him. If we can catch him unprepared, then perhaps we can bring an end to this war, early."

"We may. Evor is ready to fly a long journey."

"So soon? It has only been a few weeks."

"When you've been filling your dragon with as much magic as I have, they will eventually recover from even the most grievous of wounds. Evor is ready."

"It never ceases to amaze me, the bond between dragon and rider. I didn't realise that you had managed to get his wounds healed."

Elanor tapped her foot in annoyance. "If Evor can fly here then he will be fit to fly anywhere in the world."

Baldur's dark eyes locked onto Evor with a predatory focus. Evor stood his ground, shoulders squared and jaw set, meeting both Rotang's wolfish stare and Baldur's cold intensity without flinching. The air between them seemed to thicken, charged with an almost visible tension that made the fine hairs on Elanor's arms stand on end. Her breath caught in her throat as Baldur's fingers twitched at his side, hovering near the hilt of his weapon, and she braced herself for the single word that would unleash Rotang's savage fury.

"How did you come by this information, Elanor? Did you fly to the city yourself and see it with your own eyes?"

We cannot lie, Elanor. That would only serve to make further mistrust between the two of us. If you want to be in a position where we can defeat Dalton, the other Dragon Lords are our best allies at this point.

They'll distrust us anyway.

Exactly, so tell them the truth.

Elanor took a deep breath and sighed. "One of Dalton's agents has been in contact with me. He wants us to attack him in that city. He will be waiting."

"Who was this agent?"

"One of the dragons in Dalton's employment, Chorru."

Baldur snorted and chuckled. "I should have known that worm would come back when Dalton did. He was among the first defectors, and when he was nearby, the chances were Dalton usually followed."

"So, what do you want to do?"

Leyla stepped in beside Baldur, a grimace etched all over her face. "If it's a fight that Dalton Ashbourne wants, I believe it is within our best interests to give it to him. We'll ready the wyrmguard and fly out to meet him."

THIRTEEN

The days continued to pass and melted together like wax candles in summer heat. Rivulets of sweat traced paths down Ayr's flushed face, stinging his eyes and soaking the collar of his tunic as Azura observed from her stone perch, high above him. Her silhouette was sharp against the arena's torchlight. Bryne stood across from Ayr on the sand-strewn floor, his frame tensed with contained fury. His knuckles were white, pressed hard against the hilt of a proper steel sword, and Ayr caught sight of the seemingly new coiled dragon tattoo that was emblazoned on his right pectoral, identical to Dalton's.

"Is that new?"

Bryne grinned at him. "You missed out. Father gave it to me when I was sent to the Seminary."

"How come I never got one?"

"You were never ready and you still aren't."

He's just trying to get into your head, Ayr. These blades are not dulled.

I'm the better swordsman.

Are you? From what you've told me; he's bested you in every contest. Use your power to your advantage.

He's just as good.

I can guarantee you that you and I have a better connection and understanding of each other. Bryne will not be able to match my power with Zaurien.

If you say so. But Dalton gave us these blades for a reason. If I use magic, then he'll critique me for it.

Play to your strengths. If Dalton wants to use you, he'll be smart about it.

Ayr sighed as he realigned his feet into a forward stance and readjusted his grip on the hilt of the sword. "I don't think that I need to prove myself against you."

Bryne's smirk widened. "You will do as our father asks. You'll keep fighting me until he is satisfied. You wouldn't want to disappoint him, would you?"

Ayr raised his eyes towards the ceiling of the arena and saw Dalton perched equally as high up as Azura. He had no dragon with him, and sat alone, wrapped up in his cloak, his eyes narrowed as he stared at his sons on the arena floor. Ayr scowled at him as Bryne took a step forward. This would be the second round of their engagement, and Ayr had thought he had the upper hand, but he knew that Bryne was holding back, working into the fight with a steady confidence that had only come from experience. Whilst Bryne was a few years younger than Ayr, he had excelled in prowess with traditional weapons.

Ayr hesitated. All he wanted to do was stop this fight before it began again, knowing that if he lost, it was his neck on the line. "I wouldn't dream of it."

Bryne raised his sword over his head, with his grin widening. "Come on then. Show me you're worthy of his attention."

Rather than waiting for Bryne to take the offensive, Ayr ran forward, lunging with the sword outstretched. Bryne was ready for it, and his body language had changed from their first exchange. He took a wider stance and was more commanding than he had been. Bryne welcomed Ayr's sword into his arc and stepped around him. Even though he had just been on the offense, Ayr was immediately put on the defence, stepping backwards trying to deflect everything that Bryne sent his way.

Bryne was as fast as Dalton and Kita, but his youth and muscular build made him one of the most challenging fights that Ayr had ever experienced. Bryne's power was evident. He switched into a two-handed grip on his sword, and each blow, whilst slower by the margin of a hair, was twice as powerful. Ayr switched his grip, reacting to Bryne's power, but it still was not enough. Bryne launched sweeping uppercut after sweeping uppercut and whilst Ayr could read them, he was losing control of his sword.

Ayr hated the fact that he was giving ground to Bryne with every strike, even as Azura encouraged him from above. He could feel her power radiating through his power, but in this battle of pure power, he was losing. Each strike rattled his teeth, and he was running out of options. This second round was more intense than their first, and Ayr realised how outclassed he was. Bryne had been training whilst Ayr had been at the Obelisk and beyond. He only had one option left. His sword was slipping through between his fingers and one more strike from Bryne would dislodge it from his grasp.

Ayr switched his grip once again, as he avoided one final strike from Bryne, but his speed meant that he was running out of space to work with. With one hand on his sword, Ayr tried to parry one more fluid uppercut, and felt it shatter. Bryne was overbearing, but dropping the sword was just what Ayr needed. He felt his power surging through him, and he shot his hand forward. Bryne's body seized up, locking in place as Ayr's spell overtook him. Whilst his magic was not as powerful as Ayr's, he was still strong and fought against it at every turn.

Ayr needed to be commanding, and controlling, but there was only so much he could do. He stooped to the ground, collecting the sword that Bryne had knocked from his hand only seconds ago and he needed to be fast. Bryne was already freeing himself from the spell as

Ayr lunged toward him once more. Then a crack reverberated around Ayr's skull and he stopped in place as Dalton's voice was just as sharp overhead.

"Ayr! Bryne! Stop!"

Bryne was panting, each breath making his chest rise and fall. His head snapped up towards Dalton who was now standing on his feet. Bryne's head was the only part of his body that Ayr allowed to move. A frown was etched over Dalton's features, the creases in his forehead evident as he watched on. Bryne was shaking, fighting against Ayr's locking spell, his frustration growing.

"Stop? He's pathetic! How did you send him to the Seminary before me?"

"It appears that Ayr needs a little more motivation. What are you going to do when you can't rely on your magic to save you?"

"I will always have it."

Dalton snorted and shook his head. He turned his back and Ayr could see the disappointment in his eyes as he turned away. He stepped down from the arena seating without another word parting from his lips. The only sound that reached Ayr's ears was the sound of Bryne panting that masked Dalton's footsteps. As his figure faded from sight, Ayr heard Bryne in front of him.

"Fuck you, Ayr."

"For what? You know that your magic is not as potent. Perhaps spend some time with your dragon and he might be able to help you more."

There was an angry grumble from above as Zaurien started to shift in his place. "You cheated. You went into this fight knowing the rules of engagement."

"Don't pretend to be noble with him, Zaurien. Not after what I saw you do to Draxion. If you shared any decency, you would have given her a noble death."

Azura rose to her feet as well, extending her neck out to her full height. She was still larger than Zaurien, but not by much. Zaurien hissed at her and rose to his full height, trying to intimidate her. Azura steeled herself and did not back down from the threat.

"We are dragons, Azura. Draxion was my enemy. She deserved no mercy."

"How dare you!"

"You question me? If it was not for Dalton, then you would still be a slave to the Commonwealth, Azura. Perhaps your motives are not aligned with ours."

Bryne turned as he freed himself from more of Ayr's spell. "Zaurien! Stand down! I don't need this right now. Free me from this spell."

Zaurien hissed again and turned his attention towards Bryne. The burning behind his eyes was evident, "As you wish, rider."

Zaurien slinked down the arena wall, his eyes focused on nothing other than Ayr. He was loosening the spell on Bryne but could feel the presence of Zaurien starting to overwhelm him. There was no point in fighting against Zaurien and Ayr let the spell go completely. As Bryne emerged from the spell, he stepped forward again, lowering the sword at his side.

"I'd suggest you go and see him, after that abysmal display."

Zaurien lowered his head, so that Bryne could mount him. He swung himself up onto the black dragon without another word in Ayr's direction. Zaurien rolled his eyes at Ayr and in turn, Azura before exiting the arena in a huff. Ayr stared into Bryne's back as he left.

"I'll consider it."

Azura entered his mind once more. *What are we going to do, Ayr? I'm going to go see my father.*

So soon?

You don't know Dalton, Azura. That look on his face was not one that I want to see often. Considering this interaction with Bryne, he will want to speak to me.

Be careful.

Do you want me to come with you?

How is that even a question? Let's go.

Ayr did not need to mount Azura, instead using his legs to carry him towards where Dalton had exited the arena. Whilst he could no longer hear either Zaurien or Dalton's footsteps, but there was only one way that Dalton could have exited the arena. It seemed almost identical to the other arenas that Dalton had constructed across the Commonwealth during the time he had spent in exile. If it was in fact the same, then Dalton could only be in one place.

Ayr traced the steps that were very familiar to him, even though this was his first time inside this particular arena and led Azura from the sand floor after she climbed down from the raised elevation she had been sitting upon. With her footsteps echoing off the walls behind him, rather than turning left to exit, Ayr went right at the first fork in the path that crossed them. Sure enough, the dusty, sandy tiled floor started to rise in elevation.

As the path turned, it already began to level out and sure enough, exactly above the arena floor, Ayr found Dalton. Dalton, however, was not standing or sitting in a position that Ayr expected him to be. Instead, Dalton was crouched beside what appeared to be a bathtub, that was full of water, and a small jet-black dragon. Ayr raised his hand towards Azura, gesturing for her to stay put. Azura bowed her head and came to a halt in the next step.

How strange.

He's always had strange hobbies. Stay here, Azura. Let me investigate.

As you wish, Ayr.

Ayr stepped forward with intention, angling himself so that he could see what Dalton was doing. His footsteps were heavy, and if Dalton had not heard him, he did not show it.

"What are you doing, father?"

Dalton's arms were moving around the dragon, and as Ayr saw more of what was going on, it appeared that Dalton was washing it. He otherwise did not move or show any sign of acknowledging Ayr's presence.

"Something that I enjoy. Whilst dragons and their kind are magical, there is something therapeutic about helping those that can't take care of themselves. This is a moment for me to reflect on what I have done."

"And what conclusions have you come to? Surely this task would be better completed by magic, would it not?"

Dalton sighed and leaned back from the porcelain bathtub, its white surface stained with rust-coloured rings. He tugged at the thick leather falconry glove on his left hand, the material worn smooth at the fingertips. The copper-hued dragon in the tub coiled its serpentine body around itself like liquid metal, steam rising from its heated scales. It set its wedge-shaped head on the rim, orange eyes like molten amber fixing on Ayr with the practiced indifference of a predator deciding whether something was worth the effort to kill. He could incinerate it in a heartbeat should Dalton want it to attack. It would be another task that he would no doubt fail in Dalton's eyes.

"Not everything needs to be completed by magic, Ayr. I still care about the dragons, despite what those within the Commonwealth might think."

"You've always told me you have, but this is not what I expected."

"Perhaps if I had focused your training more on dragons, you would be able to see what I do, Ayr. I believe it was a mistake sending you to the Seminary of Fire before you were ready."

"And Bryne was?"

Dalton breathed in heavily once again as he removed the second falconry glove from his right hand. The dragon glanced up at him, with a disappointment in its eyes.

"Bryne is different. But then again, so is every dragon. They influence you, just as you influence them. If you had been paired with a dragon more like Zaurien, he would not have affected your judgement when it came to the Sunfire woman, for instance."

"We can't help that."

"I thought the same, once. And then I met your mother. Everything is a choice, Ayr."

"Was your dragon promised to another? Even with all my power, I still can't shake the thoughts of Elanor out of my mind."

"You're powerful, yes. But again, Ayr, your choice of dragon was not what I would have picked for you. It is your weakness as much as it is hers. Have you ever seen two promised dragons fight each other?"

Ayr shuddered at the thought. "No, nor do I want to. If Azura was to fight Evor, the results would be disastrous."

"I have seen it with my own eyes."

"Was the rebellion as horrible as you are making it out to be? Or have you just lied to me my whole life, just like the rest of them?"

"You need to be shown something, boy."

"What happened to my mother?"

The emotion in Dalton's glare drained from it, his eyes narrowing. "I told you what happened."

Ayr's response was flat. "I don't want you to tell me what happened. I want you to tell me the truth."

"You're not ready for the truth, Ayr. I have told you everything you need to know."

"Do I need to search for answers from someone that will be more forthcoming?"

Dalton snorted and shrugged, indifferent to the remark. "You can do whatever you like, Ayr. But those that can give you the answer you seek are already dead."

"Who knew?"

"Crassus, Anton, Grace. A handful of others."

"Everyone you've killed?"

Dalton's dead eyes met his. "I've killed a lot of people, Ayr. As have you."

"Don't do this to me."

"Why? You're doing your job. As I asked. You have more training to do."

"I have, but what about Kita? She won't leave me alone."

"I will speak to her. You have a lot more to show me before I let you out into the world again."

"What's my next task?"

"Never you mind. Now did you have something you want to ask me, or can I go back to washing Sprungli?"

Ayr stiffened, knowing that if Dalton was throwing this wall up in front of him that he was no longer going to give Ayr any answers.

"No, father. Enjoy the rest of your day."

"Thank you, Ayr. I intend to."

FOURTEEN

With his frustration growing, Ayr only had one being within the city that he could talk to without fear of judgement or worse. Azura was at his back, and he was walking out into the sunlight. It was a bright day outside, and so far for their entire stay in Ironrock, the weather had been perfect riding conditions. Not that Dalton had let them leave the city. It was just like it had been for Ayr whilst he had been in exile with Dalton, except when Dalton caught wind of the Commonwealth, he would flee the city that they were in. When they were outside, Ayr rounded his shoulders, trying to relax. Azura entered his mind as he stared out towards Ironrock.

I worry about you, Ayr.

It feels like I am forever stuck in this cycle. I just want to break free.

And we will. You and I are getting stronger each day. The tests against Bryne and Kita are pushing your limits.

But this can't be it. He can't keep testing me. When is the ball going to drop?

I'm not sure, Ayr, but I feel your frustration.

He's getting to me. With his riddles and non-answers.

We will find the answers you seek. They're out there.

I'm glad you think so, Azura. Should we go for a quick flight?

Always, I will be weary of Sinibad, however. Come here, Ayr.

Ayr did as he was told and reached towards Azura's neck. He grabbed a hold of her and in a singular motion, she lifted him towards his back. He was still covered in sweat from the sparring with Bryne, but he did not care. The moment he was up in the sky on Azura's back it would be blown away from his body regardless. He withdrew his mask from within his jacket pocket once he had climbed up Azura's armoured hide and settled into the saddle. When the mask was over his face, he at last, felt comfortable. Azura sensed his comfort and without another word between him, kicked off from the ground. The all too familiar sensation of gravity leaving his body filled him and joy. The emotion coming from Azura.

She kept her eyes towards Ironrock's mountain where Sinibad rested. The elder dragon had not moved much in the weeks that they had been here. Ironrock seemed incomplete without his presence looming over the city. Some days he would fly off on tasks, set by Dalton, or to feast on the local fauna. A dragon of that size needed plenty of food to sustain its bulk, and Ayr could only wonder what would keep him satisfied. Today, Sinibad raised his head as Azura flew up towards the mountain. His voice carried across the open space.

"Ashbourne. Should you be up here? Has your father given you leave?"

Azura spoke for Ayr. "He has, Sinibad. But you would know that if you were linked to Dalton in any shape way or form."

A stream of smoke pilfered up from Sinibad's nostrils as he snorted. "If you knew the first thing about me, you would know that connection with a human is not something I seek. You're lucky I did not get to you before the Obelisk fell."

"I am grateful for Drementhol's interference."

"And now you are equally as grateful for Dalton's protection. If I did not respect the man, you would make for a nice toothpick. Enjoy your flight, children."

Ayr kept his eyes locked on Sinibad, even as he put his head back down to rest on his enormous paws that were easily the size of Evor. He

did not want to become comfortable or complacent around the one
dragon in particular that would be able to snuff them out in an instant.
Even though he had slain the Dragon Lords and their dragons with the
help of Dalton, he somehow thought that Sinibad would be far too
much for him to handle. Ayr frowned behind his mask as Azura angled
away from the mountain, and for the first time in days, was showing
him the outside of Ironrock.

From their elevated position, Ayr could see it wall to wall, hidden
amongst the valley and mountains that otherwise protected it. Ayr
wondered how far away they could go before they were hunted by
someone at Dalton's command. He had half a mind to direct Azura
to the east and head back towards the Haven and contact Elanor
but knew that their efforts would be fruitless. What would happen if
Dalton requested his presence again and he was not within the city?
Whilst Dalton had not attacked the Commonwealth again yet, he
knew exactly where to go.

Instead, Ayr was resigned to enjoying the view from Azura's back
as she started looping over the city below them. The less than half a
dozen dragons that were on guard through Ironrock all paid her no
attention. Knowing that she was not a threat, they settled into their
roosts and continued to watch the sky with one lazy eye. With Sinibad
at their back, his anger was still a worry in the back of Ayr's mind,
but he tried to focus on enjoying the flight. As they flew over Dalton's
throne room, Ayr heard a familiar roar rip through the sky. He was
looking through Azura's vision, and she swung her head around to see
Manir rising up from the ground behind them.

What do they want?

*It was a challenge, there was no doubt about it and Manir was
headed straight for them. Ayr could see Kita strapped into her saddle,
growing larger as they approached. Even though Azura was by no means*

a slow dragon, Manir was catching them, even as she fought against the upward wind currents.

This better not be another test. I've had enough of them already today.

I do not think that we're getting out of this test. It is very convenient that she is coming after us after leaving Dalton.

Then fly, Azura. Put her behind us.

No sooner than he had spoken the words at Azura, she arched upwards, flying towards the sun. Grateful for not only his mask, but Azura's vision, Ayr was not blinded as they headed towards it. Manir issued another challenge and increased her wing speed. How was she faster? Not wanting to be caught by them, Ayr lowered his hand to Azura's side and pressed it against her scale. He locked himself into the saddle as he felt her surge underneath him, the particular scale he touched feeling like it had swelled in size.

With the touch of magic, Azura ripped through the sky like a dart. As the air around them started to thin, he could feel her tensing, waiting for the right moment. Azura kept flying upwards, as the pressure grew in Ayr's head, but he knew that she would look after him. As he drew in a slow breath and his ears popped, Azura hit her peak. With a snap of her body, Azura shot downwards, tightening her wings to her side as she dropped like a rock.

Sinibad looked no larger than a small rodent underneath him, but as they fell his body grew in size, back to what Ayr knew it to be. Manir roared behind them again, but due to the free fall they were in, Azura did not look back. Yet she did not need to. As they plummeted back towards the earth, Ayr caught sight of Manir's shadow, growing by the second. Azura continued to pound her wings through the air, doing everything she could to gain speed and an advantage on the larger dragon. She headed down towards the cliffs near Sinibad, but headed away from him.

Land, Azura! There is no doubt that Kita wants me.

I'm not leaving you behind!

Don't. But we both know I can handle Kita by herself.

But I can't handle Manir.

Azura, you need to stop doubting yourself. Half of your power was used by me when we killed the Dragon Lords. You are stronger than you know. If you don't want to fight her, just lead her away.

And Kita?

If I need to kill her, I will. I will pass whatever test this is from Dalton.

Ayr stood up in the saddle as Manir's shadow swarmed over them like a wave. He focused on the cliff face ahead of them. If Azura could control her speed and use her smaller turning circle at the last minute, perhaps they could cause Manir to crash into the snow-covered rock. Azura read his thoughts. She backed off and Manir's shadow loomed over them. He could feel her breath against their backs, and Azura, whilst calm, was not leaving anything to chance. She turned at the last moment, but rather than snapping forward and smashing into the rocks, Manir rose up, flying over them.

Drop me off and then go!

I'm not leaving you, Ayr!

That was a command, Azura! Do it!

Azura groaned inside his mind, unhappy with the situation. Yet, as Manir circled back towards them, she complied. A tall forest stood just back from the cliffs and it would provide Ayr with enough cover to ride and hide from Kita, or to ambush her on his terms. Azura barely touched down to the ground before Ayr was already leaping out of the saddle. In the same breath, Azura was taking off again, leaving him behind.

Good luck!

Just focus on yourself. We will win this by dividing them.

Yes, Ayr.

He heard the determination in her voice as she powered away from him. Manir was coming down, looking for a way to attack them, but now they had separated she seemed hesitant. She coiled in the air, and tried to become between the both of them, but there was no time. Ayr was already sprinting into the forest, praying to Chilijo that his plan would work. He ran forward and then turned back to check on Manir's progress. Kita was surging towards him, Manir having dropped her off in a similar fashion to what Azura had just done to Ayr. There was no time to waste.

Faster, Azura. Here she comes.

I can see her. She will not catch me.

Ayr strode into the forest, but much like Manir, Kita was faster than he was. There was no losing her without a magical illusion and unless he wanted her to catch him, he had no time to conjure one.

"Little Ashbourne!" Kita's voice followed him through the forest like a banshee's howl. "Little Ashbourne!"

Why is she this relentless?

It has to be a test. Manir is fast.

Stay ahead of her. Once I've dealt with Kita then we'll be okay.

"Little Ashbourne!"

Ayr groaned, hearing her voice once again, cutting through Azura's conversation with him. He started to slow down with purpose, now that he was deep enough in the trees that would obscure his location from Manir. Not that it would achieve anything if Kita was still within sight of him. She started laughing, knowing that she was catching him. Ayr did not need to turn to see her face in front of his. She had been more than close enough to the point where he could remember her for a lifetime.

"Aren't you forgetting something?"

Kita's voice grew closer. Ayr spun, turning on her. He wanted to strike at her, but she was too far away. "What would I be forgetting?"

Kita was still closing the gap between them, step by step. She wanted to catch him, and Ayr was letting her. "If I catch you!"

Ayr's dagger was already in his hand before Kita finished her sentence. "I don't care what your conditions are. I have a promised that I will not betray at the first sign of convenience."

"Yet you left her."

Ayr lunged forward, his tongue cutting through the empty space like his dagger. "I had no choice! What was I going to do? Deny Dalton?"

"It's what you want, isn't it? You wouldn't willingly go against the wills and whims of your promised, would you?"

"You only know my father, Kita. You don't know me."

For the first time that day their blades clashed together, the magical blades forgoing the familiar ring of steel on steel. Like always it was a battle of control and power, one that Ayr was most eager to win. Kita made him feel small. At least when he and Elanor had sparred, she had challenged him, but it had never been a struggle of fight or death. Yet against his brother or his father's subordinate, Ayr felt as if one mistake could be fatal.

As they battled against each other, her wicked smirk returned to her lips. "I know your uncle and brother as well, Ayr. You Ashbournes are all the same."

"If you know us so well you will know that we're all different."

"Are you? At your core, you all want the same thing?"

Ayr drew away from Kita, pushing back against her. She recoiled, readying another strike, but froze as Ayr spoke. "And what in your expert opinion is that, exactly?"

"Power and control."

"I don't."

Kita raised her eyebrows at him. "Really? Then why is the first thing you want to do when you're strong enough, is to stab your father in the back?"

"I came back here to serve Dalton. Not to be a slave to his will."

Kita's bark echoed throughout the forest and she lowered her dagger, letting it dissolve into thin air. "We're all slaves to Dalton Ashbourne here. But it's better to be under his rule than that of the Commonwealth."

"Yet under the Commonwealth once I proved myself, I didn't have to any longer."

"Is that what you said when they locked you in a cage just for having your last name? That doesn't sound like freedom to me, little Ashbourne."

Ayr bit his lip, unable to come back with a retort. Azura bumped into his mind, still trying to shake Manir off her tail. She was panicked, but remained calm and kept flying at a breakneck speed. Regardless of Kita's actions on the ground, that meant nothing when it came to the dragon that was still in the air.

"You know I'm right. You need to choose who you are going to serve. You can't sit on the fence forever. I'm trying to push you over one side. Dalton would not have made you kill the Dragon Lords if you weren't powerful enough."

Ayr tightened his grip, curling his fingers over his palm. "He didn't make me kill them. I wanted to do it."

There was a pause as Kita took a step back. Ayr felt the pressure from Azura in his mind weaken as she realised that Manir was pulling away from the chase. Kita's lip quivered, her one good eye assessing him like he was a strange statue, unmoving and unyielding in his approach. He felt like an animal being stalked by its prey.

"You're a strange man, Ayr Ashbourne. Nobody has ever refused me before."

"Like I told you, I have a promised, Kita. I will not betray her so easily."

A smirk came to Kita's lips as she glowered down at him. "You will, in time. Your promised will never see you alive again."

"Not if I have anything to say about it. What was the point of all this?"

"Dalton wants to know what you're made of. He still has doubts about you."

"And what's your assessment of me? You've spent enough time around me now, Kita."

With a deep sigh, Kita let her dagger fall from her hand and took a step back away from Ayr. Azura filled his mind once more, alerting him to the fact that Manir was no longer in pursuit of her. Calmness came over Azura and flowed through to Ayr, especially now that Kita no longer had a weapon in hand. Whilst he did not trust her, he felt better about the situation, knowing he had the upper hand.

"I'll report to Dalton. You show no fear or mercy when your back is against the wall. Your power will come in a time of need. You killed the Dragon Lords, that should be enough for him."

"You caught me, though. What were your rules?"

Kita puffed out her lips. "You have a promised you weren't going to betray. You have resolve, just like your father. It took years to break him before he laid with me. You've done well. Perhaps he will want me to train you properly going forward."

Kita bowed her head and continued to step back away from him. Ayr heard Manir's massive wingbeats overhead as the blue dragon settled down just out of sight, just out of the tree line.

"What now?"

"Wait for me in the tower. I'll find out what Dalton wants to do on your behalf."

What was it? Another test?

Dalton knows that I'm only going to use my full power when either you, or our promised are under threat. I think he was trying to force that out of me.

Hmm. Perhaps I need to fuel you more. What can he want from you?

Everything. Can you handle a long flight, Azura? We need to get out of here.

Where are we going?

Back to the Commonwealth where we belong. We need to see Elanor and Evor. I didn't realise that the people here would be mad.

I could not agree more, Ayr. The sooner we leave this place the better. Dalton and his wishes be damned. I will follow you.

Then we need to make preparations. I don't exactly think we're going to be received with a warm welcome.

FIFTEEN

Manir had beaten Azura to the side of the mountain, but now that their two riders were at peace, so were their dragons, Azura was still on edge, not wanting to trust Manir and Ayr did not blame her. He could feel Azura's power flowing through her, ready to strike out at Manir in self defence if the situation called for it. Yet as Kita began to climb up Manir's side, Ayr felt more comfortable with the situation. He did not want her to report to Dalton, but there would be no stopping it. They needed to be quick.

Having not removed his mask from his face during the run, Ayr repositioned it with a small adjustment so that it was in its proper place once more. He climbed up Azura, using the armour on her body as footholds and within moments, was back in the saddle.

I shouldn't have left you.

You did what you thought was right, Ayr and look at the result. There is at least a temporary peace between us.

Yes, but only until Dalton sends her after us again.

Even if he does, I would not be surprised if she asks differently next time.

I still don't trust her, Azura. We should put as much distance between us as possible.

Of course.

Ayr and Kita exchanged a glance as they settled into their saddles. The dragons also looked at each other, but nothing passed between them. There was no connection between them like there was between Azura and Evor. Manir launched herself into the air first, leaping from the cliff side into the empty open space that awaited her below. Her blue wings shot out from her side, catching her in free fall and she started back towards the heart of Ironrock. Ayr already had their quarters in his sights, and Azura coiled around herself before following Manir, throwing herself forward.

With both rider and dragon fixated on their new destination, there was no reason for them to speak to the other. Ayr remained locked in, and Azura's wings beat with a steady silence by her side as she flew back down towards Ironrock. Sinibad saw them approaching, one of his enormous eyes drifting open with a lazy roll when he realised who was headed back towards them. There was no sound except for Azura's wings and the whispers of the wind currents that rose up under them.

The journey was brief and not what Ayr wanted, but they had a job to do. The journey back to the Haven would be much longer and would give them both much needed alone time together. Ayr was thinking, running through a list of items that he would need to bring with him. If the Haven was where he expected it to be, he knew that Azura could handle the flight in a little over a day, so he could bring limited supplies and not have to worry. What he was lacking, he could make up for with his magic.

He was feeling powerful, especially now that he did not have to look over their shoulders for the threat of Kita and Manir. With that pressure valve at least temporarily released, Ayr sunk into the saddle as Azura flew the remainder of the journey back to the knock off Obelisk that Dalton had created. As the days went by, more dragons were making their presence known within Ironrock. It was clear that others had heard the word of Dalton's exploits and wanted to join the cause.

Even though more were joining them, Ironrock did not seem anymore full than what it had been since Ayr and Azura had arrived in the city. Dalton had built it in a way that everyone had adequate housing, and the dragons still took the priority even though they were outnumbered at least one hundred to one by humans. If Dalton wanted to launch a full-fledged attack on somewhere like the Haven, we would need Sinibad and at least a few more dragons with him to make it a success. The riders would be broken after the fall of the Obelisk, but they were not defenceless and in Kaladin's short time as Overlord, he had done what he could to ensure they were ready.

Azura passed underneath the cover of the Obelisk and took the path towards their chambers. They both knew by now the fastest way to get there. A red dragon stood in the corridor and looked down at them as they passed but did otherwise not speak to them. The dragon was riderless and was not one that either Ayr or Azura had a chance to speak to. When they reached their room, Azura pushed the door open and by the time she had stepped inside, Ayr was already on the way down to the floor.

He hit the ground running and headed straight for the wardrobe that had a small satchel sitting in the bottom of it. For this journey, clean clothes and luxury items were not a necessity. He purely wanted something to carry water. They would not be stopping. Inside the satchel was a waterskin and Ayr removed it from the satchel before taking it to the valve that was underneath his shower head.

Ayr turned it on and filled the waterskin with fresh, cold water that he had learned had come from the springs above Ironrock. They were warmed by Sinibad's presence, but the pipes that fed the water into the city were cooled for these purposes. With his waterskin filled, Ayr was content with what he had for the flight ahead. If he needed food, either magic could sustain him for a while or Azura would be able to hunt from the sky.

Ayr, someone's coming.

Who is it?

I cannot tell.

Ayr pivoted toward the chamber door just as it crashed against the stone wall with a thunderous boom that echoed through the room. Zaurien's enormous and scaled black head head thrust through the opening; his face contorted with contained rage. His amber eyes narrowed to slits and darted between Azura and Ayr, his nostrils flaring with each rapid breath.

"I found them, rider."

Bryne sauntered in a moment later, his hands thrust deep in his pockets, thumbs hooked just above the ornate hilt of his sword. The blade hung at his side in a worn leather scabbard adorned with tarnished silver filigree that caught what little light filtered through the chamber windows. His shoulders rolled with each step, casual yet purposeful. Bryne's eyes moved from Azura to Ayr and then he settled his hand on his sword more.

"Thank you, Zaurien."

Ayr walked towards Bryne, his shoulders squared and his jaw set like stone, his eyes fixed on a point just beyond his brother's left ear. Each deliberate step carried the weight of his resolve to pass without acknowledgment, his body angled as if already anticipating the brush of fabric against fabric when their shoulders would inevitably meet in the doorway.

"Hey! Where the fuck do you think you're going?"

Ayr shrugged away from Bryne and pushed back without further question or statement. "Away from you."

He heard Bryne grunt and felt his hand slip up to his shoulder. "I don't think so. Father wants to speak to you again."

"He hasn't up until this point, I don't know what's changed."

"Come with me, Ayr."

"No!"

Ayr spun and a blade emerged in his hand as he struck at Bryne. Not to his surprise, Bryne met him with his own and they were once again locked in combat. Ayr snarled at Bryne and turned back away, but Bryne chased him.

"Ayr! Get back here!"

"I'm not interested, Bryne!"

Zaurien snarled down at Ayr and stepped across his path, his scaled nostrils flaring with a hot breath that smelled of sulphur and ash. Azura lunged forward, her white scales catching the torchlight as she positioned herself between them. The two dragons locked eyes. Amber against brilliant bright blue. Their elongated pupils narrowing to slits while their massive jaws parted to reveal rows of yellowed teeth sharp as daggers. A low, rumbling growl vibrated through the stone floor beneath them as they circled each other, tails lashing against the walls.

"I'm not going to fight you this time, Ayr. I came to deliver a message from Father, nothing more. If you're not going to go to him, then I can't force you."

"What's gotten into you? You always want to fight."

Bryne backed away and threw his dagger to the ground. It vanished into nothing and he stood his ground, with his nose turned up. He planted his feet shoulder-width apart, his jaw clenched and nostrils flaring as he tilted his chin upward.

"There's no point. I know where it goes. Especially if there are no rules in place to stop you."

A smirk spread across Ayr's face. "Good, so let me go."

"He'll come for you."

"Let him. I don't care anymore. If he wants to punish me, let him."

"Where are you going, Ayr?"

"I already told you. We don't want to be here anymore."

"Then go."

Zaurien rose to his full height and stepped away from the door. The movement allowed Azura to pass him without incident and Ayr followed her, stepping outside. Ayr looked over his shoulder and saw Bryne standing still, looking defeated, even though their conflict had not escalated past the first exchange.

He's just letting us go?

Nothing feels right, Azura. I don't trust it. We shouldn't waste time.

You're right, Ayr. Climb on.

Azura swung her neck around to collect him, and with the momentum that he had behind him, Ayr was up in the saddle almost in an instance. He swung the waterskin around his body, looping it over his neck, and pulled his mask back down over his face. Azura was picking up the pace as they neared the exit of the Obelisk and within moments, she was outside, spreading her wings once more.

Without anything impeding them anymore, Azura took off from the ground with confidence. Ayr cast his eyes up towards Sinibad who was still perched atop the mountain. He had not moved, nor did he pay them any attention as Azura rose into the sky. Ayr did not trust him, and half expected the enormous dragon that looked to be as big as Baindussa from here, to come after them. If Bryne reported to Dalton, would he send Sinibad after them?

Ayr urged Azura on, giving her some of his power to speed them along her journey. She turned to the east, no sooner than she had cleared the height of the surrounding buildings and shot across the sky. Ayr prayed that Dalton was not watching, but he knew that they would not have long before Bryne informed Dalton of what was going on. As Azura flew, Ayr remained on edge. He kept checking over their shoulders to ensure that they had not been followed. As the minutes slipped past, there was still no sign of any other dragon like Manir or Zaurien trailing them.

Even though it was becoming evident that Dalton had not sent anyone after them yet, Ayr was still not convinced that they would make it to the Haven unopposed. There was a world out there, many of the larger dragons like Sinibad were in fact faster than Azura. Then there was also the fact that the closer that they got to the Haven, the higher the chances that they would be approached by a dragon that was still loyal to the Commonwealth. At this point, everyone would know of their defection to join Dalton, and any rider would treat them as hostile.

The sun was already beginning to slip beyond the horizon the further east that they went. Azura was making good ground, even though from where they were, Ayr had no significant landmarks to make note of any progress. Azura was confident of their heading on the other hand. Darkness overtook them, and the beating of Azura's wings had been the only sound that Ayr had heard for the past few hours. They had to be getting close to their destination, especially considering the power that Ayr had been giving her. They had not stopped since they had left Ironrock, and the night was growing longer.

Azura, call Evor when you can sense him.

Yes, Ayr. He must be getting close. I can almost see the Haven from here. Can you feel the changes in the wind?

I can Azura.

Ayr knew that they were drawing closer to the Haven. The glow of the city was just upon the horizon and somewhere within it was Elanor. If he knew a spell that would have summoned her to his side, Ayr would have cast it, but instead, he would make do with Azura reaching out to Evor. He could feel Evor in her thoughts and wondered if they were within range of the city yet. Azura kept flying and Ayr's mind turned to Elanor instead.

He kept his thoughts to himself, even though the emotion from Azura was slipping through. The sky was beginning to darken, and

Ayr saw something shooting towards them from the north-east. He looked through Azura's eyes and could see a familiar silhouette flying towards them. Azura was overcome with emotion as she knew it was Evor flying towards them. A roar escaped her throat and a surge of happiness coursed through her body.

SIXTEEN

Elanor was nervous for the first time in a very long time. Evor gave her certainty and clarity, but considering the wounds that he had suffered and how his physical prowess had been diminished, she felt insecure for the first time in her life. Yet he was getting better day by day. Elanor sat on Evor, her hand against his wound as it had been every day for the past few weeks. There was still no sign of it healing fully yet, but the fact that he could fly was enough for Elanor.

The fact that Baldur had taken her words seriously had been a shock. She had half expected him to refute her and tell her that she was imagining things, but the older rider had accepted everything. The riders still needed time due to the losses suffered at the hands of Dalton when he had attacked the Obelisk, but due to the Haven already being more than fully equipped, production was well on the way. Every dragon that was yet to receive armour did so in a prompt fashion, and now only the few that remained were not far away.

Elanor and Evor watched over the Haven as the few remaining dragons shuffled in and out of the main armoury that stood in the centre of the city. The smiths had been working non-stop since their return, desperate to ensure that every dragon was equipped for the building war that was going to come soon. Elanor was comfortable, but the looming thought of where the Ashbournes was getting to her. She had always known where Ayr had been due to Evor's affinity with Azura, but now since they were so far away, she did not know.

It unnerved her being this far apart from them and despite the decades that she had spent with Evor, never thought she would feel less than whole with him so close by. There was nothing that they could do at the moment. The other Dragon Lords were preoccupied, and Elanor still very much felt on the outside of what was going on. It had been decided that she would watch over the daily operations of the smith, ensuring nothing went out of the ordinary. She knew that they wanted to watch over her and as they flew over the city, she kept looking up at them, wondering what they were hoping to see. The sunbathing with Evor was relaxing and given her past few months, was much needed.

As the day dragged on, dragons were busy ferrying their riders throughout different places in the city. Yet as they did, one particular dragon finally paid them attention. Evor raised his head as he spotted Sinpac headed towards them. Sinpac landed on the roof beside them and Elanor sat up, as Marcello leaned forward over his saddle.

"Lady Sunfire! How goes it?"

Elanor sighed, rolling her eyes up at him. If this was all he had come for, she had no time for it. The peace that she was enjoying with Evor was precious.

"It goes, Marcello. Have we had any developments on the Ashbournes or how close we are to launching an attack on them?"

Marcello carried a satchel on his side and from within it, he removed a scroll that was as long as his forearms. He opened it, his head moving from side to side as he devoured the information that was on it.

"We are close, Lady Sunfire. We only have a handful more dragons to make armour for and we just need a handful more ballista in place before Baldur is happy with the city's defences."

Elanor rolled her eyes again. Of course, Baldur had wanted to ensure that every detail was accounted for before they launched the attack. For all his flaws and resistance to wanting to become a Dragon Lord, he did have the Commonwealth's best interests at heart. Everything had been in a flux since they had returned from the Obelisk, yet the most established rider had managed to steady the ship. For that, Elanor was grateful, even though they never saw eye to eye.

"And once he is happy will we fly on Ironrock?"

Marcello gave her a stern nod. "Yes. But both my brother and I don't want that to happen?"

"You're still loyal to the Ashbourne cause."

"Of course. Our family always was loyal and will remain so."

"You know where I got my orders from, Marcello. I think the command of the personal messenger of Dalton Ashbourne outweighs what a lonely wyrmguard and his brother want to happen. What are you asking me?"

"Due to where our loyalties lie, Malachi and I don't want to take any part in the attack on Ironrock."

"And why is that? You swore an oath to the Commonwealth. You will do as the Dragon Lords command."

"We don't want to spill blood in Ironrock. We have many friends and family there. If we are caught fighting someone that shares our values, I don't want that on our hands."

Sinpac nodded in agreement with his rider. Elanor took in a deep breath and sighed. "Yet if I somehow manage to get you excused from the attack on Ironrock, you will look like traitors to the Commonwealth."

"Surely you can think of something that you need from us. We will go, but perhaps a certain dragon and her rider need extraction from the city?"

"What are you trying to say here, Marcello? What exactly are you offering?"

"Dalton Ashbourne will have a tight grip on Lord Ashbourne, will he not? You and Evor are both missing your promised and are not living up to your full potential. If we were to somehow sneak him out of Ironrock, the balance of power would turn in our favour."

"I'm confused. Are you with Dalton or not?"

"Dalton Ashbourne is the old guard. I've heard of Ayr's power and would prefer that he takes over the legacy of his family. He would ferry the Commonwealth into a new prosperous age."

"Yet Ayr is still in servitude to his father. As we all are."

Sinpac snorted and Elanor took it that it had come from Marcello instead. "In an ideal world, they could rule side by side. But unless you were to join Dalton completely, Ayr is torn between the two."

"We will kill Dalton Ashbourne and remove his shadow from our backs."

"There's only one person that can help you with that. We need Ayr back on our side."

Elanor chewed on her lip as Evor entered her mind once more. *He's right, Elanor. You know we are not complete without our promised by our side. You know that I can lead Azura down the right path.*

If she has fallen off it.

Do you believe she has?

No. Azura is pure.

Then we will bring them back, Evor.

Elanor raised her eyes to where Marcello stood over his saddle, one gloved hand resting on the worn leather, the other stroking Sinpac's dappled neck. Sunlight caught in his dark mask and glinted off the silver clasp of the satchel where he had tucked away the scroll, its parchment now hidden from view. His mask remained impassive, but as sharp as a hawk. He did not look away, patiently awaiting her response.

"Fine. If you are present when we strike at Ironrock, I will do what I can to help you retrieve Ayr from within the city."

Sinpac's scaled lips peeled back to reveal a row of yellowed fangs, the corners of his mouth curling upward in a grotesque parody of mirth that mirrored the expression Marcello would be wearing beneath his mask. With a slow, deliberate tilt of his massive head, Sinpac gazed skyward, his amber eyes narrowing to slits against the harsh sunlight. A thin tendril of charcoal-gray smoke escaped from his flared nostrils, coiling and dissipating in the cool air like a phantom serpent.

"Then we will ride with you to Ironrock, Lady Sunfire. I will inform Malachi that our plan will be put in place with your assistance."

"If Dalton is as prepared as we think he is, don't be surprised if Ayr is guarded. It won't be easy extracting him if that is the case."

"We will see it done, Lady Sunfire. You should have faith in our abilities."

"Considering you allowed Dalton to slip into the Obelisk undetected and destroy it, I don't have much faith."

"I was not going to stop the elder dragon."

"Yet you want to evade it with a high value asset, one that Dalton almost values above all others?"

Sinpac turned back towards her and Evor. Evor grunted as Sinpac stared them down. His voice carried a threat, one that Elanor knew that he could still carry out. "Just because I am wounded, doesn't mean I can't rip you limb from limb, Sinpac."

Sinpac hissed at them, even though his words likely came from Marcello. "We will consider the plan and come back to you, Lady Sunfire."

He then turned and angled himself towards the armoury. As Evor sneered at him, Sinpac rose into the air, otherwise unencumbered. Elanor watched them leave and wish that Evor was in the mood to go on a long flight of their own. She wanted to get out of the city but was not willing to push Evor past his limits, especially if they were to attack Ironrock soon. Instead, Elanor leaned back once again and continued to pour what magic she could afford into Evor's wound, praying that today would finally be the day that they got better.

As the minutes went by and turned into hours, Elanor was beginning to grow tired of waiting around and as her magic was leaving her, so was the light. There were still half a dozen dragons in and around the smithy being outfitted with their new armour plating, and everything was moving to Baldur's schedule. Yet as the sun was beginning to dip over the edge of the mountains in the distance, Evor started to sit up. Elanor sensed something in his mind shift, as if he was focusing on something far away. She gave him a moment before he spoke to her.

Elanor.

What, Evor?

I can feel something. Something I have not felt in weeks.

Azura?

Yes, she is close.

Can you talk to her?

I can, Elanor. She is alone.

Elanor's heart spiked, but it was not just her own. Evor's emotions were beginning to pour through her like he had just turned on a valve. *And Ayr?*

Of course he is with her. There is nobody else with them. This is not a trap. They are returning to us.

What the fuck are they doing here? Returning to us? They left us.

Under sufferance, Elanor. You know what would have happened if they had refused Dalton. It is not practical for us to assume that they left of their own will.

But that's his father! He was sent here to ruin us!

Azura's heart is still pure. She still serves the Commonwealth.

You can tell that without having laid eyes upon her in weeks? You and I have served Dalton despite not stepping out of line from the Com-

monwealth. Now that they've been unsupervised for that time, what's to say that something hasn't happened?

She is still pure. She is my promised.

I will take your word for it. Can you fly?

Of course, Elanor.

Elanor climbed up Evor's side without another word, desperate to reach her saddle. Each movement brought her closer to seeing Azura again, to seeing Ayr again. The singular thought drove her forward, powering her legs and within moments she was atop Evor, slipping her legs into the saddle. Evor had a sense of urgency, and he did not wait for Elanor to be secure before he started to stand. It was the fastest he had been since his injuries.

He groaned as he had done every time he rose to his feet since the attack by Sinibad but otherwise seemed in good spirits. Elanor's mind was still full of turmoil. Had Dalton sent them back here to face the consequences for the fall of the Obelisk? Was this another step in his grand master plan?

Slow down, Evor.

No, I must hurry. Do we want them to be discovered?

It did not matter. Ayr and Azura were the closest they had been to them in weeks, and Evor was starting to act like an excited hatchling once again. Evor was usually more reserved, his emotions rarely getting the better of him. There had been nothing to keep his mind off his injuries for the past few weeks, but now there was only a singular thought in his mind. Azura. And he needed to have her. She was so close. Even though he still needed to be careful, Evor was not. He could feel where she was, even though to Elanor it was nothing more than a slight blimp on the horizon.

Evor scrambled through the air, uneven in his flight as he tried to contain his excitement. Elanor did what she could to continue pumping magic into his veins as he tried to steady himself. Within the matter of a few wingbeats, they were already high above the city and heading to the west. Evor let loose with a loud bellow that would have woken up anyone sleeping below, but Elanor did not care. If Evor was to be reunited with his promised, this was all that he deserved after the events they had been through.

SEVENTEEN

As Azura raced through the sky, Ayr did all that he could to keep himself in the saddle. He was strapped in by both his hands and his felt, yet he had never felt Azura fly faster. She had made her desperation to reach Evor clear, and as he started to approach them, Azura's excitement only grew even more as she called out to him.

"Evor!"

Azura shot past Evor like a dart, and she did not slow down squealing as she flew. Ayr tried to get her to stop, but it was like he was pulling back on a powerful mountain river, trying to stop it from running. Evor turned in mid-flight, arcing back towards them, but then stopped, hovering. Ayr noticed that his wingbeats were not as stable as they once had been and spotted the wound that Sinibad had opened on him.

Evor's voice rolled across the sky and reminded Ayr of a rolling wave of thunder. He immediately felt at ease, even though they were out in the open, somewhere between the Haven and Ironrock.

"Little one."

"Evor."

"It has been too long since I last saw you. I missed you."

"I missed you too, you have been gone from my presence for far too long."

"How have you been, Azura?" Azura did not answer straight away which pressed Evor to ask more questions. "Did he hurt you?"

Azura shook her head. "No, I had Ayr by my side. He did not allow that to happen."

"Good. I am glad that you have returned to us in one piece."

"I am not so sure about that, Evor. Everyday away from you felt like a lifetime."

A small yet verbal snarl escaped Evor's as he rounded on Azura. He brought his enormous head alongside hers, and Ayr felt dwarfed as he always did around the obsidian behemoth. With their heads this close together, Ayr could now at least speak to Elanor without needing magic to communicate across the gap. Azura pressed her head against Evor's and Ayr could feel their scales brushing against each other. Elanor rose from her saddle, and removed her mask, flicking out her hair behind her. Even in the darkness, Ayr caught the flicker of auburn against the moonlight. Her expression was flat, mirrored by her hands across her hips.

"You left me!"

A deep pit opened in Ayr's stomach as he swallowed the guilt. "Dalton expected us to go with him. We didn't have a choice. He would have killed all of us if I'd refused. You know that."

"Where is he?"

Ayr shook his head. "I can't tell you that."

"Whose side are you on, Ayr?"

The questions came one after the other, each one feeling like a gut punch. Ayr wanted to answer and to tell her everything, but it was as if a compulsion from Dalton's hand had slipped around his throat, grabbing his tongue from the inside.

Tell her the truth, Ayr. She deserves that.

Azura's comment shot through his body like a lightning bolt. Ayr exhaled and straightened his back, standing up to his full height. There was no point in arguing with her. Not with the emotions that were surging between the two of them.

"He's nearby, building his forces, readying an attack on the Haven. I can't tell you any more than that. He's thrown tests at us left and right, never giving us a chance to rest. We fled."

Ayr.

If he finds out, he'll kill me.

How will he find out? There is only the four of us here. Do you want to defend Evor and Elanor or not?

I don't want to betray my father. Even though he has been testing us, it is nothing more than what the Commonwealth has done to us.

He has blinded you. Do I need to remind you that your only loyalty now should lie with our promised?

You've been there every step of the way, Azura. You know what he would do to us if we didn't play along with his game.

Now is not the time, Ayr. Tell them or I will.

Fine!

"Elanor, he's coming to attack you soon. He plans on crushing the Commonwealth underneath his heel."

Elanor sighed and took in a deep breath. "I know. This isn't new information, Ayr. Chorru has told me as much already. I know that Ironrock is his home. We plan to attack it when we are ready."

"Do you even know where it is?"

"To the west. It can't be that hard to find. We're on the lookout for an overgrown gold dragon. Where does he hide?"

"You'd find him. He watches over the city from his roost on the nearby mountain. Ironrock is a fortress. The only reason we managed to slip free is because nobody stopped us going out. I'm not sure that you'd be able to take it, even if you caught Dalton unaware."

"Is he that powerful?"

"You saw what he did to the Dragon Lords and the Obelisk."

"He had help, from you and your brother."

Ayr shook his head and smiled at her. "That doesn't change any-thing, Elanor. If Dalton wants something, he will take it. Look at what he did to you for Chilijo's sake."

Elanor met his gaze, as steely eyed as he was. "It won't happen again."

Ayr took a step closer to her and wanted to stretch out to touch her. They had been apart for so long, and it only confirmed that he had been correct in making Azura bring him her. Just being this close to her was intoxicating. "Don't make promises that you can't keep, Elanor. Especially not to me."

"You're the one that made me a promise, Ayr."

"And I intend to keep it. Even if we are apart."

Now it was Elanor's turn to smile at him. "Don't make promises you can't keep."

"I don't have to go back yet."

"Stay with me a while. Evor find a place to land."

"Yes, Elanor."

Ayr sat back down in his saddle as Evor pulled away from Azura. They were high above a cluster of mountains and Evor navigated his way down to them, with Azura following close behind. Ayr heard the rumble beneath his feet as Evor landed, and then Azura touched down moments later. It was an all too familiar sight, dating back to their first mission together when they had sought out Dalton and Sinibad. Ayr glanced around thinking they may have been in a similar position, but they were ultimately too far north.

Evor crouched down to the ground and Elanor was already in the process of dismounting from him. Ayr lifted his leg and mirrored her movements, sliding off Azura, using her armour plating to catch himself on the way down. Elanor's boots hit the ground first, even though she had a larger distance to travel. He inhaled as he hit the ground, not knowing what to expect from her. She had been short

when she had been on Evor's back, but now that he was face to face
with her on an equal footing, was another thing all together. Azura
cooed as Evor rounded on her, and he moved closer.

"We should give these two some space, little one."

Go with him, Azura.

As you command, Ayr.

No sooner than they had been together, both dragons launched
themselves into the air. Ayr watched them go, Evor's black making him
appear like nothing more than a shadow on the horizon as they crested
one of the nearby mountains. Elanor stepped across the empty space
towards him and came to rest just outside of his arm's reach.

"You look good, Ayr."

"So do you. Nothing has changed."

Elanor folded her mask in her hands and then tucked it into her
pocket just above her chest. She stared up at him, her eyes not leaving
his as she assessed him.

"What did Dalton do to you? Did he send you back here to destroy
us on your own? I know what your power is like now."

Ayr shook his head in response. "I came to see you. Between Azura
and I, I couldn't take it anymore. I had to see you."

"So you left without his permission. He'll come for you."

"I had to see you."

Ayr took a hesitant step forward, his boot scraping against the
dirt surface beneath his feet. Elanor's shoulders tensed, then relaxed
as she stepped toward him, her arms outstretched, fingers trembling
slightly. He moved into her embrace, his calloused hands finding the
familiar curve of her waist. Their bodies fit together like puzzle pieces
long separated now joined again. Her head tucked perfectly beneath
his chin as she stooped into the hug, his heartbeat drumming against
her cheek.

Ayr buried his nose in her auburn-streaked hair, and inhaled. The hazelwood and lavender scents clung to each strand, transporting him back to the warmer evenings that they had spent together at the Obelisk. His memories cascaded through him like water breaking through a dam. Above them, Azura's white scales gleamed against Evor's obsidian ones as the dragons spiralled together in the air, their wings creating ripples of wind that stirred Elanor's hair around them both.

"I hate you." Elanor's voice was muffled against his chest.

"What?"

Elanor pulled her face out of his chest, and she looked back up at him. She shook her head and Ayr could see the restrained disappointment etched all over it. "I know it's not your fault. If you hadn't left, Dalton would have killed Evor."

"I'm sorry for what happened to him."

"It wasn't your fault, Ayr. I'm just glad you're back here."

"I can't stay for long. Dalton will know we've left already, and he'll grow suspicious that my intentions are not to be with him."

Elanor cusped his hands in hers and she guided him towards her face. "I'm not asking you to stay for long. Whilst they're off having a moment, I want one as well."

Another smile came to the corners of Ayr's mouth as he understood the assignment. He leaned forward, or was pulled, towards Elanor. She met him halfway and for the first time in weeks their lips met. All of her fire and all her bravado, the hate for him leaving her faded away as her shoulders slumped forward.

Ayr wrapped his arms around Elanor's waist, drawing her even closer as their kiss deepened. His lips caressed hers with a mix of hunger and tenderness, mimicking the warring emotions raging within both him and Azura. As Azura was getting closer to Evor, he was getting closer to Elanor. Elanor's hands tangled in his hair, her grip firm yet gentle, as if she were afraid to let go and lose him again. Her lips moved against his with a fierce determination, as if she were trying to commit the feel of him to her memory. A shiver ran down Ayr's spine at the thought that this might be their last goodbye, but he pushed it aside, unwilling to taint these precious moments.

"I need to go, Elanor. I don't want to, but we've stayed far too long already."

"You just got here. Stay a while."

Ayr shook his head. "I can't. I came to see you, to make sure that you were okay."

Elanor sighed, and smiled at him, tracing the base of his jaw with her fingers. "I'm always okay. I'm more worried about you. How has he been treating you?"

"He refuses to tell me more of his plan. All he does is test us."

"He's trying to make you stronger. You're already amongst the strongest riders that I have ever seen. You killed the Dragon Lords."

Ayr nodded as he ran his fingers through her hair. "I know, how is that going?"

A small smile spread across Elanor's lips. "I'm a Dragon Lord now. The Hormook came to the Haven to give us their blessing. I must have the Commonwealth's best interests at heart. Baldur doubts me at every turn."

"He survived the fall of the Obelisk?"

Elanor nodded, confirming the question. "They all did. We are just missing an Overlord."

"I don't want to be a lackey of my father forever. If he takes Azura from me..."

"Is he likely to?"

"He talks about breaking the bond between rider and dragon. Whilst it hasn't happened yet, I don't want him to."

"Then you need to flee."

"And go where?"

Elanor slid her hands around the back of Ayr's neck. The hairs on the back of his neck stood up. Whilst they had just kissed, the way she was staring into his eyes was something else entirely. He ran his hands down towards her hips and pulled her tight against him. He wanted there to be nothing between them and he knew that Elanor felt the same. She was close enough so that he could feel her breath on him.

"Stay right here, with me."

Their lips joined together again, and Ayr felt her fire against him. There was nothing between them as they swayed together, pushing against each other jostling for control. Elanor wanted dominance, but so did Ayr and he was not going to give up without a fight. He wanted her to think she had a chance, but there was nothing that he wanted more than ensuring that she wanted him.

"What?! You want to do it here?"

"Well, I'm not doing it on Evor's back. That's just a step too far."

"Here I was thinking you didn't have boundaries that I could cross."

Elanor rolled her eyes as she came in for another kiss. "Shut the fuck up, Ashbourne. Just fuck me already. It's been too long since I've had your cock inside me."

Ayr was not going to say no to her. If he did, it might have been his life on the line. Ayr reached forward and snaked his hands up her half naked body. With each movement of his hand, he remembered her curves and the way that her riding uniform fit to her incredible figure. There was nothing more he wanted than to rip it off her. She was right. It had been too long since they had last touched.

Now that they were back together again, the world felt complete. Elanor was everywhere, her skin touching his, her hands flying to unbutton her jacket. Ayr's hands were equally as busy, pulling at her hair, and also trying to unbutton his jacket. Elanor did the work for him, however, and Ayr's jacket was being pushed off his shoulders before he had even got hers half unbuttoned. The cold night air kissed his skin, but it was not the only thing kissing him as Elanor brought her lips forward.

She was all fire, and all passion as she touched him. At first it was gentle, teasing small pecks that did nothing but make him want more. He wanted to manhandle her, but Elanor pressed against him, controlling the tempo. As she kissed down his neck towards his chest, his nipples hardened, but he was not sure if that was because of the atmosphere or her touches. He did not complain regardless.

Ayr ran his hand along the base of her neck and pulled her close, groaning as he did. She giggled as she wrapped her mouth around his hardened nipple and bit down. At first it was tender, but the more that Ayr encouraged her into his body, the more she bit down. Ayr continued to groan as his jacket left his shoulders completely, now somewhere on the ground behind him, laying forgotten. Elanor backed off and continued to trace her tongue over his chest and before he could do anything to her, her hand was finding its way, snaking down to his trousers.

"I need you, Ayr."

Ayr groaned in response. Somehow, someway, Elanor's hand had already slipped open his belt and her grip was already tightening on his shaft. His eyes rolled back in his head as he let go of control, wondering how she had found her way to what she wanted so quickly without the use of magic. His wonderment did not last long as with another twist of her hand; Elanor fastened her grip on him and took control of him like a rider would use their saddle to control their dragon. Ayr was at her mercy.

He wanted to serve her, but any move he made towards her, Elanor rejected. Instead, she led him towards the nearest trees that stood just outside of the forest that otherwise surrounded them. It was a picturesque night underneath the stars and the moon, and Ayr could not have thought of a better place underneath the stars. There was a fallen tree branch that looked to be about hip height and Elanor pulled him towards it. Ayr was struggling to walk, nothing more than a waddle with his pants halfway down his legs. He wanted them off, but his boots kept them from sliding all the way down. Elanor turned to him as they reached the tree branch with a fierce look in her eye, one that reminded him of Evor. Her tone was urgent, her heart undoubtedly racing underneath her chest.

"I need you inside me, right now!"

There was no reason not to comply. As much as he wanted to serve her, Ayr wanted to tease her and prolong this experience as much as possible. Yet he knew that if Elanor wanted something, he needed to give it to her.

"As you wish, Elanor."

Ayr positioned himself behind her and dropped his knees so that he was at the right angle. There was a silent moment that passed between them, Elanor shifting with anticipation as she waited for him to be ready. Even under the moonlight, he could see just how wet she was for him, and there was nothing that he needed to do to further it. Time was short and she had already told him what she wanted.

The first gentle thrust inside her was electrifying. Ayr felt her tighten around him, and he almost wanted to release every bit of pent-up frustration that he had been holding in for what seemed like years. He felt Elanor move her hips as he pushed into her, her moan carrying through the night, extending the deeper he went. Ayr smirked as his hands found purchase around her thighs and now that he was situated properly, he pulled back. Elanor's low moan and the way her hand coiled on the tree branch drove him forward again

Elanor turned her head and smirked at him. "Is that all you've got for me, Ashbourne? I want you to fuck me properly."

Ayr grunted and reaffirmed his grip. "No."

It was the only word he could focus on. If he said anything else, he would have lost control, and he did not want to disappoint Elanor. It was all happening too fast. Elanor's hips bucked against his, urging him forward. Ayr complied, ramming into her again and again. He could feel Azura somewhere in the back of his mind, and her closeness to Evor was only fuelling the fire that raged between him and Elanor.

Whilst crickets chirped nearby, the only other sound that reached Ayr's ears was the sounds of Elanor's moans as she continued to whimper underneath the force of his thrusts. Ayr's fingers dug into her flesh as Elanor reached her first crescendo. Ayr slowed down, allowing her a moment to breathe, but Elanor grabbed at him.

"More! Don't stop!"

If Elanor wanted more, he had to give her more. He was struggling to hold on and what little control he had left was slipping away. Ayr thought about calling out to Azura, but she had her own concerns to worry about at this time. She was shut off to him, but he could still feel her presence, somewhere just out of sight and earshot. Ayr fought against Elanor, every time she thrust herself back on to him. There was no relenting. Ayr snaked his hand up to her hair, and grabbed a handful of it. He was not gentle, and the motion pushed Elanor over the edge again combined with Ayr's renewed thrusting.

Ayr felt her tightening around him and could feel himself getting closer to the edge. Then there was a split second where Elanor clenched around him, and it was the final straw.

Ayr groaned, bending over and moaning with everything he had into her ear as he finally let go. Elanor wriggled her hips as he felt himself finish inside her. Elanor was not one to waste a drop of his seed. She turned to look at him, her eyes swimming with admiration and lust, giggling like a girl much younger than she was.

"Fuck, I missed you."

Ayr grinned and started to laugh as well. "I missed you too, Elanor."

"What are we going to do?"

There was no moment to relax between the two of them. By the time Ayr had come to rest on the tree branch beside her, Elanor was already standing up. Elanor shifted her pants and started lifting them up around her waist. She did not look awkward or out of place, even though Ayr felt exposed here in the cold night.

"What about? The Commonwealth or Dalton?"

"Both. We can't remain this far apart for a long period of time. Azura and Evor won't cope."

Ayr raised his eyebrows as a smile came to his face. "Azura and Evor. Are you sure you don't mean you and me?"

Elanor tried to brush him off, but her eyes could not leave his. Ayr used no magic, but he thought that he could see her eyes beginning to water. Then, as if she had indeed been possessed by a spell, Elanor stopped, her eyes drying almost in an instant. Ayr was distracted by Azura as she re-entered his mind. She had finished her business with Evor, and the dragons were now flying back towards. A sadness was coming over both of them, as Ayr realised their time together needed to come to an end. This had been more than what he had expected.

"You need to go, Ayr."

"No, not like this. Don't leave me, Elanor."

As Ayr stared into her eyes, he could see that the tears had not dried completely. "I can come back with you. I am not comfortable with Baldur breathing down my neck. The Commonwealth is dying. I have seen it with my own eyes."

"And face Dalton's wrath? He'd kill you. You've got a job to do inside the Commonwealth, and I have one to do in Ironrock."

Elanor touched his face, one last time before he pulled away from her fully. "I'm going to miss you. Don't leave me waiting too long for you, Ashbourne. Otherwise Evor and I will drag you back from Dalton ourselves.

Ayr looked down at her, his smile still plastered all over his face despite the sadness that was prevalent in his eyes. "Don't threaten me with a good time, Elanor."

Elanor's voice was gentle as she pushed him away. "No. You need to do whatever you can do to accomplish what you want to. I'm going to delay Baldur acting on Ironrock for as long as possible."

"For what purpose?"

"Don't you want to overthrow Dalton?"

Ayr paused as he heard the wingbeats of the dragons overhead. He glanced up towards the stars and saw Evor's enormous dark figure cut across it. The dragons would join them in moments, and Ayr would once again be forced into the saddle to fly away from her. He sighed as he finished buckling his belt, Elanor's question still filling his ears. He was sick of caring and there was no point in remaining a servant to Dalton for the rest of his life.

As he felt Azura touch down on the ground beside him, Ayr threw himself forward once more, wrapping his arms around Elanor. She sunk into the hug with reluctance at first but accepted his embrace. Why would she willingly throw him off? Ayr felt her head in his chest as she spoke to him.

"Goodbye, Ayr. May your dragon always breathe fire."

"And may his wings always carry you on his back."

EIGHTEEN

E lanor hated watching Azura fly away, yet for the second time, there was nothing that neither she nor Evor could do about it. Evor stood beside her, his head down, not wanting to see his promised leave him once again. There was no guarantee that they would be coming back either. Elanor could only imagine what Dalton would do to them when they returned. Even if Ayr could plead his case, from what she knew of Dalton, he would not take kindly to insubordination. And then there was the matter of Azura. Whilst Ayr was his son, Azura had little importance to him.

Evor remained stagnant, watching until the last trace of Azura's silhouette had vanished, swallowed by the moon. Elanor could feel his loneliness already starting to wash over him, even though she knew that they would still be communicating with each other until she was out of range. Even though she wanted to, Elanor did not pry into their conversation. Sometimes the words that flowed between promised dragons should have been kept between them. After a while of Evor staring at the moon, she entered his mind.

What are you thinking, Evor?
That the love of my life has left me again. We should not be apart.
I feel the same way.
That's unlike you to admit your feelings, Elanor.
There's no point in hiding them anymore, Evor.

Then why did you not tell him. It would have been an opportune time. We may not get another chance to see them again before the two sides come to blows.

I'll tell him the next time I see him.

Good, that will please both Azura and I.

She knows?

Of course. What do you think I was talking to her about?

Why did you do that to me?

Because you and I both know that we are running out of time. The world is changing, Elanor. You need to act and those words should not come from Azura's mouth to his ears.

You're right.

Evor's next thought came to her in a chuckle. *I know I am. Now come, the sooner we return to the Haven, the better.*

Elanor inhaled through her nostrils and turned to face Evor, ready to pull herself up his massive side. As she planted her feet along his first row of scales, Elanor heard an all too familiar laughter rising around her, one that she did not want to hear. She turned her head and saw Chorru zoom past her and come into land just above her head on Evor's armour.

"I saw what you did, Elanor. Obviously, Dalton will know that his son left him to come and see you, but when I report back to him, he'll come for you."

"We're going to Ironrock. Let him."

Chorru was already leaving, slinking in between the shadows. "Careful what you wish for, Lady Sunfire. It will come to pass sooner rather than later."

"Dalton won't touch me again."

"We'll see if you are still singing the same tune once you attack Ironrock."

"Don't."

"Good luck, Elanor!"

Chorru started to laugh as he took flight, somewhere above her head. His laughter filled the air, a mocking cascade that seemed to vibrate the very air. Evor's scaled neck whipped around, his eyes narrowing to slits as he tracked Chorru's ascent, nostrils flaring with unmistakable irritation at the other dragon's display.

Let me kill the whelp, Dalton will not know.

He'll blame us. We must let events play out now, Evor.

Evor snorted and huffed at Chorru as he continued to fly away. Just how had he reached them so quickly after seemingly having returned to Dalton to relay more information? There was only one Chorru and despite the wyvern that he had at his command, Chorru was so far the only other dragon that she had seen come from his city.

You know that I do not agree with this course of action, Elanor.

Yet, we need to let it play out. Perhaps you will find him when we attack Ironrock.

Perhaps. Should we retire to our chambers?

There is nothing else to do now. Not without Ayr and Azura here.

I agree.

Evor waited for her to climb up his side, his eyes never leaving where Chorru had vanished to. As Elanor pondered the smaller dragon's fast travel time from Ironrock, she realised that he could have attached himself to Azura, but surely, she would have felt him on her. Had he been here the whole time? Ayr could handle himself, but what would Dalton do to Azura?

She shook the evil thoughts out of her mind at Evor's insistence, who did not want to think about Azura being targeted by Dalton for whatever vile experiment he had in mind or being fed to Sinibad. Elanor pulled her mask out of her jacket pocket once again and pulled it back over her face, not wanting to feel the insects and cold wind in her face on the flight back. Whilst it was not far, Elanor was now taking every comfort she could.

She could still feel Ayr inside her, and half had a mind to turn around and have Evor chase down Azura. If they were not willing to come with them, Elanor would instruct Evor to drag Azura back to the Haven with them. She knew that they would not be able to sneak them into the Haven and that as soon as they were spotted there would be conflict. With a heavy sigh, Elanor glanced over her shoulder one final time, hoping that they had changed their mind and were coming back. Instead, she was just met with nothing but the moon as it continued to rise over the mountains.

Evor mirrored her sadness and then turned his head, dangling down towards the ground. He took more steps as he then started to pick up leg speed, now aiming his head towards the sky. Evor went to take off, and Elanor saw something approaching from the Haven. Elanor squinted, also trying to see through Evor's far superior vision. Her heart began to sink. She identified Rotang soaring above the highest structures in the Haven that glistened far away on the horizon. There was no mistaking that Rotang was doing anything but heading straight towards them.

There was no getting around them and as if Evor redirected away, it would be far too suspicious. But with their trajectory it was far too late. Rotang let loose with a roar of greeting, his eyes locked onto Evor.

"Evor! There you are. Where are you returning from?"

"My rider and I fancied a flight outside the city for once. We are entitled to it."

"Land, Evor. We need to have words with you."

Elanor, I feel like he knows something.

Then do it. We're not here to cause conflict. If Rotang wants a fight on the ground, then that will be better suited for you, will it not.

As long as you can handle Baldur. And no, not in that way.

That way may be the only way available to us, Evor.

Evor grumbled and shook his head in agreement as he complied with Rotang's direction. Elanor could feel Rotang's eyes boring into the back of them, and this was by far not the first time that they had been in such a situation, the most recent being with Gundrag as Elanor had entered what had been Kaladin's chambers at the time. She shuddered at the thought of that memory, not wanting to remember what had come after. But then, as she remembered it, there was Ayr. He stood over her with Kaladin's blood on his hands, the dagger that he had summoned, gleaming in his fist, almost glimmering in delight with Kaladin's blood.

Baldur would not be so easily dispatched or taken by surprise. He was a man more focused on his goals, and from what Elanor could tell, he had no interest in her. There would be no distracting him. Rotang followed Evor to the ground and moved to enshroud him, jostling for position beside him. He brought his head close to Evor's so that Baldur could speak to Elanor unencumbered.

"What do you want, Baldur?"

"You need to be more careful with who you associate with, Elanor. Just because you think you were hidden does not mean your dragons weren't."

"I don't know what you're talking about."

"I followed you from the city! I saw the white dragon."

Elanor was continuing to deflect, running this for as long as she could. There would be no denying it if Baldur cut to the crux of the issue. She felt Evor surge underneath her, coiling, getting ready to strike at her command. "There are plenty of white dragons within the Commonwealth. One chose to join us."

"The only white dragon that has been sighted recently belongs to one Ayr Ashbourne."

Elanor's response was flat. "So?"

"What was he doing here? You told me that his father took him with him."

"He came to visit me. He's told me that Dalton plans to attack us soon."

If she could have seen through his mask, Elanor would have sworn that his eyes narrowed underneath it. Baldur stood up and leaned forward in his saddle. "Yet you gained that information from Chorru. If Ayr Ashbourne left with his father, he is a traitor to the Commonwealth. Allowing Dalton Ashbourne to roam free is a crime!"

"Ayr was not going to kill Dalton when the elder dragon held Evor to ransom. You're smarter than this, Baldur."

"You have no idea what that man is capable of! His son has blinded you!"

Elanor thrust her hand back behind her, gesturing to the wounds that remained on Evor's scales. "I know exactly what he is capable of! Look at what he did to my dragon for Chilijo's sake!"

"A scratch. If that dragon had wanted to kill Evor, it would have."

Elanor grit her teeth, wanting to bang her head against the nearest wall. Rotang was still circling Evor, the latter arching up, trying to make himself more imposing. They would be evenly matched if it came to blows, both as battle hardy as the other. A fight would come down to their riders.

"I am a Dragon Lord, Baldur. The same as you. I have a responsibility to the Commonwealth! The same as you."

"And yet your dragon is compromised. That is not a threat that I will allow to continue."

Elanor could feel Evor's fire churning in his throat. Just give the word, Elanor.

Only attack if you are attacked.

Baldur sat back in his saddle, but his body language did not betray any other emotion. Was he sitting back in his saddle so that Rotang could launch an attack? Elanor tried to read Rotang's body as well, but the older dragon was stoic. Elanor toyed with having Evor attack, just to get it over and done with, but then if Baldur or Rotang were to survive "Elanor Sunfire, I have reason to believe that you are fraternising with our enemy and no longer have the best interests of the Commonwealth at heart."

"Are we really doing this here?"

"I want to handle this discreetly. Nobody else has to know about what disgrace has befallen your family since your father's demise."

Elanor...

Baldur removed the mask from his face as Rotang started to step back. Rotang's expression was also less than favourable, but as Baldur removed his mask, Elanor saw that they both mirrored each other.

"The Sunfire name is still as strong as it was during the Ashbourne rebellion."

Baldur raised his hand gesturing towards the sky. Elanor's heart stopped for a moment, hoping that Ayr and Azura were returning, but Baldur was gesturing towards the complete opposite direction to where they had vanished. The hairs on the back of Elanor's back started to stand up as she realised something was amiss. A thunderous roar split the sky and drew both Elanor's and Evor's attention. For not wanting the Haven to know about what was happening here, the new dragon that was approaching was louder than it needed to be just announcing its arrival.

At first, Elanor did not see it, until Evor's keen eyes picked the beast up that was surging towards them. There was no doubt in Elanor's mind as to who this was. She recognised his purple scales against the darkness of the night sky as soon as she distinguished his outline from the horizon. With each passing wingbeat, Gundrag came more into view, Baldur and Rotang watching on with a renewed hunger. As Gundrag drew closer Elanor she knew exactly what this was about as the memories came flooding back to her during the final moments of the Obelisk still standing. The chaos as Evor had tried to chase Gundrag, to bring him down before he went mad with grief over the loss of his rider.

"I beg to differ, Elanor. I saw Gundrag flee the Obelisk only moments before Sinibad brought it down."

"So? Kaladin was a man of action. He probably knew something that we didn't. It only seems fair that the Overlord escaped before the fall."

Baldur's dark eyes sharpened on her. "Gundrag was without his rider, which meant Kaladin fell when the Obelisk did. Or should I say just before?"

"I don't know what you're talking about."

Rotang snarled as flames licked at his jaws. He started to move around Gundrag, who remained standing tall, his eyes flicking between both dragons around him. Gundrag was growing closer by the moment, and Evor was in no condition to outfly both of them.

"What happened to Overlord Kaladin, Elanor? By my count you were the last person to see him alive. I was most shocked to hear what Gundrag had to say about his death."

"It wasn't me!"

"Liar!"

Elanor!

Now is not the time, Evor! Just wait.

Baldur lashed out, throwing his hand forward and before she could raise her own hands to even think about countering him, Baldur's spell wrapped around her like a lasso. The training that he had spent with the Hormook had clearly paid off. Whilst Elanor was no slouch when it came to magic of her own, trying to fight against Baldur was as fruitless as fighting against Dalton in a duel of magic. She was trapped, but thankfully Evor was not. Evor tried to dart away as the lasso from Baldur tightened around her neck, but even as Evor backed away, Rotang followed.

If I wait any longer we will both be dead.

Gundrag was closing in on them, his shadow, even though it was dark, washed over them. Elanor was struggling as Evor tried to keep his space from both Rotang and Gundrag, but it was running out. Was he walking back towards the mountain they had landed behind, and Gundrag was coming in overhead.

"What are you two doing?"

"Doing what we should have done a long time ago, Evor."

Rotang's voice spat venom at them. He was circling Evor like a shark. Elanor had never felt so enclosed before, even when Gundrag had Evor trapped in his jaws before Sinibad's attack on the Obelisk. Elanor was starting to panic. Evor could take on either one of these two dragons alone, but if they were working in tandem, it would be a different outcome. Even Evor was beginning to grow concerned as he felt like the hunted for the first time in his life.

"I will let you have your revenge, Gundrag. As discussed, it is for all your years of service to the Commonwealth."

Gundrag was as smooth as ever and he came into land on the crest of the mountain behind them. He coiled around his own body with a snigger as he glared down at Evor.

"I appreciate your efforts, Overlord. Thank you for bringing the dragon and rider that played such a large part in Kaladin's death to me."

"Overlord? Dragons have no Overlord!"

"Times change, Evor. We are heading into a new era that you will not be part of."

Now, Evor!

The fire that surged behind Rotang's closed jaws now spilled forth and Evor turned away, leaping over the flames. Yet as he did, he leapt too high, leaping into the outstretched talons of Gundrag. Gundrag clamped down and Evor roared as Gundrag's talons ripped into his back, opening a fresh wound near where the wounds from Sinibad were. Evor twisted and contorted, breaking free as he turned his head to snap at Gundrag's legs.

Even though Gundrag had released and beat his wings away, moving up from Evor, Rotang was also on the attack. He slid forward, striking with precision, opting for his fang and claws over his fire. As Rotang moved forward, Elanor felt the spell from Baldur loosen around her neck and she could move once again. Whilst she and Evor needed to be in harmony, this was his element and he took control. Evor danced away as much as he could on the ground, only for Gundrag to strike down from above again.

With her sword not being viable in this situation, Elanor raised her hands. The day that she had spent channeling magic into Evor was leaving her feeling drained, but she managed the flow from his body into hers. It was a symbiotic relationship, and there was no need for Evor to use magic in this battle of tooth and claw and the two on one assault. Elanor raised her hands as Gundrag clamped down again and sent a surge of energy towards him. The energy jolted Gundrag enough so that he let go again, giving Evor a little room to move.

It was not enough and Rotang was crowding the space. Even as Evor turned and shrunk away to defend himself, Rotang was relentless. Elanor kept pushing her hands towards Gundrag, shooting more magic towards him, but she knew that Evor's reservoir of power would not last forever and soon she would be just as drained as when she had started. Gundrag came down again as Elanor heard an all too familiar roar break across the sky.

"Ashbourne!"

Gundrag tore his eyes from Evor and Elanor felt the release of his claws from Evor's body. As Gundrag's claws left his wounds, Evor reared his head back in pain, and almost sent Elanor flying from the saddle. She threw her hands down into the reigns but almost missed her grip. Her three fingers that remained locked in were her only saving grace, and she sent a quick prayer in Chilijo's direction, thanking him for saving her.

Azura was like a pale lightning bolt that shot across the sky, so fast that Elanor could not track her movements. Rotang also turned away, sensing the new threat overhead, which gave Evor time and space to move away. Rotang let loose with a roar of his own and rose to face the newcomers. There was a clap of thunder in the distance, as something blinding shot towards Rotang.

"You killed Kaladin! You will die!"

Elanor was lost in the blinding light that arced across the sky. She was only watching the battle unfold through Evor's eyes that were resilient to the magic that was being cast around. Baldur and Rotang met Ayr and Azura head on, a jet of magic racing out towards what came towards them. Gundrag was on them again and the focus of the moment was gone. Rotang continued to roar, as if trying to call for support from the Haven, but unless he had a promised somewhere within the city, the cry would go unanswered.

Gundrag's claws were everywhere, Evor doing what he could to fend them off. Blow after blow met his armour, most of them only glancing, but Elanor rocked with each hit. She sent blast after blast at Gundrag, trying to create separation between them. What if Azura and Ayr could not force Rotang and Baldur to submit? Then she heard a whimper that was the sound of defeat. She tried to tear her eyes away from Gundrag, but he was everywhere. Out of the corner of Evor's vision, she saw Rotang retreating, flying back towards the Haven. What had happened?

Gundrag kept coming, crowding Evor and Elanor screamed as she felt a cut bury itself deep under Evor's right eye. He groaned in pain, but could not relent. Gundrag kicked at him, his claws scratching at his softer belly, and Evor was fighting back, trying to push the violet dragon away. There was separation at last as a jet of flame soared overhead. The tables had now turned with Rotang's retreat and now the odds were in their favour.

As Gundrag pulled back, Evor snapped forward. The foremost of Gundrag's legs was trapped inside Evor's jaws, and all it took was for Evor to wrench his head back. Elanor heard the crunching of bones in Evor's mouth and felt the sensation in her own, revelling in the taste of them. This was better than when Kaladin had collapsed by her side in defeat, with Ayr standing over him with his bloodied dagger in hand.

The more that Evor bit down on Gundrag, the more that this felt final to Elanor, like there was nothing else left now. Azura rounded on Gundrag, coming in for one final pass. Elanor could see Ayr in his saddle with his hands extended towards Gundrag. With one more blow, fire tore across the sky, as both Ayr and Azura unleashed with their torrents of flame. Evor pulled away at the last second before the fire engulfed Gundrag.

If he had not already been roaring before as his leg had been torn from his body, Gundrag was now. Elanor and Evor were both relishing in his demise, as Ayr's fire combined with Azura's made a supernova, one that seemed as if it could melt through anything. Gundrag's scales were melting before their eyes and there was nothing that he could do to break free of the fire.

Evor stepped back further as Ayr and Azura took full control of the situation. Elanor scanned the sky and saw Rotang's silhouette under the moonlight. He flew unevenly, favouring his left side. Had Azura or Ayr wounded him to the point where he decided it would not be wise to continue the fight? If he made it back to the Haven in one piece, the entire Commonwealth would know that they had attacked them. Rotang had too much of a headstart. How had Baldur escaped Ayr?

The end result would be the same. With their inability to cut off Rotang's arrival back to the Haven, the Commonwealth would know of hers and Evor's betrayal. Even though they had been the ones that had been attacked, Baldur would spin the opposite tale. Had this been how it had been when Dalton had begun his rebellion? She reached down and patted Evor beside the saddle as Ayr and Azura continued to incinerate Gundrag, until there was nothing left of him but cinders.

NINETEEN

Ayr was the first to cut off his stream of power from flowing into the charred remains of Gundrag. Azura sensed his magic pulling away and cut hers off only moments later. He could feel her surging with pride and joy, seeing that Evor was now free from the sharp fangs and claws of Gundrag and Rotang. She came into land beside him and puffed out her chest.

"I didn't think that we would be seeing you again so soon, Evor."

Evor stood tall over her, grateful for her presence. "Nor did I little one, yet I am grateful for the assistance. When I called, you came to my rescue."

"I did. I would do anything for you. Chilijo himself could not keep me from your side in a time of need."

"And I would do the same for you, little one."

Ayr watched through Azura's eyes as they ran across Evor's body. "You are hurt, Evor."

Evor's tongue flicked out from his mouth and towards the wound. He tasted the air around him and snorted. A puff of smoke escaped his nostrils and he laughed. "Nothing more than a scratch. If it was not for Rotang, I could have handled that hatchling."

"There is no need to act with me, Evor. Even without a rider, Gundrag was powerful. The fight could have gone either way."

Now it was Evor's turn to puff out his chest, a hint of anger in his voice as he spoke. "Do you think me to be incapable, little one?"

"No, Evor. Sometimes you do not know your limitations. You are still injured, after all."

"Yet I can still fly."

"You will have to. I think there is only one place for us now."

"One place? Azura, that man wanted Elanor to become a Dragon Lord. She is supposed to be here. The Haven is her task to conquer."

Ayr spoke up, looking up at Evor. "What's likely to happen if Baldur drags you before the other Dragon Lords and demand you be punished for what you did today?"

Elanor was as cool and as calm as a cat. She leaned back in the saddle and removed her mask. Ayr took in a deep lung of oxygen as he looked upon her face once again. Elanor was still glowing underneath the moonlight.

"He can fight me. I'm entitled to a trial by combat."

"Can you defeat Baldur in a duel?

"He's powerful, but I can try."

"You are two Dragon Lords; I just wonder how much further your luck will carry you."

"I have a job to do, Ayr. Nothing is going to stop me from accomplishing it when Evor's life is on the line. I could not stop my father or my mother's death, but his life is in my hands."

Ayr bowed his head. "Then you know what you need to do. You need to live for Evor so Evor can live for Azura."

"You live for both of us as well, Ayr."

Ayr sighed, unable to shake the sinking feeling in his chest. "This time apart does us no good. We need to find a way back to each other."

Now it was Elanor's turn to smile at him. "You came back to us in our hour of need. This is temporary. We will get through this."

"We will. Will you return to the Haven?"

Elanor nodded, her face hardening as she went to answer. Ayr knew that her decision was final. "Yes. Whatever happens, will happen. If Baldur wants to fight, we will be ready."

"Can Evor take on Rotang?"

Evor grumbled over him, and whilst Ayr did not feel small due to being on Azura's back, he knew that if he was not Azura's rider, he would have been squashed like a bug. "Do not question my ability to fight another dragon, Ayr. I would have fought Sinibad if he had not taken advantage of my distraction."

Ayr raised an eyebrow. "Azura was fine without your help."

"Dalton had her in his grasp. There was nothing that I would not do to see her free from that."

Even though Azura held no anger towards Evor, there was some annoyance in Ayr's chest. "She is my dragon. If Dalton would have harmed her, I would have killed him."

Evor's eyes widened as he leaned down towards Ayr. "You're not as strong as you think you are. Dalton still has a hold over you."

"We came back. You know we intend to break it."

"What will break first, I wonder."

Ayr bit his lip as Azura cut into his mind. *Stop. We are on the same team.*

He questions us.

Evor is my promised, Ayr. We need to respect him. We will get through this together.

We will, but we need to be on the same page.

Then speak it into existence. You are the one that always wants to fight.

Ayr frowned and then sighed as he realised that Azura was right. "We will not break. Dalton will not drive us apart."

"For your sake and mine, I hope not. We will return to the Haven and face Baldur."

Azura nodded underneath Ayr. "Then we will return to Ironrock and face Dalton."

Ayr could see Rotang still flying above the Haven, and as he neared the city, there was lights coming up from underneath him, making him look larger than usual, even at that distance. Evor turned his head and a grumble escaped his chest again.

"We need to go. I will miss you, little one."

Azura stepped forward and rubbed her head against Evor's chest. "And I will miss you, Evor."

"I will cherish this night."

Elanor nodded in agreement as she went to pull her mask back over her face. "As will I."

Ayr smiled up at her and nodded in agreement. He spoke for both of them. "We will as well."

"I mean it this time, Ayr. May your dragon always breathe fire."

"And may his wings carry you forward."

Elanor's mask slid down over her face and Evor stretched his wings out. His size engulfed them and he turned, taking care not to hit Azura with his tail. Evor ran forwards, his footsteps shaking the ground beneath his feet. Ayr caught sight of the scars still on his back in the moonlight. Whilst they were still prevalent, they were at least healing. However, if Rotang sunk his teeth or claws into them more than Gundrag already had, with a rider as powerful as Baldur, it would have had detrimental results.

Ayr did not want them to go, but both Elanor and Evor had made up their mind. Evor launched himself into the dark, velvety night sky and Ayr could feel the wind beating from his wings. He felt a sinking sensation in his stomach, which was only amplified by Azura's feelings. Azura remained stagnant for a moment before she entered Ayr's mind again.

We need to return to Ironrock. Dalton will be waiting, Ayr.

Why are you filling our minds with doubt? We need to be clear on our mission, Azura. What do you want to do?

If Dalton does intend to break us, we need to be prepared.

We have a day's flight back to Ironrock. We will be.

I am concerned for our future, Ayr. Dalton will not be pleased when we return to him.

I don't care. We will deal with him.

Ayr! We are still not strong enough to face him.

We have to. There is no backing out of this now. If we wanted to run, we had our chance weeks ago.

It's too late to back out now. I for one do not wish for Bryne to come hunting us. Or worse, Sinibad.

I will evade them.

As long as Chilijo wills it, Azura.

Azura paused to chuckle before she continued. Ayr wondered what was so funny. *I did not think that you were religious, Ayr.*

Chilijo was a god?

He was to us. But now I doubt everything I know about him and the formation of the Commonwealth. The Keepers would have no reason to lie, would they?

I don't see why they would. They were there when the first war happened, yes?

At least that is what our history books say.

Are you ready to fly, Azura?

Azura's wings unfurling on either side of them was all the answer he needed. Ayr took a deep breath, still dreading what was waiting for them back at Ironrock. Dalton would be furious but there was nothing they could do about it. If they fled to the Commonwealth they'd face a similar fate to Elanor. Dalton would at least hear them out, unless they had reached the end of their usefulness with them. The Dragon

Lords and the Commonwealth would just try to murder them before they had a chance to explain themselves.

As Elanor and Evor were leaving them behind, Ayr continued to feel his heart sink further. He pat Azura and she shook her head as she turned back towards the west, in the direction of Ironrock. Azura shook herself out and readied herself for the long flight ahead. Not that there was any time constraint on their journey, but both Ayr and Azura wanted to be as far away from the Haven as possible. Ayr checked over his shoulder and saw Evor's silhouette slipping into the light of the Haven and knew that it would not be long until they were in danger.

Every part of him screamed at himself to go back and to save her, but he had no leverage and was outside of his power. If he wanted to flatten the city, he could, but not before the Dragon Lords or any of the other dragons within the city killed either Azura, Evor or worse, Elanor. He and Azura had agreed on their course of action and now he had to go through with it. Azura started forward and launched herself into the air, leaving where they had incinerated Gundrag behind them.

Ayr only looked forward. With Azura in the sky, Ayr felt more at peace with what was going on around them, but he could feel that Azura was not fully focused on the flight ahead. It was not that it would be a hard flight, but if they were set upon, she needed to be ready. Ayr cast his gaze towards the horizon, just waiting for more dragons to come over it. Whether they were from Ironrock or the Haven, the outcome would be mostly the same.

Ayr set himself in the saddle, not wanting to sleep, but Azura was uncertain, especially with what was happening to Evor. If they were being attacked, she was not showing any signs of distress, so Evor at this point was not in danger. That did not mean that it was not about to change. Ayr closed his eyes, allowing himself to breathe properly. If Azura was not panicked, why was he? He could not feel Elanor like

Azura could feel Evor, but considering the link between dragon and rider, Azura would know if Evor felt that Elanor was in danger.

Azura chased the moon across the night sky, and Ayr could feel her losing her grip on Evor the further they slipped away from the Haven. He knew that there was nothing more they could do and he could only focus on how he could best deal with Dalton. Ayr lost himself deep in thought and Azura continued to hum away underneath him. The flight was peaceful and steady. Ayr sank into the saddle, tired from the day's travel and his activities. He closed his eyes and allowed himself to relax, even though his mind was so far away.

TWENTY

*Y**ou still did not tell him, Elanor.*

Things have changed! We need to catch Baldur!

Ha! It takes no time at all to say three extra words. You could have told him by now. I thought you promised that you would tell him the next time we saw him.

You know as well as I do that there's every chance that you and I are going to our deaths.

Stop making up excuses, Elanor. Part of you wants to defend the Commonwealth. If they kill us after you told him how you felt, you know he'd burn it to the ground, even without Azura.

Elanor did not respond to the statement, not wanting to give Evor the satisfaction of being correct. We need to focus. We know how dangerous Baldur and Rotang are.

How much longer are you going to run from the truth, Elanor?

As long as it takes.

Hmm. You'd best pray to Chilijo that Baldur and Rotang do not kill us.

Just fly, Evor.

Elanor withdrew herself from the conversation as Evor continued forward. The lights of the Haven were ever present on the horizon, and Rotang's presence was gone, sunken somewhere into the city. As Evor got closer to it, the more that Elanor was fearing that Rotang would watch up from the city at them. Instead, as Evor flew over the first walls, the more Elanor was scanning the city floor.

Evor flew straight towards the hall of the Dragon Lords and as it started to take shape on the horizon, Elanor could make out the enormous figure of Rotang crouching by the building. As they neared, he raised his head towards them, and then snaked his way up the side of the hall. Evor came into land beside it, growling as he did so. Rotang was not alone, however. Beside him were Tempura and Gravu, both of them sneering down at Evor with him.

"You're too late, Evor. Baldur has spread word of what you have done tonight. There will be no coming back from it."

"Save your words, Rotang. I will finish what we started."

"You might want to slow down, Evor. Baldur and the others are coming to deal with Elanor."

Let me handle this, Evor. You're not in a physical state to take all of them in a fight.

There is nothing that I want more.

Stop. You're not going to win. Let me challenge him to single combat.

You will not win either, Elanor.

Let me try.

Evor grumbled underneath her as he came to a complete stop. Elanor raised her mask from her face and grumbled along with Evor. Knowing what she had to do, Elanor slid down Evor as he lowered himself to the ground. Baldur was not carrying himself in his usual manner. Instead of being upright and commanding, Baldur was keeled over, clutching at his face. Elanor knew that neither she or Evor had struck him, and that was ever was wrong with him was of his own doing.

"There she is!"

Baldur removed his hand from his face to reveal a deep red cut underneath his left eye. He glared up at her with his typical fierce intensity, but Elanor remained calm and unmoved. As Baldur and the other Dragon Lords moved towards her, Elanor felt Evor arc up, wanting to protect her, but he had problems of his own. The three dragons that were all peering at him snarled, sensing his insubordination. Their riders would have spread word to their dragons, and they were all now on the same page.

Evor, remain calm.

They want to do us harm. I will fight until the breath leaves my body. It's me and him. You will not beat Rotang.

And you will?

Elanor's boots touched the ground, and she stepped away from Evor as the other Dragon Lords surrounded her. The sword on her hip seemed to pulse at her side, even though no magic had been cast on it. She would need it soon, but for now diplomacy was the answer. If they could not sort out their differences, then steel was required.

"Dragon Lords. How can I assist you?"

Romulus snorted. "Assist us? Elanor, can you tell us why in Chilijo's name you thought it would be a good decision to attack Baldur?"

Leyla was also short with her, her face contorting with rage. "And more importantly, why did Ashbourne save you? He's not supposed to be here!"

"He only came because we were in danger. Baldur doesn't want to be equal with the rest of you. He seeks to become your next Overlord."

Romulus raised his eyebrows in surprise, whilst Leyla continued to press her, encroaching upon her space. "How do you know this?"

"Did you perhaps want to ask him why he attacked us? Kaladin's dragon returned to us and attacked along with Rotang."

Baldur's hand went back to his face, covering it as he screamed. "That's not what happened! You attacked us first!"

"Do you expect them to believe that? You were on Rotang's back? How did you get that cut on your face? It wasn't me. If it was me, I would have done the job properly."

Baldur raised his finger and pointed at her in anger. "If it wasn't for your little Ashbourne, you'd be dead!"

"Good thing he came back when he did then. But I'm over this Baldur. What exactly is your issue with me? We're on the same side here!"

"Ayr Ashbourne. You are compromised!"

"My father quite literally broke the rebellion by his own hand."

"Because Dalton Ashbourne wanted to fuck your mother! Don't try to tell me that he did it out of the goodness of his own heart. We all knew that Dalton, Grace and Crassus were friends before the rebellion and as soon as Crassus' dragon was promised to Grace's, that's when the lines became blurred and Dalton went down his path of madness. I saw your mother's body, Elanor. He killed her. Just like he did Crassus and Anton. And you're throwing your lot in with his son!"

"His dragon is promised to mine!"

Baldur sneered at her, removing his hand once more from his face. "See. By your own admission you are compromised. You can't be a Dragon Lord."

As Baldur's hand fell towards his sword, a screeching roar shook the sky from somewhere behind Elanor, and as one, the Dragon Lord's eyes rose to the horizon. Elanor turned as well, and as a second ear splitting shriek broke across the otherwise pristine night, she saw two large dragons approaching. Based off their uneven flight, she had a funny suspicion regarding who the dragons were. They approached within moments, and as the dragons set themselves on the ground, it was evident who they were.

As one, the Hormook removed themselves from their dragons, touching down onto the ground within a hair of each other. Their faces were unreadable underneath their masks. Athel was the first to step forward, her voice coming through her mask as soft as silk.

"It appears that we were summoned for the correct reason, Terenas. What seems to be the problem?"

Baldur continued to point his finger at Elanor. "Her! She lies with the enemy."

Terenas removed his mask from his face with a well-practiced grace before holding it afloat in just one hand. He ran his discerning eye over Elanor and then Baldur. The lines on his face creased as he inspected Baldur's scar. Terenas' eyes then flicked towards Elanor.

"Is what he says true?"

Do not lie, Elanor. He is more powerful than you.

You and I both know that we're past the point of no return. This is where we live or die.

I appreciate your concern for my promised, Elanor.

They are both our promised. I will fight for them.

Then see it done.

Elanor raised her eyes to Terenas before bowing her head. "It is true. Ayr Ashbourne is the rider of my dragon's promised. But I didn't attack Baldur like he claims."

"You are a liar!"

Terenas raised his hands, silencing both of them in a flash. Elanor could feel the tightening of the spell around her tongue, Terenas' mastery of magic almost as commanding as Dalton's and for the first time since their last encounter, Elanor felt afraid. She stood rigid as Terenas came between both her and Baldur. He scowled at both of them in turn, pursing his lips as he stared. There was a silence as Leyla and Romulus watched on with anticipation for what was about to happen. The former looked like a hungry hyena, licking her lips, waiting for someone to attack with the first blow.

"If a solution is unobtainable through ordinary means, then it is perhaps time we explored another option. What do the two of you think about a trial by combat? Chilijo will bless whoever is telling the truth."

Terenas lowered his hands and Elanor felt the spell slip away from her like a wave of water rushing over her body. She now once again had full body control, but it appeared that Terenas had lessened the spell on him first. Baldur snorted and at last lowered his hand from his face.

"Excellent, a chance to kill this pretender once and for all."

Elanor grit her teeth as her hand fell to her sword. This is what both her and Evor had been afraid of. There was no coming back from this. Either she would kill Baldur or he would kill her. There was no in between. Elanor nodded and Terenas caught the motion. He stepped out from between the two of them and bowed his head.

"Very well. Since you have both agreed to trial by combat, you are both granted one sword. There will be no magic allowed for this fight. You are both well versed in swordsmanship. Chilijo's divine wisdom will decide who prevails on this night. Take your weapons."

Elanor felt a cold chill at her back. The night was cold, but the chill was not because of the weather. She glared at Balur as he unsheathed his sword. He turned his back to her and if she was somewhat faster, she might have had a chance to draw hers and stab him in the back. There was no window of opportunity as he turned back around, and Terenas narrowed his eyes.

"Are you both ready? There is no going back now."

Baldur's upper lip curled. "Yes, Hormook."

Terenas flicked his eyes towards Elanor. She could also feel Athel glaring at the back of her head. The other two Dragon Lords also stood the side in a silent vigil. Both Rotang and Evor stood overhead, watching the proceedings with great interest. Elanor's sole focus, however, was on Baldur and the blade that he carried loosely at his side. He had decades more experience than she did, and Elanor did not often engage in a fight that she thought she was going to lose. Sparring Kaladin had never been dangerous. She was more in danger of being fucked than killed, but against Baldur the threat was very real.

"Lady Sunfire?"

Elanor did not feel the need to response, just instead opting to nod her head. Evor grumbled overhead, and Elanor could feel him pressing into her mind.

Do not let him overpower you, Elanor.

Really? I thought that I would just let him do that.

He is not allowed to use magic in this fight. He will be an old man.

He has decades of experience, Evor. I can't stand against him.

Do it, or we both die, Elanor.

Terenas raised his hand and glanced at both Dragon Lords before lowering it with a shout that sprang from his lips. "Begin!"

Baldur stepped forward, slow and calculating, holding his sword across his chest like a rapier. His sword was much heavier, and Elanor wondered if she could fight him blow for blow. Baldur closed the space between them in only half a dozen strides and flicked his sword out with the speed and agility of a much younger man. Elanor almost did not see it coming at her face, and moved back, feeling the wind of the blade on her cheek. Elanor saw her opening and struck forward.

Her blade met Baldur's at a midway point between them, and already Elanor felt the struggle that she would continue to face if this fight extended past a few exchanges. Elanor retracted her blade from Baldur and in the same breath stepped back towards him, swinging her sword in an attempt to catch him off guard. Baldur stepped away, using his sword to batter her away like a fly. She kept coming, each thrust desperate, all of them trying to prove her innocence.

She knew that Baldur was toying with her. He was fencing her, with one hand behind his back, and Elanor knew there was nothing that she could do to overcome his power. Even with Evor behind her, Baldur still was empowered by Rotang, thus making the imbalance still prevalent between them. Every time he struck was just another

Elanor gasped for breath, her heart hammering against her ribs. She was tiring and knew she must end this duel soon or risk defeat. Baldur, on the other hand, showed no signs of exertion, his breathing even and his eyes were as cold as ice. He did not feel threatened, even as she struck out with her full power. Baldur circled her, waiting for an opening, his movements as fluid as water, despite his age. Elanor knew she needed to do something desperate if she was to stand a chance.

Summoning every ounce of strength she possessed, Elanor feigned exhaustion, stumbling forward as if her knees were about to buckle. Baldur was nothing other than confident in his abilities. He stepped closer, intending to deliver a finishing blow. But as he raised his sword, Elanor found her opportunity.

In one fluid motion, she dropped to the ground, twisting her body, and swept her leg out in a graceful arc. Her boot connected with Baldur's legs, sending him crashing to the ground with a thud. The air rushed from his lungs, and in that brief moment of distraction, Elanor leaped to her feet, her sword held high above her head. She heard Rotang's snarl of surprise as Baldur landed on his back, but there was still not enough alarm from him to think that Baldur was in any danger of dying. Elanor brought the sword down onto him, but Baldur thrust his up in response, meeting it halfway. Elanor began to grind down, doing everything she could to force her blade into Baldur's chest, but he was doing everything in his power to force his up into her.

They struggled against each other, sweat pooling on Elanor's forehead despite the cold dark sky above her. She felt Evor's fury building underneath her, using his power to try and drive her weapon down into Baldur. She knew that he was using Rotang's to come back at her. It was a stalemate. Even though both dragons were fuelling their riders, there was no movement between the two of them. Baldur glared up at her, his teeth grinding against each other in frustration.

"If only there was an Overlord to be the difference maker with these decisions. This would have ended by now if Kaladin were still alive."

"Baldur, you do realise we have a common foe in this fight?"

"I will not have you laying with an Ashbourne. He showed his true intentions when he went with his fucking father!"

"He came back!"

"And then attacked me. Are you going to stand there and lie to my face that you did not assist him?"

"If it is my life and Evor's on the line, I will defend it. You threatened me!"

"You threaten the Commonwealth. It is my duty as a Dragon Lord to defend it!"

"And it is my duty to defend both myself and my dragon if you attack us!"

Elanor tried to thrust down again into Baldur, but as she did, she was stopped. A thick gloved hand clamped over her shoulder as Baldur's eyes widened. Terenas' hand was guiding Elanor away from striking down, and against the power of the Hormook she was powerless. It felt like a spell straight from Dalton Ashbourne's hand as he moved her arm away, forcing her to readjust her grip on the sword.

"You will stand, Elanor Sunfire. It appears you both have legitimate reasons for wanting to kill each other, particularly if what you say is true about Baldur attacking you and your dragon. And for that Chilijo's judgement will not be passed today."

Baldur's face started to grow red as he moved away from Terenas, picking himself up from the ground. He kept his sword levelled, and at the ready, just in case there was any chance that Terenas had changed his mind. Rotang grumbled overhead, but Evor matched him, staring in his direction.

"She sleeps with our enemy whilst trying to tell us she has our best interests at heart. She betrays the Commonwealth!"

Athel snapped forward, cutting between Baldur and Terenas. "You will abide by our wishes! We speak the will of Chilijo!"

Baldur's face showed nothing but confusion and shock as he tried to process the betrayal of the Hormook. "You were supposed to be on my side! Elanor Sunfire is nothing more than a nepotism pick due to the position of both her father and Overlord Kaladin."

Terenas' eyes darkened as he started to shake his head. "You chose to attack her and her dragon. That is against your laws is it not?"

"This is war!"

"That it might be but considering you were not honest with us from the start, that is grounds for us to cancel this trial. I would expect you to finalise your differences on another occasion if this enemy of which you speak waits at your doorstep."

Baldur finally discarded his sword, sheathing it back on his belt where it belonged. Seeing that he had done so, Elanor did the same. Baldur still looked to the Hormook for confirmation. "Will you assist us in this battle?"

Athel's sour expression was all that Elanor needed to know the Hormook's decision. "Considering the waste of time you have called us here for, Baldur, no. The Commonwealth will struggle under your leadership."

"You're just going to abandon us in our time of need?"

"Yes."

The Hormook moved as one, both of them placing their masks onto their faces, as their dragons both lowered their necks towards the ground. As their cloaks wrapped around them as they climbed up, the Dragon Lords and their dragons watched on, unmoving. It was not until they had raised their head and looked to the sky that Baldur finally moved in front of Elanor. The other Dragon Lords took steps closer, both Romulus and Leyla seeming apprehensive in their approaches. Baldur's sneer was etched all over his face.

"When you are ready, we will fly on Ironrock. If your promised is somewhere in the city, we will not hesitate to bring him and his traitorous dragon to the ground."

"You wouldn't dare, Baldur."

"You've escaped my blade once, Elanor. Don't tempt fate and ask for a reprieve a second time. Ayr Ashbourne will die, just like his father and we will have peace."

"You can't kill him; he has value to me!"

Baldur glared at her. "I'll be the judge of that. Make sure Evor is ready to fly, or you'll be left alone for us to deal with later. Regardless of what the Hormook will demands of us."

"And will you be the one that answers to them when they demand more of us?"

A hiss escaped Baldur's lips that sounded like it had come from Rotang above. "That is my concern. The Hormook were brought here by myself, and I will be the one to dismiss them should I deem it necessary."

TWENTY-ONE

I ronrock was a welcome sight, but what waited for them inside it was not. Ayr could feel the shift in the atmosphere as soon as they entered within sight of the city. Whilst it was still nestled safely between the mountains, the moment that Ayr laid his eyes upon Sinibad, the golden dragon began to impose his sheer size and aura upon them. He sat upright once he spotted them, his massive form stretching out as he whipped his tail behind him. He snorted, unimpressed by their presence.

"Do you think you could sneak away from Dalton and he wouldn't know? Little Ashbourne, just because you are the son of the king, it doesn't give you leniency to go wherever you feel like it. You have obligations here."

Azura spoke for Ayr, Ayr unable to project his voice so far away. "I took him away to get away from the city for a night. Do you have that much of a problem with it, Sinibad?"

"No, but Dalton does. He is furious."

"Then we will soothe his anger with our presence."

Sinibad rolled his eyes and then snorted. An even larger puff of smoke escaped his nostrils and Sinibad collapsed back into the comfort of the mountainside. Ayr was still not used to his enormous body standing guard over Ironrock and felt nothing but scrutiny as he watched them approach. Azura was also apprehensive as they approached Ironrock, but the smaller dragons that watched their approach were otherwise unbothered. They saw that she was alone and therefore were not threatened by her presence.

Azura angled herself towards the fake Obelisk, and no sooner than she had begun to make her descent, Manir appeared from underneath its roof. She glanced up towards them, her eyes narrowing as she spotted Azura. Manir kicked off from the ground and shot towards them like an engorged blue arrow. As she drew nearer, she slowed down, making her presence felt. There was no way that Azura would be able to get around her without being caught in her jaws.

Pull up, Azura.

I can get past her, Ayr.

You know we're in trouble already, we shouldn't purposely go making it worse.

A day ago, you did not care. Now you don't want to cause more drama? Why have you gone back on your word?

A day ago, it was clear that we had an option to return to the Commonwealth. We've killed one too many dragons for that to now be viable. Especially with Baldur attempting to dethrone and discredit Elanor. Talk to Manir for me please.

As you wish.

"Manir, what brings you here? We're just returning to the Obelisk."

"You've done it now, little Ashbourne. Dalton wants your heads on a pike. If he can not trust his own son and his dragon to toe the line, an example needs to be made out of the two of you."

"Well, we won't have it. If Dalton wants us, then he can come and get us himself."

"Come with me or I'll take you out of the sky myself. It's your choice, little Ashbourne. You know I'm not fussed as to how you get there."

She seems to have made up her mind.

We should go with her, Ayr, but it's your call.

We've had a long flight, and I don't want you getting hurt. Let her lead.

Azura dipped her head, submitting to Manir. "We will follow you. Take us to Dalton."

Manir swooped around them, and if it was not for Ayr ducking his head at the last moment, Manir's tail would have connected with him. The blue dragon led the way down towards the city, in a perilous arc that if she did not pull herself up from, would have resulted in her plastering herself all across the buildings. But Manir was too old and too wise, with Kita being an equally skilled rider. They led them towards where Dalton had first held council with them. Manir touched down onto the ground, the same grass that Azura had landed upon, during their first arrival within Ironrock.

Little had changed in the weeks that Ayr had been here, except this time there were half a dozen other dragons in the field. Something felt different about Ironrock now. Each of the dragons did not have riders present with them, but Ayr could still feel their power radiating all around him. Sinibad watched from above, with one lazy eye open being the only thing that kept him from falling asleep.

Azura touched down on the ground behind Manir, still taking care to avoid her tail. It was like a whip, and the moment that Manir was on the ground, Ayr could already see Kita moving out of the saddle. Ayr could feel iron growing in his legs and he grew increasingly mobile, but he knew unless he wanted Sinibad to incinerate or eat Azura for a snack, he had to comply.

Dalton was still his father, and he still held dominion in this place. They should never have come back. Doubts filled his mind as he climbed down Azura's side. He could have directed her to flee the Commonwealth and to take Elanor and Evor with them. There had been no noise from Evor, so Elanor must have been fine. Unless, of course, she was dead. Ayr shuddered at the thought.

When he reached the ground, Kita was already waiting for him. She had removed her mask from her face to reveal her straight blond hair, as well as her eyepatch. She glowered at him, with an intensity in her eye that reminded Ayr of Elanor. He did not shrink before her, instead, he straightened his back and stood up taller. If she was going to accost him over what he had done, he did not want to hear it. Not today.

"So, you think you're funny, do you?"

Ayr groaned internally and rolled his eyes. The reaction was immediate. Kita reached out and slapped him across the right cheek, with a blow so powerful it almost made him take half a step to the side. He felt his magic surge through his body as Azura arced her back. Manir snarled above them and even though his magic was building underneath his skin, Ayr felt smaller compared to her.

Answer her, Ayr. This woman will not take a no for an answer.

Ayr turned his head back towards her, acting as if he had just been struck by a mallet. He could feel his face contorting into an unfamiliar twisted anger, an anger that he had only felt when around Dalton treating him with a similar amount of disrespect. She stepped closer, her head stopping just below his eyeline. She stared up at him with her one good eye and scowled.

"So?"

"No, like I told you before I left Ironrock, I am merely over the act that I need to uphold just to appease Dalton."

"That's too bad. Come with us."

Kita turned on her heel and led Ayr and Azura towards the first place that Dalton had taken them when they had arrived at Ironrock. Sinibad's lazy eye followed them from high above, his silent judgement being passed down onto them. Ayr still shuddered underneath his gaze, at least Baindussa back at the Obelisk had some kindness about him. Sinibad was nothing but hostile towards them. Kita noticed him staring and laughed over her shoulder at Ayr.

"Everyday when I see him lurking up there, I can't help but think all he wants to do is eat you."

"Something tells me that you and Dalton, both don't want that."

Kita continued to laugh as Sinibad grumbled overhead. "I will never claim to be able to read Dalton Ashbourne's mind. The man is an enigma. What he plans for you is greatness, yet all you seem to want to do is kick him in the teeth when he presents it to you."

"Perhaps he needs to look at how he treats the people around him. You included."

Kita's usually open chest sunk slightly as her shoulders rounded. "I will follow Dalton until I die. The man has been nothing but loyal to me and assures me of our victory."

Now was Ayr's turn to sneer at Kita. "He promised all of his followers the first time around that he would lead them to victory. Strange things can happen in war."

"He's destroyed most of those that opposed his rebellion before. That won't happen again."

Ayr cocked his eyebrows at her as they passed underneath the threshold of the main hall. "We'll see."

"I can't half tell you're an Ashbourne. You're as cocky and confident as the other two."

"We're all just playing one big game, Kita. Just be grateful you're only a pawn in it."

Kita scoffed and stopped in her tracks. "A pawn? I've had you underneath my blade so many times, boy."

Magic swirled around Ayr's hand, but he did not act upon it. He felt Azura coil behind him, pushing some of her magic towards him.

He grinned at Kita as he neared her face. "Yet you've done nothing about it."

Kita pulled back and narrowed her eye, assessing him up and down. "So where did you go? Back to your promised? This is not the same little Ashbourne that I hunted yesterday."

"Things change. I'm not scared of you anymore, Kita."

Kita's eye widened as her easy all too familiar smirk returned to her face. "We'll see about that. My terms still stand."

"Good thing Dalton wants to see me then."

"Indeed."

Ayr pushed past Kita, and he heard Azura laugh behind him. It was gentle and should not have been enough to get a raise out of either Kita or Manir. Ayr heard Kita's boots on the floor as she darted forward to keep pace with him, as he walked towards Dalton. Knowing that his father lay just out of sight, Ayr tightened his jaw and ignored Kita as she walked behind him. Moments later, Dalton's throne came into view, but from out of the shadows, Ayr spotted the all too familiar outline of Zaurien walking towards him.

Bryne was just in front of his dragon, and judging from the expressions on their faces, neither of them were pleased. Bryne had his hands on his hips as he strode forward, his ever present scowl etched everywhere.

"About time you showed up. I was going to have to come and hunt you down."

"I would have enjoyed that. Azura would have taken Zaurien out of the sky."

"Father won't be pleased. And neither will you when you see what he has in store for you."

"It will be nothing worse than what the Commonwealth put me through."

The corners of Bryne's mouth curled. "We'll see about that. Come with us."

"I know where his throne is. I don't need your help to speak to him."

Bryne neared Ayr, and was walking too directly to do anything but collide with him. Ayr kept walking and saw Bryne's arms shoot out to grab at him. Ayr reacted, latching his hand around Bryne's wrist and driving him away. The grappling exchange was brief and resulted in Bryne being pushed away.

"Get off me. I'll walk myself."

"You can't be trusted!"

"Bryne!" The voice was explicitly Dalton's, louder than it had any right to be. It echoed off the walls, making Dalton sound like he was the size of Sinibad, looming in the distance. "Let Ayr come to me. I will deal with him."

"Now he sees things outside of his eyesight."

Bryne sneered in Ayr's ear. "There are many things you don't know about him. He is more powerful than you and I combined."

"We'll see about that."

With his new entourage at his back, Ayr continued to walk towards the throne. It began to loom out of the shadows, like the statue of a dragon, just beyond his vision. It was only as he drew nearer that Ayr could finally make out the silhouette of Dalton on the throne, with his legs raised up it like Kita had been when Ayr had first been here. Ayr sighed, expecting better of Dalton, but his lax nature was almost infuriating. Dalton's hand was raised towards the sky and on it was none other than the small dragon he had been washing when Ayr had last spoken to him. Dalton ignored him at first, opting to play with the dragon above his head. It was not until Ayr cleared his throat that Dalton acknowledged him.

Dalton turned his head as if he had been disturbed whilst in the midst of something important. "Yes?"

"You summoned me, father?"

"Good of you to finally join me. I only summoned you over a day ago. Where did you go?"

"I needed to take Azura away from Ironrock for a moment."

Dalton repeated the question with a flat tone. "Where did you go? To see her?"

Ayr felt himself flush. He had given nothing away, his body language neutral, his tone measured. He felt like a child back before Dalton had sent him to the battle academy or the Seminary of Fire. Dalton had all the answers before he had even begun asking the questions. There would be no point in lying to him if he knew already.

"Yes, father. How did you know?"

"You reek of her and her dragon. You forget I was like you once, Ayr. Young, dumb and in love."

Ayr's fist curled, but he did not tighten it. "I am not in love!"

Dalton snorted as he glanced back up at the dragon. "I don't even need to see you to know that is a lie. Your dragon is promised to hers. I know what that bond does to riders, even if you do not willingly choose it. This is why I need to sever your bond with Azura. Whilst you are still bound to her through Chilijo's magic, you will not be able to live up to your full potential."

"I am stronger with her. I am out there, facing your trials, duelling with your people to become stronger. If you're so desperate to tear us apart, why do you sit here doing nothing whilst the riders regroup? Do you not want to destroy them?"

"Things are in motion, Ayr. Don't think that I sit idle whilst I allow the Commonwealth to grow in strength."

"They're already weakened enough as is. Why do you delay attacking them?"

"Your concern for the Sunfire lady is admirable, but in the end, Ayr, it will get you both killed. I will attack when we are both ready."

Dalton flicked the dragon away with a gentle nudge of his wrist and it leapt up onto the highest point of the throne. It turned towards Ayr, hissing as it coiled around the throne. As the dragon coiled, Dalton sat up slowly, swinging his legs around so that he was now facing Ayr. He leaned forward in the throne, his hands resting just under his face.

"What are you planning to do, father?"

"My forces grow stronger. Every day there are new riders pledging their allegiance to me. Soon we will hold the balance of power. Then we will strike."

"And then?"

"That is my concern. We need to speak about your abandonment of me."

"It was a mistake, father. I came back."

"Chorru was there. He returned to me not long before you did. If you're going to lie to me, make sure nobody has evidence to the contrary."

Ayr was silent. *Chorru?*

He is nothing more than a snake. We should have killed him the first chance that we got.

Even if we killed him, Dalton would have had a hundred other spies that he could send instead.

Compliment your father, perhaps it is a way to sate his rage.

You don't know my father, Azura.

But I know men. Their egos know no bounds. Dalton Ashbourne is the same.

Ayr puffed out his lips and raised his eyes back towards Dalton. "Forgive me, father. It had been weeks. I needed to see her."

Kita let out a giggle behind him, one that was half forced and half choked. Dalton raised his eyes towards her, and Kita was silenced.

Dalton stood up from his throne, with a slight hunch in his back. Ayr could feel Bryne drawing in his breath beside him.

"It's clear that you still have feelings and an allegiance to her. You've shown you can't be trusted here. For that, you will come with me, where you will wait until I have prepared the shattering spell enough."

"Enough? What do you need to do to get it to work?"

Dalton clicked his fingers and pointed back towards where they had just come from. "Follow me."

He pushed past Ayr and Bryne, his scowl prevalent on his face. Ayr knew better than to argue and as Dalton walked past Azura, she let out a gasp of surprise.

He has me, Ayr!

"Let her go, Dalton!"

"You need to prove your compliance. Now come, Ayr."

Even though no spell was wrapped around his neck, Ayr felt complied to follow Dalton. He was not going to risk Azura, not when they were this close to having been freed before. Dalton led them back through the main hall and into another chamber that Ayr had not noticed before. This was barely a quarter of the size, and vastly empty. Dalton led them into the room, still leading Azura, with both Bryne, Kita and their dragons behind them.

As Ayr's eyes adjusted through Azura to the low light in the room, he could then make out tall structures that filled the far end of the room. Each of them was no larger than Azura was, but there was no mistaking what they were.

"You can't do this to us!"

Dalton turned back towards them and yanked on the invisible chain even more. Azura lurched forward against her own will, with Ayr unable to stop it. They were nearing the cells, and step by step, Ayr wanted to stop. He wanted to throw magic at Dalton, break the spell that contained Azura and flee. It had been a mistake coming back here, and the closer that Dalton moved them towards the cells only proved that point.

Ayr must have hesitated far too much. He felt a hand, whether it was Bryne or Kita on his shoulder, he could not tell. Their second hand wrapped themselves around the back of his neck, and Ayr was pushed forward towards the portal as Dalton continued to speak. There was no fighting it and even if he did, Dalton could obliterate him in a heartbeat and regain control.

"You'll no doubt see this is similar to a void cell, but unfortunately for you, I don't have any here. That is a technology that the Commonwealth has the monopoly on."

"You've copied everything else the Commonwealth has. Why not this?"

Dalton's smirk slid across his lips. "I perfected it. Get in."

Ayr took a deep breath, remembering his time in the void cells during his early days at the Obelisk. The hand that was pushing both him and Azura inside was no kinder than what Kaladin had been, even though it should have been. Again, if Azura's life was not on the line, then Ayr would have struck at Dalton and the others, but now was not the time. Clearly, Dalton had something in store for them, and now it was time to wait.

TWENTY-TWO

There was nothing but darkness that enshrouded Ayr. Every way he turned resulted in the same thing. There was no escaping from Dalton's enhanced void cell. Ayr had wasted magic trying to batter the walls down, and to call out to Azura, but nothing was working. It was like he was trapped inside the Obelisk once again, at the mercy of Kaladin who did not wish to extend him any courtesy or life support. Ayr thought he would have been better off at the hands of Dalton, but as time dragged on, these void cells proved to be worse.

Not only did the cells drain him of his magic and his connection to Azura, but there was more. Ayr felt like he had returned to the Tower of Echoes, memories of his past battering him. His failures, his trials and his tribulations. There was worse, however. Because he was no longer connected to Azura, even though he knew she was only a few meters away, not being able to talk to her was draining his soul. Ayr had lost track of time, even though he had a suspicion that they had only been in here for a few minutes.

The torture kept coming, each new vision an assault on his mind that he wanted to have end before the memory was even complete. Ayr could not use magic to calm his mind, nor could he rely on Azura to save him. Instead, he was suspended in the void cell with no way out, until after what felt like a lifetime, he felt a hand on his shoulder. Ayr was grateful for the hand's presence, but as it dragged him outside, he felt less about it. Not to his surprise when he fell backwards, he landed hard on the ground that he had once been standing on.

Ayr groaned as his back took the full brunt of the blow. He tried to move, but instead, only found Dalton standing over him. Dalton had changed his clothes into a darkened robe that shrouded most of his body and he now looked like the powerful magic user that he was. There was nothing but a sneer on his face as he glared at Ayr.

"Get up."

"Why?"

There were hands grabbing at Ayr from behind, and he turned his head to find Bryne standing over him. Bryne was helping him to his feet against his will and Ayr wanted to resist, but Dalton's raised hand in front of his face was the only thing keeping him from striking out.

"Because I told you to. We have somewhere to be."

"Where are we going?"

Dalton refused to answer, instead walking out of Ayr's view as Bryne pulled him to his feet. Ayr felt the scruff of his collar being pulled and he had no choice but to go with it. Azura was being dragged from her void cell in a similar fashion and Ayr wanted to scream at Zaurien as he moved her around. Just like Bryne, he was not gentle and Dalton seemed indifferent to their suffering. Not that it mattered to Dalton. He led them back towards where his throne sat, and Ayr had no choice but to follow.

Bryne deposited Ayr in front of the throne with no further questions. Ayr heard him back away as his boots scraped along the tiles. Zaurien on the other hand, did not move and remained in place with Azura somewhere behind them. She was still recovering from the effects of the void cell, and their connection was weak.

Just do what he wants, Ayr. This is the only way we get out of this.

I won't if it is what costs us our bond.

I would rather see you live if that is what it takes.

There is no going forward without you, Azura.

Dalton swept forward, flexing the muscles in his hand. He only had eyes for Ayr, glaring at him as Ayr looked up at him. Ayr dared not move, wondering what type of spell lay in Dalton's mind and what he could do to combat it. If this was indeed the shattering spell that Dalton had spoken of, Ayr still had not felt the touch of the magic to know what he could do to counter it. With how long it had taken Dalton to prepare, all he could do was pray to Chilijo that it would take some time to take effect.

Dalton lowered himself towards Ayr as he continued to flex his hand. Azura was still whimpering in Ayr's mind, not ready for what was about to come. With his face close to Ayr's, Dalton began to speak. Ayr strained his ears to listen to every word.

"If freedom is what you want. I will grant it to you."

"You're just going to let us go, father?"

Dalton's expression shifted into a dark smirk. "No, I'm going to break the chain that tethers you together. I told you this from the moment I deemed it appropriate."

Even though he knew what was coming, a fierce fire began to rage inside Ayr. Azura heard the words and began to struggle in Zaurien's mouth. The shift was subtle, but Ayr could sense it inside her. She wanted to flee, but there was nothing that she could do about it. Zaurien's grip was iron. Her anger was passing through to Ayr, as was her magic.

"No. No you will not take her from me!"

"You'll do nothing, Ayr! If I want you to be no longer bonded to Azura, then that is how you will be!"

"You can't. She helps me with my power."

Dalton snorted as he raised his hand. "My son, you are an Ashbourne. You are delusional to think you need a dragon to harness your power."

"You won't take her from me!"

"You have no choice in the matter! If you had considered your choices more carefully, this would not be happening!"

"Father!"

Dalton did not speak further. His fingers tilted forward like the legs of a spider, pale and deliberate. Ayr's throat tightened as he recognized the gesture. The magic was attacking his mind. He reached for Azura through their bond, a desperate mental grasp for her power, just for something to cling onto. The first shock of Dalton's spell hit like a hammer to glass. It was a violent, splintering assault on the borders of his consciousness. Ayr flung up his mental shield that shimmered just as the full force struck. Dalton's magic crackled around the edges like lightning across storm clouds, sending tendrils of burning pain wherever it touched. From somewhere deep in their shared consciousness, Azura's scream tore through him, high and piercing as a blade between ribs. Not only was Dalton assaulting Ayr, but also Azura. The bond had to be broken.

Dalton kept pouring magic into Ayr's mind, trying to flood it and to cause a wound that he could follow. Wherever the energy surged into his shield, Ayr did what he could to stop the flood, but Dalton was all consuming. He was losing ground, as Dalton's tendrils snuck into the gaps that he had left open.

"I don't want to do this, Ayr. Let me in! I would rather keep both you and the dragon alive."

"If you sever the bond there will be nothing left between us!"

"Chilijo did not intend for this to be the way the dragons served the riders. Let me break it!"

"You can't have her!"

"I will take her from you! Relinquish your responsibility from her."

Ayr screamed for her, fighting back with every inkling of power that he could muster, but no matter where he distributed the magic, Dalton managed to sneak inside his defences. Ayr continued to batter the tendrils away as Azura screamed in his mind. There was nothing he could do to stop Dalton, until he heard a boom somewhere in the distance. Thinking that it was Dalton, Ayr thrust out with all of his power, and Dalton released the spell. He flung backwards and as Ayr realised what he was looking at, Dalton had his hand raised in front of him like a shield.

"Wait!"

Dalton raised his head towards the sky and inhaled. He closed his eyes and brought his hand to his head. "It's about time they arrived. I sent Chorru to the Haven with the instructions weeks ago. Perhaps they were weaker than I first thought." Dalton turned away from Ayr, a dark look in his eyes. His voice deepened, sounding like a dragon's rumble echoing throughout the chamber. "Rise, Sinibad. We have guests."

Even though Sinibad was perched on his jagged outcrop up the mountain, his voice cut through the thin air like a blade, each syllable reaching Ayr's ears with unnatural clarity that made the hairs on the back of his neck stand on end. Whilst he still had not grown comfortable with Sinibad's presence, his voice from so far away was still unnerving.

"I will deal with these interlopers, Dalton. Prepare yourself accordingly. Without their home to protect them, many will perish. It will be like fending off hatchlings."

Dalton glared at Ayr and beckoned for him with his outstretched fingers. "Bring your dragon and come with me. We will finish this later."

"Where are we going?"

Dalton remained silent and kept his stranglehold on Ayr. Ayr wanted to use his magic to break free, but he could feel the hold that Dalton also had over Azura. If he attempted to escape, Dalton could cut the cord that was around her neck and sever her from this world in a moment. And that for Ayr would be worse than him cutting the bond. For a man that supposedly respected dragons, he used them as leverage far too much. Yet Ayr knew that it was the only way he would have complied. If only he did not have Azura to worry about. Then he could have taken Dalton then and there. No doubt Elanor would be arriving at Ironrock along with the other Commonwealth riders. Both her and Evor would draw Dalton's ire.

Azura, is Evor nearby.

He is, Ayr. I have been speaking to him.

You need to tell him to flee. It's not worth the attack here. Dalton or Sinibad will kill them.

He's not leaving, Ayr. He refuses to be branded a traitor to the Commonwealth.

And Elanor?

She is of the same opinion.

We can't save them from this fate. If they attack us, then there is nothing we can do to save Evor and Elanor. If they die, they die.

That's not something that neither of us want.

No. That is not a result that I will accept either.

Dalton quickened his pace as he headed for the exit, but now there was more than just the sounds of Sinibad overhead. Ayr could hear other dragons, all of whom resided in Ironrock now roaring, calling to each other. It was as if the city was waking up from a mutual slumber, all of the dragons reaching out at the same time, trying to figure out what was happening to their city. As Dalton breached the outside of the building and the city came into Ayr's view, he could see the flock of dragons that he had not yet seen within Ironrock.

It was like he was seeing the Seminary of Fire again for the first time. Ironrock had never been full of dragons at any one time, but somehow, the city was now suddenly full of them. They were not dragons from the Commonwealth, none of them in the armour that Kaladin and the others had mandated the dragons wear going into combat. They were all staring off into the distance, somewhere high above Sinibad's roost. It did not take Azura long to spot what had been drawing their attention and she shared her vision with Ayr.

Azura went to speak, but Ayr cut her off. He could see it clearly enough. The swarm of dragons headed towards them was almost enough to blot out the sky. They all ranged in different sizes and colours, but it was evident that this was what the Commonwealth had sent to attack Ironrock. Neither Ayr or Azura were able to spot the all too familiar figure of Evor cutting his way through the sky. Where was he?

Are you sure that Evor is here?

Yes, Ayr. I can speak to him.

Where is he then? Are they not joining the attack?

Evor is slowed, he still struggles with the injuries he sustained from Sinibad.

Then they are easy prey for Sinibad.

They are easy prey for Dalton as well.

Can you tell them to flee?

No, Ayr. They are committed. As we must be. With whatever Dalton tells us to do. We must maintain our bond, regardless of what he says.

You know he is committed. What do we do?

Pick a side, Ayr. Now is the time.

Ayr grit his teeth as he walked out into the open behind Dalton. Riders were running in each direction, desperate to catch up to their dragons. Some waited for their riders to climb aboard, but others were already rising into the air despite their riders not being seated in the saddles that they had on them. Ironrock was filled with chaos, and panic, but it was clear to Ayr that the riders thought they had everything under control. Much to his surprise, Sinibad did not come down towards the city, but instead flew out towards the invaders on his own.

Dalton raised his head towards Sinibad, tracking his movements. Ayr could see the faintest of smiles present on his lips as he watched Sinibad move into the sun. He could feel the pressure from Bryne behind him, from Zaurien that was still no doubt watching Azura's every move like a hawk. Azura wanted to turn and face him, but now was not the time, trapped between both Dalton and Zaurien. Dalton leaned back towards Ayr, his smile still prevalent on his face.

"This is your moment. She is near, isn't she?"

Ayr nodded his head in response. "Yes, father."

"Excellent. You'll fly out there and meet her."

"Meet her and do what exactly?"

"Kill her. Her or her dragon. I don't care which. I'll be watching."

Ayr took a moment to compose himself before he continued. "I'm sorry. I'm not sure that I heard you correctly. Her dragon is promised to mine."

Now Dalton turned and gave him his full attention. Ayr froze up underneath his gaze. Whilst Dalton was no taller than Ayr, his magical presence and dark energy radiated around him making him appear as tall as Azura.

"You'll do as you're commanded, otherwise I will rip you two apart completely. I know that you were fighting me trying to keep me out of your mind, but the bond between the two of you is severed. More so between Azura and her promised."

"What have you done?"

"What was necessary. You will fall in line."

"I feel no differently about Elanor and Evor than I did before. Your spell hasn't worked."

"My spell will not work instantly. It will take time. Not every spell is a fireball straight to your face, Ayr."

Dalton stepped towards his hand next to his head. Ayr stared at Dalton's fingers as they shot towards his face, unable to act. There was one more jet of power that surged through him from Dalton. Whilst Ayr still felt no differently regarding Elanor and Evor, he listened to Dalton's next words with care. There was subversion in his words, his tongue laced with magic that filled the air around them.

"You are an Ashbourne. Kill the last of the Sunfire line and return to me victorious. Then we can truly overthrow the ruling powers of the Commonwealth."

Ayr turned his attention towards Azura and nodded at her. Azura flooded his mind with her thoughts, her voice filled with panic and concern. She had felt the spell bite him, but Ayr was resisting it with every ounce of magic he could. Dalton's words slipped into his mind like water, probing at any part of Ayr's mind that was not guarded.

What are you doing, Ayr? We're not going to kill Elanor and Evor.

No, but Dalton isn't going to know that. Let's ride.

Do you know what you're doing? If any other riders recognise us, we will be attacked. We abandoned the Commonwealth.

I will ensure that nobody will touch us.

That is a lot of dragons out there, Ayr. They have shown up in force.

And we only have eyes for one of them. Are we going to do this?

Azura finally knelt, allowing Ayr to clamber up her side. Ayr latched onto her neck and climbed up into the saddle, pulling his mask out of his jacket pocket. Azura waited for him to be seated before she coiled underneath him, her head in the direction of where Sinibad was disappearing over the edge of the mountains. Without another word from Ayr, Azura launched herself upwards, but she was not the only one. Ayr turned his head and saw Bryne mounting Zaurien. The jet-black dragon was incensed and shot up after them.

"Wait for me, brother!"

Zaurien spoke, his voice cutting through the air, but the words were all Bryne's. Ayr had no desire to be caught by them and urged Azura forward. She increased her speed, shooting over Ironrock faster than an arrow as more of the Commonwealth dragons made themselves known. Sinibad let loose with a roar, but even though he was on the other side of the mountains, the call still ripped through the sky, deafening Ayr. He winced and could only imagine how the dragons and riders nearer to him would have felt. Other smaller dragons voiced their responses, but already the carnage was on.

Azura rose higher and now, they could see Sinibad tossing and turning in the sky. He battled half a dozen dragons at once, all of whom worn armour that was not serving them any better than their own scales. Despite the battle raging on, Ayr still had not made out any of the Dragon Lords, or the most important of all, Evor. With Bryne and Zaurien still hot on their tail, Ayr opened his mind to Azura once again.

Where are they?

Coming.

Can we lose Zaurien?

I can only fly so fast, Ayr. He is not a slow dragon. Perhaps you could use some of your magic to slow him down.

From your back? I'm just as likely to hit Sinibad.

Do it or we're doomed.

Azura banked hard to the left, killing almost all of her wing speed in an instant. Zaurien who had been only a few wingbeats behind shot past them, unable to match her agility so easily. The opportunity had passed and Ayr was unable to form a spell in time. Seeing that they had stalled, Zaurien turned to the right, flying further away from Azura. The magic crept into Ayr's palms as he readied a noose that would cripple Zaurien. Without the presence of Dalton looming over him, he felt unconstricted and able to breathe. As Azura turned back he could however see where he had left Dalton, and his father was no bigger than an ant on the ground beneath them. He half expected a spell to shoot up and slow them in return, but nothing came their way.

Here he comes, Ayr!

Ayr did not need to be told twice. Zaurien was completing the loop, coming full circle, but due to the turning, was less than at full speed. Ayr sent the magic up through his body, encouraged by Azura. The noose shot out from him and snaked its way around Zaurien like an invisible snake. It latched onto his foreleg as Ayr had hoped for. He pulled down, and Zaurien missed a wing beat. He stumbled in the sky, and fell like a rock.

Go, Azura!

Azura did not need another command from Ayr and shot off, past Zaurien as he struggled to regain control of his flight. He spiralled back towards Ironrock and the motion gave Azura breathing space. Overhead, more Commonwealth dragons were attacking Sinibad, but at last, the one dragon that they wanted to see was limping into view. Evor was slower than all others around him, but his sheer bulk made him stand out from the rest of the flock. His eyes were locked onto Azura as he flew, and Azura changed direction to head straight towards him.

Azura let out a roar as fire spilled from her mouth, issuing an open challenge to Evor. Already, Ayr could tell that he was perplexed, the sign of aggression from Azura would have been unusual. He slowed down as they approached, but under Ayr, Azura showed no sign of slowing down.

Azura. Did Dalton's spell work?

No, but I am still compelled to comply with his instructions. We have to make it look like we are attacking Evor. That's what his spell wanted us to do.

Are you crazy?

No, Ayr. Whilst you guarded yourself, if we don't comply, he'll just try to break us again. This is self-preservation. Evor will understand.

What if he attacks us?

Evor will not harm me.

Azura shot in towards Evor, increasing her speed. Evor was stagnant in the sky, expecting a reunion to occur that would not come. Azura neared and outstretched her talons, diving in towards Evor. She lashed out and Evor was too slow to dart away. Azura raked his side, and Evor cried out in pain. She snapped back, and Ayr could feel her tensing for another attack. Evor recoiled in kind, limping backwards, his eyes narrowed in confusion as Azura came in again.

"Azura! Stop! What are you doing, little one!"

"Putting on a show! Dalton thinks that he's won! He thinks that he has broken us apart. Our bond is still strong!"

"I won't harm you!"

There was nothing that Ayr could do except remain locked into the saddle. He had long since given up trying to control Azura. She was in her own mind, darting towards Evor like lightning, closing the gap between them before striking. Evor did not strike back, even as he roared in pain as Azura struck him. Ayr had seen Evor struck before by other dragons and seeing him not retaliate was odd.

"Azura! Stop!"

She was not listening to him. Evor continued to plead as he was struck again and again. Azura was still only a fraction of his size and whilst she was not damaging him physically, the strain in his repeated cries were waning on Ayr.

Azura! Enough!

We have to keep trying, Ayr! Dalton is watching!

We'll deal with Dalton later! You're just hurting yourself at this point! Azura!

Ayr reached down to Azura with magic of his own, trying to pull her head away from Evor. He kept flying away, wanting to move further away from Sinibad and the commotion that was being caused behind them. Ayr heard a familiar snarl and for the first time since Azura had begun attacking Evor, realised that Bryne and Zaurien were still behind them. Azura dove forward, and Ayr just jolted out of the saddle.

He felt the wind from Zaurien flying overhead, but the proceeding roar from both Evor and Zaurien was as deafening as Sinibad had been. The two black dragons clashed in a collision of fire and claws, both of them as violent as the other. Now that Evor had been cleared from accidently striking Azura, he unleashed his full ferocity. Zaurien was bigger than Azura, but there was still a size difference between him and Evor.

Azura turned around in midair and Ayr saw Evor swipe at Zaurien. Now was the time to attack. But just as Ayr readied his magic to strike, Bryne pulled Zaurien back. Zaurien fell into free fall as if his wings had begun not working and he plummeted from the sky. Ayr watched him go, and had no desire to chase after his brother. Instead Azura hovered up to be level with Evor. As Evor opened his mouth, more shrieks broke across the sky. Evor's head snapped to the side and Azura followed. From underneath them was a swirling black mass of hundreds, if not thousands of bodies, all hurtling towards them.

"Wyvern! We're outnumbered. Flee, little one!"

Evor had only finished speaking his command before he turned and fled. There was no last word or exchange between them, Ayr unable to hear if anything was going on between them in their minds. Azura heeded Evor's instructions, Dalton spell having had minimal effect. Azura went just as limp as Zaurien had and followed him, falling towards the ground. Ayr clung on for dear life, praying to Chilijo that he would see it through this ordeal. He closed his eyes, panic overtaking him. If Azura did not want to open her wings and fly, there would be nothing he could do to stop her fall. Not at this speed.

The shrieks continued all around them and as Ayr opened his eyes, it was evident they were not what the wyvern were chasing. The wyvern were not headed for Ayr and Azura, however they were honed onto Evor, like he had a target on his back. There was only one explanation. Dalton had sent them to target him. The other Commonwealth dragons were responding to the new threat, those not currently duelling with dragons over Ironrock. Sinibad had cut a scythe through the Commonwealth dragon ranks, with many torn out of the sky, their bodies falling towards Ironrock if they were not scattered over it already. Those that remained left in the sky were hesitant to engage. The wyvern were doing their job of scaring the Commonwealth dragons away as Sinibad chewed through another green dragon that had found itself unlucky to be caught in his jaws.

Ayr shook his head in disgust. It was just like the destruction of the Obelisk all over again. And Dalton had one against almost as quickly. The battle was one sided and Dalton's pack of hungry wyvern had all but seen to that. Knowing that they could do nothing to turn the tide, Ayr clung to Azura, waiting for the judgement that would await them when they returned to him.

TWENTY-THREE

The wyvern would devour everything in their path. The pack of wyvern was much larger than any other time that Ayr had seen it. Did they breed at a faster rate to the dragons or were they just another magical illusion conjured by Dalton? Either way, they had been effective in chasing off the Commonwealth dragons. The number of dragons that they had brought to the fight had been similar to what Dalton had stationed at Ironrock. However, the wyvern presented a different threat. Between thousands of snapping jaws that could manoeuvre underneath the dragons, it was clear that they would be the difference between victory and defeat.

Even if the Commonwealth dragons had each been the size of Sinibad, they would have all fallen to the sheer volume of wyverns that Dalton had at his disposal. Where had they all come from? Ayr thought he had explored a lot of Ironrock but clearly there was more to discover. The thoughts all raced through his mind as Azura fell back towards the city, but there was another question to ponder.

Azura levelled out and he saw Zaurien ahead of them, racing back towards Dalton. There would be no chance of catching them, and even if Dalton had not seen what had transpired above between them, he would be hearing about it in a moment. Dalton would believe Bryne, like he had always done during their childhood, even though Bryne was more often than not the antagonist. Bryne would air his complaint, Ayr would be punished, and the vicious cycle would continue. There was no reprieve in the Ashbourne household.

Your father will not be pleased, Ayr.

When is he ever? At least they managed to repel an attack.

At great cost.

This is war. There are going to be heavy casualties on both sides, Azura. It was that way in the first rebellion.

It was Dalton that caused the casualties for the Commonwealth.

I was there, Azura. I saw the bodies that the dragons burned first-hand. The casualties were not all from Dalton.

Do not take your anger out on me! I'm on your side, remember? Prepare for the threat right in front of you.

Ayr kept his eyes forward as Azura came into land beside Zaurien. The black dragon snapped in her direction, but Azura did not flinch, ignoring him. Bryne was already speaking to Dalton who stood in the doorway of the main hall with his arms folded. There was nothing that said to Ayr that he was impressed with what had just transpired. Bryne was in his ear, gesturing with his free hand towards the sky where they had just come from. Dalton remained unmoved by anything that Bryne had said, his eyes tracking all Azura's movements.

When Ayr was on the ground, both Bryne and Dalton locked onto him, like a hawk watching its prey. Ayr moved towards them, not with pace, but he was not slow either. Clearly, he was taking far too long for Dalton, regardless. It was just like it had been growing up. Nothing was ever good enough for Dalton.

"Get over here, boy!"

Ayr stood tall, his chest puffed out to make himself as big of a threat as possible. Even with Azura at his back, he did not feel like one. He coiled his magic around his fists, at least just a little so that should Dalton attack him out of rage, he could have conjured a defence in a hurry. But even then, if he managed to deflect or block Dalton's first strike, there was also Bryne, who's face was turning red. Whilst Dalton was the level head of the familiar, Bryne was the other end of the spectrum, ready to explode at the slightest inconvenience. However, now the roles were reversed.

A physical lashing from Dalton would have been kinder than the assault that he unleashed on Ayr's ears. Spit and bile flew at Ayr's face and he was in no position to move away, unless he wanted the physical beating to go along with it.

"What were you thinking? Attacking Bryne?"

"I don't know what else you wanted me to do!"

Dalton snarled at him and extended his arm, wrapping it around the back of Ayr's head. "You had a job to do! One job! You failed!"

"Evor is so much larger than Azura. What hope did you think she had against him? Are you blind, father?"

"Her magic and yours is more powerful than any other dragons out there, Ayr. You don't feel what I feel when it comes to your abilities. It is rarely about the size of the dragon. Chilijo himself was not the largest dragon."

"I've been to his tomb! That is larger than any city the Commonwealth has."

Dalton snorted and brought Ayr close. "You still haven't learnt the most valuable lesson that I could have taught you. They lie!"

"As do you! About everything!"

Ayr shouted the last word, his voice thundering through the city like a physical force, the veins in his neck bulging with the effort. Both Dalton and Bryne remained unmoved as stone sentinels, although Bryne's thin lips parted, revealing a flash of his teeth as his eyes narrowed with predatory calculation. His fingers twitched almost imperceptibly toward the hilt of his sword as he recognized the weakness Ayr had just revealed.

Dalton's tone was cold and as calculated in his response. His eyes darkened and Ayr felt a surge of magic around him. "Don't ever fucking speak to me like that again. Am I understood?"

Ayr was defiant, still feeling the power surge throughout his entire body. "Or what?"

"Clearly, I didn't give you enough motivation, boy!"

"You gave me plenty. Azura was never going to kill her promised!"

"If you will not do as I command, you will be broken! I will free you from the burden you bear. It is clearly far too much for you to handle."

Ayr could sense the magic coiling around Dalton's body. He was ready for the spell that was to come. But rather than the magic seeping from Dalton's body into Ayr's, he turned, focusing his attack on Azura directly. Ayr fumbled with his defence, throwing it up around him, thinking that he was the target. Azura screamed, her cry echoing through Ironbark, louder than any piercing shriek from the wyvern. It struck a chord through Ayr, cutting him to the bone as he realised his mistake.

He backtracked recoiling his magic from himself and wrapped it around Azura like a blanket. She continued to shriek even though he was now protecting her from the worst of Dalton's spell. The magic that lingered on her was still causing damage, and Ayr was straining trying to hold back the unrelenting assault from Dalton.

"You will not take her from me!"

"You've proven yourself to be inapt, Ayr! There is no such weakness between Bryne and Zaurien!"

"Azura chose me!"

"And now I am breaking you apart!"

There was no other choice. He had to put himself between Azura and Dalton and he needed to end what he was doing to her entirely. Ayr thrust his hand out and sent a blast of energy hurtling at Dalton. There was no time for his father to react, the short range between them and the sudden change of Ayr's target meant that Dalton was unprepared. The effect, however, was immediate. Dalton was launched back as if he had been fired from a cannon, and the lapse of concentration caused him to break the hold of his spell.

Using the lapse in Dalton's presence to his advantage, Ayr turned, heading back straight for Azura. Azura ran towards him and they met halfway, Ayr vaulting up Azura's legs in a heartbeat. Dalton was already clambering back to his feet, his usual calm manner now gone, replaced with rage akin to what he was familiar with from Bryne. Ayr could already sense the magic coiling around Dalton. There was no turning back now.

Fly, Azura!

There was no hesitation from Azura, who turned and scampered away, trying to put as much distance as possible between them and Dalton. Ayr was preparing a counterattack to whatever Dalton was going to throw their way, but as Azura made her way into the sky, nothing came at them. Ayr was confused. If Dalton was so enraged, he would have brought them back to the ground. Ayr turned his head back to look towards the ground. Bryne was mounting Zaurien communicating with Dalton.

Then there was a furious beating of Zaurien's as he took off, headed straight after them. Ayr urged Azura on, desperate to get out of the city before he caught them. Sinibad was still chasing off the last of the Commonwealth dragons. Dalton still had not given him further instructions, unless there was a bond between them that allowed them to communicate like Ayr and Azura. Zaurien let loose with a fierce roar that ripped across the sky.

"You'd better fly faster if you wish to escape me, Azura!"

He is relentless.

I know you're faster, Azura. If he gets close, I'll slow him down.

We can't take the risk.

Fly low to the ground, let him come over the top. Bryne is not as magically gifted as I am.

For our sake, I hope not.

Azura kept low, headed for the easternmost point of Ironrock. The mountains came up around them, and within a matter of minutes, they had left the city behind. Sinibad was also a distant figure, still not travelling in the same direction that they were. Ayr checked over his shoulder. It was clear that Zaurien was catching them, but it was only marginal. None of the other dragons at Dalton's disposal were invested in chasing them, much to Ayr's surprise. Knowing that he needed Azura to out speed Zaurien if they were going to stand any chance of reaching the Haven alive, Ayr put his hand against Azura's scales and filled her with magic.

Azura shot forward, but as their journey dragged on, Zaurien had still not given up the chase, nor had he slipped beyond the horizon. He was gaining on them, and it was clear to Ayr that Bryne was using all of his magic to help speed his dragon along, matching what Ayr was doing for Azura. She was also beginning to tire. Whether it was as a result of the travel that they had undertaken in the recent days or of Dalton's spell, there was little Ayr could do to keep her going. The Haven was at least a day away, and they would only receive hostilities upon their arrival.

We can't keep going like this, Ayr. I need to try and lose him.

What do you have in mind?

If only there was somewhere we could hide like what we had in the Seminary of Fire.

He is much larger. Surely there is a cave amongst these mountains somewhere.

But then we will be trapped.

I can fight Bryne and force him into submission. That may be the only way to get Zaurien to give up the hunt.

Keep a look out.

As the sun dragged closer to the horizon, the chase was still on and Ayr was still searching for any kind of opening that they could use to their advantage. The mountains here were endless, rolling from one to another with deep valleys between each. It was untamed wilderness, with nothing preventing the coming conflict. If Zaurien caught them, Azura would need to fight him tooth and claw. Whilst Ayr still had magic at his disposal, he would be focused on fighting Bryne.

Ayr knew that Azura was slowing down and Zaurien inched closer. Even when Azura banked to the side to follow the valleys, Zaurien would match her path exactly, so as to not lose distance between them. One wrong move could set them back and allow Azura more breathing room. As Azura turned into the next valley, Ayr spotted a gap in between two mountains that looked like a ravine. He focused on it and drew Azura's attention to it.

That might be what we're looking for, Azura.

If I can fit.

You will.

Ayr checked back over his shoulder again. Zaurien was closer than he had ever been, his eyes narrowed in focus as he chased them. Azura continued to shoot towards the ravine, and Ayr realised it was in fact wide enough if she folded her wings in. Rather than dropping speed, Azura increased her velocity as they neared the wall. She shot into the ravine and folded her wings as she came in to touch the ground.

Zaurien roared behind him as he pulled up, the ravine only giving Azura room to turn her head back to face him. If he wanted to squeeze down it to chase them further, he could have, but Azura's slim body was already scraping the sides. Ayr stood up in the saddle, ready to use magic should he need to protect them from Zaurien's fiery breath.

Zaurien's voice was amplified by the ravine around them. "Come out, Azura! Dalton wants you back. You're trapped."

"We're not coming anywhere with you."

Bryne peered over Zaurien's head, standing up in the saddle. "Brother, why did you do this? If only you could have accepted Dalton severing the bond between you two."

Ayr was not going to remain quiet even though he knew Bryne was baiting him. "Would you accept it if he did it to you? What would you be without Zaurien?"

"You know that dragons are not meant to be in servitude to us like they are. Chilijo demanded them to be free!"

"We're not coming back with you, Bryne!"

"Fine! Then we'll wait here for you to come out."

Ayr, the ravine opens up ahead.

Can you get down there?

I can, there's something ahead. A structure of some kind.

Is there another way that Zaurien can follow us in?

Ayr raised his head to the ceiling of the ravine to inspect it. There was no gap in it that Zaurien could breathe fire through or come down at them from. Azura was right, there was a structure up ahead. Confident that they were now out of range of Zaurien's fire, Ayr turned his back on them and urged Azura to follow the path.

The ravine was shallower and even more narrow and Azura was growing uncomfortable. The walls were closing in and Ayr could do nothing to ease her pain. The structure was becoming clearer as the ravine began to open, and Ayr had a sinking feeling in his stomach. He had seen this before in the Frozen Wastelands. If it was anything like the last place, this was the home of a Keeper. Hopefully this one will stay asleep.

TWENTY-FOUR

T he fact that this Keeper's tomb had been so easily discoverable, was of concern to Ayr. It had taken them the better part of a week to find Otheria's in the Frozen Wastelands, but this was simply in their way as they returned to the Haven. Whilst the Commonwealth was expansive and many did not live outside of her cities; the riders still patrolled the vast majority of the airspace. Perhaps it was not so easily discoverable from above, but where did it lead to?

If it was anything like Otheria's lair, then this place would have had another entrance. Unlike Otheria's lair however, this was not covered in snow. As Azura continued to traverse the ravine, Ayr wondered just how a dragon the size of Nargoon would fit here. Perhaps there was no dragon inside. Azura slowed down as she approached the structure, which was just as metallic and solid as Otheria's.

I think this is another Keeper's cave, Ayr. Do you think that we should venture inside?

Another Keeper? Just how many were locked away after the first war?

I'm not sure, but if we discover that they have world bending intentions like Otheria and Nargoon, we can't let them escape.

It took a whole unit of the wyrmguard and their dragons to seal the last tomb.

I know. I'm not large enough to bury this cavern underground on my own, Ayr. I will need your magic.

And you will have it.

Can you still use it?

Ayr paused for a moment. In truth, the power that he had used against Dalton had drained him and he had been running on fumes ever since. The fact that he had been able to keep Azura flying as fast as she had for as long as she had was a miracle itself. All he had left were a few droplets that coursed between both him and Azura, as well as whatever she had left in reserve. He tried to draw on it and knew that it was not much.

I think I can manage it.

Even if we have to use some of it to get inside?

Yes. His hesitation was brief but measured. There was no rush at this point. Zaurien was unable to reach them, and even if they found another way out so quickly, there was every chance that Zaurien would catch them. If Ayr could even have a few moments rest before they continued, he would at least feel somewhat replenished. Azura plodded on towards the door, checking over her shoulder to ensure that Zaurien was still as far away as he had been moments ago.

Then they reached the door that was just as unremarkable as it had been outside Otheria's tomb. Ayr took in a deep breath, sighing at what he saw. He would need to fight his way into this tomb if they wanted to explore more about whatever Keeper lay inside it. At least, Dalton had not yet awoken this one. Or so it seemed. Azura came to a stop in front of the door, the sheer wall no different than any other part of the structure. The top of it jutted out from above the ravine, but there was no space for Zaurien to make a surprise appearance.

Can you unlock it, Ayr?

I can try.

Ayr raised his hands in front of his face as the world grew quiet around him. Considering the amount of magic that it had taken for him to open the first door to Otheria's cave, he was concerned with what it would take to open it. Not that he felt like he was in any rush to reach their new destination with Zaurien no longer able to reach them. Ayr focused on the door and reached out with the magic, probing, trying to touch somewhere that he could latch onto. He found it, like a small handle that was no longer than his palm. Despite it's size, Ayr caught on and drove his magic into it.

He was already feeling exhausted, but he needed to open it so that they could continue forward. Zaurien was still out there somewhere, and he did not want them to entice him. Ayr strained against the force of the door and continued to push it open. As it opened, Azura stepped forward and placed her claws in the gap, helping Ayr wrench it open. She groaned and grunted as she pushed against it, but as time went on it continued to slide open. When it was large enough for her to slip inside, Azura did so.

Ayr ensured that her tail was all clear of the door before he let go of the magic. In the minutes that it had taken him to unravel the spell that was laced across the door, it was suddenly undone and all of his hard work had been for nothing. Ayr felt weaker, more drained and as a result wanted to slump in the saddle while Azura carried him forward.

We've been in one of these before. Light the way please, Azura.

Of course, Ayr. As you wish.

Azura opened her mouth and fire spilled from her jaws, shooting towards what Ayr knew were the statues that would light the way forward. The flames caught onto the foremost statue and illuminated the room around them. It was unlike the entrance to Otheria's cave and Ayr realised that it was much smaller than that expansive underground network. There was only one room visible to them, and the far wall was illuminated in the slightest of shadows. Ayr spotted another statue and Azura raised her head, shooting another flame towards it.

The flame caught, and the rest of the room was now covered in the light and Ayr could make out the far wall. It was unlike Otheria's chamber where there was a dais in the middle of the room, but instead, there was a strange clear chamber in the middle of the wall. Ayr pushed Azura towards it and as they drew near, he could make out something inside the chamber.

I don't like this, Ayr.

Neither do I. Do we wake them up?

And have two threats in the world? I would have thought dealing with just Dalton and Otheria was enough.

What if this Keeper has not been corrupted by Dalton?

I think we have to take the chance.

Your magic is low. How are you going to fight a Keeper? There's only one way out of here.

Ayr ignored Azura's warning and removed himself from the saddle. He was certain that this was the course of action he needed to take. Ayr climbed down from Azura and landed upon the floor. It was tiled, just like Otheria's lair, but it felt warmer due to the lack of snow around the structure. Yet there were still chills running down Ayr's spine as he saw what awaited them in the chamber.

It was a humanoid male, much like Otheria, tall, pale and appeared dead. There was something strange about him, and unlike Otheria's chamber, there was no other tubes which held more bodies. Ayr saw nothing that seemed like a control panel, but as he raised his hand towards the man, he felt something begin to drain his energy. It was a prick, nothing more than a needle entering his hand, but it was enough to make Ayr know that his magic was being used.

His magic reacted to the chamber, and much like the door had slid open, the chamber door was now sliding up. Ayr held his breath as more magic was drained from his body, but there was only so much he could give. He dropped to a knee, Azura filling his mind trying to fill him with substance so that he could stand again. Ayr nudged her away. The drain on his body did not feel malicious, like something that

Dalton or Otheria would do to him. As the chamber reached its peak, the body underneath it slid out.

At first, it appeared that they were weak, their limbs as weak as a newborn fawn's as it stood up for the first time. Ayr felt a touch more magic leave his body and then the figure stood upright as straight and tall as a reed. His eyes were closed and he swayed on the spot until there was another drop of magic taken from Ayr. The man opened his eyes and they locked onto Ayr as if he knew where he was. Ayr wanted to take a step back, feeling the power radiate off the man as he began to speak.

"Ayr Ashbourne, you have awoken me. What brought you here?"

"How do you know my name?"

"I am Ezzu."

Ayr raised his eyebrows. "That tells me a lot. Who are you? Are you a Keeper?"

Ezzu nodded, his eyes widening as he awoke. "I am the last among my kind."

"Did you know Otheria?"

Ezzu closed his eyes again, his weathered face hardening into a mask of concentration. His midnight-blue robes billowed and snapped in a wind that seemed to touch nothing else in the chamber, the silken fabric riding up his sinewy forearm. Ayr's gaze fixed on what was revealed on his skin. It was a tattoo etched in crimson and obsidian ink just below Ezzu's elbow. The design depicted a dragon's gaping maw with its fangs bared, forked tongue extended. The dragon bore a crown of jagged horns erupting from the scaled head above it. The tattoo seemed to pulse with its own inner light, as if the beast might spring from Ezzu's skin at any moment.

"Otheria branded me. It was her way of calling me a slave."

"Yet you broke free? How did you end up here?"

Ezzu nodded again, this time it was nothing more than a shallow dip of his head. "She took my dragon from me and left me to die."

"And that's how you wound up here?"

It seemed that all the Keeper could do was nod. He was still yet to take a step forward and show other signs of life. Ayr felt another drip of magic leave him, and then Ezzu blinked.

"You are observant."

"That's something the Ashbourne family all have in common."

Now Ezzu's expression finally changed, and he opened his eyes again. He scowled, at Ayr, studying his face as his eyes flickered from side to side. "Ashbourne. I have heard of that name before."

"How? We're an old family, but it wasn't during your time. I know we came along after Chilijo's demise."

"There were whispers, about a man who would rise above all others to sit on a throne of ash. Not a dragon, a man."

"That's a coincidence. I don't want a throne."

Ezzu wriggled his eyes in delight. "That's what Chilijo said before he went mad with power and tried to seize the world for himself."□

"Chilijo never wanted the world."

Ezzu chortled. "That's what they all want you to think. Chilijo was a monster, one that was hellbent at reforming the world in his own image. He was a false god."

"Then why do so many people follow him? Whose side are you on?"

"I have no skin in the game. I came here to rest so that I may have my revenge."

"Now that you are awake, how do you intend to go about moving throughout the world? It is not a small place."

"I have no dragon of my own."

"How are you a Keeper then?"

Ezzu lowered his head, his eyes becoming full with sorrow and mourning. "She was taken from me by Otheria and her monster. It is unfortunate that she chose to side with the wrong side. But I will have my revenge."

"We know where her tomb is if you would like to come with us. We have another fight to take care of first, but if you were to join us, we could take you there."

"I'm not interested in joining someone else's fight. The only thing that concerns me is Otheria. She is my only concern."

"Come with us, and we can investigate Otheria. You have no drag-on. You could be walking for years across the surface of the world before you catch up to her."

Ezzu pondered the offer for a moment, frowning at Ayr. "Will your dragon be able to carry both of us?"

"We may be slower, but she will be able to."

I pray that Bryne and Zaurien are no longer waiting for us then, Ayr.

If they are, we will stand and fight. We have a Keeper on our side. That will be enough to deter them.

And if he cannot?

Then we will fall. Dalton won't want me killed just yet.

Ezzu interrupted their conversation, clearing his throat. He lurched forward, seemingly unsure of his footing. The first step was the hardest for him. Ezzu groaned as he took the next step. Ayr wanted to support him, but he felt another drop of magic leave his body and Ezzu straightened. The Keeper was feeding off him. If Ayr needed to cut him off, he would need to make a spell that would hopefully last. Was it proximity to the Keeper that was draining him?

"Very good, Ashbourne. Your dragon is much smaller than others that I have met in my time. What happened to their power?"

Azura rumbled overhead, hissing at the insult. "I am powerful, Keeper. Just because I am of a smaller stature does not mean that I am not apt with magic."

A smile came to the corners of Ezzu's mouth as he acknowledged her properly for the first time. Ayr could feel his eyes staring into her soul, as they both stared at each other for a moment.

"That you are, Azura. That you are."

"How do you know her name?"

Ezzu's eyes shifted back towards Ayr. "Nothing remains hidden from me for long, Ayr Ashbourne."

"You will find some things more guarded than others, Keeper."

"We'll see about that. Now, do you have room for me in that saddle?"

Ayr bowed his head and stepped backwards, throwing his arm up to guide Ezzu towards Azura. "Whenever you're ready."

Ezzu took another apprehensive step forward, his weathered boots scraping against the stone floor. It was more of a shuffle than a step, his shoulders hunched forward as if bearing an invisible weight, but at least he was moving at last. Ayr felt the familiar cold tingle as more magic drained from his body like water from a punctured skin, leaving him hollow and light-headed. He turned back to Ezzu with his mask in his hands.

"That has to stop."

Ezzu's little smile returned to his lips. "If you want me on your side, you will siphon me more magic when I request it."

"I've just broken my bond to one master; I don't need to be held in servitude to another."

Ezzu's face shifted away from the smile into something more sinister. "Having just released myself from one, I can understand this sentiment. I will release you once I can feel myself returning to my full strength. I would not fight Otheria without having some of my magic back."

"How long will it take for you to recoup your losses?"

"Days, but there is a place not far from here that I can recover at."

"As long as it's on the way to the Haven, we can take you there."

Ezzu's eyes narrowed in response to the name of the Haven. "Is that what it is called? An ancient city that is home of the dragon riders?"

"Yes, that's right."

"Then that is where we are headed. I want nothing to do with the dragon riders until my power has returned to me. I will direct you to where I want to go. Lead the way, Ashbourne."

TWENTY-FIVE

Elanor swept into the hall of the Dragon Lords with fire in her veins. The Haven was a fireball of chaos, with wounded dragons and their riders all licking their wounds. The flight back to the Haven had been one in which they had constantly been looking over their shoulder. Sinibad had chased them across the sky, hunting down dragon after dragon, tearing them from their wings. There was too much blood shed for Elanor's taste, especially for the lack of result they had achieved.

Even though it was her information that had sent the Commonwealth riding to their demise, Elanor did not feel guilty. It was what Dalton had wanted and even though Evor had been attacked by the younger Ashbourne's dragon, he was still breathing, alive and well. There had been a brief moment when Sinibad had locked his eyes onto them which sent the fear shooting down Elanor's spine, but he had turned away before pursuing them. Perhaps Dalton still wanted her eyes and ears inside the Commonwealth.

Yet for all of Dalton's ferocity and the counterattack that had been launched from the city, those dragons and their riders that had survived the assault seemed unphased. Was her job as a Dragon Lord on his behalf now finally complete? Something told Elanor that he would never let her have her freedom, just like he refused to let Ayr go. The attack from Azura had also been baffling, but thankfully Azura was nowhere near the size of Evor. Not even Zaurien had been able to damage Evor much in his assault.

Her mind was a blur, not having rested properly since Ayr had returned to them a few nights ago. She had snuck moments in the saddle when they had flown to Ironrock, trusting Evor to take care of any threats that could have arisen. But considering he had not slept properly in almost two days, it was beginning to take a toll on him as well. Dragons could often go for days without sleep but coupled with the constant fighting that Evor had endured, it was clear to Elanor that his stamina was beginning to wane.

Even though Evor was starting to tire, he was still there for Elanor as he crawled onto the ceiling with the other dragons that rested there. Through his eyes, Elanor saw that Rotang was the first to greet him, their encounter the previous evening still very much in the forefront of his mind. Evor snarled at Rotang, who responded in kind, but otherwise, Elanor watched as they settled beside each other. Elanor could do nothing to quash the animosity between the two of them, except speak to Baldur inside the hall.

Elanor, just stay calm. We don't have all of the facts.

I don't care, Evor. Baldur accused me of betraying them. He tried to kill us both, even though the Hormook have now spoken against it.

Sometimes it is better to forgive than forget, Elanor. Baldur can still be a powerful ally going forward.

He's not sorry. He will refuse to apologise, and we will just be back at square one. He made his intentions known when he wanted to remove both you and me from this world.

We have had many people and dragons try to remove us from this world that we are still working with, Elanor. Use him and become a valuable asset that he does not want to be rid of.

Elanor grit her teeth together, fully knowing that Evor was right. *Then you need to make sure that Rotang no longer wants to devour you.*

I will do my best, Elanor, but you need to change Baldur's feelings about us as well.

That may prove to be harder than changing Rotang's mind.

We are in this together, Elanor.

Elanor cut off the connection between the two of them, shaking her head. She hated the fact that Evor was correct, but dragons, in her experience at least, were a funny race of creatures. For all their nobility and for all of their inner turmoil, most dragons were similar with a sense of pride and regality that far extended what humans were capable of. They had to come together, otherwise they risked being destroyed by Dalton. Elanor thought it had been strange that Rotang had not been one of the dragons to confront Sinibad at Ironrock, but considering his rider, she should not have expected anything more.

With Evor's words still being rammed home in her mind, Elanor continued to stride into the hall, half expecting Baldur to lash out at her from the shadows. The attack never came, but that did not mean she was ultimately prepared for what was to come once she entered the council room. Rotang continued to staunch Evor, while Tempera and Gravu watched on in silence. Now that Elanor was approaching, all three of the other dragons drew closer to Evor. Elanor could feel that he was uncomfortable, but she had her part to play in this act.

Elanor stepped into the council room and found the other three Dragon Lords already in their seats. All three of them were leaning in, their backsides on the edges of their seats as they were deep in debate. Leyla was the first to look up from the debate and spotted Elanor crossing the room, walking towards them.

"Ah, here she is. The great betrayer."

Both Baldur and Romulus turned their heads, and Elanor saw at least Baldur roll his eyes. He stood up from his seat and started to pace around the platform as Elanor approached. She slowed down as she approached the steps which took her up towards her seat, but Baldur was not letting her sit down in peace. He approached her, pointing his finger towards her face.

"What the fuck happened in Ironrock? Where were you?"

"Where was I? Baldur? Where were you? I rode in on an injured dragon and was lucky to make it out alive. Why did you not challenge Sinibad?"

Baldur scoffed and shook his head. "You wanted me to challenge an elder dragon?"

"Our strongest dragons should have challenged him, yes. That included the three of you!"

"And you! Why did you not tell us what awaited us there?"

"We were underprepared! I knew Dalton had wyvern at his disposal but not that many! I couldn't have warned you!"

Romulus raised his hands and stepped in between the two of them. "To be fair, Baldur, you didn't want Lady Sunfire being part of any plans. We should have taken our time and scouted the city more."

Baldur's lips barely opened as he spoke. "We had the numbers!"

"They weren't enough! The wyvern skewed the numbers in his favour, Baldur! What about us? Where were the Hormook?"

"The Hormook abandoned us! We needed them!"

"Whose fault was it that they left? The Hormook still want to deal with us whilst we are being honourable, Baldur. Your play at becoming Overlord on your own set them on a path that took them away from us. Perhaps you should think about that."

The temperature in the room rose by a degree as Baldur took a step closer. She could see the veins on his forehead; his eyes locked onto her looking like he wanted to devour her. Baldur pursued his lips and chewed on them before answering.

"The Commonwealth needs a definitive leader! We need someone like Anton and Kaladin that could stand up and take action. Outside the four of us here, who can fill that role?"

"I can think of one man that is not a Dragon Lord."

Baldur exploded with his anger finally spilling over. "If I hear you mention Ayr Ashbourne one more time! He betrayed you! He no longer resides within the Commonwealth. He forgot his oath! All because of his fucking father!"

Romulus spoke up again from his chair. "Dalton Ashbourne has been the sole reason for this madness. We should ponder our next steps with careful consideration."

"The time for consideration has passed, Romulus."

Leyla shook her head and also rose from her seat. "Yet a brash plan to attack Dalton head on didn't work either, Baldur. We need time to recover otherwise we will be stretched to a breaking point we can't come back from."

Baldur rounded on her, a deep growl evident in his throat. "There is no coming back from this. Dalton Ashbourne will leave us in nothing but charred ruins, just like half of the cities across the Commonwealth."

"Those cities weren't destroyed by Dalton."

"Remember who you serve, Elanor."

"I'm not the one that needs reminding of that, Baldur. I took the oath to defend the Commonwealth and I have done that. I have no ambition of rising above my current station and becoming Overlord."

Baldur narrowed his eyes on her. "Yet you'd have a fucking Ashbourne lord himself over us once again?"

"He needs direction. He has Azura at his side. She is the one that can steer the course and take us into a new age."

"You place too much faith in one dragon. One that is promised to your own."

"Because I know her."

"The dragon and the rider are one in the same. If she has not been corrupted by him yet, she soon will be."

"When was the last time you spoke to him? He broke away from Dalton to come and see us."

"A rider being led around by his dragon's emotions is not a proper rider."

Elanor sighed and shook her head, knowing that this conversation was going nowhere. "If you need me, I'll be in my chambers with Evor. There's no point discussing this with you further."

Baldur snorted and looked down on her with disdain. "Of course you will be. I would expect nothing less of someone with a dragon as weak as yours."

"Evor survived a blow from an elder dragon. That's more than you can say for Rotang. Now the Hormook made me a Dragon Lord, the same as you. I took the same oath. If you ever think of what to do for our next steps let me know. There is no point standing here arguing with you, especially when our dragons are also at each other's throats. I'd appreciate it if you called Rotang off the hunt."

"He is not attacking Evor now."

Elanor stepped away. "You know what I meant. Call him off."

Leyla reached out, touching Baldur's forearm and he turned to her. "Baldur, let it go. The Hormook have said you were in the wrong regarding this matter. We are stronger together."

Baldur's jaw tightened as he glared at Elanor, realising that he was outnumbered by the other Dragon Lords. "Go then. I don't want to see you unless we have reached a decision on what we do going forward."

"I look forward to it."

Elanor turned on her heel, her boots scraping against the stone floor as she began to leave the room. The heavy wooden door loomed before her, its iron hinges gleaming dully in the torchlight. Behind her, Baldur's voice cut through the air like a blade, hurling an insult that made her shoulders tense. She forced herself to keep walking, her jaw clenched tight enough to ache, her fingers curling into half-fists at her sides. There was no point in arguing further. His words were just wind, and nothing productive would come from extending this bitter exchange. She had achieved what she had wanted. Peace, and knowing that Rotang was no longer going to be hunting Evor.

You did well, Elanor.

You think so?

You held your own in an arena against three other humans that thought you to be beneath them. Baldur had no choice but to agree to your terms.

I somehow get the feeling it won't be for long, Evor.

It does not matter, Elanor. We bought ourselves more time.

We have. Get down here. I want to go back to our chambers.

Darkness was overtaking the Haven as the sun slipped beyond the mountains. The shadows were beginning to lengthen as the night took over, but it was not Elanor's concern. The darkness would bring her peace. Evor clambered down from his roost on top of the hall, his footsteps creating a small earthquake with each movement. He felt relaxed and was ready to retire after their tiresome last few days.

The rest of the Haven was quiet as they flew over it, with dragons settling into rest. Evor knew the way back to their chambers and they flew across the city in silence. Elanor continued to scan behind them, praying to Chilijo that Baldur's declaration that he had called Rotang off the fight was not an elaborate ruse that could be used to lull them into a false sense of security. Evor did not take long to navigate the Haven and landed in front of their quarters, allowing Elanor to dismount.

They worked their way inside and found nobody opposing them. Any dragon or their riders had seemingly retreated to their own quarters, which was something that Elanor was more than grateful for. Yet she still could not shake the feeling that she was being watched by someone or something. Chorru was the most likely answer, but as she continued to scan her surroundings, she found no sign of the small messenger dragon.

Evor pushed open the door to their chambers and Elanor walked in underneath him. She was grateful for the assistance but could only imagine how exhausted he was. Evor rumbled overhead, as he stepped inside, hitting the door closed with his tail as he passed through. Elanor heard it slam shut and was now grateful that the outside world was gone at last. Nothing waited for her in the room and she crossed the floor straight to the bed. It was missing Ayr and Azura's presence, but there was nothing that she could do about it with them both trapped at Ironrock.

Once Elanor had removed her sword, tossing its scabbard to the side, she flung herself onto the bed, not wanting to put up with any more drama from anyone else today. Despite his grumbling before, Evor remained silent, feeling that Elanor wanted peace. No sooner than Elanor's head had touched the pillows, she felt a sense of calm watch over her. She knew that it was Evor's influence, and she thanked him for it. Elanor closed her eyes, now feeling her mind go blank. Evor grumbled in her mind again, settling her.

She fell into an easy slumber, and nothing but happy dreams and moments with Evor filled her mind. Elanor was drifting away, falling into deeper sleep when she was disturbed out of the void.

Elanor. Evor's voice cut through the silence that had filled her mind like an earthquake. If she had not been used to the volume from Evor, it would have frightened her. She stirred as Evor continued. *Azura is speaking to me.*

Elanor shot up out of bed, staring at Evor. She blinked hard, once, twice, as her heart hammered against her ribs. The room came back into sharp focus and Evor was lifting his head, his eyes narrowed as he looked towards the windows, their gateway to the outside world.

Azura? She's here.

Yes, her and Ayr are on their way. They have company.

Then we need to greet them immediately.

They're almost here. I will open the windows and let them in.

Let them in? They're coming here?

They're wanted fugitives. Where else are they supposed to go?

By Chilijo, are they alright? What happened to Azura? Did Dalton break their bond?

No, everything is fine, Elanor.

Elanor shifted her legs and threw them over the edge of the bed. Evor's excitement was growing as he stood up and neared the windows. She could sense Azura through him now as well. They were drawing near. But something scared Elanor. Why had Ayr come back again? Was this a mission created by Dalton or was this of his own accord. Elanor held her breath as Evor pushed the window open, waiting for what was to come.

TWENTY-SIX

E zzu was sure of his footing from the moment he dismounted from Azura. They were just outside the walls of the Haven, Azura taking care to ensure that they had not been spotted from the city. They were nestled amongst a cluster of trees, and Ezzu nodded with authority. His movement had become more fluid, and he had only drawn a touch more magic from Ayr. Ayr was feeling drained, without having had any rest, but Azura on the other hand was feeling reinvigorated.

There was a closeness to Evor that they had not properly had in months, and the fact that Azura was going to see him again only drove her forward. Now that he was on the ground, Ezzu looked up at them in the saddle, his weathered face creasing into solemn lines as he nodded, the silver embroidery on his robes catching the moonlight as they shifted in the breeze.

"Everything here is as it should be. I can feel the magic in this place is almost just how we left it. I imagine when Otheria awakes properly, she will come here for me."

"Is that likely?"

"Yes. Leave me here to recharge my magic. If you need to see your promised, go and see her."

There were no further words exchanged between them and Azura looked to the moon, waiting to launch into the sky so that she could reach Evor. Ayr ensured that Ezzu was clear of anything that Azura could kick up and once he was away from them, he pushed Azura forward. She kicked up off the ground and Ayr held onto the grips in the saddle like his life depended on it. Azura was never going to throw him off, but her excitement was uncontainable.

She flew towards the city at breakneck speed, one that she had not achieved since she had been fully rested in Ironrock. Ezzu had been an extra weight on her, but it was as if the events of the past few days had been absolved.

Stay low, Azura.

I know, Ayr. I know they will be watching for other dragons.

With any luck we can avoid them. Hopefully it is just Sinibad that they are on the lookout for.

Well, knowing our luck, we will now be enemy number one.

Perhaps you could use some of your magic to hide me then, Ayr.

You know as well as I do that I can't. If I was that powerful, I would rival Dalton.

And you know as well as I do that you already rival Dalton. In many ways, I can safely assure you that you surpass him.

I appreciate the kind words, Azura. Shouldn't you be focused on getting us safely to Elanor and Evor.

I am doing my best, Ayr.

The first wall of the Haven was just in front of them, and Azura slowed her flight to avoid overshooting it. There was no room that she could fly over the buildings without being spotted, but by some miracle, there were next to no dragons stationed on the rooftops, patrolling, looking for any sign of danger that was going to come from Ironrock.

Evor is ready to see us.

And Elanor?

According to Evor she is much the same.

Take us to them then.

Yes, Ayr. I do not want to get caught. We still need to be careful flying around here even though it is dark.

Azura knew the Haven well and if Evor was speaking to her then she knew exactly where he would be waiting for them. Up ahead, Ayr saw where he and Elanor had spent what seemed like an eternity locked in the Tower of Echoes, but also where Elanor now would have resided. The window on the side of the lodgings opened, and Ayr spotted an all too familiar jet-black scaly leg poking out from it. Azura shot towards it and within moments, she was barrelling into Evor, with all the excitement of a toddler rediscovering its favourite toy.

Evor!

The scream of excitement was meant only for him but in the moment, Azura must have sent it out to Ayr as well. His head rung with the volume that Azura yelled out at, but he recovered as Evor swept around her. Evor was more refined with his approach, careful not to crush either her or Ayr.

"Little one, it has been far too long since you have been tucked under my wings."

"I missed you, Evor."

The change in their discussion to now being a verbal one was abrupt, but Ayr adjusted. "It's good to see you as well, Evor."

Evor's tone was firm. "Ashbourne. I could go another lifetime without seeing your face again. But you are the little one's rider, so I will have to tolerate you."

"That's no way to treat an old friend."

"I would sooner call you food if it was not for Elanor. We are in this situation because of you."

"Speak to Azura and you know that is not true."

Evor huffed as Azura set herself down towards the floor so that Ayr could dismount. He saw Elanor standing beside Evor, waiting patiently for him to come down to ground level. She stood stoic, with her arms folded, appearing unimpressed. Had she forgiven him for the betrayal or was she still harbouring resentment towards him for leaving? As he touched down onto the ground, Azura moved away, Evor taking her under his wings. Her emotions were still rocketing around the room, bouncing off the walls of his mind like a dart. Between that and seeing Elanor standing before him, Ayr was a ball of uncertainty.

He approached her as she scowled at him, a smile coming to his lips. He did not know what else to do. Ayr outstretched his arms towards her, only to receive a cold reception.

"Did you miss me?"

Elanor's tone was as icy as her expression, and she looked cold to touch. She stepped back, moving for the first time since they had entered the room. "What the fuck are you doing here, Ayr?"

"We had to come back. We left Dalton."

Elanor raised an eyebrow and her expression softened. "You left Dalton?"

"He was going to jeopardise my relationship with Azura. With you."

"What are you talking about?"

"He wanted to break the chain. I was not going to accept that. If he broke the chain between Azura and I, I'd hate to think what would have happened."

"Azura is your dragon, Ayr. That would have changed nothing between us. You had an inside into his operations and whereabouts, and you just gave that up?"

"She wasn't the only thing that I was concerned about losing. If I'd let Dalton continue on with his magic, there was more than just Azura on the line."

"What was?"

"You were what I would also lose. Our connection is only there because of Azura and Evor. With Azura, there is no you."

Considering her face had been rock hard only moments ago, Ayr paused upon seeing the small tears that were already starting to form in Elanor's eyes. "So, you don't feel the same about me?"

Are you doing what I think you're doing, Ayr?

What exactly do you think I'm doing?

Ayr heard Azura's smirk in her tone. *It's taken you long enough. It's about time.*

Can you stop ruining the moment?

Sorry, Ayr.

Ayr refocused on Elanor in front of him, whose shoulders were rounding. She appeared smaller than she had moments ago, but it was not for the change in her stature. The tears in her eyes were more prevalent now.

"No, that's not what I'm saying at all. From the moment I met you, I felt like there was something between us. I don't know if it's the dragon's magic or what, but I've got something to tell you."

From the way her shoulders shuddered, Ayr could tell she knew what was coming. She had felt it as well and it was clear to him that the feeling was mutual. How could it not be? Between both Azura and Evor, their feelings were not a matter of what, but when. They had discovered the elder dragon together, fought hordes of wyvern together and she had been there for him since the start.

Elanor took a step closer to him. There was no holding back the tears now. The fire light from above caught in her hair, making it appear more radiant than it was. With Elanor within arm's reach, she finally dropped hers to her side as she looked up at him. Ayr went to speak but Elanor's competitive nature overtook him. She raised her hand to his lips, and placed her index finger over them, silencing Ayr. Elanor opened her mouth and spoke the words that he had been waiting to hear for a long time.

"Ayr Ashbourne, I love you."

The words were a release. A chill raced down Ayr's spine as Elanor's voice filled his ears. All the building tension that had resulted in weeks, and months of frustration now all came to an end. For all their time apart, the world came rushing back to him, and Ayr felt whole once again. He grabbed at her, scooping her up in his arms, pulling her tight to him. Elanor's presence was overwhelming. Her lips met his in a fiery clash, one that was unlike any other time that they had come together. This had more weight behind it, and there was now more at stake. Ayr had committed to her, but this was her committing to him.

Evor rumbled overhead, the faintest hint of happiness in his tone. "By Chilijo, I'm glad that's over. It's about time. Let's give them space, little one."

"We'll be discovered outside, Evor."

"Very well, we will stay here."

Ayr was caught up in the moment as he moved Elanor past the bed. If it was not for Azura probing his mind, he would have ignored her entirely. The culmination of the past few weeks, every single moment that he had been missing her had come to this one moment. He was back, and Chilijo himself would have to tear him away from her. Those words on her lips were everything Ayr could have hoped for and more. But he could not say it back, not when she looked at him like that.

Elanor gasped as Ayr gripped her waist and pulled her flush against his hard body. He could not find the words, but he could show her exactly how he felt. He brought his lips to hers in a tender caress, as if afraid she might vanish beneath his touch. The kiss was slow and reverent, like a quiet confession pressed into her mouth. Elanor's breath hitched as the world narrowed to the warmth of him, to the unspoken truth he poured into that fragile moment.

But like everything in this world that was fragile, their restraint broke. The kiss deepened, intensified into an inferno that threatened to consume them. Ayr lifted Elanor off her feet, and she wrapped her legs around his waist. Elanor's hips ground over his hardness.

"I can feel how much you want me, Ayr."

Ayr hissed in return, gripping her ass as he shoved her back against the wall. He pressed his lips against her throat. "You have felt nothing yet, Elanor."

The way her pulse fluttered beneath his mouth made his cock twitch. She felt so fucking good against his body. This was better than the last time that they'd met. This felt earnt, and Ayr felt like he was going to be rewarded momentarily. Even the emotions surging between Azura and Evor could add nothing to this moment. This was purely the bond between both riders.

Elanor reached between their heated bodies, her fingers trembling as they found the cool metal of his belt buckle. She worked it free with practiced urgency, the leather sliding through the clasp with a soft hiss before she tugged his trousers down just enough to free him from the confining fabric. Ayr released his grip on her, his calloused hands leaving momentary ghost-prints of warmth on her skin as he set her down. There was only one painful moment before he hooked his thumbs into the waistband of her pants and tore them downward with such force that the fabric whispered a complaint. In one fluid motion, he lifted her again, his strong hands cupping the backs of her thighs as she wrapped her legs around his waist, her ankles crossing at the small of his back to pull him closer. His cock teased her entrance, drawing a frustrated sound from her lips that made Ayr chuckle.

He deepened his tone. "Say it again."

Elanor gripped his face, tugging him closer until their foreheads rested together.

"Make me, Ashbourne."

Those three words unravelled him like a fraying tapestry. Ayr rolled his hips without warning, his muscles tightening beneath her fingertips as he slammed into her with such force that her back arched against the cold stone wall. The slick heat between them ignited, spreading like dragon's fire through their bodies, stealing the breath from their lungs and leaving nothing but desperate, ragged gasps hanging in the air between their parted lips.

Elanor threw her head back and her nails dug into his skin. Ayr hoped that they would leave a mark as he groaned. "Be careful what you wish for."

He gripped her ass with both hands, fingers digging into the soft flesh as he thrust into her with a primal rhythm. Her legs, slick with sweat, tightened around his waist like a vice, pulling him deeper as waves of pleasure radiated from her core, her release tearing through her body with the force of lightning striking water. He cursed under his breath and pulled out before it was too late. His point had not been proven yet, and the words he craved had not spilled from her mouth.

"That didn't take you long, Elanor."

But one way or another, he would hear the words that he was desperate to hear again. Her protest earned a dangerous smirk as he set her trembling legs back on the ground and bent, throwing them over his shoulders. Her thighs shuddered against his head as he took her heated flesh into his mouth, her cry of pleasure shooting straight through him. Ayr grunted as he listened to the sweet sound. He paused before he started moving his tongue, letting it work her all over her in slow, knowing circles. The taste of her was intoxicating as the rest of her body. She trembled between his mouth and the wall. Just as she was about to fall apart, Ayr pulled away.

Elanor started to complain, her fingers tangling in his hair, trying to pull him back. "Ayr..."

His tone was soft as he savoured her whimper. "Tell me what I want to hear."

"I love you, now please..."

Her words broke into a moan as Ayr sucked her into his mouth, devouring her as though he were starving.

"I want you to finish for me."

He rumbled against her overheated flesh, his voice a low vibration that travelled from his chest into hers. The words rippled through Elanor like wildfire catching on dry brush, igniting every nerve ending until her body arched taut as a bowstring. Ayr's arms encircled her, his fingers pressing into the small of her back as she shuddered against him, her release coming in powerful pulses that left her gasping and clinging to his shoulders. Now he knew that her fingernails were leaving crescent moons in his skin. Ayr was not done. There was still more that he wanted to do to her.

Ayr set her down and spun her, so her hands splayed against the wall and the curve of her ass was flush against his hips. "You did so well for me, now you're going to take my cock."

Elanor's response was weak, but the whimper in her voice only egged him on more. "Please, Ayr. I need it."

Elanor arched against him, grinding down until he was back inside her, where he belonged. The way she took him nearly tore him apart. Elanor braced herself against the wall, her palms flat against the stone as her body tightened around him. The way she took him from behind made a low sound rumble from his chest. He indulged in everything he could. The curve of her back, the helpless way she pressed into him like she needed more, stripped the last of his restraint away.

Ayr growled her name as release ripped through him, sharp and overwhelming. He bent over her, one hand braced beside her head, the other gripping her hip as he held her there, buried deep, riding out the shudder that shook him to his core. For a moment, there was nothing but her warmth, her breath, the brutal rightness of being exactly where he belonged.

When it passed, he stayed there. Ayr shuddered as he placed his forehead against her shoulder, his chest heaving as he fought to steady himself. She was still trembling beneath him. Yet in that moment, she was still his, and the truth of it settled heavy and unyielding in his chest. For a long moment, neither of them moved and only silence filled the chamber.

Elanor rested her forehead against the stone, her legs still trembling, her fingers curling loosely against the wall as the last of the intensity faded. He shifted just enough to brush his lips against her shoulder, the gesture quiet and unguarded. She leaned back into him in response, a soft exhale leaving her chest. It was not words that settled them.

It was the shared silence, heavy and certain, and the undeniable truth that whatever this was between them, it was no longer something either of them could walk away from. Even if Dalton came after him to drag him and Azura back to Ironrock, he would fight against him until there was nothing left but dust and charred cinders.

"Elanor. I've got something to tell you."

A sly smirk formed on Elanor's lips as she pressed her hand onto his chest. She was becoming more comfortable as she settled into his body. "Yes, Ayr?"

"You know I love you, right?"

She giggled and snaked her hand up towards his chin. She slid upwards and brought her lips to his as she settled onto his flank. Ayr found himself lost in her eyes, and despite the previous day's events, felt everything was right with the world. There was no other place he'd rather be than except in this moment. Her scent filled his nostrils, and his hand on the curve of her back fit snuggly, like her body had been carved just for it to rest there. Her eyes sparkled in the firelight as she came towards him for another kiss. It was slow, long, deep and passionate. Every emotion from Azura flowed into him, as she mirrored him, feeling the same way about Evor. The dragons were unspoken, but their bond was as undeniable as the rider's.

"Yes, Ayr. I love you too. We should get some sleep."

Ayr grinned down at her and laughed. "We could, or we could do something else that is a little more fun."

Elanor matched his mischievousness, with there being no misunderstanding between the two of them. "Tell me, Ashbourne, I've had a long day. Just what did you have in mind?"

Ayr was feeling exhausted from the first round, but all he needed was a touch of magic to be back in the game. He licked his lips and shifted closer to her again. "Oh, you have no idea, Lady Sunfire."

TWENTY-SEVEN

"Lady Sunfire! Lady Sunfire!"

Elanor jolted awake to the sounds of thunderous pounding on her chamber door. The heavy oak rattled against its iron hinges with each strike. It sounded like a dragon was hitting it, but the voice calling her name was very much human. Evor released a low, rumbling grunt that vibrated through the stone floor beneath them. Azura merely flicked her white tail once before curling tighter around herself, both dragons evidently dismissing the urgent commotion as unworthy of their full attention. They were enjoying the presence of each other's company. The morning had been peaceful, but this rude interruption was something she was not willing to stand for. The voice sounded familiar.

Annoyed, Elanor rolled out of the bed, dragging one of the bedsheets with her. Ayr had not moved, still on his back with his arms splayed in every direction. His snores were light, nothing outside of the usual and Elanor smiled at him as he lay there, vulnerable. She cast a side eye at Evor who raised his own.

What?

You could have done this, you know.

I'm injured, Elanor. What is it that you humans say? Give me a break.

You've had plenty of rest, Evor. What if there was a threat on the other side of that door? You'd feel bad if I opened it and walked into dragon fire, would you not?

Perhaps, but I was of the opinion that Rotang had been called off the hunt. I cannot smell him nearby at the moment.

So, who is it then?

There are multiple scents. See for yourself.

Elanor rolled her eyes and crossed the room to the door. The thudding continued on the other side of it, and Elanor was left with no choice but to open it. Wrapped in her bedsheet, Elanor flung the door open and found both Marshadow brothers standing on the other side of the threshold. Sinpac and Esher stood behind them, both dragons looking like they were ready to charge through the door.

Marcello and Malachi both stood in the doorway with their wyrmguard helmets removed. Their uniforms were both freshly pressed, and whilst they had flown to Ironrock, they both appeared as if they had not fought at all. Elanor had seen both of them slicing at wyvern with their swords, so she knew that both men had gotten their hands dirty during the fight. Marcello snapped to attention, his blonde wavy hair, billowing with the movement as he saw her.

"Lady Sunfire! We heard word that Lord Ashbourne has returned to us."

Malachi leaned forward as his expression shifted into a smirk. "Judging by what you are dressed in, our assumption is correct."

Elanor hissed at them both and flung the door open so they could get past her. She gestured them inside and one by one, both Marcello and Malachi entered the room. Elanor slammed the door shut behind them, keeping the dragons outside. She glared at both of them as they entered the room, their eyes immediately locking onto Azura as she remained curled inside Evor's wings.

"Ayr! Cover yourself!"

Ayr was still stark naked on the bed, with no covers, especially now that Elanor had ripped the sheets out from underneath him. He reached over his head, grabbing one of the pillows as both Elanor and the Marshadow brothers walked towards him. The pillow barely covered his waist, but it was enough for now, not that Elanor did not want to see it. The unwelcome interruption was still bothering her. She only wanted a few more hours or minutes with Ayr by her side to properly relax.

Ayr sat up in the bed as the Marshadows approached. His brow furrowed and he took a deep breath, eyeing both twins with a gentle curiosity. "What can we help you with, gentlemen?"

The twins snapped to attention, their heels clicking against each other. Elanor saw Ayr's eyes narrow as he awaited their response.

"Lord Ashbourne, we are glad that you returned to the city. We thought you would remain with Dalton, however. Why have you come back so early?"

Ayr's eyes darkened. "My father is no longer someone that I wish to live in the shadows of. His philosophy is outdated. He tried to take Azura from me."

Marcello was the first of the twins to speak, crying out in alarm. "He tried to take Azura away from you? How? Did he want to have her killed?"

Ayr shook his head as he responded. "There is no dragon and rider relationships in the future if we are to follow Dalton's path. He wanted to break our bond. As he does for all other dragons and their riders."

A stillness entered the room as the Marshadow brothers cast a glance at each other; their faces narrowed in calculation. With a firm nod from Marcello, he gestured for Malachi to speak for both of them. "You are the future of your family, my lord. If Dalton is not willing to put you in that position, then we can no longer serve him either."

"Did you only come here to pledge allegiance to Ayr? Why is it just the two of you?"

Malachi swallowed and continued. "Our family always pledged themselves to Dalton, but that was under the assumption that he was going to work with dragons in the future."

Ayr snorted and laughed. "He will continue to work with dragons, but only whilst they benefit him. He's shown me that he doesn't care about them."

"Then we will follow your lead, Lord Ashbourne. What do you plan to do? The other Dragon Lords would not have you lead the Commonwealth."

"I need to dispose of my father. He is the most immediate threat to us at this point in time."

"And what of the Keeper, Ayr?" Evor's voice rumbled from over Elanor's shoulder. "They should be taken into consideration."

"What do you mean the Keeper?"

"You're not the only one that Azura speaks to. As her promised I am privy to many of her secrets. She thought that I should know about it."

Ayr clenched his jaw and his back tightened as he sat up straighter than he had been before. He cast a glance at Azura and met her gaze, and there was no doubt in Elanor's mind that there was a silent conversation being carried on between the two of them. Ayr pursed his lips together and looked back at Elanor.

"When Ezzu is ready, he will be able to contain the threat of Otheria. Or so he says."

"I thought you'd have known better than to have even been tempted to bring someone who claimed they were a Keeper back here."

"I shouldn't have to justify myself to you."

Elanor flushed red with anger at Ayr's response. He had just dismissed her with an off-hand comment. She opened her mouth to let him know just how inconsiderate that he had been, but Ayr continued.

"Everyone in this room knows that Dalton is the biggest threat to all of us. He could be leading his forces back here now to attack us for all we know."

Marcello stepped forward, his back as rigid as it had been moments ago. "We stand ready to defend you, Lord Ashbourne."

"I don't need defending."

Evor shot into Elanor's mind with a sound of alarm. He moved his head and rose from his resting position. Something was wrong. Elanor turned to him as he spoke.

Elanor, someone else is coming. I think it is the Dragon Lords. I can smell them.

Elanor was equally as confused. There would have been no chance that Baldur could have come to a decision within the last few hours. More so, why would they be coming here this late at night. They would have had to have seen Azura entering the Haven.

The Dragon Lords? Here? All of them?

Yes, Elanor. We need to hide the little one! They aren't as stupid as you like to give them credit for.

There's nowhere for her to go!

Hide Ashbourne in the cupboard, Azura will have to flee outside!

Elanor broke free from Evor's thoughts and surged forward. Ayr's eyes widened in alarm as Elanor swarmed him. He fell backwards as she tried to grab his hand, but Elanor adjusted and grabbed him properly.

"What are you doing, Elanor?"

"The Dragon Lords are coming. There's no time to waste. Azura, you need to go!"

"Come with me, little one."

Evor was already up and moving towards the windows. They were still open from the previous night. Perhaps someone flying by had seen Azura in the window and had put two and two together. Regardless, if the Dragon Lords were on the way, there would be no time to do anything except get Azura out of the room. With Ayr's hand secured, Elanor spun towards the two wyrmguard who remained stationary behind her. She flung her arm out, directing them towards the door.

"You two go and head them off!"

"Yes ma'am!"

Marcello and Malachi both nodded their acknowledgement before turning on their heels and almost running out of the room. The door slammed shut behind them, but Elanor did not see it close as she was dragging Ayr to the cupboard. He was on his feet and moving, but he had not been fast enough, nor was he clothed. Azura was almost out of the window when a dark shadow appeared just outside it. The all too familiar silhouette of Rotang filled the window way, and Azura shrunk away from him without a second thought.

Evor moved to fill in the window, but Rotang touched down on the ground. The thunderous boom filled the room and Azura darted behind Evor. The two larger dragons came face to face, with Rotang poking his head inside. His eyes narrowed as he stared at Evor, the two behemoths not willing to give ground to the other. Rotang spoke first, his tone low and menacing, the threats of the past coming to the surface.

"Move, Evor. Or I will move you."

Elanor...

Do it, Evor. We won't win this fight.

I have the little one at my side.

We are trying to change the Dragon Lord's perception are we not?

I can beat him.

Stand down. Let him inside.

Evor gave ground, which allowed Rotang the space that he needed to move inside. Evor growled as Rotang entered, but without Elanor's approval, there was little that he could do. Rotang at first inspected the room, his eyes running over Azura, until they locked onto the very much naked Ayr that was standing beside Elanor, only steps away from where they wanted to hide him.

Rotang spoke for Baldur, with nothing but fury in his voice that rumbled the walls around them. "What in Chilijo's name is he doing here! He's supposed to be in Ironrock! I thought the report of his dragon being here was just a lie!"

"Your reports were incorrect, Rotang. Come in and we can discuss this."

The room was now uncomfortable with how crammed it was considering there was a third dragon inside. At least the Marshadow brothers had the sense to leave theirs in the hallway. Yet Baldur was not as sensible as some men. He was standing up in the saddle, over the top of Rotang. With Rotang still glaring a hole in Evor, he coiled around the room, making it his own.

Elanor heard the doors to the chambers opening again, and rather than the Marshadows reemerging, it was Tempera and Gravu, making their presence known. The Marshadow brothers were at the feet of the dragons, with Sinpac and Esher snorting their disapproval behind the backs of the Dragon Lords. The other two Dragon Lords made the room claustrophobic, and Evor and Azura stood with their backs to each other. Evor snarled his own disapproval, not taking his eyes off Rotang. He wanted to protect Azura, but in the two on three scenario it would not be possible.

"Get out of the way, wyrmguard!"

Baldur slid down from his saddle and landed on the floor. He stood up to his full height and stepped between Evor and Rotang. He peered up at both dragons before continuing towards where Elanor and Ayr stood. Both Romulus and Leyla were also making their way down from their dragons. The room was starting to become suffocating, with the mass of dragons all sharing it. With Azura and Evor being the only ones inside it was spacious, however the other three dragons were too much.

Rotang spoke, his voice firm and demanding. "We're here, Evor. There is nothing more to discuss. You and your rider will finally face prosecution. It is clear to us that it is well overdue."

Elanor was not going to back down as Evor and Azura became encircled by the other dragons. "You all need to stop! Why would Ayr Ashbourne return to us if he wanted to bring harm upon the Commonwealth? He has no interest with Dalton if Evor is the promised of his dragon."

Baldur rounded his shoulders and lashed out with his tongue. "You're blind, Elanor. I've been informed that he has killed many Commonwealth assets in his time here. I will not have you maintain your post as a Dragon Lord if you are this compromised. You've fought me once recently. Don't ask for it again! I will not have mercy."

"I'm not asking you to have mercy. Clearly, something has occurred since our attack on Ironrock. You would be foolish to refuse Ayr's help."

"Foolish? How would he be able to help us?"

"I told you that he was the one man that could become the Overlord. He has the pedigree for it. Look at what his uncle did for the Commonwealth, for fuck's sake."

"I never saw eye to eye with Anton Ashbourne. I disagree with what he did to the Commonwealth. He took us into an age of complacency."

"Yet there was no threat within the Commonwealth. Not everything has to be war, Baldur. Ayr can be the Overlord that destroys Dalton Ashbourne once and for all."

"Beg to the gods and Chilijo for forgiveness. Pray they are more merciful than me because I am over this game that you and I have been playing, Elanor."

"You need to stop, Baldur!"

Ayr's voice cracked like a whip across the room. Baldur's obsidian eyes, weighted with suspicion, slowly dragged away from Elanor like a sword being unsheathed. The muscles in his weathered face tensed as he shifted his penetrating focus toward Ayr, his jaw clenching beneath his silver-streaked beard.

"What are you going to do about it, Ashbourne?"

"You should speak to the man that put you in the position you're in with a little more respect."

Baldur smirked and scoffed at Ayr. He lowered his head and chortled to himself. "The man that put me in my position. What, as Dragon Lord? We all know you killed the Dragon Lords with your father. There's no denying it. Dalton is powerful, but against all four of the previous Dragon Lords. He needed help."

If Ayr was flustered, he did not show it. There was something intimidating about him normally, but now that he stood firm, naked and opposing Baldur, there was something new about him. His shoulders were squared with unflinching resolve and his jaw clenched tight as granite. Ayr's eyes burnt with a cold fire that seemed to pierce through Baldur's very soul, matching Baldur for aggression. The muscles across his chest and arms tensed like coiled springs, ready to unleash their power. It was as if he had grown three inches in height through sheer force of will, his presence expanding to fill the room like a storm cloud about to break.

Baldur continued, his tone low and dangerous. "You'll never be the Overlord. Over my fucking dead body."

Ayr spat at Baldur. "Good, I don't want to be. I want my dragon and I want my partnership with Elanor to continue. Can you offer me that? I want Dalton dead for what he tried to do to me and Azura."

Now Romulus was on the front foot, stepping forward to confront Ayr. Whilst Baldur was tall, Romulus was stocky, but Ayr still also towered over him. "You've killed many riders. This is a ruse. You're an Ashbourne."

Ayr turned his head to glare at Romulus. Elanor wondered what was going through his mind with the evil stare. Did he want to strike him down where he stood? But that would only serve to prove Romulus' point.

"I knew if I came back my life would be in danger. Why would I risk all of that for nothing? Let me help you bring Dalton to the ground. If I can do that, then the Commonwealth can move on with what it wants to do. Just let Azura and I ride free from here when this is all over. I understand how much a danger my father is to our way of life."

"Our way of life? You joined it only a few months ago. You were part of Dalton's plan."

"I was, yet I am not aware what his end game is. My role was to infiltrate the Obelisk and bond with a dragon of my own.

Leyla spoke up, her higher pitch significantly noticeable beside that of Baldur and Romulus. "This is a trap. Yet history does show us it takes one Ashbourne to kill another. I would rather deal with this runt than Dalton."

Elanor's eyes narrowed to slits as she watched Leyla. The woman's gaze lingered on Ayr's broad shoulders, tracing down the contours of his sides with such blatant appreciation that Elanor's jaw clenched. A flush crept up Elanor's neck as Leyla bit her lower lip. She was either oblivious or did not care of Elanor's mounting displeasure and the possessive heat flaring in her chest. Jealousy over Ayr? They were bonded together through their dragons. Nobody would be able to come between them. The creases on Baldur's forehead became even more evident as he pondered what Leyla had just said.

"I still don't trust him, or you, Lady Sunfire. There is nothing that tells me that you won't turn on us the moment that it benefits you."

"I brought another Keeper back from the dead."

A hiss escaped Baldur's lips. "Another Keeper? You mean there is more than one of them that are still alive?"

"It's incredible what happens when you venture outside your seat of power, Baldur. But yes, I woke him."

"You could have mentioned this earlier. Where is it?"

"He resides just outside the city syphoning magic."

"You brought him here? Ashbourne, what in Chilijo's name were you thinking? We all heard about the disaster that was the discovery of the first Keeper!"

Ayr shook his head. "If you'd allow me to get dressed, I could take you to him. He's here for the other Keeper. Nothing else."

"How do we know this isn't a trap?" Leyla's question was valid as much as Elanor wanted to stab her in the face for looking at Ayr how she had.

Ayr's response was calm and measured. "If you have to, put a blade to her throat and keep her with you."

Baldur stepped forward and snorted. "You've already betrayed her once. I'm not willing to take that chance. If you aren't genuine, I think there is a more substantial piece of leverage we can keep over you."

Ayr raised eyebrows. "You want to take Azura, hostage? How then will I show you the way to where the Keeper is?"

"Ride with your promised. Evor can see what Azura knows about the Keeper's location and take us there."

"I wouldn't feel comfortable without her nearby."

Baldur's smile darkened as the corners of his mouth turned upwards. "She will be nearby. In the jaws of Rotang."

"No!" Evor's shout was violent and sudden.

Elanor! Make sense of this situation. We have escaped the frying pan only to be thrown into an inferno. Ayr cannot agree to those terms!

Elanor went to open her mouth, but Ayr had already raised his hands towards Evor. "It's done. I'm more than willing to earn the trust of the rest of the Dragon Lords."

"Ayr! Reconsider!"

"There is no need. Baldur will learn the truth, and he will release Azura without question."

The smile that had still not left Baldur's lips told Elanor that they had other things to worry about. "Yes, Ashbourne. That is exactly what will happen. Let us investigate this Keeper and see if he can't help turn our fortunes around. Ready a contingent of the wyrmguard. I would not go into this alone."

TWENTY-EIGHT

The Dragon Lords had at last backed off and had given Ayr time to dress. Even though they were still eyeballing him, Ayr did not feel uncomfortable. The only discomfort came from Azura, who was panicking about where she now found herself. Ayr did not blame her, however. The jaws of Rotang were a place that no creature ever should have had the displeasure of being inside.

Ayr, I really must protest. This is ridiculous.

I agree, Azura. But if this is the only way that Baldur will accept what we're saying is the truth, then we have to do it. You're protected.

Forgive me if I don't trust your magic at the moment, Ayr. You were compromised when we broke Ezzu out of his tomb.

You know I've recovered since then. He is no longer draining me.

You need to be careful. I don't want you to overexert yourself. We've already seen the dangers of that.

I'm not Dalton, Azura.

I know you're not. But Rotang is not just any dragon. I pray to Chilijo that you can keep me safe.

I know the risk. I'll kill him if he so much as rips one scale from you. My shield should hold around you until you can get out of his mouth.

Do you think they suspect anything?

If they do, I don't care. Your safety is paramount. Don't move unless you feel like you're in danger.

Yes, Ayr.

Ayr was locked into the saddle in front of Baldur, and he did not feel secure by any means. It was uncomfortable, and it felt like he had the hand of Dalton wrapped around the back of his neck once again. Yet Evor led the Dragon Lords towards the grove where they had dropped Ezzu off the previous evening. Nothing had changed in the hours since Ayr and Azura had last been here, and Azura was feeding information to Evor. Evor adjusted his course accordingly, and within minutes, they were outside of the Haven's walls.

The grove came into view, and Ayr began to grow nervous. Would Ezzu still be there, or would the ancient Keeper have moved on. Evor was the first into the grove, splitting the trees around either side of his body. Rotang followed behind as did the other Dragon Lords. Ezzu was not hard to spot as they entered the grove, his midnight blue robes, stark against the greenery of the forest that surrounded him. He was seated on the ground, with his legs crossed and his arms extended as if he was meditating. Ezzu looked up when he heard the dragons but did not flinch or run away.

The Dragon Lords settled down around him in a circle, and Ezzu's eyes were drawn to Azura. Baldur directed Ayr to dismount before him, and whilst Ayr was not familiar with dismounting from a dragon the size of Rotang, he felt there being little difference as he slid down the much thicker and larger leg. Rotang snorted at him, and Azura was still in Ayr's mind praying that Rotang did not choose to bite down.

Baldur was only a heartbeat behind Ayr and as he landed on the ground, he scoffed, appearing unimpressed. "So this is the Keeper?"

Ayr nodded. "Considering that my dragon's fate is in your hands, I have no reason to lie to you."

"Why would you bring him here?"

"He requested it. It was either he come here and recharge his magic, or feed off mine. Is it any wonder why I chose that option?"

"How very Ashbourne like of you."

Ayr ignored the quick jab and moved towards Ezzu. Now that the Dragons Lords were all on the ground and approaching him, Ezzu stood up, keeping his arms extended in greeting.

"Lord Ashbourne, why have you interrupted my meditation?"

Ayr heard Baldur hiss behind him. "Lord?"

"Apologies, Ezzu. These are the Dragon Lords that I was telling you about. They requested that they come and meet you in person. As you can see, my dragon's life hangs in the balance."

Ezzu narrowed his eyes as he glanced at Azura. "Why is that dragon being held hostage? Release her at once."

Baldur was firm. "No, that won't be happening until we can verify that you are a Keeper and you wish us no harm. We've recently had dealings with another one of your kind. How can we trust you?"

Ezzu flicked the ends of his robe up, starting to reveal the brand that Otheria had left on his skin. He eyed Ayr, before glancing around at the Dragon Lords. "You didn't tell me that they would be so difficult to deal with."

"I made no promises. The fact we've gotten this far has surprised me."

"Hmm. Well, feast your eyes. I have no love for Otheria."

Ezzu rolled his sleeve up entirely so that the brand could be seen. As he did, Ayr caught another dark tattoo that ran down from his shoulder towards his bicep. It was a spider's web, one that looked like it had corrupted the skin around it. Ayr narrowed his eyes, as he tried to work out just where it had come from. He thought he had seen all of the pain that Otheria had inflicted upon Ezzu, but this was new.

"What's that?"

"More evidence. When I said Otheria branded me, I meant it. I will have my revenge like I told you, Lord Ashbourne. It corrupts me."

"Can you stop it?"

Ezzu shook his head. "Only when Otheria is dead. This spell is ancient, and once she is no longer with this world, I will be free."

Baldur still was not convinced. He stepped forward, scowling, his uncertainty written all over his face. "How do we know that you're a Keeper? You could have been anyone that Ashbourne dressed up from a hovel in the woods."

A wry smile came to Ezzu's lips, and he reached out with his hand. Ayr could already feel the magic coiling around Ezzu. Just like Otheria before him, he had an exemplary control of it, one that Ayr felt secondary to. It was like he was standing across the room from Dalton as he had watched the man summon the magic in a display of power and control. The leaves at Ayr's feet started to shift all at once, and the Dragon Lords looked down.

Romulus let out a cry of alarm and as branch shifted, hitting him on the ankle. For the most part the magic was subtle, but Ayr could feel the world shift around him. It was Ezzu's to control. Baldur remained steadfast and grit his teeth as he watched the leaves and dirt move around him,

"The Hormook should know about this."

Leyla spoke up, her eyes fixated on Ezzu as she watched him with awe. "Baldur, they left the Haven. Have you got any way of calling them back to us?"

Baldur shook his head. "No, once they're gone, they're gone. There was nothing that I could do to call them back now."

Ezzu grunted as he turned away from them. "If you turned the Hormook away from you, you must have slighted them."

"You know about the Hormook?"

"Honorary riders, perfect examples of what it means to be bonded with a dragon. I fear that they have lost their touch if they were to help one such as yourself."

"I won't stand here and be insulted."

"You will. My magic returns to me presently. Ayr, I will help you when Otheria comes to smite you as repayment for you releasing me from my tomb."

"Thank you, Ezzu."

"Now, Lord Baldur, can you tell me where I can find housing and nourishment? It has been many years since this body has had anything in it besides magic."

Baldur paused and glanced at the Dragon Lords. His gaze did not linger on Elanor. "Thoughts?"

"It's rare that a man can have an affinity for magic like that without a dragon. The chances are he is a Keeper. I am willing to believe Ashbourne, this time around."

"I pray that we are not making a mistake, but I agree with Leyla. If this man is indeed a Keeper and is willing to fight against the one that wants to destroy us, I see no reason in not having him around. The Hormook are gone. A Keeper even without a dragon is sure to be of more use to us."

Rotang and the other dragons all rumbled overhead. Ayr still had his shield wrapped around Azura, ready to activate it and remove her from his mouth should Rotang choose to bite down. Whilst he felt like there was now enough evidence on their side to dictate that there was no need for it anymore, he still did not trust Rotang and Baldur as far as he could throw either of them, even with magic.

Baldur's eyes darted between Romulus', Leyla's and then lastly Elanor's. His jaw tightened as the sounds of the birds and other wildlife returned to the grove. The dragons all looked down at their riders, waiting for their verdict to be passed.

Romulus filled the silence with his thoughts. "Our backs are against the wall, Baldur. You saw what awaited us at Ironrock. I know the four of us don't have the raw power to stop Dalton Ashbourne on his own, especially with that elder dragon at his back. You saw what it did to our ranks."

Baldur's teeth would have been turning to dust inside his mouth with the amount of grinding he was doing. His tongue would not have been safe either. Ayr could almost hear him mulling over the thoughts going around in his brain.

"We can't afford anymore mistakes. We have to be sure that this man is a Keeper and what both he and Ashbourne say is genuine."

"I would have no reason to lie to you, Baldur. Not now."

"Yet you deemed it appropriate before you left to go and be with your father."

"I didn't have a choice!"

Beside Ayr, he heard Ezzu cough at the most opportune moment. The first cough, Ayr ignored, but the second cough made him turn. Ezzu's eyes were wide open, not out of embarrassment, but out of fear. Ezzu shifted where he stood, snapping forward like he had been struck by lightning. He cried out, a groan escaping his lips. Ezzu slipped forward onto his knees like he had been struck in the back of the head by a mallet. He tried to keep himself upright, but another shock tore through his body. Ayr raced towards him, ignoring the hand of Baldur that tried to stop him.

"Ezzu! What's wrong! What happened to your magic?"

Ezzu's voice was weak, cracking underneath the strain of whatever was going on in his body. "It's Otheria. I can sense her."

Romulus started forward, stuttering over his words? "Do you mean the other Keeper? Otheria? She was left in the tomb."

Ezzu shook his head and for the first time, Ayr saw fear in his eyes. The brand on his forearm had changed colour. What was once black was now a subtle shade of crimson red, like blood was starting to pool in the wound.

"Believe me when I say she is close. She is coming!"

Elanor hissed as she clicked her tongue out. "This is what we wanted to avoid when Dalton made the wyrmguard seal it. How did she break free?"

"Mere snow and ice were never going to contain her. She is more powerful than anyone here. Myself included."

Baldur placed his hands on his hips. "Say that this Keeper is coming here. What does she intend to do? Is this the one that sided with Dalton."

"Yes, Baldur. She was the first Keeper that was awoken.

Ayr turned back towards Baldur. Whilst there was no confusion on the older rider's face, he was still cold and calculating. "If that Keeper is coming here, you need to let Azura and I go. Dalton will not be far behind her. If you want to stop him, I need to have no restrictions."

"You'll refuse to confront him."

"In this state, yes. I need more time to recover. I've fought Dalton once in the past few days. Send out scouts to the west. See if he approaches. Don't sit here and take no action like the previous Overlord did."

Leyla interrupted, cutting across Ayr, not allowing him to finish. It was clear that she was not the only one that was sick of the conversation. She wanted Baldur to make up his mind. "Ashbourne is right, Baldur. The longer we sit idle, the closer we are to our destruction. If it's through his hand or his father, if we lose the Haven, we lose the Commonwealth. This equation is simple in my mind."

Ezzu was moving towards Baldur, crawling along his belly, like he was dying of thirst. He stretched out with one spider-like arm that splayed across the ground as he spread his fingers.

"Please... heed this warning. Otheria will destroy everything in her path. Don't let your ego get in the way of defending your home."

Leyla glared at Baldur. "Decide to do the right thing, Baldur. For all our sakes."

Baldur finally stopped grinding his teeth and grunted. "Fine. See Ashbourne and the Keeper back to the city. I want every dragon ready for an attack!"

A groan came from Azura and Ayr felt her falling to the ground. Rotang had at long last removed her from his jaws without an external prompt from Baldur. There had been no hesitation and now that Azura was back on the ground, she could not believe that she had survived. Ayr could see the saliva from Rotang dripping off her and knew that would be something to clean from her later on. But for now Azura was in one piece. Ayr dove into her mind with a smug tone.

See I told you there was nothing to be worried about.

You play a dangerous game, Ayr.

There was no game. You know that I don't gamble with your life. You mean too much to me.

Well, you've got a funny way of showing it.

Neither of us died, and we have gained Ezzu as an ally, Azura. Everything is fine. We just need to be sure of when Dalton decides to attack us.

TWENTY-NINE

It was a strange thing to see someone else on Azura's back along with Ayr. Whilst Elanor had done it, there was almost no sense in doing it on a regular basis. Ezzu had chosen her as his preferred mount, and something told Elanor that she was similar to the dragon that he no longer had possession of. How Ayr had managed to find not one, but two Keepers within the space of weeks was astounding. Obviously, he had help with Otheria, but from what he had told her the previous night, finding Ezzu had been all him and Azura. How many more Keepers still slept buried underneath the Commonwealth and more importantly when would they rise?

Elanor watched as Ayr got Ezzu into place on the saddle. The Keeper was almost stagnant, taking his time to fit into position on the mount. Elanor could relate to what he was most likely feeling, however. Riding on another dragon was always an odd sensation, but she could not imagine what it would feel like without access to a dragon of his own. When Evor had been sick, she had felt useless and less of a rider, but if Evor was dead. Elanor shuddered at the thought. They would die together or not at all.

The magic that had brought Ezzu to his knees was still coursing through his body as Ayr helped him up. Ayr's grip was not physical, but rather it was all through his magic. Ezzu was lifted up into the air like a ragdoll and placed upon Azura's back. Ayr had done all of the heavy lifting himself, including helping Ezzu into the saddle.

Baldur and Rotang led the Dragon Lords back towards the Haven. Even though nothing had changed, Elanor kept checking over her shoulder, searching for any sign of what had caused Ezzu to slow down. If Otheria could do that to him, could she do it to anyone that she chose or was it strictly because of their bond. Regardless, Elanor did not want to find out. They were unbothered by the dragons on guard, but Elanor could see through some of their expressions that they had not expected the Dragon Lords, along with Azura, to be coming back into the city so early in the morning.

The Marshadows were among the wyrmguard that had escorted them in and out of the city and brought up the rear of the sizable contingent. Rather than heading towards the hall of the Dragon Lords like she expected them to, Baldur led them towards the Amphitheatre. Elanor was taken back to the last time she had stood within its walls, facing down Baindussa as they stood accused of killing Crassus, only for Dalton Ashbourne to swoop in at the last second and burn Anton Ashbourne to a crisp.

Today, the Amphitheatre looked different. It stood as it always did at the core of the Haven, but today the Amphitheatre was no longer a killing arena. Instead, as they approached, it was clear to Elanor that it was being used as a nursery for the injured. The other infirmaries were overflowing as a result of the attack on Ironrock. Those dragons that had not been fortunate enough to get into one of the infirmaries was being worked on here.

There were over a dozen dragons, all scattered over the arena floor. Shade sails and shelters had been constructed for them, with both their riders, for those that still lived and the medics were busy attending to them. Dragon assistants were busy ferrying supplies to and from the other infirmaries, and beneath them the Amphitheatre was a hive of activity as all the players moved around in the sand and dirt. Elanor was just glad that Evor was not one of the dragons lay on the ground in the hot sun. She had already done it more than once and was not so eager to return to that time in her life.

Some of the larger dragons that had been mauled in the Ironrock had bite marks that lined their flanks. The smaller bite marks were from the wyvern, but there were several dragons with claw marks down their entire side. Rotang led the group of Dragon Lords and the wyrmguard into the Amphitheatre and sat himself down. All of the other dragons followed, making sure that they did not tread on any of the wounded dragons.

Once they had all touched down, Rotang looked down at the other dragons and sighed. "So many fallen soldiers. Many of them will not make it. What a disappointment."

Evor snorted in return. "As a result of your actions, Rotang."

The animosity had done nothing to go away, and they were right back at square one. Rotang coiled around Evor and Elanor sat up right in her saddle. At least this time she had Ayr to protect her, and the two Marshadow brothers had also made their allegiance clear to this point. They would turn the tide of a battle if it was to come, but the three other Dragon Lords were no joke when it came to fighting. Unlike their predecessors they were still of a proper fighting age and their magic was not lacking.

One of the medics that had been under one of the shelters, strode out from underneath it. She was as tall as Elanor was and wore a simple medical garb. Elanor imagined that underneath the shelter there were a dozen riders that were also all being treated for injuries sustained in the assault. The medic made her way straight across to Baldur and Rotang. Rotang let Baldur down and he walked towards the medic.

She thrust her arms out and threw them around him. Baldur sunk into the embrace like the entire weight of the world had been lifted off his shoulders. Elanor could see them exchanging words and asked Evor to lower her to the ground. He obliged and Elanor slid from his neck onto the sand, making her way towards Baldur and the medic. As she approached, Baldur turned toward her, his expression unpleasant as normal.

"What do you want, Lady Sunfire?"

"Why did you bring us here? The Amphitheatre is not the best place for us to mount our defence of the Haven if we are indeed under attack."

"It's not, but it is the most central hub to everything in it. We can coordinate and see what the city needs from here."

Behind Baldur, Ayr was trying to assist Ezzu from his place in the saddle, but using only physical force, Elanor could see that he was struggling. She wanted to urge him to use his magic, but she had a feeling that there was a reason that he was not. Ezzu stood straighter than he had done before, but he was still moving at a snail's pace out of the saddle. Baldur took Elanor's attention again.

"Unless you have a better solution, I would suggest you keep your mouth shut. Mirian was telling me what the situation was here."

"That's not what it looked like to me, Baldur. Since when have you had someone you cared about other than yourself?"

"That's none of your concern. Mirian is the best healer we have available in the Commonwealth."

Elanor raised an eyebrow. "Yet I've never heard of her."

"We don't have time for this, Elanor. What do you want?"

"I still don't believe this is our best course of action. Kaladin has the city set and ready to fight against any foreign threat. How are we improving the situation here?"

"Fine, we'll do it your way if that's what you so choose. I'm not about to have my authority undermined here when this is the situation that calls for strong leadership!"

Baldur's gaze darkened like storm clouds gathering over a winter sea, with the lines around his mouth deepening into crevasses of displeasure. He stepped away from Mirian with the deliberate slowness that Elanor was accustomed to. When he raised his thick and calloused finger towards her face for the second time, Elanor's palm tingled with the visceral urge to strike it away, to feel the satisfying impact of flesh against flesh and watch his arrogant gesture crumble. She resisted, but only because of the grinding her top teeth were doing against the bottom ones.

"Speak to me like that again, and I'll feed you to Dalton himself. I don't care what it costs us anymore."

"You'll lose Evor if you do that."

"I don't need him to beat Dalton."

"Really? Because it seems to me like you and I can use every asset we can get our hands on at the moment."

Baldur hissed at her, the sound like a blade being drawn from its scabbard. His eyes then became fixed on something beyond her. His weathered face froze mid-snarl, and his jaw was beginning to slacken. Elanor whirled around, her hair whipping across her face, to follow his gaze. Through the haze of tension, she heard Ezzu's voice that was low and melodic and almost hypnotic drifting from where he stood. She crept forward on the balls of her feet, straining to catch his words as they floated on the air. Even though he was trying to project his voice, she could tell from the intimate timbre of his tone and the way his eyes locked with Ayr's that these whispered words were meant for no one else.

"Ayr...stop and look." Ezzu's voice was faint and he raised his hand towards the horizon. "She's here."

Elanor turned, following Ezzu's point and her heart sank. There on the horizon, was a dragon that she had hoped not to see again. Yet it was all too familiar and very much free of the icy prison that had one entombed it. Whilst Elanor could not see the figure that rode upon it, it was clear to Elanor that the dragon was none other than Ragoon.

Now that he was out of the tomb that had kept him, Elanor was seeing his size for the first time.

Ragoon was still far on the horizon, yet from what Elanor could see, he was as large as Sinibad, if not more so. It was no wonder why he had taken so long to be removed from the prison. Why had Kaladin been so insistent on awakening her? Now they were going to pay the price for his incompetence and his greed in something that should have never happened. Even if Dalton had awoken her originally, there was a chance that she could not be heading there now.

Elanor prayed to Chilijo that Ayr was correct and that Ezzu was in fact a Keeper. But without a dragon would he be able to stand up to her power? She glanced down at Ezzu as he steadied his feet underneath him. There was a surge of magic as he waved his hands in front of him and Elanor had no idea what it had done. Ragoon let loose with a roar on the horizon. If the Haven was unaware of his presence, they were well aware of it now.

The rest of the Dragon Lords all turned their attention towards Ragoon as he came in, settling in on the nearby mountain range that overlooked the Haven. Elanor felt her throat constrict, as she watched the enormous dragon settle into what he was evidently declaring his new home. She was surprised that he did not venture forward.

Another roar came from somewhere behind her, and this roar was familiar to her. A chill ran down Elanor's spine as she turned around to investigate the sound. Even though her heart was already sunk, it was Evor's that now plummeted into the sand. Elanor could not see who had made the roar, but Evor raised his head and could see just over the edge of the Amphitheatre to confirm just what was coming towards them.

Sinibad had arrived and was nestling himself in the mountains to the south. The ground shook as he landed, and even though everyone was concerned with Ragoon to the north, there were more heads that turned to the south. As Elanor watched through Evor's eyes as a swarm of wyvern all made their presence felt around Sinibad. There seemed like there were more here than what there had been at Ironrock, as well as the other dragons that Dalton had at his disposal. The Haven was caught between a rock and a hard place.

We are not ready for this fight, Elanor. The riders have not recovered yet.

We were never going to be ready, Evor. Unless Ayr and Ezzu can do something to save us, I fear today marks the end of the Commonwealth.

I will fight to protect our home.

Our home is already lost, Evor. We lost our home when we lost the Obelisk.

That angers me, Elanor.

Then use it, Evor. Our backs are against the wall. You and I are at a point that we have nothing to lose anymore.

We can lose Ayr and the little one. We have something very real to lose.

Then we will fight for them. Before we lose them entirely.

THIRTY

A yr had not wanted this day to come. He should not have expected anything less though. His departure from Ironrock would
have only served to infuriate Dalton and knew that his father could
be anywhere in the city at this point. Whether he had come earlier
and was now simply allowing Sinibad to provide the distraction was
anyone's guess. The medics and healers that had once been tending to
the dragons and riders underneath the shelters were coming out from
them to stare off into the distance.

He could feel the whole of the Haven pausing to examine the two
gargantuan dragons that had just made their presence known. Whilst
dragons were nothing new to the Commonwealth, the thunderous
arrival of the two behemoths that now surrounded the city had drawn
the attention of every person and dragon within sight. Ayr wanted to
turn and run from them, but standing in the middle of the Amphitheatre with Ezzu by his side meant that it was not an option.

Ayr had his eyes on Ragoon, but he knew the real threat would
come from behind Sinibad. Unless Dalton had somehow changed his
mind about what he wanted, he was going to assume that Dalton still
wanted him alive. Ayr held Ezzu steady beside him and waited for the
Dragon Lord to act. Yet as both Sinibad and Ragoon coiled around
their respective mountains, Azura was a calm presence in his mind.

We can take Dalton head on if you would like, Ayr.

That would require us to head into the mouth of many hungry wyvern. Are you sure you want to risk that? You can see what they've done to every other dragon that is laying here, can't you?

Dalton directs them and if he directs them to attack us, so be it. We will have done everything we can to defend what remains of the Commonwealth.

I thought we didn't want to do that.

So far, they're the only group of people that haven't wanted to tear us apart. I think the least we can do is do something to help them in this situation.

Otheria and Ragoon will prove to be more than enough for most of the riders and dragons here, I would think. She showed her power in the tomb.

I somehow feel that was only a fraction of what she was capable of.

Exactly. I am glad we have Ezzu here then if his intentions are true.

There is only one way to find out. Should we deal with Dalton?

If we can find him. If we can stop Sinibad, then yes, that will put a dent in his plans.

Sinibad reared his massive, scaled head from the jagged mountain peak, his crimson eyes blazing like twin suns. His jaws stretched wide, revealing his rows of gleaming obsidian teeth before he unleashed a roar so powerful it sent avalanches of loose stone cascading down the slopes. The very air vibrated, trees bending as though caught in a hurricane. Across the valley, Ragoon's midnight-black form rose against the clouds on the opposite mountain, his answering roar splitting the sky with equal fury, the collision of their voices creating a thunderous harmony that echoed through the mountains long after their jaws had closed.

The Haven was trapped between them, and nobody on the ground within the Amphitheatre wanted to move. Ezzu was the first, as he slowly moved away from Ayr. The black magic that was still etched into his skin was still pulsing, but Ezzu was now mobile.

"You need to deal with your father if he is the threat to you. I will deal with Otheria and send her back to her tomb."

"Are you sure. I could help you defeat her."

"I am a Keeper. It is my job to contain threats, whether it be something like your father, or one of our own. I will not let you down."

"How will you get to her to do battle?"

"She will come to me. Now trust the process. I will use what magic I have here to smite her. If I am unable to kill her, then the rest of the riders will need to combine their efforts to contain her."

"Contain her? Are you crazy? She can't be let out again."

"Then I need to kill her outright."

"And the chances of that?"

"I will have the element of surprise on my side, but once I start using my magic, Otheria will know exactly who I am. But I can deal with her here, on the ground."

"She'll crush the city."

"Not if I have anything to say about it. Now go. Take the fight to your father. He has the power here."

Ezzu stepped away from Azura, his dark robes billowing around his ankles as he retreated. Now that he was clear of her, Azura flexed her iridescent wings and tensed the powerful muscles along her spine. Ayr felt the familiar ripple beneath him as her shoulder blades shifted, preparing for that first mighty downstroke that would launch them skyward. Around them, the Dragon Lords formed an intimidating circle, their faces hard as stone, each of the dragons, towering over Azura.

"Where do you think you're going Ashbourne?"

Ayr grit his teeth, annoyed that he was stopped at every turn. Azura grumbled underneath him as she felt uncomfortable.

These dragons are fools. How can they not see what's going on, Ayr? We will teach them.

Baldur was striding towards them as Rotang sneered down at them. Baldur spoke, his mouth opening, but Ayr was too far away to hear the words. So Rotang spoke for him. "Are you so eager to return to your father so quickly? I knew we should have ended your existence!"

Azura in turn spoke for Ayr. "You're stopping us from stopping the threat before it destroys the Haven! Let us go!"

Rotang snorted at them, smoke shooting from his nostrils. Ayr could see the fire building within his jaws, ready for the command from Baldur to end them. Ayr called magic to his hands, ready to raise a shield should he choose to strike. "You're not stopping that elder dragon on your own. Azura would be eaten in a mouthful."

"You're forgetting who is on my back, Rotang. Ayr will be the one that directs our power towards ridding the world of Sinibad."

"That elder dragon is not the same as the Dragon Lords and their dragons that you killed."

"We've lived under his shadow for weeks. If there is anyone that is well aware of that fact, it's us. That dragon needs to be stopped."

"And what of the Keeper?"

Ezzu raised his voice, speaking clearly for the first time. "I will deal with Otheria. You deal with the rest of the horde coming this way."

"The rest of the horde?"

"Do you think that's all that Dalton has brought with him if he has his biggest weapons out to play? Think Rotang, don't let your rider do all the thinking for you."

"I can sense them coming. I can hear them."

Rotang lifted his massive, scaled head and turned it towards Sinibad, his neck muscles rippling beneath iridescent crimson plates. His amber eyes narrowed to dangerous slits, pupils contracting to thin black daggers. He grumbled, a sound like boulders grinding together deep in his cavernous chest, the threatening vibration echoing throughout the Amphitheatre, making the very sand beneath their feet tremble.

There were shrieks on the horizon, ones that Ayr recognised and ones that he had only heard a few days ago. Except now, there were more of them. Even though Ayr could not hear them, Azura raised her head towards Sinibad. As he remained coiled around the mountain peak, wyvern were beginning to appear on the horizon. They were swarming like moths, all to a lantern. It was clear from their direction that Sinibad was that lantern.

Are you ready, Azura?

I never thought you would ask, Ayr. I am ready to see this through to the end.

Then prepare yourself. This is going to be the hardest thing that we have ever done together.

Yet this will be the most rewarding if we can pull it off.

Are you confident with your newfound power that you can kill him?

Azura, you've seen me murder the Dragon Lords. Now that Sinibad no longer scares me and threatens the only two things that I care about in the world, I will end him. If Dalton wants the Haven and the Commonwealth, he's going to have to kill us first.

I will assist you.

I know you will. The bond between us is still strong.

Nothing will ever come between us. Not whilst I still have the power that I do inside me.

Ayr felt Azura smiling. Anticipation surged through Azura's body as she coiled, ready to launch skyward. Evor grumbled behind her, and Azura turned her head to him. Ayr could feel her sparkling blue eyes running up and down his body. She was curious, but did not expect Evor to be so ready to help her. Ayr could tell through Azura's vision that he was still not at one hundred percent.

"Yes, Evor?"

"You don't have to do this alone. I will be there for you."

"One more attack from Sinibad will finish you. I'll need help getting to him."

Evor snarled as he glanced in the same direction as Azura. He lowered his head and collected Elanor from the ground. She threw her mask over her face and threw Ayr a nod. Ayr responded in kind, as Rotang raised his leg again in front of Azura.

"You fly out alone?"

"Will you bring the rest of the dragons? Sinibad needs to fall first if we are to stand any chance against them. I can't get there without the wyvern getting in my way."

"If you are confident in your ability to bring him from the sky, then yes, we will assist you. The Haven is our home, and we will defend it with everything we have."

The other Dragon Lords grunted in agreement. Romulus and Leyla were still in their saddles, and they were waiting for Elanor and Baldur. Baldur gave one final quick hug to the medic that stood by him, and he turned on his heel, headed towards Rotang. Rotang snarled and ducked to collect him and within moments Baldur was back in the saddle.

"Baldur says we are to ride against Dalton and the rest of his horde. Are you confident you can destroy Sinibad?"

Ayr flushed more magic from his system and down into Azura. She was already glowing from the power he had used before, but now she was even more radiant. Where he ended and she started, Ayr could almost not tell. There was only their goal, which waited for them at the top of the mountain. He felt Azura grin underneath him as she responded to Rotang.

"Yes. With Ayr on my back, we will bring Sinibad to the ground or die in the attempt."

Evor was still sceptical. He stood over Azura, offering her protection from the sun in the meantime. "I will not lose you, Azura."

"Then protect me."

Evor cooed, even though it was a rumbling sound like distant thunder, and he brought his massive obsidian head closer to Azura. His midnight scales, each the size of a shield, scraped against Azura's pristine alabaster ones with a sound like metal on stone. Ayr watched, still unsettled by their proximity, the stark contrast between darkness and light as ancient as the mountains themselves.

"Little one, you know that I will die for you."

Ayr felt Azura grow warmer underneath him as a result of Evor's words. "And I you, Evor."

Elanor was close enough to them, and she was leaning out of the saddle. Even though she was underneath her mask, Ayr could feel that she only had eyes for him. Ayr could sense the intensity of her gaze burning through the narrow eye slits, fixed solely on him. Her gloved fingers gripped the pommel so that the material stretched across her knuckles, her entire posture betraying what her hidden face could not. She was not ready, just like Evor.

"What are you going to do, Ayr?"

"Kill Sinibad. Ensure my father's plan doesn't come to fruition. We've got too much at stake here to give it up now."

"Too much to give up?" Elanor leaned back in her saddle and Ayr could hear the sarcasm in her voice. The blue crest that he had grown all too familiar with bobbed up and down with the movement of her head.

"You know what I mean."

Ayr could hear the enjoyment in her voice, even though the task before them was nothing short of monumental. They were too far apart, and the lasting contact that they had taken in the morning when waking up together had been the last time they had touched. Ayr wanted to reach across the gap between them and touch her, but she was just too far away. Instead, Elanor could offer him nothing. She leaned back in her saddle and looked towards the sky.

"May your dragon always breathe fire, Ayr."

Ayr tried his best not to choke up underneath his mask. It was only because of Azura's reassurance that he managed to say the words loud enough so that she could hear him. "And may your wings carry you forward, Elanor."

THIRTY-ONE

Azura was the first to rise, kicking off from the ground and shooting into the air like an arrow. Ayr could hear the wingbeats of Evor just below them and could feel his looming presence right behind them. By the time they had already come over the roof of the Amphitheatre, Ayr could already see Sinibad staring at them. The corners of his mouth started to curl as he stretched his wings out behind him. From this distance, Sinibad was already appearing to be as wide as the Haven, his wingspan casting shadows over the surrounding landscape. He was ready for them.

"Come, Ashbourne. Meet your fate. Your father demands you come home."

Azura was too far away from Sinibad for her voice to carry. Instead, she issued a roar, as she headed straight towards him. It was a direct challenge, and one that he could not ignore. The wyvern formed up behind Sinibad, spreading themselves out across the sky. The dragons from within the Haven were beginning to grow restless, with roars and groans from the dragons ready to defend their home growing.

Ayr checked over his shoulder, and through Azura's vision could also see those same dragons taking to the sky. One by one, more dragons rose up around the Haven, all of them heading towards Sinibad and the wyvern. Where had this fight been when they had attacked Ironrock? Azura felt secure and confident with Evor behind her, even though they were heading towards the jaws of Sinibad. Ayr, on the other hand, was thinking the opposite.

The closer we get to him, the more I regret this decision.

Do you want to end this or not, Ayr?

Of course I want to end this. This is the only way we get to live our lives together in peace.

Then no matter how scared either of us are, we have to do this.

I'm not scared, Azura. I know I can fry that dragon with my power.

That's not what it feels like to me.

Then you are mistaken. This is something I have been waiting a very long time to do.

Ayr felt Azura pause mid thought as she considered her answer. There were dozens of thoughts flooding her mind, all at the same time, and Ayr could not make any sense of them, despite their closeness.

We both know what we have to do. See it done. I will take you there.

Azura dove down, gaining more air speed as she did. If it was not evident already that Sinibad was tracking them, it was abundantly clear now. The wyvern that were closest to him changed the angle of their flight. Whilst some were headed directly for the rear of the Haven, under the guise of Ragoon, there were just as many now headed straight for them.

"Get behind me, little one!"

Evor's thunderous roar shattered the air above Haven, vibrating through Ayr's bones as the black dragon's massive wings beat harder, propelling him forward with terrifying speed. His obsidian scales gleamed like polished armour as he surged past Azura, taking point position with his razor-toothed maw opened wide. The approaching wyverns, which by comparison were all thin-winged and serpentine, scattered before regrouping, their yellowish eyes fixed on their prey. Through the chaos, Sinibad remained perched on his mountain throne, lips curled back to reveal ancient fangs in a smile that promised death, watching as his minions swarmed forward like a plague of locusts, their collective screeches nothing but insect buzz compared to Evor's earth-shattering battle cry.

Here they come.

Evor on the other hand was ready for the wyvern. As he streamed forward, molten fire erupted from his jaws in a blinding torrent that split the sky like liquid lightning. The foremost wyvern beat their leathery wings frantically as they shrieked their battle cries, but that was not enough to save them from Evor's rage. The first dozen or so were engulfed in Evor's flames instantly. Their scaled bodies writhed in midair, becoming nothing more than charred silhouettes against the inferno before plummeting toward the ground like fallen stars.

Sinibad was unbothered by Evor's display of power and had not taken his eye off Ayr and Azura. He was more upright than he was before, and Ayr could see the power in his legs, ready to launch him forward. There was still no sign of Dalton, but Ayr was focused on the monstrous threat in front of him. As Evor tore through the first of the wyvern, other dragons were making their presence known from the Haven. Streams of fire shot across the sky as dragons of every size and colour entered the fray. The sky had gone from a clear baby blue to being covered in streams of red and orange, coming from both sides.

Now that the wyvern were thinning, Ayr could see more behind Sinibad. There were more dragons now inside the horizon, dragons that Dalton had at his disposal. Ayr recognised some from his time in Ironrock, but many of them were unfamiliar to him. The tables had turned and it was now the Commonwealth that was on the backfoot. Ayr heard a monstrous roar from behind him that could have only been Ragoon. He took his eyes off Sinibad for a moment and saw Ragoon diving towards the Haven. Fire streamed from his jaws, and the screams from the city below did not reach his ears.

Ayr could only pray to Chilijo that Ezzu was taking care of Otheria and Ragoon. Sinibad at last had launched from the mountainside and was now coming towards them. Ayr focused, Azura's vision highlighting just what was coming towards them. Ayr coiled his magic around his hands, his sole focus on Sinibad. Sinibad's neck recoiled, as fire built in his belly. Azura saw it coming and looped directly upwards. Ayr felt the fire beneath him, the heat radiating up his back. He clung onto the saddle with all of his strength as Azura shot straight up, looping over Sinibad.

Ayr had lost all sight of Evor, but the shrieking of the wyvern and the other dragons was still prevalent behind them. Sinibad was as fast as Azura, even more so due to his massive size. Ayr knew that he was gaining on them, and the fact that he would catch them was a matter of if, not when. Ayr urged Azura on, and was waiting for Sinibad's jaws to get closer. The magic was growing around them, but Ayr wondered if it would be enough to stop him. The Dragon Lords had been one thing, but Sinibad was different. There was an increasing vacuum as Sinibad drew nearer and Ayr was ready.

"Stop flying, Ashbourne! Come here!"

Azura flipped and turned, doing whatever she could to avoid Sinibad's clutches. There was only so far, she could go in terms of altitude before both she and Ayr would start to pass out and fade. Azura pulled up and leveled out. Sinibad went roaring past them, his size making his turning circle so much larger than Azura's. Yet they were not out of the woods yet. As Azura became level, Sinibad dropped into a sharp descent. He wanted to rip them from the sky.

Now was Ayr's moment. Sinibad was coming at them like an oversized arrow, straight and true. Ayr had enough magic coursing through his body and now that Azura was level, he could aim his magic properly. Ayr used Sinibad's momentum against him. His spell locked around Sinibad's head like a vice. With the downward momentum of

Sinibad, all Ayr had to do was pull. Sinibad shifted in the air, knowing that he was under a magical attack, and Ayr could feel him resisting against it, but there was nothing that he could do. Ayr grit his teeth as he fought against Sinibad.

"Let me go, Ashbourne!"

Azura was moving towards the ground too, but at a slower pace. Ayr kept all of his magic focused on Sinibad's head. The enormous golden dragon was roaring as he twisted through the sky, fighting Ayr with everything he had in his body. Whilst his wings still worked, Ayr then traced the spell down Sinibad's body until he hooked the magic underneath his wings. The effect was immediate.

Ayr pulled down and Sinibad was gaining more speed as he plummeted towards the ground. As Sinibad roared, Azura was now dealing with another threat. Some of the wyvern that Evor had not ripped from the sky were now turning to attack her. Sinibad had directed them towards them. Whilst Ayr was relying on Azura for some of her magic to control Sinibad, she was now focused on the wyvern that were coming towards them. Azura reared her head back, feeling comfortable that there was space between them and Sinibad, and let loose with a stream of fire of her own that rivalled the ferocity of Evor's.

Wyvern were caught in it, and those that fell away were only replaced by more that were coming out of nowhere. The dragons from the Haven were now jousting with the Ironrock dragons in a dance that lit up the sky. Ayr was still far too focused on Sinibad, and Azura was keeping him out of danger as he continued to force Sinibad to the ground. A wyvern came near, and Azura jolted upwards to snatch it out of the air. Ayr jolted in the saddle and almost lost his grip on the spell.

Sinibad would have felt him lose control and tried to pivot to gain leverage, fighting not to go to the ground. Yet as he tried to regain control, Ayr gripped his head and turned him into a spin. There was a snap in the spell, and finally Sinibad had given up. Azura roasted more wyvern as they came at them, but Ayr was now trying to reposition Sinibad, so he did not head towards the city. It was too late. His momentum and Ayr's magic had carried him too far.

Sinibad crashed into the Haven with a thunderous boom that was reminiscent of what had happened to the Obelisk. Except this time, there were no other dragons in his clutches, nor was he in control of his fall. The impact sent a shockwave rippling across the ground that knocked any remaining dragons within the Haven scattering. The fall appeared to happen in slow motion, Ayr now releasing the spell entirely. The few dragons that stood on the remaining buildings that Sinibad was tracking towards identified the threat and abandoned their posts. Due to Ayr's attempted redirection with his spell meant Sinibad was only just within the city. Even though he had come down on the outermost wall, his momentum carried him forward and his shockwave extended well past the Amphitheatre.

The screams and cries of desperation from the city below reached Ayr's ears and he leaned back in the saddle, asking Azura to come to a stop. She did so in a heartbeat, and it allowed Ayr to survey the damage that he had caused. Ragoon was still hovering over the city, beams of energy and light shooting up from where Ezzu still stood. He was no longer in the Amphitheatre but rather seemed to have either been taken away by a dragon or moved under his own steam.

Ayr could see Otheria atop Ragoon casting her own magic, raining it down upon the city. Some dragons and their riders were attempting to stop her, but with the Keeper's combined might, they were not getting close to them. Dragons fell all around Otheria, even as Ezzu worked overtime. Ragoon was beginning to look slower, with many cuts and scratches etched all over his body that he otherwise would not have had. He wanted to help those against Otheria, but Sinibad was still moving despite his fall from grace.

We need to deal with him, Ayr.

I know. But I don't see anyone. How am I going to destroy him?

He is stunned, but you have more power. End him and then we can focus on Dalton.

Ayr took a deep breath as he stared down at the fallen elder dragon. He felt like there was nothing more he needed to do, but there were other dragons approaching Sinibad. Sinibad turned his head towards them and released a jet of flame. The burst was short and sharp, but it was enough to make those dragons on the ground leap out of the way to avoid being caught. That did not stop some dragons being roasted, however.

The screams and roars of pain reached Ayr's ears and he winced. There was no need for this to continue on the way that it was going. Ayr urged Azura to go forward but as she took her first wingbeat, something enormous cut across their path. Ayr recoiled in the saddle, sending a blast of magic towards the dragon that had swooped upon them. He blinked, realising that it was Manir. She spun around laughing as she went.

"Close call, little Ashbourne. Perhaps the next passing will take you out of the sky!"

Ayr snarled as did Azura underneath him and their attention was taken as Manir turned. Then Ayr heard a familiar roar from behind them. Expecting another dragon like Zaurien to attack them, Ayr ducked, holding his hand up ready to cast his magic. A black shadow shot overhead faster than he could react to and he realised that it was Evor behind them.

Ayr, Evor will deal with Manir! We need to get down to Sinibad! Then fly, Azura!

Evor and Manir collided midair with a thunderous impact that sent shockwaves across the Haven. Evor's obsidian scales scraped against Manir's blue hide, throwing sparks into the wind as their massive bodies twisted against each other, both of them trying to assert dominance over the other. Their razor-like fangs sought to tear their vulnerable flesh from each other while their dagger-like talons ripped through the air, each dragon fighting with primal fury that made the very heavens tremble.

Azura increased her velocity as she shot downwards, in a desperate attempt to reach Sinibad. Ayr saw him starting to move, his muscles and scales all surging as he tried to push himself up from the ground. Ayr readjusted his spell, letting the magic run down his arms and then out through his fingertips. All he needed to control was Sinibad's head and he wrapped the spell like a lasso around it. Sinibad's body rose, until Ayr felt a crack in the spell. Sinibad let out a pained cry, one that was more like a whimper than the ferocious roars that he usually unleashed upon the world.

Ayr kept the spell locked around him and Sinibad continued to scream out in pain, sounding more like a wyvern than the monster that he was. Azura flew down into the Amphitheatre, shooting straight past one of his legs and came into land on the sands beside the corpse of a dark green dragon. The dead dragon had been lacerated with at least a dozen deep wounds, each of which could have been the fatal blow.

The dragon was crumpled on its side, and in this form was smaller than Azura. There was a strange peaceful feeling despite the death and destruction that encircled them. Ayr looked up at the roof of the Amphitheatre that was cut in half by Sinibad's body. Ayr was thrown back to the last time he had been this close to the enormous dragon, his leg crashing down and destroying the ceiling of the Obelisk. Except this time, he'd been the one to bring it down.

Go to him but stay out of reach.

What are you going to do, Ayr?

We're waiting.

Ayr kept his hands up, his magic still channeling through his system to the outside world. Now that he had the spell secure around Sinibad, all that it required from him was maintenance. Azura started to step forward and Sinibad was no longer struggling. It was as if the crack that Ayr had heard had broken him. There was no movement from Sinibad, except from his head, as he moved his neck around so that his eyes were firmly locked on them once again. Ayr drew himself to his full height, standing up out of the saddle as Azura moved across the sand. The sand was pilfering from the Amphitheatre as the wind took it, with nothing left to contain it within its walls.

Sinibad's tail flicked somewhere behind them, Ayr sensing it because of the spell wrapped around him. The battle still roared overhead, but with no immediate threats, Ayr felt at peace. Azura's eyes were scanning the sky, whilst Ayr kept his on Sinibad. The monster stared him down, and all of the fear that Ayr had felt the first time he had seen him was gone. Sinibad was no more threatening to him now than Azura was.

"Sinibad! Yield before me!"

"You are a worm! I will smite you!"

"With what power! You have nothing left! I don't care if Dalton fuels you, but you are finished. You lay there, unable to strike a hatchling from this world!"

"I would still crush many dragons with my power. You are fortunate that you are just out of reach, Ayr. Your father is on his way."

"Good, I don't care. He'll see what I've done to you and call off his attack."

Sinibad was weak, but he still chuckled, his chest heaving with each movement of the rest of his body. He sounded like he wanted to give up, but the elder dragon clung to life. Even though Ayr had been thorough in his assault, he had been sure to leave just enough of

Sinibad left so that Dalton could see what he had done to him. If that would not be a wake-up call for Dalton, nothing would be.

"You didn't have to do what you did, you know."

"You were going to attack my city."

"Your Commonwealth attacked my home. What do you expect me to do when invaders try and claim my kingdom? Not fight back?"

"You are delusional, Sinibad. What drew you to Dalton? His power?"

Sinibad showed remorse for the first time. He bowed his head, unable to hold it up any longer. "Dalton promised a better one. A world in which I could thrive in. I thought that would be achieved."

"And yet in your defeat you are only further away from it."

"Indeed. You have broken me, Ashbourne."

"I did what I had to do. You attacked us."

"Only under direction from Dalton."

"Speaking of my father, where is he? I would have thought that he was overseeing this attack personally. It is unlike him to strike from the shadows, leaving others to do his dirty work with such a display of force."

Sinibad tried to shift again but groaned in pain as his body did not want to cooperate under the influence of Ayr's spell. He then let out a sigh, followed by a chortle. "You clearly don't know your father then. He trusted me to lead the assault, but considering that you brought me to ground, he comes."

"Where is he?"

Sinibad's sigh turned into a smile. "What are you going to do, little Ashbourne? Kill me?"

"I would certainly like to. Yet something tells me that killing you will not get Dalton away from me."

"I can still feel your spell all over me, Ashbourne. My fate is in your hands. You had best decide quickly. Dalton grows nearer."

I can see what you're thinking. We cannot let him go, Ayr. He's too dangerous to be left alive. Look at what he did to the Haven, to the Obelisk.

It's a waste of life. I know what he's done.

If we remove him from the world, then that is one less asset that Dalton has at his disposal. Please do not tell me that after all we've been through that you're considering leaving Dalton tools that he can use against us.

Sinibad can be turned to our side. I can feel it. He wants a better life. To me if we don't hunt him, he will be amicable.

This is your judgement, Ayr. If you believe that, then I am with you. We are one in this decision and all others.

If Ezzu can't bring down Ragoon, Sinibad is our next best option. Then free him!

Sinibad was waiting for his response, his ancient reptilian eyes fixed on the horizon where the sun cast long shadows across the jagged peaks. A smugness crept across his scaled face, the corners of his massive jaws curling upward as his nostrils flared with a wisp of smoke, the dragon equivalent of a victorious smirk.

"Have you reached your decision yet, little Ashbourne?"

Ayr grit his teeth together and found no extra reassurance from Azura. She was comfortable with his decision, even though she did not fully believe that Sinibad could be turned to their cause. He turned and glanced towards where Sinibad was looking. Zaurien was just inside the horizon, coming straight towards them.

"If I release you, will you leave the Haven and not attack us again?"

Sinibad snorted as he struggled in his place. "You're bargaining with me, worm?"

Ayr was not going to be mocked. He grunted and clamped down on the spell that held Sinibad in place. A moment later, Sinibad grunted in response, a testament to the pressure that Ayr was applying to him. His eyes narrowed as he squinted.

"Do you think I'm bargaining with you, dragon? Are my terms acceptable?"

Sinibad hissed, his frustration rising to the forehead of his expression. "If you apply anymore pressure, you will crush me."

"That is my intent. Do you agree to my terms?"

The hesitation from Sinibad was evident. His eyes were still on the horizon, hardly paying Ayr and Azura any attention. The great dragon's nostrils flared, releasing twin plumes of steam into the cold air as he waited, perfectly still save for the slow, deliberate rise and fall of his armoured chest.

"I choose life, little Ashbourne. Your terms are agreeable."

"Betray me, and I will hunt you to the ends of the Commonwealth."

"I heard you the first time, Ashbourne. I will respect you as I respect your father. Release me."

With Sinibad now accepting defeat, Azura coiled around her own body as Ayr released the spell. It was like he was raising his foot off a pressure valve and Sinibad groaned with the release. He started to rise the more that Ayr gave him the freedom to and there was another loud crack that came from him. Sinibad roared in pain, as he stood up on his front foot and Ayr knew why he had roared. Even from where he stood, Ayr could see how his foot was not sitting correctly in the socket. There had been an unintended consequence with his magic.

At least, should Sinibad attack now, there was at least an opening for Ayr to cripple him with. Ayr watched as Sinibad rose, careful not to put any pressure on the foot that was broken.

He won't be bothering us again any time soon, Azura.

How are you so sure?

Look at him. He wants nothing to do with you or me.

That does not mean that a dragon once scorned will not come back and strike again. He's an incredibly intelligent creature.

One that has been taking orders from my father. Another issue that we will solve presently.

Sinibad was indeed looking dejected. Ayr kept the spell on him, just as a precaution, but he could see that Sinibad was doing his best to get out of the city. With his injured foot, Sinibad stretched his enormous wings that appeared to cover most of the city that was still standing. The Commonwealth dragons were still engaged overhead, striking at the wyvern and what dragons Dalton had brought to the fight. Evor was still clashing with Manir high above them, and Ayr wanted to help, but with how close they were together, at this range, his magic would miss.

However, a new shadow fell across the Haven, darkening the already blood-stained ground. Ayr's stomach clenched as he followed Sinibad's lingering gaze toward the northern horizon. There, silhouetted against the smoke-streaked sky, Zaurien descended in a spiral of midnight scales and unfurled his wings that blocked out the sun. The dragon's molten amber eyes burned with such concentrated hatred that the air itself seemed to waver around him, his massive talons flexing as they reached for the Amphitheatre's stone rim.

Once again, there were two riders in his saddle and Zaurien roared as he dropped down from the Amphitheatre ceiling. He slid down the rubble and Ayr felt Azura tense underneath him. She was ready to engage, but Zaurien's considerable bulk and the presence of both Dalton and Bryne was enough to deter her.

This is it, Ayr.

Let me handle it, Azura. They've just seen us face down Sinibad, perhaps that will buy us a reprieve.

THIRTY-TWO

Despite trying to instil Azura with confidence, Ayr still did not believe the words in his head. They were surrounded by the broken Amphitheatre. On one side of them was a wall of rubble that had been born from the shattered seating that had once towered above them. If Ayr closed his eyes, he could have imagined being in the arena, with Elanor by his side as they faced down Baindussa. The shattered sky over them continued to rain down death upon the Haven as wyvern and dragons alike dropped from their high altitudes.

Whilst Sinibad had taken a portion of the city with him, the dragons and wyvern that continued to fall were taking other parts of it with them as well. None were anywhere near the gargantuan size of Sinibad, but explosions continued to rock the Haven as they fell. Crimson flames streaked across the sky as shrieks and the bellows of dying dragons reached them. Despite all that was happening above, Ayr's sole focus was on the dragon that stood in the sand opposite them.

Ayr tensed as Dalton raised his hand. Zaurien in response lowered his head down to the ground. Dalton slid from him in one smooth motion, seemingly unbothered by the spines and spikes that riddled Zaurien's body. As per usual, he wore no mask, unlike Bryne, who was pulling his off his head. As his eyes came into view, he was already glaring at Ayr, just waiting for a command to attack.

Wait here, Azura. I will deal with him.

Do you want me to incinerate him, Ayr?

No, not today.

He wanted to sever the bond between us, Ayr. I want nothing more than to reduce him to ashes. He disrespected us, he disrespected you.

That doesn't mean he needs to die today.

Ayr felt Azura coil underneath him as she lowered herself to the ground. The tension in the air was rising around them, and she let out a low hiss. We do not agree on this.

We don't have to, Azura. You will listen to me.

I thought we were one.

We are, but not in this. Listen to me. Even if I can overpower Dalton, killing him outright is another story.

I will help you.

Ayr smiled as he slid out of the saddle. He brushed his hands across her scales and felt her warmth underneath his fingertips. I know, and I am grateful for everything you do for me.

Then let me.

Patience, Azura.

Ayr's boots struck the sand and he sunk into it, half expecting Dalton to drag him down into it. Instead, Dalton remained stoic, with no hand gestures and Ayr could not sense any magic swirling around him suggesting an attack. Dalton's robes kissed the sand at his feet, and as Ayr walked towards him, he did not feel comfortable. Azura pushed him forward, giving him the courage he needed, but why was facing Dalton harder than facing down Sinibad? The only magic he sensed came from Bryne, but nothing came his way yet. Ayr stopped five paces away from Dalton, who stood still with his arms folded, his expression demanding answers of Ayr.

"What have you done to my dragon, Ayr?"

"I sent him on his way. He no longer serves you."

"This is the first I'm hearing of it.

"You have no proper bond to Sinibad, so you wouldn't have heard through him."

Dalton kicked down at the sand and snorted. "And what do you know of our bond? Were you there when Sinibad pledged his allegiance to me?"

"No father, I was not. I'd assume that when Sinibad came to you it was one of your many expeditions that you left us for weeks at a time for."

"Sinibad took several visits before he finally pledged allegiance to me. But yes. I was always busy when we were in exile. There's a reason why I told you nothing about my plans with him."

The winds started to pick up around them, whipping up grains of sand and dust. Ayr's hair blew in the wind, and he knew where the wind was coming from. Bryne's glare darkened and Ayr readied a shield to protect him if Bryne was to strike out at him. Dalton's brow furrowed even more than it already had as he spun around.

"Do nothing, Bryne! You will have your moment!"

Dalton's voice cracked over the arena like a whip and the result was immediate. The winds started to die out as Bryne sat back in his saddle, his hands falling to the wayside. Ayr glared back at him, ready to throw magic towards him if he needed to contain either him or Zaurien. Ayr could feel Azura inside his mind, hissing at Zaurien. Whilst Ayr trusted that Bryne would not act out against Dalton's instructions, she did not trust his dragon at all.

"Father, he has betrayed us!"

Dalton grit his teeth as he turned back to face Ayr. "This was always going to be the way when he bonded with that dragon."

"So how do you want to do this, father? I will not be moved on my position."

Dalton's arms fell to his side. A silver blade appeared to have slid from underneath his robes into his right hand. The blade was made of pure magical power and Dalton thus far had not formulated any other spells to attack him with. Ayr took a deep breath as he eyed the sword. He'd sparred with Dalton and a similar blade many times before. The hand and a half sword was Dalton's preferred length and allowed him to not only be agile with it, but should he need to overpower Ayr, he could do so with ease, changing his grip.

Dalton sighed and turned his wrist over twice, flicking the sword out into the open. "I never thought it would come to this, but I am glad it has. A true test of your power, at last. I won't be holding back. You have served your purpose, however if you don't come back to the table, then you are just another dragon rider of the Commonwealth that has gotten in my way."

"You wanted to separate me and my dragon from our promised. I told you that was not acceptable, but you didn't want to listen! That was my one demand!"

"Yet my command was for you to infiltrate the Commonwealth and become a rider. Not fall in love with one! Your dragon was to have no promised! Speaking of, perhaps this will encourage you."

Dalton raised his hand up towards the sky. Ayr followed his eye and saw Evor directly in the line of fire. He was still sparring with Manir, diving in and out of combat, their claws extending to rip scales from each other's flesh. Ayr was too far away to see any visible wounds on them, but Evor's movement slowed in a heartbeat. Dalton tightened his grip and a shriek escaped his open mouth as Manir moved in for another attack. Evor started to plummet towards the ground, just like Sinibad had done before him. Before Ayr knew it, he had a sword in his hand, one that matched Dalton for size and its composition. He leapt forward, closing the gap between them, his magic flowing through every fibre in his body.

Even though Dalton had his sword ready first, he was immediately on the defensive, Ayr swinging wildly without rhyme or rhythm.

He struck high, he struck low and everywhere in between. Dalton's one-handed grip immediately went to two as he tried to parry every one of Ayr's strikes. Ayr was still only one handed, but each power had the weight of Azura behind it. He could feel her pushing him forward, allowing Dalton no room to move on the sand except backwards.

He's released Evor! Keep going!

Ayr had no time to look up to see if Evor had regained his altitude or not. Even though his offense was keeping Dalton on the backfoot, Dalton still had time to counter a parry into a strike of his own. He thrust forward, interrupting Ayr's rhythm, and now it was Ayr who stepped back. Dalton's offense was just as formidable as his defence and Ayr had not felt it properly since the days before he had met Azura for the first time. He knew from experience there would only be so much of this that he could take.

Each step backwards he took was calculated and measured, not wanting to give Dalton anymore space than he already had. Ayr took one of Dalton's two-handed attacks square on his blade and held it tight against his own two-handed grip. Dalton grunted and it was evident that he was in fact now trying to kill Ayr. Every strike had to be precise. Ayr thought he saw an opening as Dalton stepped forward again, but as he struck, he realised that the mistake was his own.

Dalton jabbed forward and Ayr did not get his sword up in time. The blow was glancing as Ayr dropped his knees ever so slightly. He still cried out in pain as Dalton's blade removed flesh from his shoulder. Seeing this, Dalton smirked and did not let up on his pressure as he crowded Ayr's space.

"I see that you've learnt nothing!"

Rather than playing into Dalton's goading, Ayr slipped forward, dropping one of his hands from his sword hilt. Azura already had anticipated his movements and had given him the power. Ayr felt it surge into his body and rather than waiting for Dalton to attack with his own magic, Ayr launched it at him. The bolt caught Dalton square in the chest and was not something he had been anticipating. Dalton doubled over, coughing and wheezing as Ayr tightened his grip on Dalton.

He surged forward, his feet feeling like they were barely touching the sand underneath him. Ayr flicked his sword up to Dalton's throat as he felt him struggle against the bonds of the spell that was a smaller version of what he had wrapped Sinibad up in. Ayr almost lost his grip straight away. Dalton was stronger than Sinibad, and that was evident as Ayr struggled to hold onto him. Ayr closed the gap between the two of them as he felt Dalton begin to break. He thrust his sword out, placing it against Dalton's throat.

Despite being barely able to move against Ayr's restraints, Dalton was enraged. "I thought we were fighting with honour!"

"The Haven is my city, father. The Commonwealth is mine. I will defend it against all threats. You threatened me and you threatened Elanor! Enough is enough!"

Dalton rounded his shoulders and stood with a smirk upon his face. "As much as I can see the similarities between us, Ayr, you are beginning to live up to your destiny."

"I am not what you made me."

Dalton went to extend his hand but then retracted it as if considering his touch. He hissed at his hand, and Ayr frowned, uncertain if Dalton had just manipulated his spell or not. Ayr had felt nothing against it, but with Dalton he could never be certain.

"My son. You are an Ashbourne. You bow to no man, or dragon for that matter. I saw what you did to Sinibad today."

"You taught me that."

"I'm glad you listened. I'm proud of you, Ayr. You will surpass me."

Ayr scoffed and lowered his sword. "Proud of me. Are you fucking joking me? The only time you're proud of me is when I've done something to knock you from your pedestal? Dalton, Sinibad is almost dead because of you! I broke him!"

"Almost. He will recover. You're not the only one with the ability to heal your dragon, Ayr. I will do the same for Sinibad."

"Then what's all this for? You've killed almost everybody that has had a hand in defeating your rebellion the first time. The Commonwealth doesn't need to burn anymore. The Dragon Lords can be replaced until you find suitable people to lead."

Dalton's face twisted and he poked his own sword forward with an accusatory gesture. There was no mistaking the gesture. He was pushing the boundaries of Ayr's magic with his own, except this time, Ayr could feel Dalton's magical signature pushing against his own. Ayr tightened his grip and Dalton snapped back to where he had once been.

"No, Ayr! That's where you're wrong. I taught you better than that. You only agree with the Commonwealth now because you can see yourself at the head of it."

"It would be a better world than what you have in store for it. I spent over twenty years hearing what you wanted to do. You threatened what I have become. I'm not willing to let you lord over me anymore!"

Dalton scoffed as he lowered his sword. It was against his will, but Ayr at least felt better that he was forcing Dalton to back down. The sword itself was beginning to dissolve before his eyes.

"I know you already have your supporters. Those that have heard of your acts thus far and think you can lead them into a better future. You have my temperament, but without the loss of losing a dragon."

"I don't know what you're talking about!"

"I have spies everywhere, Ayr. Many think that given enough time, you will be able to lead the Commonwealth as Overlord. I know that the Lord Ashbourne they were speaking of was not me."

"Then who was it, me?"

A thin smile spread over Dalton's lips. "Yes, at first, I thought it was Bryne, but it is clear to me that the dragon has at least changed you. Perhaps I was wrong in wanting to shatter your bond."

Ayr tightened the spell around him, and Dalton groaned in pain. Zaurien snarled, but Dalton shook his head as much as he could. Azura tensed behind Ayr, ready to take on the larger black dragon should any further confrontation arise. For the first time in his life, Ayr had Dalton at his mercy, and for the first time in his life, he did not know what to do with him. He had envisioned this exact situation dozens of times over the years, but now that he held Dalton, he was stuck.

"What are you going to do to me, boy?"

Ayr grunted, this name coming from Dalton's lips, stirred something inside of him. It was almost like he was back in the many training arenas that they had sparred in over the years, and for the first time since killing the Dragon Lords, Ayr felt useless. The Haven was safe for now, and if he crushed Dalton in the way that he had wanted to crush Sinibad, Ayr expected a fight back, one he was not sure he could have won. Especially with Bryne nearby. The two of them would have been able to overpower him with ease, and they had done it before during Ayr's training. Azura was screaming into his mind, but Ayr was set on his path.

The magic slipped from Dalton as if he had just stepped out of his robes. Ayr let it go, no longer scared of his father. If Dalton struck back, Ayr was ready. Yet despite what he knew of Dalton and what he was expecting, nothing come back at him. Instead, Dalton remained rooted to the spot just like the magic was still gripping his body. He raised an eyebrow at Ayr, wondering if that was it. Ayr had no more words, and dismissed him with a wave of his hand.

"Leave! Before I change my mind."

Dalton nodded, accepting defeat, even though Ayr felt like he could have escaped, even without Ayr letting the spell go. "You've proven that I couldn't beat you today. For that you've earnt my respect. I will recoup my losses, and when I have healed, I will return and have my revenge. This isn't over between us."

"You live because I chose to show you mercy. Something that can't be said for me. You put me into the Seminary of Fire and every day since I have struggled. You brought this upon yourself, father."

Dalton's expression remained unchanged, even as water began to swim in his eyes. He nodded once more and turned back towards Zaurien. Bryne and his dragon had not moved since Dalton had told them not to. Bryne's face was still scrunched in anger, and Ayr could see his hand was on his sword, just underneath the lip of the saddle. Bryne wanted to speak, but Dalton waved his hand, silencing him.

When he placed his foot in the first rest hold of Zaurien's leg, he turned to look over his shoulder. "Good luck, Ayr. I hope you know what you're doing. We will meet again very soon."

Ayr froze, the sound too unfamiliar to his ears reverberating off his brain like a gong. He was dumbfounded and did not respond to Dalton. Dalton had called him Ayr. That was a rare occurrence. Ayr kept his breathing level as he allowed the sword that he had summoned to dissolve. He wanted to flee reality, and chose to do so, diving into Azura's mind.

So do I, Azura.

They had given their enemies mercy, and Azura was not all that pleased. She disagreed and Ayr could still feel the fire burning inside of her. She was a dragon after all, and she felt threatened by Dalton, even though he was retreating back to Ironrock. But for now there was nothing that she could do, so she nodded her head and was peaceful. Her response was kind and gentle, even when it had no right to be.

Me too, Ayr. I am worried that you will be the death of me.

TO BE CONTINUED...

ACKNOWLEDGEMENTS

Wow! What a start to the year we've had. It's already shaping up to be better than last year! Thank you so much for getting this far into the Ashbourne Saga. I hope you are all ready for the explosive last book that is to come. Rest assured I am already working on it, because I want this whole series in your hands sooner rather than later.

I'm going to keep this short and sweet like I usually do. First off, to the street team. We've had a bit of a revamp, but you are one of the primary reasons as to why I keep doing this. If there's any new update you hype me up on, any cool decision you guys help me make, I love it. You're making my life easier and I can't wait to build further going forward with you all. I wouldn't be able to do this without your support. There are a few names, but I think each of you having your own dedication on a new book in the future will be awesome. Again, thank you.

One lady that stands above the rest is awesome. Not only is she a great author in her own right, but is also an awesome PA, and that is Autumn. Without her guidance and help none of this would be possible. Or it would be, and I'd be even more on struggle street than I already am. I can't thank her enough. Hopefully by the time you read this I've also had my first real life trip to the USA. Hopefully there's been some book signings and Autumn would have organized that. Again, thank you so much.

And with that, that's enough on the acknowledgements. I know you are all eagerly waiting for Demise of the Dragon and that is coming very soon. The less time I spend here means I can spend more time getting that ready for you. I'm so looking forward to finishing off the Ashbourne Saga and I'm sure you're not all ready for the emotional trauma that is to come in the last book, or in Kingdom of the Dragon. Enjoy it and I will see you all in the next one.

About the Author

Matt Mememaro is an Australian author that exists somewhere in the void in Australia, as he battles with the unsettling fact that he is no longer a true spring chicken and is experiencing grey hair growth all over his head. He constantly stresses about his books and whether or not the meaning of life is in fact fourty-two.

In his spare time when he is not at his day job that he wishes to retire from, he is probably writing, playing paintball or working out. Matt wishes to one day soon become a full time author, but he cannot do that without your help.

If you enjoyed Desolation of the Dragon, please consider leaving a kind review and or checking out Matt's other works and social medias in the QR code below. Matt would also very much appreciate it if you subscribed to his newsletter in the link below so you can keep up with his new releases.